Terms of Engagement

KATE HOFFMANN
MIRANDA LEE

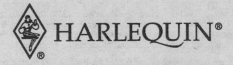

HARLEQUIN®

TORONTO • NEW YORK • LONDON
AMSTERDAM • PARIS • SYDNEY • HAMBURG
STOCKHOLM • ATHENS • TOKYO • MILAN • MADRID
PRAGUE • WARSAW • BUDAPEST • AUCKLAND

HARLEQUIN BOOKS

by Request—TERMS OF ENGAGEMENT

Copyright © 2002 by Harlequin Books S.A.

ISBN 0-373-21728-5

The publisher acknowledges the copyright holders of the original works as follows:
WANTED: WIFE
Copyright © 1994 by Peggy Hoffmann
MARRIAGE IN JEOPARDY
Copyright © 1993 by Miranda Lee

This edition published by arrangement with Harlequin Books S.A.

Visit us at www.eHarlequin.com

Printed in U.S.A.

When the Name of the Game Is Marriage...

Wedding planner Elise Sinclair
has the perfect wife picked out for her client,
Jordan Prentiss. Conveniently, it's her!
Now to convince her notorious client that
a merger is in his best interests....

Juliana Preston is shocked to discover
that she's fallen in love at last with
her own husband! But she'll have to
keep the news to herself....

Kate Hoffmann started reading romance when she was an elementary school music teacher. She started writing romance when she was an advertising copywriter. And in 1993, the year her first Temptation novel was published, she quit the nine-to-five world and became a full-time romance writer. Since then, Kate has published more than thirty stories with Harlequin, including Temptation and Duets titles, continuity series and anthologies. Kate's first single-title release, *Reunited,* will be published in 2002. Kate lives in Wisconsin with her three cats and her computer. When she's not writing, she enjoys gardening, golfing and genealogy.

Miranda Lee's success as a romance writer stems from her professed insistence that she "refuses to bore the reader." Accompanied by a passionate yearning to write, this high standard has fueled the creation of more than twenty-three novels and novellas. As a "full-time housewife with time on her hands," she began writing romances in 1981, and persevered in developing her craft until her first romance, *After the Affair,* was published by Harlequin Mills and Boon® in 1990.

A native of Australia, Miranda now lives in Lisarow, New South Wales, with her husband, Anthony, and her three daughters. When she isn't writing, Miranda enjoys reading, watching TV, going to the movies and finding inspiration in romantic getaways with her husband.

CONTENTS

WANTED: WIFE

Kate Hoffmann

1

"YOU COULD always try dating a woman for longer than two months," Pete Stockton commented.

The Sunday edition of the *Chicago Tribune* lay across the wide glass-topped desk, open to the society pages. Jordan Prentiss sat in his leather chair, staring at a photograph of himself and his current companion at a recent charity affair.

When his executive assistant spoke, Jordan looked up in surprise, having forgotten that Pete was still in the room. "I've dated a lot of women for longer than that," he replied.

Pete smiled and shook his head.

"I haven't?" Jordan asked.

"No, I'm afraid not."

"What about Clarise Sheppard?"

"Seven weeks."

Jordan frowned. "It seemed like years," he said absentmindedly as he picked up the paper and scrutinized the brief article beneath the photo:

Jordan Prentiss, bachelor-about-town, with his current lady-in-waiting, Alicia DuMont, attended the recent opening of the new orthopedic wing at Children's Memorial Hospital. Prentiss and his firm, BabyLove Baby Foods, were major contributors to the project.

His gaze drifted back to the photo. After a long pause, he spoke again. "This isn't good, is it?" he murmured. The rhetorical tone of his statement solicited no response from his assistant. When it came to business, Jordan rarely sought or accepted the advice or counsel of others.

Prentiss has the uncanny ability to assess a situation in one second and integrate a fully refined business strategy in the next. Prentiss, a loner by nature, runs his company with absolute authority, maintaining a reserved distance from his management staff. His business tactics are cold and competent, and unquestionably brilliant.

When nosy reporters weren't examining his personal life in the society pages, their counterparts from the business news were carefully dissecting his professional life. He had taken over the helm at BabyLove four years ago, and at the age of thirty-four had become the youngest CEO in the history of the food industry. The business press had hailed him as a wunderkind and watched with interest as he turned a failing, family-owned company around. The following year, the gossip columnists named him one of Chicago's "most eligible." Yet through it all, Jordan thought he had managed to keep his private and his professional life completely separate. Until today.

The bad news had filtered through the office grapevine and ended up on his desk in the form of a ten-page report from Pete. "Are you sure about your information?" Jordan asked, glancing down at the report.

Pete regarded him seriously. "If I wasn't sure, I

wouldn't have brought it to you. Your cousin is maneuvering for control of BabyLove and he has some influential board members behind him. He's got until the next board meeting to plead his case. That's just three months away. Edward may not have much business sense, but the guy has a real knack for exploiting a situation. He's convinced the board that as a bachelor, you couldn't possibly represent the wholesome, family image that BabyLove Baby Foods needs to convey to the public. The media's fascination with your marital status hasn't helped. You've been photographed with six different women in as many months."

Jordan stood and walked to the wall of windows. He gazed down at the bumper-to-bumper Chicago traffic from his vantage point twenty-three stories above Michigan Avenue. "They think Edward would make a better president simply because he's married and has four children." His voice was even and unemotional. "This company was on the edge of bankruptcy when I took over the presidency. Give me another four years and we'll own the baby-food market. I'm the one who's saved this company, not Edward."

"And you've done it by bullying the board into doing things your way. They're a conservative bunch, Jordan, and they've never felt comfortable with your progressive ideas about running BabyLove—both you and I know that. You've convinced them to overextend the company and they're scared. Edward would make a much more malleable president."

"Edward would fail inside of a year," Jordan said dryly. "He'd take the company my grandfather founded right along with him. And when Edward failed, the board would be free to appoint someone outside the family. BabyLove has always been run by a Prentiss. I'm not about to let that change."

The office was silent for a long minute before Jordan turned around and took his place behind his desk. He neatly folded the newspaper and dropped it into the wastebasket. "What do you suggest?"

Pete looked taken aback for a moment, then regained his usual composure. "You want my opinion?" the young man asked guardedly.

Jordan nodded. "Of course I do. That *is* what I pay you for, isn't it? Show me some of that Harvard M.B.A. stuff."

Pete sat down across from Jordan, an earnest expression on his face as he spoke. "First, I think you should meet individually with each of the board members, preferably in a neutral setting. Feel them out, find out where they stand. Then lay the facts out on the table and remind them of what you've done for this company. Throw some numbers at them. Play up your close relationship with your grandfather. They loved the old man."

"Is that all?"

Pete shifted uncomfortably in his chair, then handed Jordan a manila envelope. "If that doesn't work, you should consider using these."

Jordan opened the envelope and pulled out a stack of glossy eight-by-tens, each one featuring a buxom young woman, in various stages of undress, and his cousin Edward, in various stages of undressing her. The young woman was not Edward's wife, but by the looks of the photos, she was performing well beyond what was expected of one's marital partner.

Jordan placed the photos back in the envelope and

slid them across the desk. "Burn those. Be sure you get the negatives and destroy them, too."

Pete took the photos, his face coloring slightly. "I'm sorry. I just thought—"

"Don't be sorry. You were doing your job. I'm impressed by your instincts about Edward. I never would have suspected."

"But using these photos would put Edward right under your thumb. You could end his interference here and now."

"Edward isn't the problem. The board is." Jordan laughed. "You've got to admire the old man," he added in a cynical voice. "He still controls this company, even from the grave. He chose the board before he died. They're all pillars of the community, happily married, active in their churches, carbon copies of my grandfather, right down to their conservative little business minds. To them, a stable home life equates with a stable business life. It's me they're uncomfortable with. If they couldn't replace me with Edward, they'd find someone else. Some mundane, middle-aged corporate yes-man with a wife, a house in the suburbs, and 2.3 children."

"So what are you going to do?"

"I'm going to woo them individually as you suggest. I'm going to pander to their conservative natures." Jordan paused before he continued, wondering if the decision he had made was too rash. But his company was at stake and he would do anything in his power to save it. "And I'm going to get married."

Jordan was amazed at how easily he said the words. He had never thought marriage was in his future, but when faced with the possibility of losing his company, the decision seemed unavoidable. If possessing a wife would ensure his control of BabyLove, then that's what had to be done. He had no choice in the matter.

The look of shock on Pete's face gradually turned to undisguised admiration. "That's not a bad idea, but the next board meeting is on April 23. They might still vote you out."

"April 18 is a Saturday, isn't it?"

Pete nodded.

"That's the date, then. I want you to start to make plans for the wedding. It has to be very big and very traditional. And I want it kept under wraps until the invitations go out."

Pete held out his hands in a gesture of reluctance. "Wait a second. I don't know anything about planning a wedding."

"Then find someone who does."

Jordan watched his assistant mentally scrambling for an alternative plan. Though he had asked Pete Stockton to do a great many things over the past two years, planning a wedding was the only task well outside his job description. But the young man was hungry and Jordan knew he would find a way of pleasing the boss.

"My sister got married last year," Pete said, his expression brightening, "and she used a wedding consultant."

"Good, get the name of the place and have my secretary make an appointment for you. I think we can trust Sandra to be discreet about our plans. But she's the only other person I want to know about this wedding, outside of you and your wedding person."

"And the bride, of course," Pete added. "Jordan,

she's supposed to plan the wedding, not her fiancé's business associate. Don't you think Alicia is going to want some say in the matter?"

Jordan looked at him coolly.

"You're not going to marry Alicia?"

Jordan didn't shake his head, merely raised an eyebrow in reply.

"You don't have a bride yet, do you?" Pete groaned in frustration. "Why do I feel like I'm always operating one time zone behind you?"

"I'll take care of finding a bride. You make up the guest list and hire that consultant."

"You're going to have to get involved in the planning. There are all sorts of decisions to be made and it's going to look very suspicious if neither the bride nor the groom is involved. If it leaks out to the press that you're short a fiancée, every unattached female in the city will be pounding down your door. And the board will be right behind them, questioning your motives. Don't you read your own press? Last year you were named Chicago's most eligible bachelor."

"Don't exaggerate the situation. I wasn't the *most* eligible bachelor. I was third on the list."

"That was the year before," Pete said.

Jordan scowled. "All right, I'll go see the wedding consultant, make a few decisions, then let her take over. Have Sandra make an appointment for me this afternoon. In the meantime, I want you to get me a short list of candidates by the end of the day."

"Candidates?"

"Women. Brides-to-be. Preferably over thirty, never married, spotless reputation, well educated."

"I haven't seen any unmarried saints strolling down

Michigan Avenue lately," Pete said, a hint of sarcasm in his voice. "But I'll call Rome and have them send five over on the next boat. Anything else?"

Jordan ignored his assistant's remarks. "Yes. They have to be practical. I'm looking for a corporate wife. Someone who understands that this marriage is strictly a business arrangement and nothing more." He picked up a copy of the *Wall Street Journal* and opened it on his desk. "After all, I'm thirty-eight years old," he added distractedly. "It's about time I got married. But I've got a business to run, with precious little time to spend pleasing a wife. So just be sure to avoid incurable romantics with dreams of wedded bliss."

"Five frigid saints. I'll get right on it." Pete walked to the door, but Jordan's next command halted his retreat.

"And Pete, have Sandra send Alicia two dozen roses and my regrets that I won't be able to see her in the near future. You know, pressing business matters..."

"Your standard 'Dear Joan' letter?"

He looked up from the newspaper. "Just do it."

Jordan watched the office door close behind Pete, then rose slowly and walked to the windows. His dispassionate gaze traced the path of a bright-yellow cab as it wove its way through the traffic.

Had he made the right choice? Was marriage the only answer? For the first time in his professional life, Jordan found himself questioning one of his business decisions. And the plan to marry *was* purely a business decision. What else could it be? Certainly not personal.

Jordan had never invested much time or effort in his relationships with the opposite sex. Throughout his entire adult life he had found women disturbingly unpredictable and illogical, and frustrating to say the least.

Though he tried to maintain a discreet distance from the fair sex, women seemed strangely attracted to him. He couldn't understand why. He gave them no encouragement, no indication of an interest in a long-term relationship, yet he never lacked for female companionship.

Jordan had come to the conclusion that the only thing that kept the women coming back was his money and the power it represented. And the blind hope that they might one day assume the role of Mrs. Jordan Prentiss and thereby capture the keys to the Prentiss family fortune.

If only he had a better understanding of women. Maybe then, the decision to marry wouldn't cause such unaccustomed self-doubt. But his ascent to the presidency of BabyLove had left little time for polishing his social skills. His father had died prematurely of a heart attack when Jordan was sixteen, and from that moment on, his grandfather had begun to groom a shy and rather clumsy teenager to take over the reins of the family business.

Tutors had been hired to accelerate Jordan's prep-school graduation. He completed his college business degree in only three years, studying frantically and working part-time at BabyLove. His M.B.A. had followed two years later, achieved while holding down a junior management position in the marketing department. There had been barely enough time to eat and sleep, certainly no time for school dances and dinner dates.

Over the next twelve years, he had become single-minded in his goal, to the exclusion of anything that remotely resembled a personal life. Jordan had wanted the presidency more than anything. And as a defense against the rampant rumors of nepotism, he had distanced himself from his co-workers. Each business decision had been watched and analyzed by every manager above and below him on the corporate ladder. To avoid the chance of a misstep, he had studied every piece of relevant data before making any business decision, then made the decision with an icy competence that even the most vociferous of his detractors could not fault. After a time, he had gained the respect he deserved. And with it, he had also gained a reputation as a total enigma.

No one knew the real Jordan Prentiss. And at times, he wondered if he even knew himself.

But he did know one thing. He would do anything to save his company. And if that meant getting married, so be it.

THE SUNDAY EDITION of the *Chicago Tribune* lay across Elise Sinclair's desk, open to the society pages. She scanned the engagement listings, scribbling down names as she read.

"Here's one," she said out loud. "Scott and Perkins. Her father is president of First Chicago Investments. And here's another one. Carruthers and St. James. Her father is Warren Carruthers of Carruthers, Trent and Stone."

"So, now that you have the names, what are you going to do?"

Elise looked up at her best friend, Dona Winters, and smiled. "What are *we* going to do," she corrected. "You're going to help me with this."

"I bake cakes, Elise."

"Not just cakes," she replied. "Incredibly romantic confections, masterpieces wrought from flour and eggs. That cake you baked for the Welton wedding was so beautiful it brought tears to my eyes. Those precious sugar-paste rosebuds and the ivy-leaf garland. Four tiers of exquisite beauty." For a moment, Elise lost herself in the memory of the Weltons' cake. The Welton affair had been such a lovely wedding, her best effort yet.

But she was well aware that's what she said about every wedding she'd planned, from the day she opened her wedding consulting business, right up to the nuptials she coordinated last Saturday. Each wedding was more special and more romantic than the last, each bride more perfect, each groom more dashing.

Elise's firm, A Tasteful Affair, was gaining recognition in Chicago, but the process was slow. Over the past three years, she had built a respectable portfolio of weddings, but she had yet to land a big one. A Gold Coast wedding. A wedding that combined a Chicago high-society bride and groom, a stellar guest list, visibility in the media and an unlimited budget.

"So how are my cakes going to help your business?"

"I figure we'll make some miniature wedding cakes, package each of them up in a pretty box and have them hand-delivered to the young ladies on this list. We'll put my business card inside the box. Then, a few days later, I'll make a follow-up call."

"That's not a bad idea. I think it might work."

"It'd better work. If I don't take on a few more clients in the next couple of months, I'm in serious trouble. This house might just come crashing down around me, and my business right along with it."

This house. Her house now. When her father and

new stepmother had moved to Florida, they had happily turned the title to the crumbling Victorian town house over to Elise. The three-story brick house, located in Chicago's trendy Old Town neighborhood, had been the only home Elise had known and she was thrilled to have it for her own. The spacious first-floor parlor, with its huge bay window overlooking the street, made a perfect office. The dining room directly behind the parlor made a convenient workroom. And the lovely mahogany dining table served as a large work area, covered with sample books of wedding invitations, cakes and floral arrangements.

She had redecorated the house to match her romantic nature, in rich Victorian florals of muted rose and green. Every surface, from the walls to the tables to the floors, displayed a carefully calculated clutter, giving the rooms a warm, cozy feeling.

She always felt closer to her mother in these surroundings. Maybe that's why she was so determined to keep the house.

Elise's mother had also been a romantic at heart, taking pleasure in life's sweet and pretty moments. She had died nearly seventeen years before, when Elise was sixteen. Martin Sinclair had been devastated by his wife's death and for years Elise had wondered if her father would ever recover. But she had felt compelled to stay near him, so she gave up her dreams of going to New York to study art and instead completed a degree in design at Northwestern. She continued to live at home, keeping the household running as her father spent more and more time out of town on business. She suspected that he simply couldn't bear to be in a house that brought back memories of the wife he had cherished, yet he wouldn't consider selling it.

Then five years ago he had met Dorthi. They'd married after a short courtship and Elise had made plans to move out of the town house. But to her surprise, her father announced his retirement and within weeks he and Dorthi moved to Florida, leaving Elise with ownership of the house in exchange for sole custody of Dorthi's two prized Persian cats, Clorinda and Thisbe.

"The Girls," as Dorthi called them, were now sprawled across Elise's desk, taking one of their customary catnaps. Though Elise loved animals, she barely tolerated the presence of these two felines. They were fussy and aloof and selfish. And with their squished-in noses, Elise considered them the ugliest cats she'd ever seen.

Elise grabbed the drowsing Clorinda and unceremoniously set her on the floor. The fluffy white cat glared at her and with a sniff walked out of the room, her tail swishing haughtily. Thisbe, who never let Clorinda out of her sight, followed, shooting Elise a menacing glare as she left the room. Elise had learned to bear their hostility by reminding herself they were only cats.

"What about that mailing you did last month for corporate parties?" Dona inquired, a note of concern in her voice. "Did you have any response on that?"

"Out of one hundred sent, not one response. I made follow-up calls, but most of the companies were already dealing with an event planner. So much for my attempt to diversify."

"Hmm. Too bad." Dona paused, then rubbed her

arms through her bulky knit sweater. "Is it cold in here, or is it just me?"

"No, it's cold in here. The boiler is on the fritz again." Elise walked over to the radiator and touched it. It was barely warm. Outside, a damp January wind rattled at the multipaned windows, each gust sending drafts of cold air though the sash to stir the lace curtains. "Great. I've got a new client due in ten minutes and this place is beginning to feel like a meat locker. A beautifully decorated Victorian meat locker."

"Why don't you get the boiler fixed?" Dona asked innocently.

"For the same reason I don't get the leaky roof fixed and for the same reason I'm two months behind on my utility bills. I need more clients. I hope this Jordan Prentiss decides to book with me. If it's a big affair, it would sure help my financial situation. You took the message. Does that name ring a bell with you?"

Dona shook her head. "I just assumed she was already a client, so I didn't ask questions."

"I know I've heard the name before. You'd think I'd remember." Elise shrugged and glanced at her watch. "Miss Prentiss is due in ten minutes and I've got to get this house warmed up."

"Well, I have to go." Dona grabbed her jacket and hurried to the door. "Call me tonight. We can get together and watch a video, maybe order a pizza."

"Only if we can watch *Indiscreet*. I just love that movie."

"We watched that last month," Dona protested.

"I know, but a girl can never have too much Cary Grant. And it's such a romantic movie."

"I'll think about it," Dona called ⬚⬚⬚⬚⬚⬚ "See you later."

Elise heard the door close behind he⬚ rushed over to the fireplace. She quickly a⬚⬚ paper, kindling and two logs to the grate, then ⬚⬚⬚ a match to the paper and watched as the flames l⬚⬚ed at the logs. A nice roaring fire would add the perfect ambience to her meeting with Miss Prentiss. And it would also take the nip of winter out of the air.

She hurried through the foyer to the stairway. There was just enough time to change from her faded blue jeans and baggy sweatshirt before Miss Prentiss arrived. But her swift trip up to her third-floor bedroom was cut short by the sight of Thisbe. The smoke-gray cat sat with her nose pressed against the bottom of the front door.

"I'm not going to let you out," Elise scolded. "You're not an outside cat."

Thisbe looked up at her and meowed, then scratched at the door.

"Don't you remember what happened to Clorinda when she snuck out? She came back covered with grime and had a big scratch across her nose. Cats of your careful breeding do not socialize with street cats." Elise looked around the foyer. "Speaking of Clorinda, where is the little tramp?"

Thisbe scratched at the door again and let out an insistent howl. Elise's stomach tightened and her heart stopped. Oh, no! Clorinda must have snuck out when Dona left. If anything happened to one of "The Girls" her stepmother would never forgive her.

Elise grabbed a jacket from the hall closet, then ran to the kitchen and opened a can of tuna fish, letting the can rotate twice before releasing the lever on the electric can opener. The familiar humming sound brought Thisbe running for dinner, but there was no Clorinda. Elise ran back to the foyer and slipped out the front door. The cat couldn't have gotten far. Dona had left just minutes before.

Elise called Clorinda's name a few times before she got down on her hands and knees at the far edge of the house and crawled though the thick, leafless bushes that lined the front facade. This was where she'd found the runaway cat the last time. But this time the ground was soft and soggy from a brief winter thaw, and after only a few minutes, her hands were coated with mud.

"Here, kitty, kitty, kitty. Come on out, Clorinda." Elise waved the can of tuna through the air. Clorinda was a glutton for Chicken-of-the-Sea. She'd never be able to resist. Elise pushed through the heavy growth, cursing the entire feline species as the branches snapped back against her face like stinging whips and tangled in her hair. She reached the front stoop without finding a trace of the wayward cat.

Sliding though a small opening in the tall shrubbery, she grabbed the ornate cast-iron railing on the front steps, then pulled herself up and away from the clutching branches. As she brushed her hair out of her eyes, she realized someone was waiting on her front step.

A man stood with his back to her, stamping his feet against the cold. The wind ruffled his dark hair, brushing it against his collar. His wide shoulders were clearly outlined by the luxurious navy cashmere topcoat he wore.

"Can I help you?" she asked, shivering as a gust of wind swept past her.

He slowly turned around. His pale-blue eyes widened slightly upon seeing her. "I'm Jordan Prentiss. I have a two o'clock appointment with Elise Sinclair." He didn't smile, just looked at her, a tiny frown furrowing his brow. "I believe this is the right address." He pulled a piece of paper from his coat pocket and showed it to her.

Elise glanced down at the paper. This was Jordan Prentiss? This incredibly gorgeous, solitary man standing at her front door? On occasion, her clients would bring along their fiancés, but in most cases, the bride's mother or sister or best friend would be present.

Feeling more than a little self-conscious, Elise pulled herself over the railing and landed next to him on the stoop. In her haste to straighten her jacket, the can of tuna fish slipped from her hand, tumbled through the air and spattered over the shiny polish on his shoes. Mortified, she stared down at the oily mess for a long moment, then glanced up at him apologetically.

"Tuna fish," she mumbled and bent to brush the smelly goop off his shoes. Nervously she stood and, without thinking, held out her mud-caked hand. "It's a pleasure to meet you, Mr. Prentiss. I'm Elise Sinclair," she managed to blurt out.

He reached to take her hand, but at the last moment, she pulled it away. Blushing profusely, she gave a wan smile. "Mud," she explained, wiping her hands on her jeans.

Elise groaned inwardly. Jordan Prentiss had obviously come with the thought of using her consulting service, but with the way things were going, she would be lucky if he even stepped through her door.

As she sheepishly glanced up at his handsome features, a spark of recognition teased at her memory. Jordan Prentiss. Suddenly she realized where she had heard the name before—and seen the face. Jordan Prentiss, one of Chicago's most eligible. Man-about-town. Wealthy businessman and philanthropist. So, what was he doing on her front stoop? Alone?

His voice interrupted her scattered thoughts.

"It's cold out here. Do you think we could move inside?"

Elise smiled at him and pushed open the door, allowing him to enter. "I'm sorry. Please, come in." She took one last hurried look for Clorinda before closing the door, then turned to him.

"Have I come at a bad time?" he asked. His voice was soft and rich, but a bit icy around the edges.

"Of course not. I was just looking for my cat." Elise motioned for him to follow her into the parlor and indicated a chintz-covered sofa. "Please, sit down. Would you like to take off your coat?"

She watched Jordan shrug out of the topcoat and toss it across the back of the sofa. He was dressed in a finely tailored suit, also navy, with a blindingly white shirt and a red silk paisley tie.

The absence of the standard fiancée on his arm all but ruled out wedding plans. Could he be here on behalf of his daughter? He appeared to be in his mid-thirties, not old enough to have a daughter of marriageable age. Her confusion deepened. Maybe he wanted her to plan a corporate party. She tried to recall whether she had contacted his company and was nearly certain that she hadn't. She couldn't even recall the name of his company.

Why was he here? And why was he standing there, staring at her in such a puzzling fashion?

"Can I get you a cup of coffee, or maybe some tea?" Elise offered, hoping that he would refuse and she could move on to the next question—the question of what he wanted from her.

"No...thank you," Jordan answered, his gaze locked on her face. He opened his mouth to continue and she waited, offering him an encouraging smile. Finally he spoke, his voice detached, his expression composed. "You have something on your face." He reached out to brush his index finger along her cheek.

She felt a shiver run through her at his touch and wondered why she would have such a reaction when the room suddenly seemed so warm. He pulled his hand back and held out his finger. His fingertip was muddy.

Oh, no! She reached up and rubbed her cheeks furiously. Her fingers came back dirty. Then her hands swept to her hair and she heard the unmistakable crunch of dry leaves. "I—I was looking for my cat. She got out. Oh, I must look a mess." Beneath the mud, she could feel her cheeks flushing to a crimson shade.

A small smile quirked the corners of Jordan's mouth, but it quickly vanished and she wondered if she had only imagined it. "No, you look fine," he insisted, his voice the model of reserved politeness. "You just have a few smudges on your cheeks."

"If you'll excuse me, I'll just go clean up. Please, sit down and relax. I'll only be a moment."

She waited until Jordan had settled onto the over-stuffed couch, then hurried from the room and ran up the stairs to her bedroom. The mirror above her dresser reflected her disheveled appearance.

Just a smudge? Dry leaves and tiny twigs clung to her strawberry-blond hair, framing her dirty face. She looked like something out of *A Midsummer Night's Dream*. There was no time to shower, so she brushed the debris from her hair, snatched a clean towel from the rack, wrapped it around her head and scrubbed her face clean. She would have to forgo makeup. There was no time. Jordan Prentiss did not look like a man to be kept waiting.

Elise dressed quickly, yanking on panty hose and shimmying into a pale-green sweater dress. She searched frantically for her ivory shoes. When she realized she had left them downstairs beneath her desk, she pulled another pair from her closet, slipped into them and stumbled from the room.

Nervous anticipation fluttered in her stomach as she slowly descended the steps. She took a deep breath to calm herself.

JORDAN CASUALLY surveyed his surroundings, amazed by the disconcerting clutter. The floral patterns of the couch, wallpaper and rug clashed in a riotous outcry of decorating madness. Added to the cacophony of color and pattern was an annoying variety of bric-a-brac scattered about the room and embellishing the walls. How could someone function in these surroundings?

His own office was spare and modern, each piece of furniture functional and adorned with only utilitarian accoutrements. His co-op on East Lake Shore Drive was the same, serenely clean and elegantly urban, leather and glass and tile, calming neutral colors.

This was definitely a place only a woman could love. A frivolous, feminine woman like Elise Sinclair.

Despite her baffling behavior, it had been immediately clear that beauty lurked behind her mud-streaked mask. The dirt couldn't hide the striking cheekbones or the wide, sensuous mouth. And her hair was the color of spun gold touched with copper, falling about her face in a tousled mess. She was soft and curvy in all the right places. He remembered her hand as she brushed it over her cheek, long, slender fingers and perfect pink nails.

Jordan blinked hard, startled by the direction of his thoughts. What had gotten into him, carrying on over a woman like that? Elise Sinclair wasn't even his type. He had always been attracted to women with a hard edge who accepted his pragmatic attitude toward relationships beyond the physical. Elise Sinclair didn't have a hard edge on her; she was all woman, with a vulnerability that was reflected in her liquid green eyes. The kind of woman every man wants for his wife.

Except him.

Jordan felt something brush against his leg and he looked down to find two cats at his feet, staring up at him with round amber eyes. Though he made no overt invitation, the cats leaped up onto the couch and settled themselves on either side of him, purring contentedly.

Cats. What had he expected? A big, bruising German shepherd? Or a yapping poodle? No, cats suited Elise Sinclair. He reached out to stroke the white cat on his left, scratching behind its ears. Birds would also be her style. Canaries or parakeets in brilliant colors and singing sweetly.

"I'm sorry to be so—"

Jordan turned to see Elise standing in the doorway, her face freshly scrubbed and rosy pink. She was staring at the cats, her gaze darting back and forth between the two furry creatures and Jordan.

"Where did you find her?" she asked.

"Is this the missing cat?"

She nodded.

"I didn't find her," Jordan replied. "She found me."

Elise narrowed her eyes and shot the white cat a venomous look.

"Are they not supposed to be·on the furniture?" he asked.

Elise smiled, and Jordan relaxed a bit as he felt the warmth penetrate his icy composure.

"No, they're always on the furniture. They think the furniture in this house exists solely for their enjoyment. It's just that those cats don't like anyone. Not even me, and I feed them. In the five years that I've known them, they have never shown me, or anyone else for that matter, an ounce of affection." Elise sat down on the couch next to Jordan and tipped the gray cat's chin up to look into the animal's hooded eyes. "I wonder if they're sick."

The cat responded with a nasty hiss and a swipe of its paw, before indolently closing its eyes again.

"They appear to be quite healthy," Jordan said solemnly.

"You wouldn't want to take these cats home with you, would you?" she joked. "They seem to have taken a real liking to you."

"No," Jordan answered. "I'm not much of a...cat person."

"I didn't think so," she murmured, her attempt at levity ignored. She primly folded her hands in her lap and looked at him. "Well, Mr. Prentiss. What can I do for you?"

"I'd like you to plan my wedding." For a fleeting second, Jordan thought he saw disappointment shade her face, but then she smiled widely, her heart-shaped mouth curving up at the corners.

"I would love to help you plan your wedding. Why don't we set up a time for you and your fiancée to come in and discuss the preliminaries?"

"I'd like to take care of that right now, if that's agreeable with you."

"But wouldn't you rather have your bride here to participate in some of the decision making? It is her wedding, too."

Jordan stared at her for a moment before he spoke. "My...bride and I have discussed the matter...and she has agreed to let me make all the arrangements. With your help, of course. When decisions must be made, I will discuss them with her and pass along her wishes."

"This is most unusual, Mr. Prentiss. A woman's wedding day is the most important day of her life. Are you sure your fiancée wouldn't be happier working with me directly? If she can't, perhaps her mother or her sister would agree to help."

"Miss Sinclair, there will be a great deal of attention focused on this wedding. I do not want my fiancée exposed to any undue pressure or inconvenience. If you have a problem with this, I'm sure I can—"

"Oh, no, Mr. Prentiss," she interrupted, a conciliatory smile on her lips. "Whatever you and your fiancée have decided is fine with me."

"We want a large, traditional wedding. I would expect approximately four hundred guests." He saw Elise's eyes widen with shock. "Of course, you will have an unlimited budget for the wedding. Whatever you feel is appropriate is fine with me...and my fiancée," he added quickly. "But you must be extremely discreet in making your plans. I do not want anyone learning of this wedding until the invitations are sent. Can you do that, Miss Sinclair?"

Elise nodded mutely.

"Then you accept the job?"

"Yes...yes, I accept."

"Good." Jordan stood up and extended his hand. Elise slowly rose and took it. "I look forward to working with you, Miss Sinclair. Now, I really must be going." He reached into his breast pocket, withdrew a business card and handed it to her. "If you have any questions, just call me. But most of the decisions I leave up to you. I trust your judgment on these matters. Send me whatever papers I need to sign along with an invoice for your expected expenses and charges and I'll be sure you are compensated immediately."

Jordan nodded to her, effectively ending their meeting, then picked up his coat and walked into the foyer. She followed a few steps behind him.

"Wait. You can't leave yet. We have so many more things to discuss."

Her hand touched his elbow and Jordan turned to her with a questioning look. When she snatched her fingers away, he felt a strange sensation of loss.

"Have you chosen a date for the wedding?" she asked.

"April 18."

She relaxed and smiled in relief. "That gives us plenty of time. That's over a year away."

"This April 18."

"Three months from now?" Her voice betrayed a hint of alarm. "You want me to plan a wedding for four hundred guests in three months?"

"Is that a problem?"

She looked at him, astonished, then covered her expression carefully. "No. I'm sure I can take care of it. But wouldn't you rather have a June wedding? April can be such a terrible month for weather. And June would give us a little more time to plan."

"The wedding date is set, Miss Sinclair," Jordan said as he pulled on his coat. "It must be April 18."

She sighed in resignation. "Have you made *any* plans? Have you booked a location for the reception?"

"Isn't that part of your job?"

At first she seemed put off by his curt reply, but her expression of dismay was quickly replaced by one of cool efficiency. "I'll work up some budget figures for you and take care of finding a place for the reception. Why don't we plan to meet later this week to go over the preliminary plans. Would Friday be all right?"

"Fine. Call my secretary and set up a time. I'll let her know to expect your call." Jordan opened the front door. "Goodbye, Miss Sinclair."

"Goodbye, Mr. Prentiss."

Jordan pulled the door shut behind him and scanned the narrow street for his driver and limousine. As he stepped into the car, he looked back at the house. Though the fussy decor had made him uncomfortable at first, he had sensed a certain warmth and contentment sitting in Elise's flower-strewn parlor. He had been tempted to stay longer, but had found his mind wandering from the wedding plans and lingering on Elise Sinclair's beautiful features.

As the limo pulled away from the curb, Jordan made another instant business decision. He would not turn over plans for the wedding to Pete Stockton. It would look too suspicious, and Elise was already questioning the absence of the bride. No, Jordan would work with her personally.

He smiled to himself as he realized that this was the only business decision he had made all day that gave him the slightest bit of pleasure.

2

SEVENTEEN BRIDESMAIDS, not to mention the junior attendants. All of them dressed in a different color. Purple, pink, pumpkin, periwinkle. It would be laughable, a disaster of catastrophic proportions. Like an explosion in a paint factory.

"Seventeen bridesmaids? I've never planned a wedding with that many attendants." Elise groped for a gentle way to dissuade the bride. "A wedding party that size could be very...unmanageable." She had wanted to say ostentatious or even tacky. But brides were a very unstable breed and one wrong word could result in torrents of tears. "There may not be room for all of them at the front of the church."

"Then we'll get a bigger church," Minny chirped. "There is no way I can leave any of my friends out. *No way.* They would hate me forever and I just couldn't stand that. Besides, Daddy said I could have whatever I wanted and this is what I want."

"All right," Elise said patiently. "But why don't we rethink the color scheme. With that many attendants, it might be best to choose one color for the bridesmaids' dresses." She hesitated, considering how an art-deco wedding might look. But seventeen bridesmaids standing at the front of a church in black would probably resemble a flock of crows perched on a phone line. A snowball wedding would be just as bad, enough white to send the guests home blinded by the sight. "How about having all the girls in emerald green? Or deep magenta?"

"But I really, really wanted a rainbow wedding," Minny whined. "Mother, tell her."

Elise looked to Grace Marbury, long-suffering wife of Crazy Bill Marbury, Chicago's king of discount appliances. Though Grace had endeavored to inject a bit of class into her daughter's wedding, her every suggestion had been overruled by Minny and her indulgent daddy. Grace smiled at Elise and shrugged. It was clear she had given up the fight long ago. Maybe it was about time for Elise to throw in the monogrammed tea towel, too.

No, Elise scolded herself, there was a wedding at stake, along with her reputation. She had to give it one last try.

"With a rainbow wedding, you have to be very careful how you assign the colors," Elise began, fixing a deeply concerned look on her face. "What if someone doesn't like the color you've chosen for her? What if she wants the color you've chosen for someone else? If you give the best colors to your best friends, how will your other attendants feel? They might really, *really* be mad at you. Wouldn't it be best to choose your favorite color? After all, it is your wedding."

Elise could see the wheels turning in Minny's head as she weighed this new dilemma. Finally the girl sighed dejectedly.

"All right, we'll dress them all in one color, even though I think it's really, really boring. But it's got to be purple, 'cause that's my absolute favorite color. Do you think tuxedos come in lavender? Wouldn't that look cool—purple dresses and lavender tuxedos? And we could even dye those boring white roses purple."

"Purple would be lovely, Minny." Elise unclenched her hands and relaxed her jaw. She had won the day's battle, but she knew she was losing the war. After the Marbury wedding, she might be forced to change the name of her business to A Taste*less* Affair. "We'll discuss the men's colors next week. Let me know when you'd like to shop for the bridesmaids' dresses and we'll choose something stunning for the girls. Usually the bridesmaids accompany the bride on the shopping trip, but I think seventeen girls would make it impossible to come to a decision."

"Oh, no. We have to take them all along. I promised. If I don't, they'll hate me forever."

Elise stood up and walked the Marburys to the front door, collapsing against it after she shut it behind them. At times like these she wondered what had possessed her to get into the wedding business at all. Why hadn't she followed her childhood dream of becoming a bus driver? Or a princess? Or a cowgirl? Any one of those careers would have been better than what she had chosen.

If she hadn't desperately needed the income from the Marbury wedding, she would never have taken the job. But Crazy Bill had deep pockets, bottomless pockets when it came to his only daughter. Thank God she had the Prentiss wedding to outweigh the Marbury debacle. An unlimited budget and little interference from the bride or the groom. She would plan a wedding the likes of which Chicago had never seen.

Elise glanced at the clock on the mantel. She was due at Jordan Prentiss's office in an hour for their first planning meeting. The cab ride downtown during the afternoon rush could take half that time. She ran up the stairs to change, a hum of anticipation pulsing in her head. After their last meeting, she wanted to look her best. But she stopped midway up the second flight of stairs with a sudden realization.

She was worrying about her appearance like a lovesick teenager! Jordan was an engaged man. Elise slowly sat down on the stairs, winding her fingers around a pair of balusters and resting her forehead between them.

She was attracted to him. From the moment she saw him standing on her front stoop, she had felt an undeniable connection, a tiny current that drew her to him. His image had drifted through her thoughts over and over during the past four days and she had found herself fantasizing about the feel of his soft, dark hair and the touch of his finely sculpted lips.

But it was his eyes that had drawn her to him, his unsettling habit of looking directly into her gaze as if he could see her soul. Though he maintained the outward appearance of a cool, detached businessman, she'd noticed something more simmering beneath the surface. It was as if the man on the outside was a careful affectation to cover the man inside. And the only hint of the inner man had been in the eyes. Those stunning pale-blue eyes. A boyish, almost innocent feature on such a sophisticated and worldly man.

What had she seen in those eyes? Her first impression had been doubt. But he was such a confident man; nothing could rattle that ironclad composure. Pain? Elise let the thought swirl in her mind. Romantic images of a long-lost love, a broken promise, a man betrayed drifted through her thoughts.

Elise shook her head. She was letting her imagination run away with her again. Why did she always try to romanticize life? Jordan Prentiss was probably an ordinary man with ordinary problems. Maybe he had stubbed his toe as he'd gotten out of bed that morning or maybe his fiancée was driving him crazy as brides had a tendency to do. Or maybe the stock market was down.

She had attached a mystique to the man, then let her fantasies take over. It hadn't been the first time. Elise had an amazing knack for stumbling upon tortured souls. Every man she had dated boasted a painful past. And those who didn't, well, she managed to invent one for them. Then she threw herself into healing them with love and affection. And when they were healed, Elise found herself with an ordinary man and his ordinary problems, not the romantic, happily-ever-after hero she had hoped for. The infatuation would die and Elise would be left with just another name to add to her list of male "friends." At last count, she had more male friends than Minny Marbury had bridesmaids.

Elise sighed. She had let her fantasies about Jordan Prentiss go too far. It was no wonder. Jordan was an incredibly attractive man, probably the most handsome man she had ever met. He exuded an air of tightly leashed sensuality, carefully controlled and hidden behind his indifferent facade.

She would have to put a stop to her crazy infatuation—they were very unprofessional feelings for a wedding consultant to have toward her client. Though unrequited love was a very romantic notion, she was sensible enough to know that it could only lead to heartache.

Elise raised her head and looked up the stairs to see Clorinda and Thisbe staring down their ugly noses at her from the third-floor landing. "Oh, what do you know?" Elise shouted, sending the pair scurrying for the safety of the linen closet. "If you're not careful, I may accidentally leave the front door open and you'll both find yourselves eating out of garbage cans and associating with alley cats on a permanent basis."

A half hour later she was seated in the back of a cab, weaving through traffic on Division Street, dressed in a simple suit topped with a conservative wool trench coat. She had decided that dressing to attract the attention of Jordan Prentiss would only be inviting trouble, so she had even gone so far as to pull back her wavy hair into a simple businesslike knot at her nape.

The cab dropped her off in front of an impressive glass-and-steel high rise on the east side of Michigan Avenue near Water Tower Place. She gave the security guard Jordan's card, and after he confirmed her appointment, she was directed to a bank of elevators. The elevator opened on the twenty-third floor and Elise found herself facing the wide glass doors of the corporate headquarters of BabyLove Baby Foods. The company name was painted on each door in gleaming silver script wrapped around the familiar BabyLove logo, a heart-shaped silver spoon.

Elise stepped into the reception area and a pretty young woman behind a circular desk greeted her with a smile.

"Good evening, Miss Sinclair," she said as she stood up.

"Good evening. I'm here to see Mr. Prentiss. We have a five-thirty appointment."

"Mr. Prentiss is just finishing up a meeting. He asked that I show you back to his office."

Elise followed the receptionist down a wide hallway. The woman pushed open a pair of mahogany doors at the end of the hall and stepped aside to let Elise through.

The corner office was huge and starkly modern. A wide glass-topped table served as a desk and two sleek leather guest chairs sat before it, with a more imposing desk chair behind it. Two of the four walls were solid glass, with the interiors of the offices across Michigan Avenue visible through the tinted windows. The other two walls were adorned with large postimpressionist paintings.

Elise recognized the artists immediately and wondered what paintings of museum quality were doing in the office of the president of a baby-food company. If Jordan was a collector of art, he had very good taste. But it was hard to believe that the taciturn businessman she had met four days ago would collect art for its beauty alone. A man like Jordan Prentiss was more apt to collect art for its investment value.

"Could I get you anything to drink, Miss Sinclair?" the receptionist asked.

Elise shook her head. "No, thank you."

"Then I'll let Mr. Prentiss know you're here."

She walked from the office, closing the doors behind her. Elise placed her briefcase beside one of the chairs, slipped out of her coat, and draped it over the arm, then strolled over to the windows. The twinkling lights from the rush-hour traffic outlined the street below as the cars, cabs and buses crawled home from the Loop on Michigan Avenue.

"Hello, dear."

Elise spun around to find a plump white-haired woman standing before her. She was smiling, her eyes sparkling behind wire-rimmed glasses and her face alight with undisguised curiosity. She wore an elegant pink suit with pearl buttons down the front of the jacket. Elise wondered how she had managed to enter the room without making a sound then looked down at her shoes. A pair of high-tops completed her outfit.

"Hello," Elise replied. "I was just waiting for Mr. Prentiss."

"You're here for Jordan? You must be Elise." The woman walked to Jordan's desk and carefully flipped through his calendar. "I'm sorry Jordan has kept you waiting. He sometimes gets so involved in business matters that he forgets the time." She began to sort through the file folders on his desk, peeking inside one every so often, then putting it carefully back in place before continuing her search.

So this was Jordan's secretary, Elise thought. Somehow she had imagined Jordan with a much younger, more coldly efficient woman, not someone who looked like everyone's favorite grandmother.

"I suppose you're here to discuss the wedding," the woman said, engrossed in the contents of a large white envelope.

"You know about the wedding?" Elise asked.

The older woman smiled, the corners of her eyes and mouth crinkling into deep grooves, as if smiling were the predominant expression on her face and had been her whole life. "Of course I do, dear. I'm well aware of what Edward's been stirring up. Although I can't say that I approve of Jordan's plans. I would hate to see him in an unhappy marriage. What do you think?"

"About what?"

"Why, Jordan's happiness, of course," she replied, acting as if Elise should know exactly what she was talking about. "He takes on too much and now this."

"This?"

"Yes, this. What are we going to do about that boy, Elise?"

"I—I'm not sure I know what you mean."

The woman reached out and patted Elise on the hand. "I'm sure you don't, at least not yet. But you will, my dear, you'll see. I'm counting on it."

The woman gave her a cheerful wave and bustled out of the room, leaving Elise with a sense of utter confusion. What had she meant by her cryptic statements? She'd mentioned Jordan as a little boy. Would his secretary have known him as a child? And her words had almost implied that she was against Jordan's marriage, that it would cause him unhappiness. And who was Edward? Elise was still staring at the doorway in befuddlement when Jordan walked in.

"Miss Sinclair," he greeted, stepping to her and shaking her hand in a firm, impersonal manner. "I'm sorry to keep you waiting. I hope Kay made you comfortable."

"Comfortable" was hardly the word for it. In fact, her conversation with Jordan's secretary had made her quite uncomfortable.

"My secretary was out sick today so I had Kay stay at the front desk until you arrived. Did she offer you something to drink? Coffee or tea, perhaps?"

"No," Elise answered, quickly covering her confusion. If Jordan's secretary was sick, who was the sweet little woman she'd encountered just minutes ago in his office? She seemed quite at ease shuffling through the papers on Jordan's desk. And she was obviously close to Jordan—she knew about the wedding.

"No, she didn't offer you anything?"

"No...I mean yes, she did, and no, I don't need anything," Elise replied, stumbling over her words and glancing up at him. He was gazing at her in that same intense way she remembered from their encounter in her parlor, as if he were trying to read her thoughts.

He was as handsome as she recalled. His hair was dark brown, nearly black, and was combed neatly back. She imagined it windblown and falling in waves over his forehead, imagined him with a cheerful, boyish smile instead of his usual cool, prepossessed expression. But right now the only clues to his state of mind were a questioning arch of his eyebrow and a tiny upturn of the corners of his firm lips, not nearly enough to constitute a smile. She found herself blushing slightly.

"Well," he said, "why don't we get started, then?"

He took his place behind his desk and Elise sat down in one of the guest chairs, grabbed her briefcase and extracted a file folder and pen. She looked up at him and found him staring out the window. Elise cleared her throat and waited for him to turn to her.

"I'm listening," he said softly, toying with a small jar he had pulled off his credenza.

"All right," she replied. "First of all, I'll need your full name as well as your fiancée's."

Jordan paused for a moment, staring at the baby

food jar he held in his hands. "Jordan Broderick Prentiss."

Watching his long, slender fingers grip the glass, she tried to imagine what his hands might feel like touching her. She bit her lower lip, disturbed by the direction of her thoughts, and hastily scribbled the name on her file form. Then she paused, her pen poised, and listened for the next name. "And your fiancée's?" she prompted.

"Is that necessary?" Jordan asked, directing a cool blue gaze at her.

"The fiancée or the name? It's usually standard practice to have a fiancée if one plans to get married. As for her name, if I'm to order invitations, it would definitely help." Elise shifted uncomfortably in her chair, realizing her answer sounded mildly sarcastic. But why was he so secretive about the bride's identity? First, there was his insistence on the April wedding date, and now, his reluctance to give her a simple name. What possible reason could there be for all this subterfuge?

The reason came to her like a bolt from the blue. Jordan's bride was a celebrity! In his much-publicized bachelor days, he had dated his fair share of famous women, she had learned, including several well-known movie actresses and a famous pop singer. That could be the only reason for attempting to keep the bride's name out of the press. What a chivalrous gesture, Elise thought with a smile. It was the first spark of romanticism she had seen from the aloof Mr. Prentiss.

What a delicious thought! Jordan Prentiss, white knight, protecting his lady fair. But why the quick wedding? Maybe the future Mrs. Prentiss had to get back to Hollywood. Or maybe she had a concert tour coming up. Or maybe...she was pregnant. Oh, dear, a high-society shotgun wedding. She stopped herself. Her imagination was running rampant again.

Still, if Jordan Prentiss really was marrying a celebrity, this wedding would bring her the kind of publicity she had only dreamed of. The front page of the society section. Society brides fighting for her services. What did she care whether the bride was pregnant or not?

But she *did* care.

"You'll just have to put off ordering the invitations for now," Jordan said.

Elise nodded reluctantly. She could wait for the name, but she would get it out of him sooner or later. "We can put off ordering them for at least another month, and if you're willing to pay a bit extra, another two months."

"As I told you earlier, Miss Sinclair, money is no object."

"Yes. Well, then, I'm sure the invitations will be no problem. Next, we need to discuss the location for the reception. Since you are firm on your wedding date as April 18..." She paused, hoping he might offer an explanation for the early date, but not really expecting a straightforward reply.

"Yes," he said. "April 18."

Her hope for a brief reprieve fell. "An evening reception is out of the question. All the hotels that can accommodate four hundred guests are booked. That, in turn, rules out an afternoon wedding. We could consider your country club, if you have one."

Jordan shook his head. "No country club."

"Or your home or family estate."

He shook his head again. "No room."

"I did happen upon one bit of luck, though. The Drake had a cancellation in their Gold Coast Room for the early afternoon of the eighteenth. It's the city's most elegant location. I would suggest a morning wedding with a champagne brunch following. Although that's not quite as traditional as you had hoped for, it would be acceptable given the time constraints."

"Fine," he answered. He looked over at her. "Is there anything else?"

She held back a gasp of shock. Did he think this wedding was going to plan itself? Lord, the man could be aggravating! "Yes, of course there is. I have a whole list here. Are you sure you wouldn't rather have your fiancée here to help?" she asked, wondering just how far she could push the issue.

He looked down at the jar in his hand and opened it, then swiveled the lid back and forth distractedly. "Go on," he ordered, blatantly ignoring her question.

"Where do you plan to have the ceremony?" Elise asked. This was an easy question, one she was certain to get a solid answer for.

"A church," he replied. "That is where one is supposed to get married, isn't it?"

Elise ground her teeth. "Yes and no. Churches are sometimes harder to schedule than receptions. If you have a church of choice, I can check on the availability. If not, you can hold the ceremony at the hotel."

"No, it has to be a church. My grandfather belonged to Fourth Presbyterian. Try there."

Elise wrote the name of the church on her form. Fourth Presbyterian was one of Chicago's most beautiful churches, a truly romantic spot for a wedding. Elise could already picture the floral decorations she would choose for the picturesque Gothic church, swags of greenery and white satin ribbon decorating the sanctuary and sprays of roses with candles at the end of each pew. And a huge arrangement of her favorite flowers, Casablanca lilies and white roses, adorning the altar. It would be stunning, a wedding to remember for years.

Elise drew herself back to the present and glanced up at Jordan. Now they were getting somewhere. An actual decision had been made. "Fourth Presbyterian would be perfect. And since most Protestant weddings are scheduled for the afternoon, the church might still be available at—" She silently watched him remove the lid of the jar he was playing with and hold it under his nose, sniffing at the contents. "This late—" He wasn't listening to anything she was saying. "Date." She might as well be planning a wedding for two mannequins in the window of Marshall Field's.

"As for the menu," she continued smoothly.

"Yes, the menu," he murmured, nodding. Suddenly, he set the jar down, turned to his computer and began tapping at the keys.

"Mr. Prentiss?" Elise watched his intent study of the screen. "Mr. Prentiss?" He made no move to resume their meeting.

"Fine," Elise muttered. "I'll just work on the menu while you do whatever it is you're doing. For the main course, I would suggest sardine sandwiches and grits. Of course, if you would prefer hot dogs, that's fine, but hot dogs don't have the same...oh, I don't know...panache as a good sardine sandwich." Jordan showed no reaction. "And for dessert, instead of cake, we could have cotton candy. Wait! I have a wonderful idea. We could dress the bride and groom as clowns and make this wedding a real circus."

The room was silent. Elise waited and wondered how long it would take for him to realize she had stopped speaking and return his attention to the wedding. Finally he looked up.

"I'm sorry, what were you saying?"

"We should discuss the color scheme," Elise replied evenly, hoping this would elicit more interest from him. "I would assume your bride has chosen her bridesmaids. What about the dresses for them?"

"No bridesmaids," Jordan responded.

No country club, no family estate, no bridesmaids. What was with this guy? "You mean no dresses?"

"No dresses and no bridesmaids."

No bridesmaids? What was a wedding without bridesmaids? Elise rubbed her temple, feeling one of her I-wish-I-drove-a-bus-for-a-living headaches coming on. Gee, maybe Minny Marbury could lend a few bridesmaids to the future Mr. and Mrs. Prentiss. Their wedding was promising to be much more bizarre than Minny's. "You have to at least have a maid of honor and a best man."

"I do—I mean, we do?" Jordan asked. He shrugged. "All right."

His sudden acquiescence surprised her. "Your bride and her honor attendant will need to go out and look for a bridesmaid's dress."

"Can you do that?"

"Of course, I do it all the time. But usually I'm accompanied by the bride."

"Well, you'll have to do it yourself."

Elise's frustration shot to the boiling point. If he gave

her one more evasive or obtuse answer, she was sure she would scream. How was she supposed to plan a wedding with no cooperation from the bride or the groom? She had once thought their lack of interference would make her job easier, but now she was beginning to regret her earlier enthusiasm.

"All right," she said with practiced patience. "What is your bride's favorite color?"

Jordan paused.

"You don't know your fiancée's favorite color?" Elise calmed herself. She had learned that Jordan Prentiss cared little about this wedding, but now she was beginning to believe that he cared even less about his fiancée. She quickly reconsidered her opinion of the man before her. Chivalrous? Hah! He was quite possibly the most unromantic man she had ever met. It was a wonder he had even found a woman to agree to marry him and incomprehensible that the woman, pregnant or not, would have the romantic fortitude to put up with him for life. The image of a shotgun, pointed at his head, flashed through her mind.

"Black," he finally said, as if this was the only answer he was really sure of.

"Black," Elise repeated.

"Yes, she wears black all the time. I would assume it's her favorite color."

"Black is not an appropriate color for a morning wedding." Elise heard her voice rise several decibels. "Black is better suited to funerals."

"Hmm. Then it should be black," he muttered as he stared into the jar.

She watched in amazement as he stuck his finger inside and then put it in his mouth. He grimaced, turning in his chair to face her.

"Here, smell this." He reached over his desk and pushed the jar at her.

She drew away.

"Go ahead," he urged. "Smell it."

Elise sniffed at the contents of the little jar. "It doesn't smell like anything."

"Exactly," he replied, a note of triumph in his voice.

"Taste it." He dipped his index finger into the jar again and held it out to her. Without thinking, she drew his finger into her mouth. When he didn't pull his hand away, she looked at him with wide eyes, realizing just what she was doing. Slowly Elise pulled away, conscious of the erotic tingle that touched her lips and tongue. He, too, seemed suddenly aware of what had passed between them and hesitantly drew his fingers away, letting his touch linger for just a moment on her lower lip.

Elise let the taste of the baby food and his finger mingle in her mouth before swallowing convulsively. "It— it doesn't taste like anything."

"Precisely," he said, his voice low, his gaze locked with hers. Then he shook himself out of his daze and smiled.

A tiny thrill rippled through her as she watched the corners of his mouth turn up in a charming grin.

"We know for a fact that babies can tell the difference between strained peas and banana pudding. Any mother will tell you that. And if they're aware of that difference, they probably differentiate between good carrots and this tasteless orange mush we package as carrots.

"The problem is in the canning process," he explained, pushing himself away from his desk to pace before the windows. "We try to avoid the use of preservatives, salt and sugar, cook the hell out of the food and then grind it up. It ends up bland and tasteless. Would you eat that?"

Elise shook her head, watching as he paced before her.

"Then why would a baby?" he continued, not waiting for an answer. "I've been thinking about adding a line of frozen, microwaveable baby foods to BabyLove. It's going to take a tremendous amount of investment in new processing and packaging equipment, plus a big marketing and advertising budget, but we could make baby food that tastes good. What do you think?"

She could hear the excitement in his voice, see the passion in his eyes, and she wondered whether that same burning passion she saw now had ever been directed toward his fiancée. She wondered what it would feel like to have that passion aimed at her. "I think it's a wonderful idea."

"My board of directors disagrees with you, me, and the research. Our research shows that ninety percent of our product is consumed in the home and eighty percent of our customers own microwaves. The only drawback to frozen microwaveable baby food is that it doesn't travel well. The board feels that this is enough to kill the idea. I think they're being stupidly short-sighted."

"Well, I think it's a brilliant idea. I'm surprised no one has thought of it before."

"Someone would have if babies could talk. They would have told us long ago why they feel compelled to spit up their dinners all over their parents' shoulders."

Elise giggled at Jordan's serious expression. Could it be that Jordan Prentiss had a sense of humor? Though he wasn't smiling, she could detect a hint of sardonic wit in his voice. It was a small chink in the impenetrable armor he hid behind and she felt as if she had been allowed a glimpse of the real man, a man she found utterly intriguing.

"Do you and your fiancée plan to have children after you're—" Elise stopped. The words had just popped out. The question was such a natural one, but combined with the evidence she had already gleaned about the future Mrs. Prentiss, she realized that it might appear overtly nosy. "—married?"

Jordan looked puzzled for a moment. "I don't know. We haven't discussed it. But yes, I think I would like to have children."

She stifled a sigh of relief and her mental picture of the shotgun disappeared in a puff of smoke. For some unknown reason, she was glad Jordan wasn't being forced into marriage. But then she realized the idea of a shotgun wedding was preposterous. Jordan Prentiss was not the kind of man to be forced into doing anything against his will.

"How many would you like?" Elise asked, regaining her composure.

"Two. Two would be best."

"Two sounds like a nice number. I was an only child, so two sounds like a good number to me." Once again, Elise's words escaped her mouth before checking in with her mind. What was she saying? "Not that I meant that you and I—I mean, me and my husband—

when I find a husband, that is—after I'm married—I'd like two children, with my husband." Elise flushed.

Jordan grinned at her as he slid into his chair and studied her openly. "You changed your hair," he said, shifting the conversation in a manner that was becoming increasingly familiar to her. "I liked it the other way."

Elise reached out to touch her hair. "The other way?"

He motioned, waving his hand near his shoulder. "Down. Loose and curly. The way you had it the last time I saw you."

"Oh..." The word hung in the air between them. Elise's mind raced, wondering how they had gotten so far off the subject of the wedding. Her only excuse was that Jordan Prentiss was the oddest client she had ever had. And the most irresistible. Maybe all grooms are like this, she thought. It certainly explained why they were all getting married.

"I think we should get back to the wedding plans, Mr. Prentiss," she suggested.

"Jordan," he said, his gazed still locked on her. "You can call me 'Jordan'...Elise."

She liked the sound of her name on his lips, the way it sent a shiver skittering down her spine. "Jordan," she repeated, trying to calm her pounding heart. "Now, about the budget."

"What about the budget, Elise?"

"Three hundred per person should cover everything." She expected a reaction—shock, discomfort, disbelief. After all, she was proposing a total budget of $120,000. But his gaze never wavered from hers. "Of course that doesn't include the wedding dress."

"That sounds quite reasonable to me."

Reasonable? It was enough to buy the most lavish wedding Chicago had to offer and then some. Elise looked down at her notes, frantically searching for the next subject of discussion and thoroughly rattled by his outward show of calm. She glanced up and found him watching her intently. They stared at each other a long moment before she finally spoke.

"I—I think we've covered everything I need for now," she said, suddenly feeling an intense need to escape Jordan's magnetic presence. "I'll check on the church and I'll make arrangements to meet with the caterers at the Drake to discuss the menu. If you'd like to be involved with the choice of—"

"I'll be there," Jordan said, a crooked smile touching his lips. "Call my secretary with the time and date."

Elise stood up and pulled her coat from the chair beside her. She fumbled with her briefcase, then held out her hand to Jordan. "All right...fine...I guess that's it, then." She pulled her hand from Jordan's warm grip, the heat searing her palm. "I'll talk to you sometime next week, Mr.—er, Jordan."

Elise turned for the door. Jordan followed and pulled it open for her. "Good night," she mumbled as she brushed past him.

"Miss Sinclair?"

She turned back to him.

"Just one more thing. About this clown idea of yours..."

Elise felt her face flush. *Oh, no. He had been listening!*

"The idea has merit, especially the cotton candy for dessert. I'll give it some serious thought." He smiled

again, this time a devastating, heart-stopping smile.
"Good night."

JORDAN WATCHED her hasty departure down the long
hallway and smiled to himself.

God, she was beautiful. Even in that button-down
suit he could still make out the soft, lush form beneath—full breasts, a tiny waist, curvy hips and legs
that wouldn't quit. Those eyes, like a cat, green and set
at a slight upward tilt, and that mouth, full and expressive. There was no doubt about it. He wanted Elise Sinclair. The flicker of attraction he had felt at their first
meeting had turned into a fire.

A fire he would have to snuff out.

In the past, it had always been a matter of control, a
matter of containing the desire. As long as he was in
absolute control of his basic urges, there was no chance
that the relationship would go any farther than he
wanted it to. He would not be swayed by lust and emotion. He would not make the same mistake his father
had. He would not allow a woman to ruin his life.

He had never experienced a sexual attraction as
deep and intense as he felt for Elise Sinclair—and as
dangerous. Jordan drew a deep breath and attempted
to smother the flames Elise had ignited. He would put
her out of his mind.

Besides, having her was impossible now that he was
an "engaged" man, he rationalized. Elise Sinclair did
not seem the type to play fast and loose with her clients, or any man for that matter. She was more likely
the kind of woman to give herself only to a man she
loved, a man who loved her in return.

And Jordan could not be that man. An unexpected

stab of disappointment twisted in his gut at the realization that she was the first woman he had ever truly wanted and the only woman he couldn't have.

"So that's Elise Sinclair. I can see why you decided to take me off the planning committee." Pete Stockton stood in the hallway, and had obviously enjoyed the same view of Elise's retreating form.

Jordan walked back into his office, with Pete at his heels. He slid into his chair and leaned back, closing his eyes and rubbing his forehead.

"How did it go?" Pete asked.

"Playing out this charade is a lot harder than I thought it would be," he said, his voice shadowed with exhaustion. "I've never been good at lying, especially to women. She is definitely suspicious. We have got to find a fiancée for me and fast." *The sooner I get engaged,* he thought to himself, *the sooner Elise Sinclair is forgotten.* "What about the party? Any responses from your list of five?"

"Even on such short notice, they're all planning to come. You don't throw many parties, but when you do, it's the hottest ticket in town. It should be quite an affair. Thirty-five of Chicago's richest and most powerful and five prospective brides, all seemingly gathered to salute your newest cause, the Children's Museum at the Art Institute. And, of course, I'll be there to help you out."

Jordan glanced at him. "Help me out?"

"You're going to need me, unless you plan on charming all five of them at the same time. I do respect your skills as a bachelor, but that's beyond even you. Somebody's got to pay court to four of them while you're interviewing the fifth. And if they bring guests, you'll need me to run interference."

"I don't think that's necessary. I'm sure I can handle the situation by myself."

Pete sat down across from Jordan. "May I speak candidly?"

"You've never asked my permission before. What's stopping you now?"

"Let's face it, Jordan. You're not exactly Mr. Romance. In fact, when it comes to matters of the heart, you haven't progressed beyond the Dark Ages. In order to make this plan work, you've got to convince a woman to marry you in less than two months, *before* the wedding invitations go out. You've never had a relationship with a woman that's lasted that long."

Jordan considered Pete's statement soberly. He was right. He'd heard the same accusation from nearly every woman he'd had a relationship with, short-lived though the association may have been. Women did not consider him romantic in the least. And he hadn't a clue as to what women did consider romantic. But Pete did.

"All right," Jordan muttered. "You can come. Are all the arrangements made?"

"The caterers will be at your place tomorrow by four. The party starts at eight. I've called your cleaning lady and she'll be in early tomorrow morning. All you need to do is show up. It's formal dress, by the way."

"I hate parties," he grumbled. "All that small talk drives me crazy. How long is this supposed to last?"

"Three hours, maybe four."

Jordan sighed and pushed himself out of his chair.

"If it weren't for Edward, I wouldn't be in this mess. Anything new on him?"

"He met today with Cyril Carstairs. They had a very cozy lunch at Belle Maison. Edward had the veal and Cyril had a Caesar salad. The way I figure it, Cyril is the swing vote. He's the one you need to get to first. The others can wait."

Jordan opened his briefcase and began to toss file folders into it. "I'll call him Monday. Do you have the regional sales reports finished?"

Pete held out a file folder that he'd picked off of Jordan's desk. "Isn't it a little early for you to be leaving? It's only six o'clock. You're usually here until at least ten."

"I'll be in early tomorrow morning. We can go over the reports then." Jordan grabbed his coat from the closet.

"Do you want me to call your driver?"

"No, I think I'll walk home. I could use the exercise. See you tomorrow, Pete."

Jordan strode to the elevator, pulling on his coat and fishing in his pockets for his cashmere-lined leather gloves. As he pushed open the wide glass doors of the ground floor lobby and stepped outside, the wind that howled unceasingly between the buildings on Michigan Avenue hit him squarely in the chest. For a moment, he regretted the decision to walk. But thoughts of Elise still nagged at his mind and he would do anything, including walking in a subzero wind chill, to rid himself of this unwanted attraction for her.

The brisk ten-minute walk home along the lake did nothing to drive Elise's lovely face from his thoughts. The biting lake wind didn't dispel the heat that burned deep inside of him. The double scotch he had with his dinner didn't numb the uncomfortable craving he felt.

Jordan Prentiss would choose a bride in less than twenty-four hours, yet he fell asleep that night with an image of Elise Sinclair on his mind.

3

HER PERFECTLY MANICURED hand slithered down the front of Jordan's pleated shirt, a vicious red nail flicking at an onyx stud before she dropped her questing fingers farther, to his belly and then beyond.

"Why don't we find some place where we can be alone," she murmured, emphasizing the word "alone" with the firm pressure of her palm at the juncture of his thighs. She rubbed her sequined-clad body against his, thigh to thigh, breast to chest. "I know you want me and I want you, so let's forget the silly preliminaries and get to it."

Jordan wrapped his fingers around her bare shoulders and gently pushed her away from him. "Excuse me," he said, his voice cold and dispassionate. "There's someone I need to speak to. Here, drink this." He pushed a glass of champagne into Sirena Marsh's hand as he stepped away from her. "And try to relax," he added. "This is a party, after all."

Pete Stockton stood across the room, grinning from ear to ear, surrounded by three of Jordan's potential fiancées. He raised his glass to Jordan and Jordan nodded back grimly, inclining his head toward the kitchen door, a signal for Stockton to meet him there. Pete extracted himself from the group and made his way across the crowded living room to join Jordan.

"Four down, one to go," Jordan muttered as he

pushed the swinging door open. Weaving through the chaotic mess in the kitchen, Jordan led Pete through the breakfast nook and out to the balcony. The icy air and pristine quiet were a soothing balm to his ragged nerves. He took a deep breath and let it out slowly, a cloud of vapor drifting into the night.

"Don't tell me. Let me guess," Pete said. "You don't like her."

"At least you're right about one thing. Where did you find these women?" Jordan asked, his jaw tight with tension. "First, she shoved me into a dark corner, then she practically emasculated me with those fingernails of hers. I have never met a more aggressive woman in my life. I have to tell you, Pete, that one actually scared me."

"So I missed the mark on Sirena Marsh. What about the others?"

"Lucy McMahon spent twenty-five minutes telling me about her last boyfriend. They broke up six months ago and she's carrying a torch the size of the Statue of Liberty's for the guy. I'm not going to marry a woman on the rebound."

"Yeah, she told me about Larry. I got the condensed version, though. What about Amanda Witherspoon? It looked like you were getting along fine with her. She's intelligent and a knockout."

"She's also engaged. She and Nick Trent's son just announced their engagement last weekend. He's just taken over his father's New York office. Unlike poor Lucy, Amanda is deliriously happy."

"All right, I'll admit my intelligence on Amanda was a little out of date. That leaves Lauren. She looked like a good candidate. I noticed she had a cold, so she probably wasn't at her best. What did you think?"

"Lauren has allergies. She spent our entire conversation blowing her nose and listing the multitude of substances that set off her sneezing and sniffles. My shampoo and my cologne appeared midway down the list. She also informed me that the carpeting was giving her hives and the smell of shellfish was making her nauseous." Jordan rubbed his forehead with his fingertips. "I think it would be best if I met number five and then called it a night."

"Ah, that's not going to be possible," Pete said, turning to gaze out at the lake. "She left."

"She left?"

"Well, actually, she was carried out. It seems Miss Caroline Simmons has a propensity to overindulge in champagne. It happened while you were occupied with Sirena. Count yourself lucky, though. Amanda told me the last party Caroline attended she finished the evening on top of the dining-room table singing her rendition of 'Some Enchanted Evening.' It was not a pretty sight."

"I thought I could trust you to take care of this matter," Jordan said.

"All these women looked great on paper. And I didn't have enough time to check them out personally."

Jordan tipped his head back and sighed, realizing that his assistant wasn't at fault. "Send them all home, Pete," he said, his voice betraying his weariness. "This party was a waste of time."

"Okay, boss. Whatever you say."

As Pete stepped through the sliding-glass doors, Jordan leaned to rest his elbows on the railing and looked out over the lake. On the horizon, the constellation Orion was barely visible through the spill of light from the city. Jordan stared at the hunter stars, finding Rigel and Betelgeuse, the brightest stars in the constellation and recalling his father's patient instructions in astronomy.

They had gazed at the stars on a night much like this nearly thirty years ago and they had talked of Jordan's dreams. "Someday I'll fly in a giant rocket to one of those stars," Jordan had promised, "and I'll steal one from the sky and bring it back to you in a jar." His father had laughed and ruffled his hair, then hoisted him up on his shoulder. "Show me which star you'll steal," his father had said, and Jordan had pointed to the heavens, picking out Rigel.

He remembered that night with such clarity; it was the first time he had seen his father smile in a very long time. It would also be the last, for the morning after that crystalline night, Jordan's mother walked out for good. At first, his father had tried to explain. He had been working too much, Jordan's mother was lonely; he wasn't able to give her what she wanted in a husband; she would be back soon. But then he had stopped trying to make excuses and lapsed into a long silence.

James Prentiss had become more and more preoccupied, spending his evenings alone, closeted in his study while his son waited outside. Most nights his father had never come out. Once, Jordan had sneaked in and found him sprawled on the couch, an empty crystal decanter in his hand.

There had been arguments between his grandfather

and his father, the frequency increasing as his father's growing ineffectiveness as president of BabyLove began to show.

His father had succumbed to a heart attack when Jordan was sixteen. By that time, the company his grandfather had founded had floundered. The old man assumed the presidency, but he was unfamiliar with the changing market climate, with the baby boom and broadcast advertising, with supermarket-chain distribution and the competition from the major food conglomerates. Jonathan Prentiss kept the company running just long enough for Jordan to gain the skills and the experience needed to run BabyLove. Upon his grandfather's death four years ago, Jordan was handed the presidency of a company that was on the brink of failure.

No one had ever asked him whether he wanted it or not, it was just given to him as part of his legacy. The Prentiss legacy. And it was the only tool he had left to erase his mother's desertion and his father's mistakes. The company was his life. He knew every corner of the business. And he had been the one to snatch it from the jaws of death to make it what it was today.

He would do anything to preserve that legacy. Anything. He owed it to his father. The little boy who had dreamed of becoming an astronaut still lived inside him, but that boy had grown to be a man and had learned to appreciate what his grandfather and his father had built for him. He was not about to let it go. Not without a fight.

Jordan closed his eyes and let his tense neck muscles relax. When he had first decided on this plan, it seemed acceptable considering the alternatives. But now, the thought of marriage set his senses on edge. It should have been so simple, a business arrangement, a partnership between a man and a woman, with no expectations of love and no need for emotional surrender. She would offer him stability and he would offer her security. It would be a fair trade.

But now that plan no longer seemed workable. Why not? his thoughts demanded. Just what was it he was looking for? Could it be that he wanted more than a business arrangement? Jordan shook his head, trying to sort out the melee of contradictions that plagued his mind. One image, one name, surfaced over and over again, breaking through the muddle.

Elise. Elise Sinclair.

Dammit, why was she doing this to him? Until he had met Elise Sinclair, he had never considered romance a necessary part of a relationship. But she seemed to thrive on it, as if it were a necessary component of life, like breathing or eating or sleeping. Everything about her exuded romance, her soft, melodic voice, her graceful movements, her rose-colored view of the world.

A week ago, he would have written her off as some poor starry-eyed fool with nothing better to do than fantasize about love, an emotion that would never survive in the harsh, real world. But she had turned the tables on him. The fact that he appeared deficient in her eyes because of his lack of romantic skills bothered him. He always prided himself in being a highly educated man. Now he found his education sadly limited in the one area that counted to her—and to hundreds of other women, as well.

So what did he want? He wanted Elise Sinclair. But

he needed a wife. And if he couldn't separate the two, then he was in worse shape than he'd imagined.

Jordan pushed himself away from the railing and stepped back into the kitchen. After adjusting to the cold on the balcony, he found the heat from his apartment smothering. The caterers rushed around the kitchen, clattering trays and clinking glasses, the noise grating against his nerves. Jordan peeked through the swinging door. The crowd had thinned considerably, enough for him to make it through the living room and to the door without much notice, he thought.

Jordan checked his pocket for his keys, then headed for the front door, grabbing his coat on the way and mumbling his goodbyes to the remaining guests. Five minutes later, he turned his Mercedes onto Lake Shore Drive and headed north, the sunroof open to the winter wind and the radio tuned to an all-night jazz station. He drove along the lake as far as Ravinia Park, then turned around and wove his way back through the city.

It was after midnight when he pulled up across the street from Elise's house. Jordan silenced the engine, but left the radio playing softly in the background.

At first he refused to look at the house, angry that he had been drawn to this place against his typically unyielding will. But slowly, he let his gaze drift along the sidewalk and up her front steps. The first and second floors were dark, but a light burned in the window of the third floor. Was she awake?

His imagination slowly played with the possibilities. He would walk to the front door and ring the bell. She would answer and he would pull her into his arms and kiss her. She would be surprised, but she would return his kiss, opening herself to him. He would lead her to the bedroom, undressing her along the way. And then they would make love.

His fantasy came to a grinding halt. Make love? No, they wouldn't *make love*; they would have sex. He had never made love to a woman in his life. Love had nothing to do with the physical release he felt with a woman.

But that wasn't what he wanted to feel when he imagined moving inside of Elise. He wanted a deeper connection; he wanted to surrender himself, to take shelter in her warmth. Suddenly, he wanted to feel more than just the release, he longed to appreciate the significance of the act, to strip away the physical pleasure until all that was left was the pure emotion behind that pleasure.

A shadow suddenly appeared at the window and he instinctively slouched in his seat, trying not to be seen in the feeble glow of the streetlight above his car. He held his breath, then slowly released it when he saw that it wasn't her. The outline of a cat became clear against the light that filtered through the lace curtain. The cat seemed to be looking directly at him.

Jordan straightened in his seat. With his eyes still fixed on the window, he turned the key in the ignition, then pulled the car away from the curb. He dragged his gaze from the house at the last minute.

Thank God it had only been a cat at the window, Jordan thought, because if it had been Elise, he wasn't sure if he could have stopped himself from going inside.

ON TUESDAY MORNING, Elise stood in the center of the Gold Coast Room, her gaze gliding up the huge columns to the ornate gilt plaster ceiling and sparkling chandeliers above. The woman from the Drake's catering staff had left her alone to await Jordan's arrival, rushing off to handle an emergency. Elise was glad to have a moment of solitude. Though Jordan wasn't due for another fifteen minutes, she could sense her rising anticipation.

With a frustrated sigh, she tried to put his image out of her mind for what seemed like the millionth time that day. Instead she closed her eyes and imagined the room as it would look for the Prentiss wedding.

The room would be flooded with midmorning light from the huge windows that overlooked the Oak Street Beach. The rough wooden tables that cluttered the room would be covered with crisp white linen and table runners of white brocade edged in gold, then topped with gleaming silver, china and crystal. She would crown each table with a towering vase of calla lilies and blush roses interlaced with tropical greenery. Uniformed waiters would serve a luscious brunch of lobster medallions on a puff pastry with a light hollandaise sauce. And during brunch, a small orchestra would play soft, romantic music.

She could almost hear the music, the lyric strains of a Gershwin ballad. She hummed a few bars, swaying to the tune, the words passing her lips in a soft song. With a sigh, she moved to the piano at the edge of the dance floor and slid onto the bench. The tune meandered through her mind and she searched for the notes on the keyboard.

Ten years of childhood piano lessons and hours of painstaking practice had paid off. She added the harmony line to Gershwin's "Isn't It Romantic?" and lost herself in the music, embellishing the tune more with each repetition. At first, she hummed along with the piano, then quietly sang the words, slightly off-key. As the music progressed, Elise sang a little louder, her wavering voice cutting though the silence of the ballroom.

She closed her eyes as she played and sang, an image of Jordan appearing in her mind. He was dressed in the formal attire of a morning wedding: gray cutaway coat, striped trousers and paisley ascot. His dark hair fell across his forehead and his mouth was turned up in a warm smile. His bride stood beside him, resplendent in a dress of ivory silk organza and Alenqn lace. Out of the haze of her daydream, the bride's features materialized and Elise found herself staring at her own image. She forced her eyes open, shocked by the direction of her dreams.

But her innocent dreams were much less disturbing than the reality of Jordan's presence. He stood beside the piano watching her, one eyebrow raised questioningly.

Elise jumped up from her seat with a startled yelp. The piano bench tipped over behind her with a loud thud. Catching her balance, she grabbed for the music rack, only to send the cover crashing down over the keys. She stepped out from behind the keyboard and nervously smoothed her skirt.

"I didn't hear you come in," she said, an accusing note in her voice.

"I know," he replied. He took a step closer. "You play very well."

Elise smiled tremulously. "Thank you." She took a

deep breath and met his blue eyes squarely. "Aren't you going to compliment my singing?"

His expression became serious. "Ah, that's what that was. Singing. A very interesting approach, though I hope you don't have your heart set on a career in opera."

Elise caught the glint of humor in his eyes and laughter bubbled from her throat. "If you were truly a gentleman, you would have complimented my singing, as well. It would have been the polite thing to do."

"I prefer honesty over the conventions of etiquette. And I was being honest about your playing. You are quite good."

"Then I accept your compliment, on behalf of myself, my mother and Mrs. Merriweather."

"Mrs. Merriweather?"

"My piano teacher. She lived down the street from us and I used to go to her house every Tuesday after school. When I played well, she put a gold star at the top of the page. And when I played poorly, she would upbraid me thoroughly and send me straight home. I'm lucky I never sang for her. I'm sure she would have either scolded me senseless or moved out of the neighborhood, never to be seen again."

Jordan's expression softened and his smile lit up his eyes. "My childhood nemesis was Miss Winifred Ivey. She was a tyrant in tap shoes and she ran a dancing school. On Saturday mornings, she would hold me and nineteen other boys and girls hostage, teaching us the social graces and the box step."

He stepped in front of her, placing one arm behind his back and one over his stomach, bowing stiffly from the waist. "May I have the pleasure of this dance, Miss

Sinclair?" He held out his hand and she placed her fingers in his, her laughter echoing through the ballroom.

Suddenly the cool, reserved man had disappeared and Elise found herself looking at a different Jordan—smiling, teasing, at ease. The tension she usually felt when she was with him dissolved and she returned his relaxed humor. "I would be delighted, Mr. Prentiss." He took her to the middle of the dance floor and led her though a clumsy version of the box step, holding her at arm's length. For a short time, she thought he was being deliberately uncoordinated, treading on her toes on purpose. But when she looked up at the determined expression on his face, she realized that he really couldn't dance.

"You're almost as bad a dancer as I am a singer."

"Miss Ivey's Saturday-morning assemblies were not my idea of fun. I did my best to forget everything she taught me."

"Don't you get to practice at all those society functions you're always attending? I read about the Lyric Opera Ball and it sounded so romantic, a masque ball with Viennese waltzing and champagne. You must have danced at least once with Danielle Langley."

Jordan glanced down at her with a puzzled expression. "Who?"

"Danielle Langley." His expression remained the same. "Your date," she explained.

"She was my date?"

"Yes," Elise cried. "I saw a picture of you both in an old issue of *Town and Country*."

Jordan shrugged. "I don't remember."

"You've dated a lot of women, haven't you?"

"You seem to know more about the details of my social life than I do. *You* tell *me*. Have I dated a lot of women, Miss Sinclair?" His gaze met hers.

She looked away and studied her fingers spread across his upper arm. "Yes, you have."

"Is there anything wrong with that?"

"No. In fact, it's probably good. You were sowing your wild oats."

"I was what?"

"You know, playing the field. Getting it out of your system."

"'It?'"

Elise looked up at him and saw the laughter in his eyes. She smiled. "You're teasing me. And you're also not concentrating on your dancing. You really should try to learn."

"Since dancing is not a prerequisite for business success, I guess I'll survive."

"But what about your wedding? You'll have to dance with your bride. It's tradition. The first dance is the highlight of the reception. Maybe you could take dancing lessons. Just a few until you feel comfortable."

"Or maybe we could waive the tradition."

"Oh, no," Elise cried, stopping suddenly. "You can't do that. Your bride would be so disappointed and so would your guests. And it is such a romantic part of the whole wedding. I just love to watch the first dance. It always brings tears to my eyes."

"Then teach me," Jordan said in a warm tone. "Right here, right now."

Elise looked up at him, trying to hide her sudden discomfort. She felt herself grow tense as she realized the impact their innocent dance was having on her senses. Being in the same room with Jordan Prentiss was hard enough, but being in his arms one moment longer would be unbearable—and highly improper. Dancing lessons were certainly beyond her duties as a wedding consultant. "There's no music. I can't teach you to dance without music."

"What was that song you were singing when I came in? Sing that."

Elise shook her head and tried to pull away from him, but he held fast.

"Teach me," he urged. "I need to know these things."

He began to hum the tune, faltering slightly at first until she hummed along with him. She paused in her humming to offer him instruction. "First, you need to relax. Don't hold your arms so stiff." He loosened his grip on her and let his arms relax, but instead of gaining distance, she found herself slipping closer to his body.

"Now, start moving like this, back and forth with the music." He followed her swaying footsteps. When he had mastered the basics, she moved him in a slow circle on the dance floor. "When you dance with your bride, you will lead her, and she will follow your lead."

"Why?" Jordan asked, staring at his feet. "I'm the one who doesn't know how to dance."

"That's the way it's done. Don't you remember anything Miss Ivey taught you? Now you try. You lead me where you want to go." He slowly drew her in a circle around the dance floor and she smiled. He was a quick student. Already his movements were becoming smooth and more natural. "Don't watch your feet. Look into your bride's eyes when you dance with her.

Show her that she's the most beautiful woman in the world to you."

Jordan lifted his chin and his gaze locked with hers. She stumbled slightly. Her mind raced as they stared at each other, her thoughts a jumble of confusion. For an instant she thought she saw desire in the depths of his pale eyes, and a wave of apprehension rippled through her body. What was he doing? What did he want? Her heart hammered in her chest and her breath caught in her throat. Slowly he drew her nearer, still moving to the silent music that passed between them, tipping his head as if to prepare to kiss her.

Elise tore herself from the circle of his arms and turned her back on him. With her knees shaking and her nerves humming, she walked to the relative safety of the piano. "I think you have the idea. Maybe you should practice with your fiancée."

"Maybe," she heard Jordan say in a soft voice.

Elise turned to face him. The mask of reserve again covered his expression.

Lord, her imagination was running away with her! That hadn't been desire in his eyes. He was an engaged man, in love with his bride-to-be. And she was a lovesick fool, transforming his every word and action into some gesture of reciprocal feeling.

"Why don't we discuss the wedding plans?" Elise said, moving to the table near the dance floor that held her briefcase. "Let me tell you about the menu first." Elise efficiently recited her recommendations, keeping her eyes focused on her notes and glancing up only briefly to catch Jordan's replies to her questions. When she finished reviewing the menu, she described the decor she had planned for the ballroom. As her presentation progressed she found herself getting caught up in the excitement of the wedding plans. She pushed her feelings for Jordan to the back of her mind and let her professional expertise take over.

"I think your wedding will be the most romantic affair Chicago has ever seen," Elise concluded, her voice filled with pride. She put her papers in her briefcase and snapped the lid shut.

Jordan regarded her with a serious look. "Romantic. You use that word a lot."

"Do I?" She shrugged. "I never noticed."

"It's important to you...this romance?"

"Of course. Not just to me, but to all women. Romance makes love exciting. That's what I enjoy about planning weddings—adding romance to people's lives, making their weddings like a dream come true."

"I'm not a very romantic person," Jordan admitted in a sober voice. "At least, that's what I've been told."

Elise hid her amusement at his confession. "I sensed that about you," she replied. "From the moment we met, I wondered how you ever got your fiancée to agree to marry you."

"You make marriage to me sound like a prison sentence. I'm not such a bad guy."

"I'm sure you're not. You're practical and honest. But terribly preoccupied and definitely not a romantic."

"You know a lot about romance, don't you? You're something of an expert in the field."

"I know how I like to be treated. I guess I feel pretty much like other women do. I like to be courted, to feel special, like the most desirable woman in the world."

Jordan paused for a moment before replying. "And how would a man go about doing that?"

Elise looked at him incredulously. "You're asking me?"

"Yes. Tell me what to do. Tell me how to be more romantic."

Elise considered his request for a moment. Teaching him to dance had gotten her in enough trouble. What would advising him in the art of romance lead to? She made her decision in a split second—she would have to refuse. This was not part of her professional responsibilities.

But, then, she was in the business of planning the perfect wedding. And the perfect wedding required a perfect bridegroom, a wonderfully romantic bridegroom. Maybe it wouldn't hurt to give Jordan a few pointers.

"All right. Tell me your idea of a romantic evening."

Jordan's brow furrowed as he considered her request. "Dinner at a nice restaurant?" he began, seeking her approval immediately.

"That's a start."

"Flowers."

"What kind?"

"Roses." He looked at her again for an indication of her assent, but she made no move to agree with his choice.

"And champagne," he continued. "Champagne is very romantic, isn't it?"

"It can be." She was silent, waiting for him to go on. "Is that all?"

"Isn't that enough?"

Elise shook her head. "That's all so ordinary. Real

romance comes from the unexpected. Dinner at a hot-dog stand, a bouquet of dandelions and a bottle of root beer can be much more romantic than what you described. Remember, you want her to feel special. Be spontaneous. Now, what would you consider a romantic gift?"

Jordan regarded her warily before he answered. "Diamonds."

"No, no, no. Diamonds are ordinary. They're boring. Think of something special. It doesn't have to be expensive."

"Rubies? Wait, no, that's not the right answer," Jordan said. "Hell, I hate tests. Garnets. That's what I meant to say."

Elise groaned in dismay. "Generic jewels are about the most unromantic gift a woman could receive. I'd much rather get a unique pair of inexpensive earrings—earrings that a man picked out because they reminded him of me—than all the diamonds in the world."

"I don't believe you," Jordan scoffed. "All women love diamonds."

"I know it sounds trite, but it *is* the thought that counts. It doesn't matter how much a gift costs. If it's a gift from the heart, its value is priceless. Do you understand?"

Jordan shot her a skeptical look. "No, I don't. What woman in her right mind would want cheap earrings instead of a diamond necklace? That's just idiotic...it's baffling..." He sighed. "And it's just like a woman."

Elise grinned. "You're learning." She stood up, pulled on her coat and grabbed her briefcase. "Come on. We're finished here. There's a flower shop off the lobby. Let's go down there and you can pick out something for..." Elise paused. "You could at least tell me her first name. I'm getting tired of calling her 'your fiancée' or 'your bride.' What should I call her?"

Jordan hesitated before he spoke. Surely he hadn't forgotten her name! Or maybe he was just trying to decide whether he could trust her. He regarded her with a suspicious look before he finally spit out a name.

"Abby. My fiancée's name is Abby."

A sudden surge of guilt coursed through Elise's body. Abby. Before she had been a nameless, faceless woman, someone who didn't exist in Elise's mind. Now she had suddenly become real, and Elise felt a rush of self-recrimination flood her soul.

He was an engaged man, she told herself again, the meaning finally hitting home. Somewhere on the planet was a woman named Abby who would stand beside him at the altar, make love to him in his bed and bear his children. Somewhere there was an Abby who loved Jordan Prentiss. And here she stood, Elise Sinclair, ridiculously enamored with Abby's fiancé.

Elise forced a smile to her lips. "Abby," she repeated. "Let's go find a romantic bouquet of flowers for Abby."

She walked through the ballroom, her steps brisk and businesslike, and descended the stairs with Jordan at her side.

The flower shop was unoccupied except for the young woman who stood behind the counter. The woman eyed Jordan appreciatively as he stood before her, and Elise stifled an unwelcome twinge of jealousy.

"We'd like to put together a bouquet of flowers,"

Elise said, trying unsuccessfully to draw the girl's attention.

"Romantic flowers," Jordan added with a crooked smile.

"All our flowers are romantic," the salesgirl answered flirtatiously. "What would you like? How about some long-stemmed roses?"

Jordan turned to Elise and leaned closer. "I guess she isn't a graduate of the Sinclair School of Romance, huh?" he whispered, his breath tickling her ear.

She ignored the shiver that ran through her and silently repeated the name "Abby" again and again, an incantation against her perfidious feelings.

Elise looked over the girl's shoulder to the refrigerated case behind her. "Let's start with a dozen of those daffodils." The girl retrieved the daffodils and placed them on a wide piece of paper on the counter. "Then let's add some of the freesia."

Elise picked up a stalk of the freesia and held it under Jordan's nose. "Here, smell *this*," she ordered.

He breathed in the scent and a smile lit his face. "Lemons. It smells like lemons."

Elise took the freesia and placed it under her nose, brushing the soft petals beneath her chin and inhaling the fresh scent of springtime. "It almost makes you forget it's winter, doesn't it?" Elise turned back to the salesgirl. "Add a few of those daisies, too. Then wrap them up."

When the flowers were securely wrapped against the cold outdoors, she handed the bundle to Jordan. "Next time, try this on your own. Avoid the roses and choose something that reminds you of her. It will be much more thoughtful that way."

As they walked through the lobby and out the front doors onto Walton Place, Elise was smiling. She had helped Jordan, in a small way, to understand what would make Abby happy. Somehow the gesture made up for her traitorous behavior.

"I'll call you in a few days," Elise said in a business-like tone. "We'll need to get you, your best man and your ushers in for a fitting for your cutaways. You'll need at least four ushers, preferably six, considering the size of your guest list. I'll also put together a check-list of things you'll need to take care of and another list for you to discuss with your fian—Abby."

"Can I give you a ride home?" Jordan asked.

"No, I have a couple of more errands to run and I have an appointment uptown for lunch. I'll talk to you soon." Elise stepped into a waiting cab, closing the door behind her. She waved to Jordan through the window, then fixed her gaze on the street in front of her.

An odd feeling of loneliness descended on her as the cab sped away, and she was tempted to look back, to look at Jordan one more time. But she resisted the temptation. It was best to put as much distance be-tween them as possible, both physical and mental. And the best way to accomplish that would be to put Abby directly in between them.

Abby was the key to eliminating her attraction to Jor-dan. Elise made a silent vow to force the issue of Abby's absence at the next available opportunity. If she didn't, she could not continue working with Jordan. For she knew, deep in her heart, that she would never find Jordan anything but an endlessly fascinating, hopelessly unattainable man.

JORDAN WATCHED Elise's cab disappear around the corner onto Michigan Avenue, then looked up and down the street for his driver. The limo was parked halfway down the block. Before his driver could catch sight of him, Jordan turned and walked in the opposite direction, avoiding a return to the office.

Oak Street Beach was deserted except for a few hearty joggers who passed him on the wide walkway. The strident noise of the city traffic blended with the soothing sound of the waves rushing against the dunes of ice that covered the beach. Jordan pulled the collar of his coat up and hunched his shoulders against the numbing wind coming off the lake. He breathed deeply of the frigid air, and it rejuvenated him physically, but his thoughts were still centered on his disturbing encounter with Elise Sinclair.

Though he had tried to deny his feelings at every turn, Elise was becoming a constant presence in his thoughts. They were polar opposites, yet his attraction to her was magnetic, dangerously overpowering but completely irresistible. She was everything he had set his mind against, but still he wanted her with a thirst that couldn't be quenched and a hunger that refused to be sated. He knew she had captured his mind the moment they met and now his body had begun to betray him, too.

He could still feel the warmth of her long, slender fingers wrapped in his, could still smell the fresh floral scent of her hair. He ripped open the package of flowers and withdrew a stalk of freesia. Touching the soft flowers to his lips as she had, he inhaled their scent. When they had danced, it had been nearly impossible to keep himself from pulling her firmly into his arms and taking what he wanted. He knew instinctively how her sweet, soft lips would taste to his tongue, how her warm, pliant body would respond to his hands.

Jordan sat down on a low stone bench and stared abstractedly at a small flock of pigeons that had gathered at his feet. He wanted Elise and he needed a wife. So why couldn't they be one and the same? She fit all the basic requirements and she possessed an added attribute—she was sexually attractive to him. Maybe he could combine the best of both worlds. Elise could make a perfect wife and a perfect lover.

Yes, Elise would meet all his requirements, but could he meet all hers? He had known her only a week, but he knew precisely what she wanted from a husband. She wanted love. Not just ordinary everyday love, but unconditional, undying, twenty-four-hour-a-day love. Love served up with a healthy dose of romance. She wanted the hearts and the flowers and the violins playing in the background.

She wanted exactly what he could never give her.

He had never been in love in his life and considered the prospect of falling in love a remote possibility at best. Love was an emotion that was entirely unfathomable to him. It defied logic and reason, it was unpredictable. Worst of all, love was something he could not control, and Jordan did not allow anything into his life that he could not control.

So what were his options? Jordan ticked them off in his mind, considering each and drawing a conclusion regarding its chances of success before moving on, an approach he used every day making business decisions at BabyLove.

Option one: he could tell Elise he loved her. It would

be a lie, but it seemed like the simplest way to get everything he wanted. But the thought of deceiving Elise was shockingly distasteful. Lying to her about his fiancée's name had been deceitful. Lying to her about love would be criminal.

Option two: he could tell Elise the truth about his immediate need for a wife and hope she might accept a business partnership over a loving marriage. There wasn't much possibility of her going for that considering her starry-eyed vision of love.

Or he could go on with his plans to find a bride and try to seduce Elise, as well. Chances for success? Less than zero.

Or he could just forget Elise altogether.

All things considered, the last option seemed the most likely. Elise was a complication he did not need, an inconvenient detour on the direct route to his most important goal—saving his company.

So he would put her out of his mind, he determined. But not completely. She did have one thing he couldn't do without. Her romantic advice could prove to be quite useful in his search for a bride. Time was running out and anything that could secure the future of Baby-Love was definitely worth trying.

Jordan stood up, scattering the pigeons, and walked back toward Michigan Avenue. In a heedless motion, he tossed the bundle of flowers into a trash can along the way. He took several steps, then stopped and returned to the trash can to retrieve a stalk of freesia.

With gentle fingers, he tucked the scented flowers inside his coat and turned away, a smile curving his lips. Then he picked up his pace, anxious to return to the office and resume his search for a bride. With an organized approach, and a little romance thrown in, he was sure he would have a fiancée within the next month. After all, how hard could it possibly be to learn what really pleased a woman? He just needed a few pointers and a little practice. And what better way to start than with a simple gesture of appreciation in return for Elise's help?

The only immediate problem was where to find dandelions in the dead of winter.

4

"Now I know why we don't let the grooms plan the weddings," Elise railed as she slammed the phone into the cradle. "It must have something to do with a missing chromosome in the male of the species. They have no comprehension of the importance of the event, no understanding of the necessity for schedules." Her voice rose in volume, taking on a slightly hysterical note. "If we left weddings to the men, no one would ever get married. Society as we know it would cease to exist. The entire human race would slowly disappear. We'd all be doomed." She paused in her tirade for a moment before continuing in a shriek, "I thought I told you to get off the counter!"

Clorinda glanced up at her, taking a short respite from licking out an empty frosting bowl to shoot Elise a malevolent look. Elise stepped toward her, wielding a wooden spoon with enough menace to make the feline think twice about remaining in the room. In a flurry of fur, the cat jumped from the counter and raced out of the kitchen. Thisbe trotted out after her.

"Not so loud," Dona said calmly, her concentration centered on the sugar-paste lily she was sculpting. "These flowers take a steady hand." When she finished the flower, she carefully transferred it to the top of one of Elise's tiny engagement cakes, then let out her pent-up breath. "There. Perfect." She turned to Elise. "Now, what has you so upset?"

"Jordan Prentiss, that's what...or who! And his mysterious bride, Abby. She cares even less about this wedding than he does, if that's possible. I just called him to give him the name of the formal-wear shop where he and his wedding attendants need to go for their fittings. Then I naively asked him to find out where his bride bought her wedding gown. I'm in charge of selecting the maid of honor's dress, so I wanted to find something that complemented the bridal gown. Do you know what he told me?"

Dona shook her head, her attention now focused on placing the finished cake in a small foil box.

"He told me she hadn't selected her gown yet. The wedding is less than three months away and she doesn't have a wedding gown. And then to top it all off, he told me I should choose the bridal gown along with the honor attendant's dress."

"That sounds nice," Dona replied.

Elise could tell her best friend wasn't paying a bit of attention to her dilemma. Whenever Dona was in the same room with a bowl of cake batter, all else took a back seat to her art, including Elise. In fact, she sometimes believed that her friend had batter running through her veins and butter-cream frosting for brains.

Dona pushed the box across the counter. "Isn't that pretty? This is sure to get you some new clients. Tell me, what woman could resist a precious little lily cake like that?"

Elise sat down on a kitchen stool, cupped her chin in her palm and picked up a frosting-coated knife. "It'd better work," she mumbled as she licked at the creamy icing. "After what I just said to Jordan Prentiss, he may be looking for a new wedding consultant."

"What are you talking about?"

"I told him it was against my policy to choose the wedding gown for the bride. I told him this was not the proper time to be speaking for his bride and that he should tell Abby she must choose her own dress."

"And what did he say?"

"Nothing at first. Then he said, fine, he would pass along my advice and that I should choose a variety of appropriate gowns and have them delivered to his office to be shown to her privately."

"So, what's the problem?"

"Don't you find it a bit strange that the bride hasn't shown one ounce of interest in the most important day of her life? And isn't it odd that I haven't been allowed to meet the bride? Why is her identity such a big secret? I had to practically twist Prentiss's arm before he would even tell me her first name. And I know he makes all the decisions on his own, without even consulting her. This whole wedding is positively weird."

"I've heard that the rich and powerful can be a little eccentric. As long as he's paying you, I wouldn't worry too much. And is it absolutely necessary for you to meet the bride?"

"No, not absolutely," Elise replied, her mouth pursed in an indignant pout. She grabbed a rolling pin and attacked a ball of fondant, rolling the doughlike frosting out to the proper thickness. As Elise worked, her pout slowly transformed to a sly smile. "But, I have a plan," she continued, "that might just flush the future Mrs. Prentiss out into the open. And I have a feeling once she gets a taste of wedding magic, she'll jump right into the excitement, head-first."

Dona took the sheet of fondant and covered a tiny cake, sealing the edges to keep it fresh and provide an even surface for her frosting art. "How are you going to accomplish that?"

"I'll set up an after-hours appointment for her at The Ideal Bride. Sheila will be happy to keep the shop open for a commission like the one she'll get on this dress. Then I'll be there to help in the selection. I'll take the opportunity to discuss the wedding plans with the mysterious Abby and figure out why Prentiss is so protective of his fiancée."

"Sounds like a good plan to me. Now, on to more important matters—what do you have planned for my pretty little cakes?"

The doorbell sounded from the front of the house. Elise jumped up and dusted off her hands on her striped apron. "Melvin, the owner of Lakeshore Florists, is sending over one of his delivery boys to pick them up later this afternoon," she said. "I promised him the florals on the Prentiss wedding plus any of the weddings we get from this promotion in trade for delivering fifty cakes."

Elise hurried to the foyer and swung the front door open. A young man stood on her stoop, his cold-reddened fingers clutching a small white box. At first, Elise thought he was from Melvin's, but then she noticed the name of another florist embroidered on his jacket.

"I have a delivery for Miss Elise Sinclair," he said.

"I'm Elise Sinclair."

He thrust a clipboard at her and she signed for the flowers.

Elise walked back to the kitchen with the box, her curiosity piqued. Who would be sending her flowers? It wasn't her birthday and there wasn't a man in her life. That eliminated both causes for a gift of flowers. And the box was not the typical elongated package that usually carried long-stemmed roses. There was no cellophane window to allow a glimpse into the contents and no card to give a clue to the sender's identity. She pushed open the swinging door to the kitchen.

"Who was at the door?" Dona asked, her attention now focused on coloring a bowl of sugar paste the proper shade of green.

"A delivery boy from Colin's Florals. He brought me some flowers."

"Who would be sending you flowers?" Dona's attention wandered for a moment in Elise's direction. "You haven't been holding out on me, have you? Are you dating someone I don't know about?"

"No," she answered, continuing to stare at the box. "You know how long it's been since my last date. You remind me of it at least once a week."

Dona dropped what she was doing and walked over to examine the box closely. "Well, why don't you open it? Maybe you have a secret admirer."

Elise slid her finger under the flap and popped open the top. Wading through layers of tissue paper, she finally came upon a tiny bouquet, festooned with ribbons and lace, nestled in the bottom of the box.

A tiny bouquet of dandelions.

"A very sick secret admirer," Dona commented as

she grabbed the box. "Is this some kind of joke? Who would send you dandelions? They're weeds."

"No, they're not," Elise cried defensively, snatching the box back. She pulled the wilted bouquet from the tissue paper. "They're very...romantic." The greenery surrounding the yellow flowers looked fresh and alive, but the dandelions had seen better days. She brought the bouquet to her nose and instinctively inhaled deeply. An irritating smell tickled her nose and made her eyes water. She sneezed, once...twice...three times, before she dropped the bouquet back into the box.

"Very romantic," Dona repeated, her voice dripping with sarcasm. "The guy who sent them must be a real catch."

Elise reluctantly closed the box, pushing it away from her. "He is...or will be after I get done with him."

"Then you know who sent these?"

"Yes."

Dona watched her, waiting for her to continue. Elise knew her friend wouldn't let the subject drop so easily. They had no secrets between them when it came to men—except for one now.

"I'm waiting," Dona said.

"All right. I know who sent them." Elise sighed. "Jordan Prentiss."

"The man with the missing chromosome? The man you called a loathsome Lothario? The Caveman Bridegroom? I thought you were exaggerating. I didn't think any man could be that bad, but I guess you were right."

"He isn't that bad. He just doesn't understand women. I gave him a few pointers about romance and he took them a bit too literally."

"He sent you dandelions, Elise. I think you need to send him back to Remedial Romance 101."

"Jordan can be very romantic. When we were dancing at the—"

"You went dancing with Jordan?" Dona eyed Elise suspiciously. "And when did he go from 'Prentiss the Pain' to 'Jordan the Romantic?' And why is he sending you flowers? What's going on between the two of you?"

"Nothing! It's not what you think." Elise felt her face color. "The flowers are simply a thank-you for my help. If there were really something romantic between us, don't you think he would have sent roses? You're letting your imagination run away with you."

"Am I imagining that blush on your face? Come on, Elise, tell the truth. Are you and Jordan Prentiss having an affair?"

"No!"

"Are you in love with him?"

"No." Elise heard the lack of conviction in her voice. "Not exactly."

"What does that mean?"

"I just have—I just *had* a little crush on him, that's all. It was nothing, just a silly infatuation."

"He's engaged, Elise."

"I know that. That's why it's over. It was entirely harmless. But he's a very compelling man. Any warm-blooded woman would find him attractive, including you. So don't get worked up into one of your mother-hen snits."

Dona shot her a long-suffering look. "I won't. Just as long as you don't let yourself get carried away in one of your romantic fantasies."

"It's a deal." Elise relaxed, hoping the subject was closed. "Now, let's finish up these cakes. The delivery boy will be here in a few hours."

Elise set to work encasing another cake in fondant, but her thoughts were drawn to the dandelion bouquet that lay wilting in its tissue-paper bed. Dandelions in the middle of winter. Where had he gotten them? He had probably paid a tidy sum to have some bemused florist pick them and ship them north to another florist who had the onerous task of fashioning the weeds into a bouquet. What had at first seemed like a simple gift suddenly took on complex proportions. Were they really just a gesture of appreciation, as she had told Dona? Or were they more?

As hard as she tried to deny it, an odd feeling of apprehension gnawed at her mind. Could Jordan Prentiss possibly have another motive for sending the bouquet?

THE SHOWROOM of The Ideal Bride was shrouded in shadows when Elise arrived. Sheila led her through the dimly lit salon, past mannequins dressed in their white wedding finery and past long racks of wedding gowns. They headed toward the spacious fitting rooms that lined the rear of the store.

"Is she here yet?" Elise whispered.

"No," Sheila replied in an equally quiet voice. "But he is."

"'He?'"

"Yes, the bridegroom. Your Mr. Smith. He arrived ten minutes ago. He's waiting in the Bourbonnais Room."

"Alone?"

"Yes. He said his fiancée had an unexpected schedule conflict. I told him she could have called to cancel the appointment, but he said something about wanting to get this over with as soon as possible. What does that mean?"

Elise strode toward the illuminated fitting room, her irritation rising. "I don't know, but I'm about to find out."

"You know your way around," Sheila called after her. "I'll be in the office if you need any help."

Elise stepped into the mirror-lined fitting room to find Jordan lounging on an upholstered settee, his briefcase open and a file folder spread across his lap. He looked up at her and smiled and her irritation rose another degree. Even more annoying was the skip in her heartbeat as she met his gaze.

"You're late," he commented. "I thought the appointment was for seven-thirty."

Elise returned his smile stiffly, gathering her resolve and refusing to give in to the overwhelming attraction she felt for the man. "I got caught in traffic and yes, the appointment was for seven-thirty—with Abby, not you. Where is she?"

"She had an—"

"Unexpected schedule conflict?" Elise finished, unable to hide the skepticism in her voice.

"Yes," Jordan said. "She asked that I convey her apologies and requested that we go ahead and choose a gown for her."

"No," Elise snapped. "I will not choose her wedding gown. We'll just have to reschedule the appointment."

"That won't be possible," Jordan replied, his voice even. "She's...left the country...on business. She won't be back...until just before the wedding."

Elise sensed an undercurrent of tension in his words and her anger died. He, too, seemed irritated by his bride's absence, his bluntly spoken words holding a hint of suppressed aggravation.

"She's very devoted to her career," he explained coolly. "An attitude I wholeheartedly support. Her business comes first. And since plans for the wedding can be completed without her, she didn't find it necessary to cancel her trip. I'm sorry if that inconveniences you in any way, but that's the way it has to be."

Elise studied his expression, trying to detect another clue to his feelings. But it was as if his features were carved from granite, hard and unyielding. She slowly shook her head and her shoulders slumped in resignation. "All right, you win. But if Abby can't be here to pick out her dress, then you'll have to."

"I know nothing about wedding dresses," Jordan countered. "That's what I hired you for."

"You may not know much now, but you will by the end of the evening," Elise assured him. "Come on, let's get started." She walked out the fitting-room door and into the showroom, then waited for him to join her. When he did, she casually strolled along the racks of dresses, pulling several out and examining them.

"First, I'll need you to describe Abby's figure type."

"Her what?" Jordan asked. His voice sounded oddly panicked.

"Her figure, the shape of her body. How tall is she? What size dress does she wear? Is she slender or more voluptuous? What color hair does she have? Does she have fair skin or is her skin olive toned?"

Jordan stared at the wedding dress Elise was holding. "You need to know all that just to pick out a wedding dress? Why can't we just take this one and be done with it? It's white and it has lots of that frilly stuff on it. I like it."

"This is a one-of-a-kind dress designed by Daniel Evans and this frilly stuff is Schiffli lace." She sighed. "We have to choose something that will look stunning on Abby. Now, tell me, how tall is she?"

"I don't know her exact height," Jordan answered.

Elise tried valiantly to control her frustration. How could such a brilliant businessman be so incredibly obtuse when it came to women? "Compared to me, is she taller or shorter?"

Jordan stepped toward her. He clasped his hands around her upper arms and pulled her close, the frothy skirt of the wedding dress the only barrier between their bodies. She could feel his warm breath against her forehead, his beard-roughened chin bumping against her nose. He pushed her back.

"She's about the same height as you are."

Elise tried to calm her pounding pulse, a rhythm set in motion by the touch of his warm fingers. "I'm five foot six," she said. "About how much does she weigh?"

She jumped slightly when she felt the touch of his hands on her waist and hips.

"Her figure is a lot like yours," he said, his voice deep and rough. "She has curves in all the right places, but she's not overweight. She's just right. What size are you?"

"I'm a size ten."

"I'm pretty sure that's her size, too," he said, his hands still resting on her waist.

Elise kept her gaze fixed on his chest, unwilling to allow herself to give in to the intense pleasure that his touch aroused. She cleared her throat. "And her hair color?"

Jordan moved his hand to touch her hair, pulling a strand from behind her ear and letting it slip through his fingers. "Spun gold," he murmured, "Touched with copper." She felt his fingers brush her cheek. "And her skin is like fine Chinese porcelain with a tint of pink. Very smooth. Very soft."

Elise pulled away from him and turned to replace the dress in the rack. Suddenly, as if his words had pulled a plug, she felt her self-esteem drain from her body. His glowing description of Abby made her feel like an ugly duckling being compared with a beautiful swan. No wonder Jordan was in love with his fiancée. Abby was curvaceous; Elise was slightly pudgy. Her skin was luminous, while Elise's was merely pale. And her hair shimmered like gold; Elise's was simply strawberry blond.

"She sounds like a very beautiful woman," Elise said, her back still to him.

"She is," Jordan answered. His voice sounded choked.

Elise turned and caught a fleeting look of discomfort cross his face. For a brief moment, she saw passion cloud his eyes before it evaporated behind his clear, blue gaze. She swallowed, the bitter taste of envy burning its way down her throat. How lucky Abby was to have a man like Jordan, a man who raved about her beauty as he had. Somehow she hadn't expected Jordan to be able to paint such a stunning picture of his fiancée. But his eloquent words were vivid proof of his love for Abby.

"With paler skin, I'd recommend a gown in ivory. Pure white would make Abby look a little washed out." She walked down the rack, pulling a variety of dresses out and handing them to Jordan. At the last moment, she chose her favorite gown, the gown she gazed at longingly every time she entered The Ideal Bride, the gown she would choose for her own wedding. When his arms were full, she grabbed several more dresses, then headed for the fitting room.

She quickly hung the dresses she carried on an extended hook, then took the gowns from Jordan's arms and hung them up, also. "This is a lovely gown," she said, pulling the first dress from the hook and holding it out to him. "It has simple lines that give it a medieval quality. And this is Chantilly lace," she explained, fingering the fine florals and scrolls embroidered on net. "It has gigot sleeves and a bateau neckline."

He sat down on the couch and leaned back in a relaxed manner with his arm stretched across the carved wood back. "Gigot sleeves?"

"Yes. See how they're wide and rounded at the shoulder. Then they taper down to a snug fit at the wrist. They're sometimes called leg-of-mutton sleeves."

"A rather unappealing name, don't you think? Sheep's leg sleeves."

Elise shrugged. "I guess so. But I like gigot sleeves."

Jordan nodded. "Then so do I. But I don't like that dress much. It doesn't have a waist."

Elise replaced the dress, happy that they had made at least some progress toward a choice. She pulled another dress out. "This has a very narrow, fitted silhouette. It has the gigot sleeves and a high neckline. This is made of silk charmeuse with a Venise lace overlay."

Jordan considered the dress, then looked up at her. "What do you think?"

"It isn't the dress that I would choose for myself, but with Abby's figure, it would probably be a perfect choice."

"Which dress would you choose?" His gaze was penetrating.

Elise drew the gown out from behind the others. "This one," she answered, her voice breathy with sentiment. "This is silk shantung. It has a basque waist. See, it's fitted and comes to a point in the front. The bodice and sleeves have an Alenon lace overlay and are hand beaded with these tiny pearls." She swept her arm under the dress, dragging it along the floor to show off the five-foot train. "And it has a sweetheart neckline. See how it looks like the top of a heart." Elise pointed to the low neckline, her fingers following the gentle curves at the front of the dress. "And at the shoulders are these roses with little sprays of pearls." She touched the roses reverently.

"And it has gigot sleeves," Jordan added.

"Yes, it has gigot sleeves." She smiled, her eyes still fixed on the dress.

"I like it," Jordan said firmly. "That's the one."

Elise looked up at him in shock, an uncontrollable rush of resentment coursing through her. "No!" she heard herself say. This was *her* dress. This was the gown *she* would walk down the aisle in. It wasn't meant for Abby, it was meant for *her*.

"No?" Jordan asked. "I thought you liked the dress."

"I—I do. But I don't think it would be right for Abby."

"I think it would be perfect for my bride. But before I make a final decision, I'd like to see it on."

"On?"

"Yes, I want you to put it on. It's hard to tell what it will look like when it's hanging on the hanger."

Elise shook her head. "I can't."

"Why not? Is it the wrong size?" Jordan stood up and grabbed the tag that dangled from the sleeve. "It's a size ten. Perfect. Go ahead, try it on. I'll wait here."

"But—"

"Go ahead," he said, pushing her out the door, the dress clutched in her arms. "Before I spend—" he grabbed the tag again "—four thousand dollars on a wedding gown, I want to see what it's going to look like on my bride."

Elise stepped into the adjoining fitting room, closed the door behind her and slowly sank onto a reproduction French chaise. She hugged the dress to her and the crisp skirt rustled against her legs.

She was torn, one part of her wanting to put the dress on and the other wanting to hide it from Jordan, hoping desperately to convince him not to buy it. She had been tempted to try the gown on every time she walked into the shop, but had refused to give in to the fantasy. What good would it do, dreaming of a wedding that might never happen? Though she was a pure romantic, her romanticism did have its limits. She was practical enough to realize that without a man in her life, there would be no hope for a wedding.

Yes, she was also practical. And she was smart

enough to separate fact from fantasy. So why not try the dress on? Why not enjoy the moment?

"Is that the one?"

Elise looked up to see Sheila standing in the doorway. She nodded and Sheila grinned.

"Nice choice. Big commission. Why don't you give me the dress and I'll hang it up? Then we can go write up the sale."

"He wants me to try it on first," Elise said dismally. "He's waiting in the other room." Elise stood and began to unbutton her blouse with numb fingers. She pulled off the rest of her clothes, letting them drop in a heap at her feet on top of her discarded shoes. With Sheila's help, she silently slipped the dress over her head, her grim expression staring back at her from the floor-to-ceiling mirrors.

As Sheila worked the tiny buttons from the small of her back to her nape, Elise felt the bodice gradually mold itself to her figure. She stared at the reflection of her face, refusing to shift her gaze to the dress.

"Stunning," Sheila said in a tone of genuine admiration. "Let me get a veil." She returned moments later with a fingertip veil that flounced and cascaded from a cap of pearls. She pulled Elise's hair back into a knot and secured it with bobby pins, then placed the veil on Elise's head and anchored it with two combs.

"Exquisite!" she declared, sighing as she straightened the veil. "It's like the dress was made for you."

Elise finally let her gaze drift downward over her reflection. She could barely believe the vision that met her eyes. For the first time in her life she felt truly beautiful. She watched as Sheila fastened a string of pearls around her neck. Elise reached up to run her fingers along the cool ridges of the necklace. Her fingertips came to rest at the base of her throat where her pulse drummed frantically.

"Shoes," Sheila muttered. She rushed out again and returned with a box under her arm. Kneeling, she found Elise's toes under the voluminous skirt and slipped a pair of beaded slippers onto her feet. The shoes were a size too big, but the design was a perfect match for the dress.

"There you are," Sheila proclaimed with a flourish of her hand. "The ideal bride."

Elise graced her with a wavering smile. "I'm afraid I'm only the stand-in model for the ideal bride."

"Oh, who cares," Sheila said with a laugh. "We've been playing dress-up since we were little girls. It was fun then and it's even more fun now. So enjoy it."

Sheila took a final look, her hands smoothing a fold in the skirt before she left Elise alone in the fitting room. Glancing at her image once more, Elise drew a nervous breath, then walked out the door.

She was completely unprepared for Jordan's reaction. He looked up from his file folder. His gaze traveled slowly from her toes to her face. His eyes met hers and they stared at each other for a long moment. The space between them crackled with a current of tightly leashed excitement.

Jordan stood up, his gaze still locked on her face. "You look...incredible," he said as he let out tightly held breath.

Elise dipped her head, as a blush crept up her cheeks. "Thank you," she said softly. "I feel incredible."

"Turn around," Jordan ordered. "Slowly."

Her legs wobbled as she began an agonizing pirouette. She had almost completed her turn, when her eyes caught Jordan's again and she stumbled. Her foot twisted out of the oversize shoe, and she found herself listing precariously to one side.

In a swift, sure movement, Jordan stepped to her side and grabbed her waist.

She smiled in gratitude, the heat from his fingers burning through the heavy fabric of her bodice. "I—I lost my shoe." She searched the space under her skirts for the missing slipper, sliding her unshod foot over the carpet in a clumsy quest.

"Let me get it," Jordan offered. He bent down on one knee to lift her skirts up and retrieve the shoe, then held her foot in his hand and slid the slipper back onto her foot.

To steady herself Elise placed her hands on his broad shoulders, her sensitized fingers feeling the bunched muscle through the fabric of his suit.

Her breath caught in her throat as his firm fingers wrapped around her ankle. Slowly, very tentatively, he ran his hand from her ankle to her knee. She suppressed a tiny moan that threatened to escape from her throat.

He looked up at her. "There, that's better."

"Yes," she whispered in a wavering voice, meeting his gaze. "Much better." Her fingers clenched unconsciously and she felt Jordan's shoulders stiffen in response.

He stood, then suddenly turned from her and walked across the room. For a long moment, he didn't move. Then, with a muttered oath, he turned back and strode toward her, his expression grim and determined. He pulled her against his hard body and his lips descended over hers to cover her mouth.

In a single, shattering explosion, her mind lost the ability to reason and she opened her mouth to his. His probing tongue tangled with hers, sending tremors of delight to her core. She abandoned herself to his kiss and let the need wash over her in waves, pushing and pulling and driving her to seek more.

He groaned against her mouth and pulled her hips firmly against his, straining through the layers of silk and petticoats.

Suddenly, reality struck her, a sharp slap in the face, a chilling douse of icy water. She opened her eyes wide and tore her mouth from his.

"No," she said, her voice a strangled cry.

He opened his eyes and she could see fire burning in their depths. "Don't stop me, Elise," he growled, his words more a warning than a request. "Let it happen."

"I can't," she pleaded, her voice barely audible. "You can't. You're engaged. This is wrong. You don't love me—you love her." She buried her face in his shoulder.

"I don't love her," Jordan said in a matter-of-fact tone.

Elise snapped her head up and stared at him, too astonished to speak. She finally found her voice, but her words came out in a whisper of disbelief. "You can't mean that."

"It's true. I don't love her." He paused. "And she doesn't love me."

A tiny spark of relief touched Elise's heart at his words, but she stopped the reaction immediately. It didn't matter. Jordan was still engaged. "Why are you getting married if you don't love each other?"

"These are the nineties, Elise. Love isn't a requirement for marriage. People marry for other reasons all the time."

Elise stepped away from him, hurt by his patronizing tone. "What other reasons are there?"

"Security, stability. I'm thirty-eight years old. It's time I got married and started a family." He shrugged. "I have a great deal of money. My wife will be able to buy whatever her heart desires."

Elise felt her anger rise. How could he be so cold and unfeeling? "You think your money really matters? What if her heart desires love?"

"It doesn't and neither does she. She knows exactly what to expect from this marriage and she's satisfied. She's getting what she wants and I'm getting what I want."

"Then why this elaborate wedding?" Elise demanded, indignation coloring her voice. "Why this?" She held out her skirts. "It seems like a ridiculous waste of money for a marriage in name only."

"It's necessary," Jordan stated.

Elise shook her head in bewilderment. He was making a mockery of everything she believed in, her dreams, her career, her life.

"And I suppose this is perfectly acceptable to you," she said.

"What?"

"This...this episode, this...lapse in judgment."

"Yes," he said with a wry expression. "I'd have to say that it is quite acceptable."

Elise's fingers clenched into fists around the crisp

fabric of her skirt. "Where do you think this will lead?
Do you expect me to just happily agree to carry on
some tawdry little affair behind your fiancée's back? Is
that why you sent the flowers—to smooth the way for
this seduction attempt?"

Jordan frowned. "That's not the way it is. I sent you
the flowers..." He shook his head. "Hell, I don't even
know why I sent the flowers anymore. But it wasn't
part of some scheme, if that's what you think. Elise,
you can't deny that there's something going on between us. I want—no, I need to find out what it is."

"And what would Abby say?"

Jordan's features tensed, yet she saw indecision
color his expression. He rubbed his brow with his fingers and paused, as if considering his next words very
carefully before uttering them. "Abby would say nothing because Abby doesn't—"

"No," Elise warned, holding up her hand to stop his
words. "Don't you dare speak for her again."

"Elise, let me explain. Abby doesn't—"

"I don't want to hear your lies!" she shouted, covering her ears.

Jordan grabbed her wrists and pulled her hands
away from her ears. "Then maybe it's time for the
truth," he growled. "I want you, and I know you want
me. How's that for the truth?"

Elise glared at him. "No, I don't want you!"

He yanked her to him and his mouth covered hers
again, this time in a rough, demanding kiss. Elise
pushed at his chest, but he tightened his hold on her.
Her body screamed for his touch, begged to let him
continue, but her mind refused to give in. It was
wrong!

He dragged his lips to her throat, murmuring, "Tell me you don't want this, Elise."

Tears burned at the corners of her eyes, but she blinked them back, drawing on her resolve. "It doesn't make any difference what I want. You're an engaged man."

With one final burst of defiance, she shoved against his chest, catching him unaware. Then she grabbed her skirts and ran from his presence. Racing through the showroom, she wove her way around the dress racks scattered across the dark salon. Maneuvering in the heavy dress was difficult and as she turned sharply, she stumbled.

Elise kicked off the shoes and and reached down to grab the train and throw it over her arm. Jordan emerged from the fitting room, ran his fingers through his hair, then started in her direction.

Elise grabbed the shoes and stood up. "Stay right there," she commanded.

Jordan paused. "Elise, we need to talk. I want to explain."

"I don't want to hear what you have to say."

"Dammit, Elise, running away from this is not going to make it go away." He started toward her again.

"I said, stay there!" she cried. Acting instinctively, she threw one of the beaded slippers at him. It sailed across the showroom, missing Jordan by a good three feet. He continued in her direction and she hurled another warning shot. This time, the slipper came dangerously close to his ear.

"You're out of ammunition, Elise. Now it's time to negotiate."

Elise took a tentative step back. "There won't be any negotiation. My mind is made up."

He looked at her with a tight expression. "I'm not going to stop until we—"

She held up her hand. "No! What happened in there was wrong. I was wrong to allow it. And you were wrong to begin it." With that, she spun on her heel and headed toward the front door.

She passed Sheila on her way and before she could make good her escape, Sheila grabbed at her elbow. "Elise, where are you going?" Elise eluded her grasp and pushed open the door of the shop.

"Hey, what about the dress?" Sheila cried.

"We'll take it," Elise shouted back. With that, she ran down the steps and out to the street, her skirt held high and her stocking feet tripping across the cold concrete.

With a frantic wave, she hailed a passing cab. It screeched to a halt in front of her. The cabbie slid across the front seat, rolled down the window and grinned at her. "You left him at the altar, right, sweetheart?" He glanced down. "Let me guess. Cold feet?" He laughed at his joke.

"Very funny," she snapped as she yanked the door open and tumbled inside.

"So, now that you've dumped the creep, I've got a live-in brother-in-law that's looking for a wife. No reason for that pretty dress to go to waste."

"Just shut up and drive," Elise replied. She gave the driver her address, then watched the door of the bridal shop, hoping that Jordan had decided against following her.

The cabbie punched the accelerator and Elise was thrown back against the seat. She closed her eyes and tipped her head back, steadfastly refusing to give in to the tears that threatened.

Good Lord, what had she done? She had kissed him. Even worse, she had enjoyed it.

How could she have allowed herself to lose control, to find herself in the arms of an engaged man, and a client at that? And to believe that her feelings were merely a harmless infatuation. She now realized she'd felt more than infatuation when he'd held her in his embrace. She was falling in love with Jordan Prentiss.

Elise groaned and covered her eyes with her arm. Deep in a hidden corner of her mind, she had secretly harbored a fantasy that she was to be Jordan's bride. And through it all, she had planned his wedding as if it were *her* wedding, as well. Her favorite flowers, her favorite music, even her favorite bridal gown. Every choice had been made with her own tastes in mind.

And suddenly the fantasy had sprung to life before her eyes. Jordan wanted her as much as she wanted him.

It was bound to happen. The attraction had been there from the start. She had just refused to recognize it. But was that all her fault? The mysterious Abby hadn't donated a single ounce of help in planning the wedding. Her absence had provided ample opportunity for them to get carried away with each other.

And Jordan was also partially to blame. Elise had simply made a slight error in judgment. She had let herself get caught up with a picture perfect wedding and a handsome and undeniably sexy groom.

And now the dream wedding had turned into a nightmare. She was supposed to give her clients a "happily ever after." But instead she was standing directly between a man and the woman he planned to marry. In any other situation she would have bolted, but she couldn't afford to give this job up. Besides losing a great deal of money, quitting at this late date could ruin her professional reputation.

Her head told her she couldn't quit. But her heart told her she certainly couldn't go on.

5

JORDAN STRODE to the front window of the shop and caught a glimpse of Elise's bare foot and the lacy white hem of the dress before the cab door slammed shut. When he stepped out onto the sidewalk a moment later, the cab was halfway down the block, its glowing red taillights disappearing into the night.

"Damn," he muttered. Motionless, he stared down the street until the cold began to seep into his consciousness. Then, with another curse, he turned and walked back inside the shop.

He headed directly to the fitting room, ignoring the shop owner's quizzical look, and slammed the door behind him. Pacing the perimeter of the tiny room, he tried to repair his shredded self-control.

What had possessed him to kiss her? He knew Elise well enough to have predicted her reaction, yet he'd still felt compelled to test her resolve. And she had been wearing that damned dress. All he had wanted was to see what she looked like in it, to appease his curiosity and enjoy her incredible beauty. And the dandelions? He had rationalized the gift as a mere thankyou for her help and attention. But now he realized that he had sent them with the hope that they would pave the way to something more. In truth, he had fantasized that once confronted with his desire for her, she would happily capitulate and accept a simple affair with no strings attached. Since Elise, with her romantic ideals and storybook view of marriage, was not appropriate wife material for him, a discreet liaison was the next best option.

But if he looked deep into his heart he knew the prospect of a discreet affair was as distasteful to him as the suggestion would have been to Elise. But why? He'd always been satisfied with these types of casual arrangements in the past.

Yet whenever he was around Elise, he found himself wanting more, throwing caution out the window to consider what life could be like with her at his side. All common sense fled when he looked into her wide, expectant gaze, and he found himself savoring the possibilities of the two of them, together, always. He had kissed her, and in that single instant, his self-control had shattered into a million irretrievable pieces.

How could he possibly consider marriage to a woman who had such a disconcerting and dangerous effect on him? In the rush to satisfy his craving for her, he had almost admitted the truth about his lack of a bride. Elise had a way of making him want to open the doors to his soul and show the secrets inside. She made him want to believe that endless love and absolute trust between a man and a woman were achievable. She made him want to take a risk.

Jordan sank down on the settee and, with an impatient sigh, raked his hands through his hair. How had such a simple plan gone so far astray? He had set his goals, arranged his priorities and developed a clear strategy. Yet nothing was going right. Finding a wife should have been no more difficult that completing a basic business acquisition. Locate the target, analyze the target's weaknesses, attack those weaknesses and take control. Just where had his plan gone wrong?

For starters, the target phase had fallen woefully short. He hadn't found a woman who came close to meeting his criteria. It wasn't like he was asking for perfection. He just wanted someone practical, level-headed and logical.

A woman nothing like Elise.

Jordan tipped his head back and drew a ragged breath. Somewhere along the line, he had lost sight of his primary purpose. And it had happened right around the time he had met Elise Sinclair. From the start, she had been a wrench in his plans; she had turned a simple process into a chaotic mess.

He hadn't counted on this overwhelming desire he felt for her. He wanted her, completely and absolutely, without regard for the consequences. To hell with his plan, forget the wife, forget the wedding. Right now, his one-and-only goal was to bury himself in her warmth, to take her body and to possess her heart.

But that was the essence of the problem, this over-powering need to have her heart as his own. He wanted her love and loyalty, yet he knew he couldn't give her the same in return. All he could give her would be what his money could buy: jewelry, a huge house, fancy clothing...dandelions in the dead of winter. He imagined her reaction to the flowers. He saw her smile, heard her gentle laugh. God, how he loved to see her happy. But how long would it be before that smile vanished and that laughter disappeared? How long until she felt trapped in a one-sided relationship, devoid of a shared love and commitment?

He had watched his mother's smiles and laughter

disappear as his father had become more distant and preoccupied with work. All she had wanted was his father's love, yet he had seemed oblivious to her needs until it was too late. She had gone looking for what was missing in her life and had found it with another man. Would Elise do the same?

A raging flood of jealousy coursed through his veins. Once Elise was his, she would be his and his alone. For when he had something in his hands of great value, he protected it above all else. Until now, only his company had deserved such a single-minded defense. But if Elise became his, he would allow no one to take her from him.

Ruthless. The word had been applied to him more than once and he took pride in the description. He approached each corporate battle with cool precision and a deliberate lack of emotion, for emotion had no place in his business life—or in his personal life. Misplaced loyalties and sentimental choices had destroyed others, making their companies vulnerable to people like Jordan. They were fools, all of them. Emotional fools.

But wasn't what he was feeling for Elise coming dangerously close to real emotion? Jealousy, frustration, desire. All of these were feelings that could lead him to lose control.

Jordan snapped his briefcase closed and pulled on his coat. He needed to devise a solution to his problem, a damage-control plan that would put his search for a wife back on track.

He searched his mind for a strategy as he settled the bill for the wedding dress. By the time he got into his car, he was still groping for a game plan. Ten minutes later, as he drove through the traffic on Michigan Avenue, he realized that any plan to put Elise Sinclair completely out of his life was not going to be simple.

He wanted her and he would stop at nothing to have her. Yet he was at a complete loss. He hadn't a clue as to how to go about making her his. In the past, he had diligently avoided the emotional aspects of relationships, leaving him with no understanding of the complicated mechanics that could exist between a man and a woman. And now, when some insight into the tender side of a woman's psyche might help his cause, he had nowhere to turn, no experience to draw upon.

Jordan circled the block and headed toward Lake Shore Drive. As his Mercedes sped north, he opened the sunroof and turned up the radio, hoping the drive would clear his head.

Damn Elise Sinclair! Damn her lovely face and her expressive eyes, her lush figure and her kissable mouth.

And damn him for letting her into his life.

FROM THE SILENT DEPTHS of the house, the mantel clock chimed, bringing Elise's foggy mind back to reality. She groaned and pulled herself up from where she lay sprawled in the middle of her parlor floor, a quilt wrapped around her shoulders. In one hand, she held a glass of wine and in the other, her cordless telephone. The billowing skirt and petticoats of the bridal dress surrounded her like a fluffy white cloud.

She was trapped. Caught in the confines of a dreamy dress that had turned into a straitjacket. She put her wine and the phone down beside her, then crooked her arm behind her back and tried once again to unfasten the row of tiny buttons between her shoulder blades.

But her grasping fingertips could reach just so far. Clorinda and Thisbe observed her from an overstuffed chair, reveling in her plight and smiling their smug little cat smiles.

"You think this is funny, huh?" she muttered, glaring at the cats. "As I recall, you didn't think it was so funny when you locked yourselves in the linen closet."

Maybe she should call 911. Or the fire department. If someone didn't rescue her soon from this four-thousand-dollar prison of silk and lace, she would have to cut the gown off her body. She grabbed the phone, dialed Dona's number and waited for the message on her friend's answering machine to run through.

"Hi, it's me again," Elise said with desperation in her voice. "Where are you? It's midnight. Please come over here as soon as you get in. I need your help." She switched off the phone, picked up her wineglass and gulped down the last of the warm Chardonnay, then wiped the back of her hand across her lips. With a deep sigh, she stretched out on the floor. The ceiling seemed to slowly rotate above her and she closed her eyes. The combination of two glasses of wine and sheer emotional exhaustion had made her numb and a little light-headed.

Her mind drifted back, as it had over and over in the past three hours, replaying the disastrous turn of events in the bridal salon. She recalled each moment with such clarity that she wondered if it would ever be possible to banish the memories from her mind. The warm spread of Jordan's fingers across her back, his firm mouth covering hers, the musky scent of his cologne, the vibration of a moan deep in his throat.

Though she tried to deny her feelings at every turn, she knew another full-fledged assault on her already shaky moral standards would end in her surrender to Jordan Prentiss. She wanted him. It no longer mattered that he was engaged. She wanted him with a passion that blotted out the real world, leaving them alone, together, in a fantasy world where there were no barriers between them.

What she felt for him was like nothing she had ever experienced before—every nerve in her body was alert to his touch, her pulse pounded in a maddening rhythm. But her mind was at war with her heart. Love, hate, desire, denial. Wrong, right, pleasure, pain. And surrounding it all, a whirlpool of confusion.

He had said he wanted her, but where did his feelings begin and end? Was it just lust that drove him to kiss her? Or was there true emotion behind his actions? Did he care for her? Did he love her? Would he break his engagement?

Elise drew in a deep breath, then released it slowly. It had happened before. She had planned more than one wedding that had ended long before the altar. Engagements were broken all the time, for any number of reasons—cold feet, incompatibility, another man... another woman. Though canceled wedding plans were a tremendous bother, she always felt relieved that a mistake had not been made, that love and commitment had not been compromised. A marriage without love was inconceivable to her, a travesty of the wedding vows, a lie, a sham.

But wasn't that what Jordan was embarking upon? He had spoken of his marriage like a business deal, cold and calculated, an exchange of money for services rendered. Poor Abby, she thought. Caught in a loveless union.

No! She couldn't feel sorry for her. If Jordan was telling the truth, Abby was well aware of what she was stepping into. They were consenting adults, after all. And they were both getting what they wanted out of the deal, as mercenary as it might seem to her eyes.

Who was she to judge? She was only their wedding consultant, hired to turn the most important day of their lives into the most memorable day, also. But she couldn't do it, not anymore. Not after what she had experienced with Jordan.

If he planned to proceed with his wedding plans, she would be forced to quit. She couldn't watch silently as the man she was falling in love with married someone else. There would be pain, but no guilt.

But what if Jordan chose to cancel the wedding and break his engagement? This might seem like the ideal situation. But maybe Jordan was wrong and Abby did love him. If he chose Elise, then there would be guilt, but no pain.

Either way, Elise knew her life would never be the same.

The shrill sound of the doorbell jolted her upright. Dona! She struggled to her feet, dragging the quilt with her, and stumbled over her skirts in her haste to reach the foyer. As she yanked the door open, the cold winter wind swirled in around her. Her smile froze as she came face-to-face with Jordan Prentiss.

He stood on her stoop, a grim look on his face. He wore no coat; his hands were shoved into his pants pockets and his suit-jacket collar was turned up against the wind. His silk tie was loosened, his dark hair windblown and wild. Elise was momentarily stunned at his appearance; his usual impeccable grooming was nowhere to be found and his practiced facade of complete control was gone.

She reversed her motion and swung the door shut, but at the last second, he braced his foot against it and forced it open a crack.

She peeked through at him. "Why are you here?"

"Elise, we have to talk. Let me in—it's cold out here."

"Answer one question. Do you still plan to go through with this wedding?"

"Yes."

His baldly stated reply was like a slap in the face. She shoved against the door with her shoulder and flipped the dead bolt. Had she really expected any other answer? A wave of self-recrimination washed over her. When was she going to learn? Love did not conquer all. There was no such thing as love at first sight. And love was definitely not a many-splendored thing.

The doorbell sounded again, this time more insistently.

"Just go away," she shouted through the door. "I don't want to talk to you. I don't ever want to see you again. I quit. You can find someone else to plan this wedding."

"Let me in, Elise." She could hear the rising irritation in his voice. "I have something I need to say to you. I'll stand out here all night if I have to." He pounded on the door and rang the bell again. "If you don't let me in, I'll kick this door down."

Elise quickly reconsidered his demand. Could he really kick the door down? She'd seen it in the movies all the time, but had never believed anyone would attempt it in real life, except maybe the police. Though the threat conjured up very romantic images, the thought of her lovely old oak door splintering on its hinges moved her to action and she reluctantly obeyed his demand.

Jordan stalked through the foyer and into the parlor, heading for the fireplace. Finding no warmth there, he began to pace the room restlessly, rubbing his hands together.

"It's colder in here than it is outside," he muttered, glancing her way.

Elise watched him from the parlor door. She wrapped the quilt more tightly around her, hoping to quell the nervous flutter in her stomach and the goose bumps that accompanied it. "The boiler's broken again," she murmured. She took a deep breath, then met his gaze squarely. "Whatever you have to say is not going to change my mind. I still quit."

He ran his hands through his hair, his pale eyes intensely blue. "Elise, I've made a decision. I want you to marry me."

"Didn't you hear what I just said?" Her voice rose in volume. "I quit. You can take your wedding to another consultant. I'll even help you find my replacement."

"I want you to marry me, Elise," he said, enunciating very clearly, as if she were hard of hearing. "I want you to be my wife."

"I can hear perfectly well," she answered, crossing her arms in a defensive posture. "You're the one who appears to be deaf. I said, I—" She looked at him, dumbfounded, as the meaning of his words sank in.

No, she couldn't have heard right! "You want me to be your what?"

"My wife."

The two simple words set up a pounding in her chest and she groped for a logical reply. His wife? "But...but you're already engaged. What about Abby?"

"Abby's a dog."

A stab of anger shot through her. "How can you say that about the woman you're going to marry? How can you be so cruel?" Earlier, he had described Abby as beautiful. Come to think of it, he had said Abby resembled Elise. And now, he was comparing Abby with a dog? Elise felt a sting from the insult.

"Elise, there is no Abby." He rubbed his forehead in a way that had already become familiar to her, an action that signaled his frustration. "No, that's not quite true. There was, but she's dead."

Elise's brow furrowed in confusion. This conversation was becoming more bizarre by the moment. "You've been planning a wedding to a dead per—" A shattering feeling of alarm raced through her. "Oh, my God. You didn't. You—you murdered her!"

Elise backed slowly out of the doorway. But her cautious retreat from a man who could very likely be a homicidal maniac was stopped when her heels tangled in her skirts. She cried out as she fell squarely on her backside in the middle of the foyer. Jordan appeared above her and she scooted away from him until he grabbed her arms and hauled her to her feet.

"Elise, what has gotten into you? I didn't murder anyone. Abby died of old age when I was fifteen. She was my cocker spaniel. You wanted a name and that's the first name that came to mind."

Her thoughts remained a jumble. "You're planning to marry a dead cocker spaniel?" She tried to wade through her bewilderment to understand what he was saying. He wasn't a murderer; he was a...a...well, she wasn't quite sure what the term was for a man who intended to marry an animal, and a dead one at that. "This is sick. Get out of my house before I call the police."

"Listen to me. There is no Abby. There is no fiancée. There never was." He grabbed her hands and pulled her toward the couch. Hesitantly she sat down beside him, keeping a careful distance. "It was a lie," he continued. "All part of a very complicated plan. And a very stupid plan now that I look back on it."

Elise frowned. She wondered whether forgoing the two glasses of Chardonnay earlier would have made a difference in her understanding of this conversation. Somehow she didn't think so. "Why am I planning a wedding if there's no fiancée?"

"I know this sounds strange, but the bottom line is, I need a wife." Jordan took a deep breath before continuing. His next words came out in a rush. "You and I seem to have some sort of attraction to each other. I should have acknowledged it right away. But I've never been good at this sort of thing. I need a wife, so it might as well be you."

"As opposed to a dog?"

Jordan sighed. "Forget the damn dog. Will you or will you not marry me?"

For a moment, she was speechless, staring at him through uncomprehending eyes. Then she found her voice. "Just like that? We barely know each other."

"I know, I know. But that really doesn't make any

difference." He held up his hand to stop any further comment on her part. "Just listen to the whole deal before you make up your mind. If I don't get married, I'm probably going to lose my company. My cousin Edward has been maneuvering for control of BabyLove and he's managed to convince the board of directors that I don't represent the family image that our company needs to convey to the public. I really don't think my marital status has anything to do with this shift in loyalties, but they're going to use it to force me out. They've decided they want a more stable, conservative president. To them, marriage means stability."

"A marriage proposal is supposed to be romantic," she mumbled as she studied her fingers.

Jordan continued his explanation, not hearing her softly spoken words. "I decided that a quick marriage would be the best defense. I called you to begin plans for the wedding and I started looking for a suitable bride. But things just haven't gone as smoothly as I anticipated. I'm not quite sure why, but they haven't."

"You're supposed to get down on one knee and confess your undying love for me." She talked to herself, aware that Jordan was too intent on his sales pitch to listen.

"I'm offering you a tremendous opportunity. I'm a wealthy man, Elise. I can give you anything you want. You'll never have to work again."

"And a ring," she said wistfully, glancing up at his determined expression. "There should be an engagement ring. In a little black velvet box."

Jordan looked at her strangely, finally acknowledging her words. "Yes, of course. You can go out and buy the most expensive ring in Chicago. There are a lot of other benefits involved here, too. You'll have a house-keeper so you'll never have to worry about housework. After we have children—we need to have children, at least two. A boy and a girl would be nice, a boy first and then a girl. Of course we'll hire a nanny. You'll have a very comfortable life, Elise. It's a very generous offer."

"This isn't romantic at all," she said, shaking her head. He had their entire life mapped out like one of his business plans.

"Of course, if the marriage doesn't work out, you'll be well compensated. So you see, there's really no risk involved. Either way, you come out much better finan-cially than you are right now." He paused. "And I get to keep my company."

"This isn't the way it's supposed to be," she pro-tested, twisting her fingers together nervously.

"Elise, whatever it is that you want, it's yours. We can put all the details into a prenuptial agreement if it would make you feel better. All you have to do is ask."

She focused on his eyes. "Do you love me?"

Jordan's expression remained remote, but she could see his reaction in the shift of his gaze, as if he were weighing the merits of a lie versus the truth. "Elise, I think it's important that we always be honest with each other."

"Do you love me?" she repeated more firmly, al-ready knowing the answer.

"No, I don't. But that doesn't really matter. It doesn't impact the problem at hand."

Elise shook her head. "It has everything in the world to do with the problem at hand. How can you propose marriage to a woman you don't love? And knowing that, how can you expect me to accept?"

"I think you're confusing two very different issues here. Marriage is a legal agreement. Love is an emotional commitment. The two can be mutually exclusive. Elise, we're attracted to each other—that's a start. But I won't confuse lust with love."

Elise wondered if she could say the same. Was what she felt for Jordan actually the beginnings of love or merely a nasty case of lust? "They may not really be that far apart."

Jordan shook his head. "I'd be lying to you. I'm just not capable of that type of emotional investment."

Elise felt her temper rise. "You talk about love like it's some kind of business liability. You're writing it off like a bad debt, before you've even tried to collect."

"Elise, I've explained the deal. You know all the terms. Will you marry me?"

She shook her head indignantly, her answer coming to her lips without a second thought. "No, Jordan. I will not marry you."

Jordan stared at her, his handsome features frozen in a mask of utter disbelief. "No? You're refusing me?"

Elise nodded.

He jumped up from the couch and began to pace the room again. "Why?" he shouted. "What the hell is wrong with me? I'm wealthy. I'm not a drunk or a cheat. I'm a good-looking guy." He slapped his palms on his chest. "I'm Chicago's most eligible bachelor! Women like me. You like me, and don't try to deny it."

Elise fought an outrageous urge to laugh. She had suspected Jordan had an ego, but she had never before seen it manifest itself. "Just because you're the most eligible, doesn't make you the most suitable. And I'm sure women do like you, Jordan," she agreed, "but that's not enough to base a marriage on. At least not for me."

Jordan stood before the fireplace, gripping the mantel, his back to Elise. "Suddenly, it's like I've contracted the plague. Before I decided I needed a wife, I had all the women I could handle. Now I can't seem to find an eligible woman in the entire city of Chicago, not one who's smart enough to see the up side of marrying me."

"Maybe it's your approach," she shot back.

Jordan turned to her with a look of surprise. "My approach? What's wrong with my approach?" He returned to the couch and sat down beside her, his gaze curious. "I'm very straightforward about what I want and what my wife can expect." He laughed dryly. "Women are always talking about honesty in a relationship and I'm being very honest. Are you saying I should lie?"

"No, of course not. I'm just saying marriage to you would be a little easier to...accept if you offered something beyond basic financial security. Your proposal sounded more like a retirement plan than a romantic declaration. Marriage is not a business deal. It's more than that. Much, much more."

"Like what?" he asked sullenly.

"Affection and trust. Commitment. These things aren't available on demand, Jordan. They take time. People don't just jump right into marriage. There's a logical reason for a period of courtship. It gives a man and a woman time to learn about each other."

Jordan considered her suggestions for only a moment before continuing their debate. "But I haven't got time," he answered. "The wedding has to take place as scheduled. I need to find a way to bypass that...that whatever you call it."

"Courtship phase," Elise repeated. "But that's the most romantic part of a relationship. There aren't very many women I know who would want to give that up."

"Ha! So we're back to that again. Romance."

Elise shrugged. "You have to admit, your proposal was lacking in that area."

Jordan studied her closely. "So if I would have been more romantic you would have accepted?"

"No," Elise answered stubbornly. "But I might have given it a second thought."

His expression turned hard and a muscle twitched in his jaw. "I knew this wouldn't work."

"Well, I think we had better cancel the wedding plans. I really don't think it's possible for—"

"No," Jordan stated coldly, turning away from her to pace the room. "I have to get married. If you won't marry me, then you have to help me."

"Help you what?"

He turned and fixed her with a pointed stare. "Find a wife."

Elise's jaw dropped and she gasped, unable to believe what he was saying. Just moments ago, he had asked her to marry him and now he acted as if the words had never passed his lips, as if she were no more than a passing whim in his grand plan. He expected her to help him find a wife? He had to be joking.

"I don't know why I didn't think of it before. You know all about romance and you can give me insights into the tangle of the female mind. With your help I can intensify my efforts and breeze right through this courtship phase."

Elise's heart constricted in her chest. It was as if he had suddenly turned to ice, colder and harder than the man she first met on her front stoop. He was serious. And he obviously had no idea how she felt about him or he wouldn't have asked such a thing. She crossed the room to toy with a vase of silk flowers on an ornate Victorian fern stand. "Jordan, really, I don't think—"

He followed and stood behind her. "If you help me and I manage to pull this off by my deadline, I'll double your fee. And if the wedding doesn't happen as planned, I'll give you your regular fee, anyway. It's a generous offer, Elise. Think about it."

She turned to look at him. Her eyes skimmed the sculpted contours of his face, a face that had haunted her thoughts from the day she'd met him. She was tempted to reach out and warm his frozen expression with her touch, but she resisted the impulse, balling her hands into tight fists, instead.

Could she do it? Could she bury her silly feelings for this man and help him find a wife? After all, there was no hope for a relationship with him; that fact was painfully clear. He had already forgotten his offer to her, brushing it off like a passing fancy.

Jordan Prentiss hadn't a clue as to what she needed in a husband and she was a fool ever to think that he could make her happy. So why not take him up on his offer? She could certainly use the money and she had already invested too much time in this wedding to let it go now. A new roof, a new boiler and utility payments were part of real life. Her infatuation with Jordan was simply a dream.

Elise bit her bottom lip, then nodded hesitantly. "All right," she said in a thin voice. "I'll do it."

Jordan nodded curtly. "We have a deal, then."

"Yes," she said, trying to force a bit of conviction into her reply. "We have a deal."

"All right." Jordan turned and walked to the door. "I'll call you tomorrow and we'll set up a schedule of...romance consultations." He grabbed the doorknob. "This will work. I know it will."

He turned to her once more, his gaze catching her wide eyes. Elise thought she saw a flash of regret cross his face. "You do look incredible in that dress," he murmured.

Elise swallowed convulsively and smiled. "Thank you."

"Why are you still wearing it?"

A blush warmed her cheeks. "I can't seem to get myself out of it. It's the buttons. They're so tiny and I can't reach..."

Jordan strode back into the parlor and firmly took hold of her shoulders, then turned her around so that her back faced him. With deft fingers, he released each pearl button from its tiny loop. His thumbs grazed her bare back and sent tingles of sensation shooting to her toes and fingertips. As the last button was undone and the dress threatened to fall from her shoulders, she clutched her hands to her chest and spun around to face him.

For a fleeting moment, she caught an expression of pain on his face, but then it disappeared, replaced by his normal detached facade.

"I'll call you," he said in a subdued voice.

"Fine," she answered, watching his return to the door.

He didn't turn back this time, only paused a moment before saying a blunt and businesslike "Good night."

As the door closed behind him, Elise sank to the floor, the dress ballooning out around her. She grabbed a throw pillow from the couch and buried her face in it. When she raised her head, she saw Clorinda and Thisbe sitting in front of her, eyeing the pearls scattered across the skirt of the bridal gown. She tossed the pillow at them and sent the pair retreating to a safe distance across the room.

In her wildest dreams, she had never imagined a marriage proposal like the one Jordan had made to her. Nor had she ever dreamed that the one and only time a proposal was offered, she would flatly turn it down.

THE RESTAURANT on the sixth floor of the Bloomingdale's building was nearly empty when Elise arrived. She chose a small table along the floor-to-ceiling windows and watched the midmorning traffic from high above Michigan Avenue as she sipped at her coffee. She stifled a yawn behind her hand and rubbed her scratchy eyes, wondering how much sleep she had actually gotten the night before. As far as she could recall, it had been less than an hour. A frantic two a.m. call from Dona had interrupted her only slumber.

She waited patiently for the caffeine to kick in, hoping that she would recover some of her faculties before her appointment downtown with Melvin, the florist, for Jordan's wedding.

Jordan's wedding. The plans would proceed, full

steam ahead, with or without a bride. She felt as if she had hopped on a runaway train headed straight on a collision course. Would she be able to pull herself from the rubble afterward or would she be buried alive? Could she bear to watch him walk down the aisle with another woman, knowing that she could have been his bride? It would have taken only one simple word to change her fate.

Yes. Yes, Jordan, I will marry you. Even though you don't love me. Even though this marriage means no more to you than a simple business deal.

Elise groaned and rubbed her eyes again, then ran her fingers through her hair, brushing the strawberry-blond strands away from her face. She had made the right decision. Jordan was not the man for her.

"Hello, dear."

Elise looked up as an older woman stopped before her table. She tried to place the face, then realized it was the woman she had met in Jordan's office. She was bundled from top to toe in a pale-pink wool coat with a pink muffler wrapped around her neck and a jaunty tam of the same color perched on top of her head. She had on the same high-top sneakers that she'd worn the night Elise had met her. Her cheeks were rosy and her eyes twinkled merrily.

"Hello," Elise said warily. "How are you?"

"Why, I'm quite well. Thank you for asking. May I sit down?" Not waiting for an answer, she slid into an empty chair across the table and folded her gloved hands in front of her, staring sharply at Elise. "You don't look well at all. Is something wrong?"

Elise opened her mouth to speak, then snapped it shut. Who was this woman? Normally Elise would be offended by such blatant nosiness from a virtual stranger. But after a terrible night of tossing and turning, she found the woman's concern somehow comforting.

"It's Jordan, isn't it?" the woman continued.

Elise contained her look of surprise. "I—I don't believe we've ever been introduced. I'm Elise Sinclair."

The woman laughed and shook her finger playfully at Elise. "I knew that. Don't you remember, we met in Jordan's office? I never forget a face, or the name that goes with it."

"Of course I remember. But I'm afraid I don't recall your name."

"Well, maybe that's because I never told you."

She felt a sliver of irritation at the woman's deliberately evasive answer, but it dissolved in the face of her warm smile. "Who are you?" Elise asked bluntly.

The woman gazed out the window, intent on the hustle and bustle below, her words soft and direct. "The important question really is 'Who are you?'— isn't it?"

Elise calmly placed her coffee cup back in its saucer. "What's that supposed to mean?"

"Are you the woman who can teach Jordan to love again? Or are you like the other women in his life, interested only in his money, his position." She fixed Elise with a probing stare. "He asked you to marry him, didn't he?"

This time Elise knew her expression was one of shock. "How did you know that? Did Jordan talk to you?"

"Jordan is very secretive about his personal life. I think that has to do with his childhood. Did you know that his mother left him and his father when he was nine? Just up and walked out on them one day. No, I suppose he wouldn't have told you that. He loved his mother very much, though he'd never admit it. He tried so hard to maintain that stiff Prentiss upper lip." The old woman sighed, a faraway look in her eyes. "She died a year later in a car accident. Very tragic. I believe that's why Jordan has such a difficult time trusting his feelings."

Elise felt her heart twist in compassion for him. "You knew Jordan when he was a little boy?"

"Oh, yes. I knew him quite well."

Elise shook her head in bewilderment. "And you know about Edward and his attempt to take over BabyLove?"

"Of course I do," she replied, then laughed lightly, a lovely bell-like sound. "I can just imagine Jordan's proposal."

Elise couldn't help but smile. "It was a little bit odd. He listed all the things he could give me—cars, clothes, money. He's pretty desperate to save his company."

"Hmm." She nodded. "That's good. I knew he would feel that way. Now, I know this is probably none of my business, Elise. And I do make it a practice never to interfere in other people's lives. But I feel compelled to give you one little piece of advice. Don't be concerned about what he says he can give you. Be more concerned with what you can give him. The rest will come, I promise you."

The woman glanced at her watch and then stood up suddenly, her hands aflutter. "Well, there it is. I've said what I have to say and now I'll leave you to your coffee." She reached out and patted Elise's hand, then turned for the door. "Don't you worry," she called back over her shoulder. "Everything will turn out just fine. You'll make a lovely bride."

"Wait," Elise cried. "Come back here. You don't understand. I turned him down." Elise fumbled for her purse and tossed some money on the table. She pulled on her coat as she hurried out the door, trying to keep her eyes on the pink-clad form a hundred feet in front of her.

Whoever this woman was, Elise was determined to find out how she knew so much about Jordan Prentiss. She had to be a relative. Or at least a close family friend. Either way, she was privy to Jordan's marriage plans.

Elise kept the bobbing pink tam in sight as she followed her down the escalators, gaining on her until she was only fifteen feet behind her. Then the woman stepped into the revolving doors leading out to the street. Elise waited behind several other shoppers before she passed through the spinning door. She scanned the sidewalk for the woman in pink, but her frantic search revealed only drably attired shoppers and conservatively dressed business people, their heads bent to the wind, their eyes fixed on the sidewalk.

The old woman had vanished as she had appeared, only staying long enough to pass out a bit of grandmotherly advice. Elise stood outside the Bloomingdale's building for a full five minutes, searching the crowd, before she gave up and went back inside.

6

"'WEALTHY CHICAGO businessman, SWM, 38, seeks corporate wife, SWF, 25-35. Impeccable manners, good breeding, college degree and a practical approach to marriage required. Send list of qualifications ASAP to Box 13707, Chicago, Illinois.'"

"A singles ad?" Jordan asked. "You want me to run a singles ad?"

Pete Stockton nodded. "Just as a backup. Listen, boss, we're running a little short on time here. We've got to consider all the options at our disposal. Did you look at the files on the latest list of candidates yet? Maybe you could take them home tonight and review them, then make a few appoint—er, I mean dates—for this weekend."

Jordan glanced over at the stack of manila folders on the corner of his desk. He had been avoiding the task for two days, but he knew he could put it off no longer. Pete was right. Time was running out and he was no closer to finding a bride than he had been a month ago. "I'll go through them tomorrow. I've got plans for this evening."

Pete gave him an exasperated look. "I get the feeling you're having second thoughts about this, Jordan. Are you sure you still want to proceed?"

"I have no choice," Jordan snapped. "The board is wavering in their support for Edward, but I'm not in the clear yet. This marriage could turn the tide in our favor."

"According to my schedule, you should at least have the list narrowed to a few candidates. You've got to make a proposal soon, and have an alternate in case your first candidate refuses."

"She already did," Jordan muttered, snatching a file folder from the pile and flipping through it.

"What are you talking about?"

He threw the folder down on his desk and pushed back his chair. "I've made one proposal and collected one refusal already."

"Who?"

Jordan stood up and walked to the windows. "It doesn't make any difference who she is. She said no."

He had gone over to Elise's house expecting as much, but had decided to give his marriage proposal a shot. He had figured his odds of an acceptance were least one in three—good odds by business standards. But then he had blown the execution, and the odds had plummeted to zero.

Other business deals had fallen through for him in the past, yet none of them had disturbed him in such a severe way. Jordan hated to lose. And he had lost because of a lack of preparation on his part. Her refusal made him angry and frustrated, feelings he had never allowed to enter into his business dealings.

If only he had been able to make her see his reasoning and the advantages to his plan. But her decision was based on emotion rather than reason and he knew from experience that when a business decision was made with the heart instead of the head, the results were unpredictable at best. In this case, there was no use beating a dead deal. There wasn't a chance in a million that she would change her mind.

He'd tried to convince himself that it didn't matter...but it did. He could still feel the harsh sting of her refusal. But that was the downside. This crash and burn had an upside. He hadn't lost everything. Like the shrewd businessman that he was, he had taken his loss and turned it around, finding a way to salvage something from the wreckage. Elise had said his proposal was less than romantic and he knew she was right; the trouble was, he had no idea what she really meant by romantic. But after tonight's romance consultation he *would* know and he wouldn't make the same mistake twice.

"Just no? Didn't she give any reasons?" Pete persisted. "Did you try to change her mind? Was it a definite no or an ask-me-another-time no? Did she throw you out on your ear and tell you never to darken her door again? Or did she leave the door open a crack?"

"What the hell are you talking about?"

"How did she say no?"

Jordan shrugged. "I don't remember. All I remember was her answer and no means no."

"In most cases, I'd agree. But in the case of a marriage proposal, there might be room for negotiation. If you still want this woman, you shouldn't give up so easily."

Jordan turned and stared skeptically at his assistant. "What are you saying? You think I could change her mind?"

"It's worth a try. Right now, we don't have a better deal on the table. But I think you'd stand a better chance if you listened to a little advice."

Jordan laughed. Why was it everyone felt compelled to give him advice on romance? Did he have "bumbling idiot" tattooed across his forehead? "Since when did you become an expert in the field of marriage proposals? The last time I checked, you were a terminal bachelor."

"I don't claim to be an expert. I do, however, know how a woman likes to be treated. Just let me give you a few general pointers. What could it hurt? The worst she could do is say no again."

Jordan sat back down and kicked his feet up on the edge of the desk, then clasped his hands behind his head. Maybe Pete was right. What *did* he have to lose? In reality, he had an incredible amount to gain if Pete could help him: Elise, a wife and his company. He had already managed to make a mess of things on his own. Right now, he was willing to try anything. "All right, Stockton, fire away."

Pete clapped his hands enthusiastically. "Okay. First, a woman likes a man to be a man."

"I think I've got that one covered," Jordan replied dryly.

"I mean they really go for the rugged man—blue jeans, flannel shirts, cowboy boots. Three women..." Stockton shook his head in disgust. "*Three women* dumped me for blue-collar types. For some reason, women are attracted to the strong, silent, brooding guys. Lose the suit and tie and get yourself some blue jeans. And practice your brooding."

"Brooding?"

"Yeah," Stockton answered. "Sort of like this."

Jordan's assistant furrowed his brow, narrowed his eyes and clenched his teeth. To Jordan's eye, he looked as if he had just contracted a severe case of constipation.

"It makes a man seem mysterious. Women eat that stuff up. Mystery is a big turn-on."

"I'll remember that," Jordan replied. "Anything else?"

"Never, ever be late. For anything. It's like throwing a match on gasoline. I think it's something hormonal. It doesn't matter where you were or why you're late. I was late picking up Andrea, the woman I was dating before Jennifer, and she refused to let me in. I never saw her after that night."

"How late were you?"

"Three days. But that's beside the point. They live—and you die—by the clock."

"And what if I *am* unavoidably late?"

"Bring a gift. They're suckers for presents and it will give you a perfect excuse for being late—you were shopping. When I was dating Lisa, I kept a supply of gifts in the trunk of my car. In fact, if you really want to impress a woman, bring her something every time you see her. And something for her family, too. It never hurts to butter up the relatives. You may need them in your corner someday."

"What kind of presents would you suggest?"

"It doesn't matter, as long as they're expensive. Women go for those kitchen gadgets—you know, coffee makers and blenders. They like jewelry and clothes more, but those kind of presents are too risky in my opinion. You may get something she doesn't like and then you're in trouble because you didn't know she wouldn't like it. With an electrical appliance, you can't go wrong. What's not to like about a food processor?"

"A food processor." Jordan considered this information carefully, trying to remember what Elise had told him about gifts. Don't buy generic jewels, she had said. Buy her something that reminds you of her. Somehow a food processor was the last thing that came to mind when he thought of Elise. But maybe, if she liked to cook, it did make sense.

"And compliment her a lot. On her dress, her hair, her cooking. It makes no difference, just be profuse and sound sincere. Tell her she smells good, like a spring rain or a tropical breeze."

Jordan shot him a doubting look.

Pete waved him off. "I know, I know. It sounds stupid, but I use that one all the time and it works like a charm. Finally, be assertive. Don't ask her to marry you, tell her. Women like men who take charge. Sensitivity in our gender is highly overrated. Sweep a woman off her feet, like on the covers of those romance novels they're always reading. Don't be a wimp."

"Don't be a wimp," Jordan repeated.

"Show her who's boss. Be a man, a stud, a go-to guy."

"A go-to guy."

"Right," Pete urged.

"Right."

JORDAN PUSHED Elise's doorbell, then glanced down at his watch. Though he was twenty minutes early, at least he wasn't late. Usually he made it a practice to be punctual, always arriving at the agreed-upon time. He had thought about waiting in the car for a few minutes, but if women hated men who were late, they would probably love a man who was early. He would just tell

Elise that he couldn't wait another minute to see her. This romance business really wasn't so difficult, after all.

Until his discussion with Pete that afternoon, he hadn't realized how little he really knew about pleasing a woman. He had always considered women an entirely different species, wonderfully satisfying in bed, but totally foreign to his mind. He had never taken the time to care about what they liked or disliked. His relationships with the opposite sex had never progressed far enough to make that data imperative.

But he was in the driver's seat now. Pete's insights were helpful, but Elise was about to provide him with everything he needed to turn the situation to his advantage. Though she wouldn't know it, she was about to hop on the Prentiss express, headed straight to the altar. Elise's lessons in romance were about to be put to work on the teacher herself. How could he go wrong? With a concentrated effort, he would have a confirmed deal with Elise Sinclair in a matter of days.

Jordan shifted the packages in his arms and rang the bell again. A moment later, the front door swung open to reveal Elise, her face flushed and moist, her hair wet and puddles of water forming at her feet beneath the hem of her shapeless bathrobe.

She looked at him in annoyance, then turned to the huge grandfather clock in the foyer. Slowly she returned her gaze to him. "You're early," she said. "I told you six o'clock. It's five-thirty. You got me out of the shower."

"Five-thirty-eight," Jordan corrected.

She arched her brow and stepped aside to allow him to enter. "You're still early."

"Sorry," he muttered. "I was anxious to get started." He followed Elise into the parlor, his eyes fixed on the provocative sway of her hips beneath the bulky bathrobe. What he wouldn't give to be able to pull the tie loose, push the robe off her body and explore the hidden curves beneath.

She turned to him and casually surveyed his appearance as she spoke, her expression showing mild surprise. "All right, let's start here and now. Never be early. It makes you appear too eager. Women want a man, not a lap dog. If you can't be on time, then be a little late." She ran her eyes down his length again. "Women expect that. Men are incapable of arriving on time and women factor that into their schedules. I expected you...to arrive at—what are you wearing?"

Jordan followed her gaze from his leather bomber jacket and flannel shirt, past his prewashed jeans to his feet. The pointed toes of his brand-new cowboy boots gleamed in the soft light of the parlor. "You like them, don't you?" he said as he held out his foot.

She shook her head and studied his footwear. "I'd be careful with those boots, Tex," she murmured. "You could put a person's eye out." Drawing a sharp breath, she pulled the belt of her robe tighter and nodded toward the couch. "Sit down. I'll be back in a few seconds."

He placed his packages on the coffee table and sat down, then pulled off the leather jacket and tossed it beside his gifts. So far, Pete was zero for two. He closed his eyes and leaned back, sinking into the soft depths of the couch. She didn't like men who were too prompt and she wasn't hot for the cowboy type. Stifling a groan, Jordan pushed himself off the couch and wandered restlessly around the room, picking up Elise's possessions, searching for a clue to her likes and dislikes.

She liked small objects. Nearly everything he picked up fit in the palm of his hand: a marble egg, an inlaid box, a delicate porcelain chickadee. And she liked flowers. Every surface was decorated with some type of floral design. Silk flowers spilled from vases and bowls scattered about the room. And a subtle floral scent wafted through the house. From what he could tell, her favorite color was either pink or green. He carefully filed the facts in his mind, then realized how trivial the information was.

Jordan walked to the fireplace and stared down into the cold ashes on the grate. What did he *really* know about her? He didn't know her favorite foods or what type of music she liked. He didn't know anything about her family or her childhood. All he knew of Elise Sinclair was the softness of her lips and the musical sound of her voice. He knew the exact color of her hair in sunlight and the way she bit her bottom lip when she was nervous. But she had revealed little solid information about herself in their business dealings. How the hell was he supposed to make this work?

He felt a soft nudge against his leg and looked down to find Elise's cats at his feet. Their tails switched back and forth on the Oriental carpet and their attention was transfixed by the shiny metal toes of his cowboy boots. He wiggled his foot and the white cat pounced, trapping his toe beneath its paws.

"At least there are a few females left in the world

who find macho irresistible," he murmured, bending down to playfully poke at the furry feline. "You are ladies, aren't you?"

The gray cat approached, pushing her head beneath Jordan's hand before rolling over on her back. "You live with her," he whispered. "Maybe you could put in a good word for me. I'll make it worth your while. A lifetime supply of fresh tuna and catnip." The cats stared at him with vacant looks.

Jordan gave each cat an affectionate pat, then continued his survey of the room. As he passed the mirror above the mantel, he met his reflection with a critical glare. Stockton had spent a ridiculous amount on the clothes he wore and Elise hadn't been impressed. To tell the truth, Jordan hadn't been impressed, either, but his assistant had been adamant.

Maybe it was all in the attitude. Clothes, after all, didn't make the man. Jordan furrowed his brow. He narrowed his eyes and clenched his teeth trying to replicate his assistant's version of brooding.

"Are you all right?" Elise's reflection appeared in the mirror beside his, her face etched with concern.

Jordan quickly cloaked his contorted features with a bland smile. "Me? Yes. I'm fine." He turned to Elise, his gaze locking with hers. She shifted uncomfortably, running her fingers through the damp tendrils of her hair. "What about you? Are you all right?"

"What? With these lessons?" Elise asked. She shrugged. "Sure. As long as we keep this on a professional level. You need a wife in a hurry. It's as simple as that. I'll do what I can to help you." She raised her gaze to meet his.

"Good," he murmured. He stared into her liquid

green eyes, unable to break a connection that suddenly crackled like a high-tension wire between them. An uncontrollable surge of desire washed over him and he felt his body draw closer to hers. His hand moved of its own volition, coming to rest on her silken check. Slowly he lowered his head to kiss her.

He brushed his lips gently across hers. When hers parted slightly to protest, he took advantage and covered her mouth to slowly sample her moist warmth with his tongue. To his surprise, she allowed him to continue his tender assault and he deepened the kiss, the wave of heat in his body now a raging tide.

Gradually, through his hazy passion, he realized that she wasn't responding. Her hands rested limply at her sides and her body stood unmoving before him, a pillar of reticence. He dragged himself from the drugging effects of the kiss and looked down at her. She opened her eyes and stepped away.

"That was very...nice," she murmured.

"Very nice," Jordan breathed, sliding his hands along her arms to her waist, drawing her to him again. And very romantic, if he did say so himself.

"Except..." she began.

"Except?"

"Well, this is just a suggestion, but you may want to...to impose a bit more...self-control. A kiss of greeting should be a bit less...less passionate. Less...wet."

Jordan froze. "What?"

"Not what. Wet," she said with emphasis. "Though it was, on the whole, a very romantic kiss. On a scale of one to ten, I'd give it a seven. Or maybe you'd prefer letter grades. That would be about a B-minus."

"You're grading me?"

"That's what you're here for, isn't it? Lessons in romance. I think it's best if we grade your efforts. That way, we can judge your progress."

Jordan glared at her, unable to speak, his temper threatening to explode. What kind of game was she playing? Her expression was cool, composed, as if she had suffered no effects from the dizzying kiss. He was tempted to yank her into his arms and give her an A-plus for effort, but instead he turned away and stalked to the couch.

So this was the way it was going to be. She was going to keep him at arm's length. He considered it a silent challenge—love her or leave her alone. He would play along. But Elise Sinclair had no idea what she was up against. Jordan never backed down from a challenge.

He had one advantage. She wanted him as much as he wanted her; he could see it in her eyes. He would have Elise Sinclair as his bride and without any admissions of undying love and eternal fidelity from him. Nothing would stand in his way.

Grabbing the largest gift-wrapped package from the coffee table, he turned and held it out to her. "Here, I brought you a present," he said smoothly.

Elise stepped toward him and took the brightly wrapped package from his hands with a winsome smile. "This is for me?"

Jordan watched her coolly. Two could play at this game. "No. It's for my future fiancée. I just thought I'd try it out on you first. You know, so you can grade me on it." She looked up at him and he shot her a tight grin. "Go ahead—open it."

Elise gave him a sideways glance as she tore into the paper. When the gift was unwrapped, she held the big box up in front of her and surveyed it with a confused look. "An ice-cream maker?"

Jordan nodded. In the store it had seemed like a brilliant idea. The saleswoman had gone on and on about the convenience of this particular model and the taste of homemade ice cream. And ice cream did remind him of Elise, sweet and delicious, smooth and creamy, cool, yet able to melt to his touch. And it fit Pete Stockton's suggestion of a small electric appliance.

"How...original," she said hesitantly. "Very unexpected."

"Unexpected is good. You told me that once."

"Yes, but usually one would buy a more personal gift for his future bride. But an ice-cream maker is very...original." She placed the box on the coffee table and picked up the remaining package. "What's this?"

Jordan tried to grab it out of her hand. "That's nothing."

"I'll be the judge of that." She pulled off the ribbon and foil paper, then lifted the lid from the smaller box. Digging through the tissue paper, she withdrew a tiny leather mouse. The confused look she had given the ice-cream maker was replaced by utter bewilderment. Then she withdrew a plastic ball with a bell inside, a miniature punching bag and a stuffed bird on an elastic string. "These are...cat toys."

"I know," Jordan answered defensively. "They're not for you—or my fiancée," he quickly added. "They're for your cats."

"You brought Clorinda and Thisbe presents?"

Jordan shrugged. "Sure. Why not?" They were the closest thing Elise had to a family. He didn't have much to work with, so he worked with what he had.

Elise frowned and opened her mouth, then snapped it shut, smiling at him, instead. "Thank you. It was a very thoughtful gift. I'm sure they'll enjoy these." She paused as if uncertain how to proceed, then took a deep breath. "Why don't we get started?"

"I thought we already had," Jordan said under his breath.

She sat down on the couch and looked up at him, waiting for him to join her. He sat down at the opposite end and watched her closely.

"All right," he prompted. "What do you have planned?"

"Close your eyes," she ordered.

After a brief questioning look, he complied.

"Now, describe what I'm wearing. No, don't look. Close your eyes. Tell me what I'm wearing."

Jordan concentrated hard, trying to bring up an image of Elise's clothing, but he drew only a blank. The problem was, from the moment she'd walked into the room, he had been captivated by the exquisite features of her face, the emerald depths of her eyes and the lush curve of her mouth. Hell, he had no idea what she was wearing. The only thing he knew was that right this minute, he wished she weren't wearing anything at all.

"Are you wearing a sweater?" he asked.

"Am I?"

"Yes, you're wearing a blue sweater," he said with more confidence.

"What shade?"

"I don't know," Jordan muttered. "Light blue, sky blue."

He opened his eyes to see if he was right, but she

quickly placed her palm over them. "Keep them closed," she warned.

"So, was I right?"

"I'm wearing a white blouse with a green-and-black tapestry vest. It's important to be observant. You need to remember the little details of your relationship. It will help you be more romantic."

Jordan groaned in frustration. "Why don't you ask me something I know?" he protested in an angry voice. "Ask me about how your eyes sparkle when you smile or how your hair shimmers like spun gold in the sunlight. Ask me about how your mouth feels beneath mine or how your skin is like satin under my fingertips. Ask me—" Jordan snapped his eyes open just as she snatched her hand away from his brow, suddenly aware of what he was saying.

Elise watched him, wide-eyed, her lips parted and her breath coming in shallow gasps.

"Ask me something I know," Jordan repeated, his gaze penetrating hers.

Elise stood up and walked across the room to stand at an ornate lowboy, where she picked up a tiny vase filled with a spray of silk flowers. "That was very romantic," she said in a soft voice, plucking at the flowers nervously.

"So does it deserve a ten, or was it worth just a seven or eight?" he asked in a calculating voice, his earlier anger resurfacing at her swift retreat.

She spun around to look at him, her eyes registering a flash of hurt before she buried it beneath a blank facade. Jordan was startled. Had he really said something romantic? Had his words actually affected her?

"Jordan, I really don't think this is such a good idea, these lessons."

"Why not, Elise?"

"Because, I...it's just that you..." She sighed. "I can't help you be something you aren't. No matter how hard you try, some frogs just don't have prince potential."

Jordan stood and walked over to her. "Is that what you want, Elise? Some real-life Romeo who'll speak all sorts of flowery gibberish and kiss your feet."

"You know what I want. I want a man who loves me. A man I can depend on. A man who needs me."

"You want a lap dog, Elise, and life with a lap dog can be very dull."

"Well, maybe it will be, but at least I'll know where I stand."

"What about me?" He grabbed her by the arm and drew her against his chest. "*I need you*, Elise."

She twisted in his arms. "You don't need me, Jordan. You need a body, someone to wear a wedding dress in return for a generous salary. I already have a job. I don't need another."

"That's not the only thing I'm offering. I can give you more."

She met his gaze. "What can you possibly give me that I really want?" she asked.

"I can give you this." In a swift, sure movement, Jordan captured her mouth, moving his lips against hers in an erotic dance of sensation. His tongue traced her lower lip, then plunged into the warm recesses of her mouth.

With a weak shove, she pushed away and glared at him defiantly. "Three," she uttered, her eyes blazing with anger.

He dropped his mouth to hers again, this time plundering with greater force, sliding his hands along her spine until he cupped her buttocks. With gentle pressure, he pressed her hips into his. He suppressed a groan, skimming his mouth along the curve of her throat, his lips coming to rest over a thrumming pulse point. He bit her neck softly and she gasped.

"Five," she murmured, her voice shaky.

"Tell the truth, Elise. Are you willing to give this up just for some pretty words?" He pressed his hips into hers, his arousal an unyielding ridge of heat against her belly. He wanted her to feel the extent of his desire—the driving, uncontrolled inferno of passion that spread from deep inside him like a wildfire. But her next words doused the fire as quickly as a cold summer downpour.

"Yes," she croaked. "I'm willing to give all this up."

Jordan gazed down at her, meeting her arctic stare. A tear glimmered in the corner of her eye and a rush of self-contempt washed over him.

"Dammit, Elise. I know you want me. Don't try to deny it."

"I don't deny it," she replied, her voice barely above a whisper. "But it's not enough. I'm sorry, Jordan, but I can't play by your rules. They just don't work for me." She stepped to the coffee table and picked up his jacket, holding it out to him. "That's the way it is. I can't change the way I feel any more than you can change the way you don't feel."

"And what if you never find your perfect man, Elise?"

She shook her head. "That's a risk I have to take. I grew up with parents who were more in love with each other every day they were together. When my mother died, my father almost died from grief. A few years ago, he remarried. I think he was hoping to find the same kind of love he had with my mother, but it just wasn't there. He's happy, but it isn't the same. It's second best. I don't want to settle for second best. I want the whole thing."

"My parents married for love," Jordan recalled, his voice steeped in bitterness. "At least, that's what they thought. Then my father needed to devote more time to the business and my mother started looking for...diversions. She fell in love with the tennis pro at their country club and ran off with him. Don't you see, Elise? I need a woman who understands the demands on my time, a woman who won't go looking for diversions. Someone I can trust to be there when I need her, someone who won't be ruled by her emotions."

"So you've ruled out love completely. Just because it didn't work out between your parents isn't enough reason to renounce commitment entirely. What would life be without love?"

"A hell of a lot simpler."

Elise shook her head in resignation. "Somewhere out there is a woman who's a perfect fit for you, a woman who shares your bleak opinions. You have to find her, Jordan. I'm not that woman, and I never can be."

Jordan felt a sharp pain in his chest at her words. He wasn't ready to let her go yet. "I can't find her without your help."

"Yes, you can. You can be a very romantic man when you put your mind to it. You don't need my help to find a wife. Anyway, I think it would be best for both of us if we didn't see each other again until the wedding."

Suddenly he didn't care about anything but keeping Elise close to him. She was the one he wanted. No one else would do. An odd mixture of fear and desperation grew in the pit of his stomach, weighing his words down like a rock in a rushing river. "What about the wedding plans?"

"Most of the plans are in place. We can accomplish everything else over the phone."

"No," Jordan said. "This wedding is very important. I want to at least have a weekly status meeting. And we can combine the meeting with a romance lesson. We'll just meet at my office or in public."

Elise regarded him suspiciously. "Jordan, that's really not necessary. Everything is well under control. And I don't think romance lessons are going to help. Not if you don't believe in what's behind the romance."

"If I say it's necessary, it's necessary. I have a lot riding on this plan."

She sighed, then closed her eyes for a moment. When she opened them again, Jordan saw a new determination in their green depths. "All right, we'll meet once a week. And we will keep it strictly business."

Jordan nodded. Of course he would keep it strictly business. And his most important business at the moment was convincing Elise to marry him. "Strictly business," he replied. "I promise."

ELISE CLOSED the door behind Jordan, then leaned back against it. Tears threatened to spill from her eyes, but she controlled the urge to cry with a steely resolve. She had made her decision and now she would have to abide by it. No matter how attracted she was to Jordan Prentiss, he was not in love with her. And she could not consider marriage to him.

Yet she couldn't tolerate the thought of him marrying someone else. If only he didn't have this ridiculous deadline, maybe there would be a chance for them. But without time, she had no hope of making him fall in love with her. The deck had been stacked against them from the start. It just wasn't meant to be.

She had hoped her lessons in romance would put their doomed relationship into perspective, but she hadn't counted on the intensity of her feelings for Jordan. It wasn't easy to put them aside, to ignore the rush of desire she felt whenever he looked at her, the shiver of passion she felt at his mere touch. He was everything she wanted and everything she didn't want, all wrapped up in one.

But he didn't want *her*; he wanted a wife.

Why couldn't she put him out of her life once and for all? She would still be faced with meeting him once a week until this silly charade of a wedding was over. Why did she agree? Was she still clinging to the hope that he might fall in love with her?

The ring of the phone interrupted her melancholy thoughts. Elise picked up the receiver and uttered a halfhearted "Hello."

"Lizzie, is that you?"

The sound of her father's voice calling her by her childhood nickname brought another surge of tears to her eyes. "Hi, Daddy. Yes, it's me."

"You sound upset. Is everything all right?"

"Everything is...just fine." Elise drew a deep breath. "Just fine."

"It's eighty degrees here today. What's the temperature in Chicago?"

"It's cold," Elise said softly. "Very cold."

"Did you get the boiler fixed yet? Make sure you call Max Constanza to get an estimate. And while he's there have him take a look at that leaky drainpipe in the upstairs tub."

"Yes, Daddy. I will." Even from a thousand miles away, her father was still as protective as ever. During the past five years they had switched roles again. As a small child her father had been her hero, riding to her rescue at every scraped knee and terrifying nightmare. After her mother had died, Elise had been fiercely protective of him, trying desperately to make life easy for him. But around the time he'd met Dorthi, their roles had once again shifted back to a traditional hero-daughter relationship.

"You have enough money, don't you? I can send you a check for the boiler repair if that's the problem."

"I have plenty of money, Daddy. I just got a terrific wedding to plan. The biggest and best ever." An image of Jordan's handsome face swam in her mind and she pushed it away, concentrating on her conversation with her father. He was going on about her financial situation and she listened distractedly, interjecting a "Yes, Daddy" or a "No, Daddy" where appropriate.

"Honey, Dorthi wants to say hello. Let me put her on."

Elise's attention snapped back to the phone conversation. "No, wait. Daddy?" There was silence on the other end of the line. "Daddy?"

"Hi, Elise. It's Dorthi. How are the girls?"

Elise stifled a groan of dismay. Why couldn't her father realize how uncomfortable these conversations with her stepmother were? It wasn't that she didn't care for Dorthi. Dorthi was a kind and generous woman who had never even tried to become a mother to Elise. Elise was grateful to her for bringing her father out of his long mourning. But it was hard to talk to the woman who had attempted to step into her mother's place in her father's life. Dorthi had settled for being second best when she'd married Martin Sinclair and the most Elise could feel for her was a small amount of pity.

She answered the standard questions about Clorinda and Thisbe, then listened to her stepmother chatter on about the weather and their golf games, before she heard her father's voice on the line again.

"Are you sure you're all right, Elise? Dorthi says you sound a little down."

"I'm fine." She paused, then impulsively gave voice to a question that had plagued her from the day her father had remarried. "Daddy, would you answer a question for me and answer it truthfully?"

"If I can, Lizzie."

"Why did you marry Dorthi if you didn't love her?"

"Elise, what kind of question is that?" Her father sounded shocked. "Whatever gave you the notion that I don't love Dorthi?"

"I know you don't love her the way you loved Mother."

"But that doesn't mean I don't love her at all. Elise, love can come in many different ways. The love your mother and I shared was very special. And my love for Dorthi is just as special."

"But you never kiss her or hold her hand like you did with Mother. There's no romance between you."

"Romance isn't the most important part of love. There's respect and security. And a deep friendship and commitment. Maybe we didn't exactly love each other at first, but we were great friends. I needed her and she needed me. And I grew to love her more and more every day."

The phone line was silent for a long moment before her father spoke again. "Lizzie, what's wrong? Tell me where this is all coming from."

Elise was stunned by her father's admission. She was certain he hadn't loved Dorthi when they'd gotten married. But she had never considered that his feelings could have changed over the years.

"I need you, Elise."

Jordan's words echoed in her mind. He needed her. But was that really enough to make a marriage work? They were attracted to each other; that much was clear. And she did respect Jordan and considered him a friend. But would he, could he grow to love her as her father had grown to love Dorthi?

"Elise?"

"Daddy, I have to go now. I have an appointment and I'm late. I promise I'll call you in a few days... Yes, I love you too... Yes, I'll call Max Constanza. 'Bye, 'bye." Elise hung up the phone and placed it on the floor beside the couch. She flopped down on the chintz cushion and pulled a pillow over her face, pressing her hands to her ears and squeezing her eyes shut.

"I need you, Elise."

His words were joined by a second voice.

"Don't be concerned about what he says he can give you. Be more concerned with what you can give him. The rest will come, I promise you."

Would love really come later? Could she afford to take such a risk?

7

"GO AHEAD," Elise urged. "Just walk in and look around. When you see something interesting, take it to the counter and buy it."

Jordan glanced at the shop window, then back at Elise. "What if I don't see anything I like?"

Elise smiled. "You're a man. I can guarantee you'll find something you like."

"Do I have to do this?" he grumbled. "Don't they have mail-order catalogues for these kinds of things? Wouldn't it be much better—educationally, I mean—to be able to study the products and discuss this particular area of romance before I jump in?"

Elise's expression was unyielding. This was one argument he couldn't hope to win. He had asked for romance lessons and now he was getting them. He never thought he would so soon have cause to regret his ploy to stay close to Elise.

Jordan glanced up at the name of the shop: Unmentionables. Around him, the evening shoppers at Water Tower Place strolled past, oblivious to his plight. In front of him, a series of scantily clad mannequins, surrounded by baskets of colorful underwear, seemed to regard him with haughty eyes. And through the huge plate-glass window, he could see a number of women shoppers inside the store, but not a single male patron.

This shop was the fifth they had visited that evening

and Jordan knew why Elise had saved it for last in her lesson on gift buying. He had breezed through the first store, choosing an exotic, flowery perfume. He didn't mention that the scent reminded him of her. She had approved of his choice, then hustled him off to their second stop, a jewelry store, where he chose a hand-crafted pin of silver and jade, shaped like a cat. That choice had won him the reward of a hesitant smile. A candy store was next and he bought a pound of gourmet jelly beans, the exact color of her eyes. When he explained his reasoning, an uncomfortable look swept across her face and she avoided his gaze.

Store number four was a bit of a challenge. The import gift store offered a wide selection and Jordan spent nearly thirty minutes looking for just the right gift, something unique, something that Elise would consider romantic. He left with an ornate gold filigree key nestled inside a velvet-lined rosewood box. Her first reaction to his choice was one of confusion. But then he explained that the key was very special. It was the key to his heart. He had been proud of that effort, but when Elise had quickly excused herself to find the ladies' room, he wondered if he had inadvertently made another blunder.

Staying close to Elise through these romance lessons should have made his job easier. He had already gained incredible insight into her romantic nature, information that he could now use to break down her resolve. Over time, he had hoped that she would finally give up her silly notions about love and marriage and realize that he would make a good choice for a husband. Unfortunately, he hadn't made much progress in a positive direction. She kept each consultation on a business level, never giving a clue to her real feelings.

Jordan knew she had understood the significance of his purchases. They weren't generic romantic gifts chosen for a phantom fiancée, but gifts chosen especially for her. Throughout the night he had searched her expression for some crack in her indifferent facade. He was certain the gold key would do it. But after she had returned from the ladies' room, she had simply complimented him on his choice and the sentiment, then hustled him off to the next stop—a lingerie store.

Jordan looked down at his watch and, to his dismay, found at least a half hour left before the stores closed. Shopping for perfume was one thing, but shopping for ladies' underwear was an entirely different matter. He would just have to walk in, choose a romantic gift as quickly as possible, and hope that whatever he returned with was acceptable. With an encouraging smile from Elise, he pushed open the glass doors and walked inside.

Feigning an careful air of nonchalance and prior experience, he strolled slowly through the shop, stopping now and then to examine a lacy item before moving on. At first the sexy underwear held no interest. But then he came upon an incredibly transparent black robe and he caught himself wondering what Elise might look like wrapped in the filmy gauze. He imagined her perfect breasts pushing out against the sheer fabric, the feel of her hardened nipples through the thin barrier. And lower still, the lush curve from her waist to her hip, the shadow of soft hair where her thighs met.

A wave of heat raced through his body and a telltale throbbing began just below his belt. Stifling a groan,

Jordan spun away from the robe and scanned the store. A rack of plastic-wrapped packages caught his attention and he strode over to a display of ladies' silk stockings. He grabbed a package labeled Misty Midnight and hurried over to the counter. The saleslady smiled as he slapped down his credit card.

"Is this a gift?" she asked.

Startled by her interest, Jordan met her friendly gaze. "What?"

"Is this a gift?" she repeated. "Would you like a gift box?"

Is this a gift? What else would it be? She didn't believe he planned to wear these himself, did she?

"Ah...yes. A gift. Thank you."

"You know, we have some lovely garter belts on display. Maybe you'd like to take a look at those. Or, if you prefer, I can show you some of our Merry Widow ensembles."

"Garter belts?" Jordan asked.

"To hold up the stockings," she whispered.

Jordan leaned closer. "Just how many garter belts would one need to hold up these particular stockings?"

"Just one. Or you can buy a Merry Widow. That comes with garters and panties."

He shifted uncomfortably on his feet and glanced around the store. "A Merry Widow would be fine. Why don't you choose one for me."

"What size?"

Was there no end to this? Jordan wondered. He felt like he was under the Spanish Inquisition. If this was the price he had to pay for learning to be romantic, it wasn't worth it. "Ten," he blurted out. "And I'm not answering any more questions. Just ring the blasted thing up so I can get out of here."

The sales clerk scurried off to retrieve his selection and returned a few moments later with three of what he assumed were Merry Widows—rather revealing items of underwear—in black, red and white. He pointed to the black and within a minute he had exited the store, with his Merry-whatever tucked safely in a box.

He found Elise sitting on a bench outside the shop, picking through the bag of jelly beans. She smiled and stood as he approached. "See, that wasn't so bad, was it?"

"Compared to what? Ripping my clothes off and jumping naked into the Chicago River from the top of the Wrigley Building? Or taking a nap in the middle of Division Street during rush hour?"

"Jordan, lingerie can be a very romantic gift. I just thought it would be good for you to try your hand at shopping for it. What did you buy?"

She reached for the bag, but Jordan snatched it away and hid it behind his back. "Never mind."

"Come on," Elise teased. "You did so well on the other gifts. Let me see."

"No. I'll just have to accept an incomplete on this part of the lesson. Let's get out of here. I've had enough shopping for one night."

Jordan grabbed Elise's elbow and steered her toward the exit. When they reached the street, she stopped and pulled out of his grasp, their easy-going banter suddenly gone. "I'll just catch a cab home," she said in a cool voice.

Jordan bit back an irritated reply. This had become a

regular ritual with them at the end of each lesson. A warm hug or a passionate kiss could have put a proper end to the evening. But as much as he wanted to wrap her in his arms, her prickly attitude invited no intimate contact between them. A handshake was the best he could expect.

Damn, he was running out of time. This plan to break down her resolve was quickly losing steam and he was no closer to changing her mind than he had been after her refusal. Why did she have to be so damn stubborn? Why couldn't she admit her desire for him? He knew they would be good together, knew that their marriage could work. But she was holding out for a declaration of love, something that he wasn't prepared to give her. He sighed inwardly. Maybe it was time to turn up the gas, to be more aggressive.

"I'll drive you," Jordan replied. "My car's parked at the office."

"That's really not necessary. I can find—"

"I'm driving you home, Elise. End of discussion."

Surprised by his tone, she nodded and they turned and walked briskly down Michigan Avenue.

"You did quite well tonight," she said, breaking the silence that had lasted a city block.

Jordan's irritation slowly dissolved at the soft, musical sound of her voice. "Thanks. It was fun."

She returned his smile. "Yes, it was."

Jordan yanked her to a stop, grabbed her shoulders and turned to her to him. "I always seem to have a good time when I'm with you, Elise. Why is that?"

She avoided his probing gaze, watching a pedestrian pass by instead. "Maybe it's because we're friends now. There's nothing between us but business and it makes it easier to relax, to be ourselves."

She looked up at him with wide green eyes, silently pleading for confirmation. Jordan smiled tightly and quelled an urge to argue the point. "Yeah, right," he said. "We're friends. That must be it."

The balance of the walk to Jordan's car and the ride home were spent in inane conversation about the weather and Chicago politics. Jordan could tell Elise had something else on her mind by the nervous set of her smile. He pulled the Mercedes to the curb in front of her house, shut off the engine, and waited for her to speak.

She drew a deep breath. "How is your search for a bride coming along?"

"Fine," Jordan replied.

"Does that mean you've found someone?"

"Not yet. But don't worry, I will. There's still time."

"I don't think we need to continue the romance lessons," she blurted out. "You've done very well and I think it's time to...end them." She reached for the door handle, but Jordan grabbed her arm to stop her.

"Elise, wait."

She looked down at his hand on her arm, her expression cold and distant. But this time he refused to pull away. Instead Jordan reached up and brushed his palm against her cheek. God, she was so soft, like warm silk. Slowly his thumb traced the outline of her full lower lip and he watched as her eyes widened in alarm. A kaleidoscope of conflicting emotions glittered in their emerald depths, but she didn't pull away. She opened her mouth to protest, but he placed his thumb across her lips, gently teasing and caressing the soft flesh.

Then he saw the signal he was waiting for. Desire flickered across her expression and he moved to cradle her face in his hands. His mouth came down upon hers in a touch more intimate, more demanding, more satisfying than that of his fingers on her lips. She opened to him and he deepened his kiss, drawing her closer, absorbing the feel of her in his arms and inhaling her sweet scent, tasting the tentative touch of her tongue against his.

The urge to look at her, to assure himself of the longing he felt in her kiss, was overwhelming and he drew away. Was she finally ready to admit they belonged together? Had they finally broken through the insurmountable wall that seemed to separate them? His gaze locked with hers and they stared at each other for what seemed like an eternity, paralyzed by the passion that washed over them both. But then the guarded expression returned to her eyes and she spoke.

"I—I have to go in now," she said. Her voice was empty of emotion and his heart twisted in his chest. What would it take to get through to her? Why couldn't she see how much he cared? Reluctantly, he released her and watched as she moved to open the door.

Before she had a chance to step out of the car, he reached into the back seat, collected his purchases and pushed them at her. "Here, take these. I bought them for you."

She hesitated, as if she were going to refuse, then nodded and clutched the packages to her chest. He watched her hurry up the front walk and disappear inside the house. Then, in a flash of temper, he slammed his hands against the steering wheel and cursed.

The romance lessons were over. And now it was time to put a quick and painless end to this ridiculous search for a wife, as well.

JORDAN STOOD over Elise's shoulder, pretending interest in the huge book of wedding invitations that lay open on the conference table in his office. His attention was drawn, instead, to the soft curve of her neck. His fingers ached to touch her there, but he clenched his fists at his sides.

"What about this one?" Elise asked, her slender finger coming to rest on another alternative, which to his eyes looked no different from the last hundred they had considered.

"Nope." Jordan bent closer, inhaling the fragrant scent of her hair.

"This one?"

"No." His chin brushed against her hair and the intimate contact sent a jolt of heat pulsing to his lap.

"How about this one?"

"I don't think so." His breath teased at the soft strawberry-blond strands tucked behind her ear.

Elise slammed the book shut and stood up suddenly, unaware how close he was. Her shoulder collided with his chin, snapping his teeth together and sending him stumbling backward. She spun around to face him, backing up against the edge of his conference table and regarding him warily.

"We've looked at every book of wedding invitations in the city of Chicago. *You* were the one who wanted to be involved in this decision. I would appreciate it if you would make a choice sometime this century."

Jordan caught a glint of suspicion in her eyes. He wondered when she was going to catch on to his new stalling tactics. After the abrupt end to their romance consultations, Jordan had insisted on becoming involved in the most minute details of the wedding, disagreeing with every choice Elise made and demanding another set of options for every decision. Phone calls were not enough to cover all the information Jordan requested, so they had met first once a week, then twice and now three times a week. Jordan found the plan quite clever in its simplicity. The more involved he became in the wedding, the more time he got to spend with Elise. Unfortunately, each encounter left him craving her warm, willing body—and settling for a cold shower.

Elise, however, steadfastly maintained a chaste distance between them, as if their encounter after the shopping trip had only served to strengthen her determination. She was polite, if somewhat reserved, ignoring evidence of his desire for her, as she had done just moments ago.

The stress was taking its toll, though. Jordan could see the lines of tension that outlined her perfect features and the dark smudges beneath her eyes. She looked like she wasn't getting much more sleep than he was and that was precious little. With each meeting, he became a bit more aggressive in his pursuit, tempting her here and there with an innocent brush of his hand or a long, potent stare. If he could just wait her out, he was sure she'd give in.

"If you don't choose an invitation tonight, I'll do it

for you," Elise threatened. "This is the last decision that needs to be made, so let's just get it over with. If I don't order the invitations this week, they won't be ready in time. The wedding is little more than a month away."

The last decision? Did that mean there would be no more reason for them to meet after tonight? Even through her reserved facade, he could tell Elise was close to capitulating. But without an excuse to be near her, the odds of getting her to agree to his marriage proposal were virtually nil. And without Elise, there would be no wedding. From the moment he had asked Elise to marry him, he hadn't made a single attempt to find another bride.

He had placed everything he cherished, his company and his future, on the line in the hopes that Elise would come around, that she would finally agree to marry him. And now, the whole mess was on the verge of falling apart.

If only control of BabyLove wasn't tied into the whole deal. Without the need to save his company, Jordan could wait forever for Elise. He could give her the time she needed to realize they belonged together. But the entire idea was really a moot point. He could never give up his company.

Or could he?

Jordan banished the ridiculous thought from his mind. BabyLove was his life, his future. And what was Elise? She was his— He swallowed a rush of denial at the words that came to mind. His happiness. No, she was a woman, he rationalized. A desirable, fascinating woman. A woman he wanted more than he had ever wanted anyone before. That was all.

Jordan stepped back to the conference table and casually flipped through the album of invitation samples. He paused over one page, then pointed to it. "This one," he ordered, his voice tight.

Elise turned to the table and nodded at his choice. "That's a very nice invitation."

She stood beside him for a long time, her posture stiff, her eyes fixed on the album. He bit back a hiss of frustration, then spun on his heel and walked over to his desk. Keeping his attention directed at her, he sank down onto his chair.

With a barely perceptible sigh, Elise sat down on one of his guest chairs. "What about the copy?" she asked, avoiding his glance with a concentrated study of his desk clock.

"I'll leave that up to you."

She hesitated before she spoke, then proceeded in a shaky voice. "I need the bride's name."

"As I said, I'll leave that up to you."

Her head snapped up and she looked at him with wide eyes. "You haven't found a bride yet? But I thought..."

Jordan shrugged. "I have five weeks. I didn't want to rush into a decision. Marry in haste, repent in leisure. Isn't that how the saying goes?"

"But the invitations..."

"Send them out without a name. Jordan Broderick Prentiss and his fiancée cordially invite you to their wedding. Short and to the point and certain to pique interest in attending. Who will Prentiss marry? Show up at the church and see." The last was said with more than a hint of sarcasm.

"I cannot send invitations out without the bride's name."

"There's a simple solution to the problem, Elise. Just put your name on the invitation."

"No."

Her answer was uttered without emotion, though it caused a rising flood of frustration in Jordan. In a blaze of anger, he grabbed a stack of file folders from a pile on his desk and tossed them in her direction. They scattered across the desk in front of her. She stared at the folders for a moment, before glancing up at him with a cautious look. "Go ahead," he challenged. "Take a look. I'll leave the decision up to you."

"What decision?"

"My bride. You choose and you'll have that name you need for the invitation."

With a contemptuous arch of her brow, Elise pulled a folder off the pile and flipped through the contents, lingering for a long while over the photograph. The defiance chiseled in the hard set of her mouth softened, then faded completely. "She's very beautiful," she said in a strangled voice.

Jordan shrugged. "They all are."

She took another folder from the pile and perused the papers within. "And well educated."

"Yes, very well educated."

She grabbed a third folder and examined Stockton's summary and the picture carefully. "From very prominent families, too."

"Of course. Only the best."

She sighed wearily and placed the folders back on his desk, fixing her eyes on her folded hands.

"So, who would you choose, Miss Sinclair? You've

made so many fine choices in planning this wedding, certainly you could make just one more. Traci Van Slyke is a beauty. Jane Kirkpatrick holds a master's degree in architecture. And I'm sure you're aware of the benefits of marrying into Eileen Pomeroy's family."

"I—I think you should marry whichever woman you want."

Jordan shot to his feet and slammed his palms down on his desk. "And I think you know who I want to marry. Stop avoiding the question, Miss Sinclair. Who will it be? Who should I marry?"

Elise stood and placed her palms opposite his, leaning over the desk in a threatening posture that matched his own. The disinterested look in her eyes had been replaced by flaming anger and Jordan felt a sudden stab of relief. He still had the ability to draw her feelings to the surface. She still cared.

Her soft, heart-shaped mouth was drawn into a tight line and her voice was low and even. "I don't give a damn who you marry. I don't care if you marry Traci or Staci or the man in the moon. All I care about is getting this wedding over and done with." She snatched a pad of paper from his desk and grabbed a pen, then scribbled down a phone number and tossed the pad back at him. "When you've made a decision about the invitations, call the printer. You've got until Tuesday morning to give him a name. I'll pick the invitations up on Wednesday afternoon and send them out."

She pulled her coat from the back of a chair and tucked her briefcase under her arm. "It's been a pleasure doing business with you, Mr. Prentiss. I'll see you and your bride at the wedding."

She stalked out Jordan's office door and slammed it shut behind her.

ELISE PUNCHED at the down button for the elevator with her finger. When the doors didn't open immediately, she tapped it again and again, her frustration level at its breaking point. Glancing over at the lit panel of numbers beside the doors, she saw that none of the three elevators was near the twenty-third floor. Afraid that Jordan would follow her, she hurried to the fire-exit door, pushed it open and stepped into the brightly illuminated stairway.

Leaning over the railing, she looked down between the flights. The dizzying twenty-three-story drop caused her already nervous stomach to lurch. With a deep breath, she started down the stairs. As she rounded the landing for the twenty-first floor with her eyes fixed on her feet, she came to a sudden stop as she nearly ran into another person heading up the stairs. A cry of alarm burst from her lips and she frantically grabbed for the railing to save herself from tumbling down the next flight of stairs. She regained her balance by sitting down with a painful jolt on the edge of a concrete stair.

"Ouch!"

"Oh, my!" a familiar voice exclaimed. "Are you all right?"

Elise looked up to see a figure in high-top tennis shoes and a pink sweatsuit holding on to the railing on the other side of the stairwell. She closed her eyes and shook her head, but the woman was still there when she opened them again.

"Wha-what are you doing here?" Elise sputtered, trying to bring her racing heartbeat under control.

"I'm exercising," the woman answered brightly, plopping down beside her. "It's all the rage, this stair climbing. You should give it a whirl. Exercise would do you a world of good. You're looking a little stressed out, my dear."

"I nearly fell down twenty-one flights of stairs!" Elise gasped, rubbing her sore backside. "How am I supposed to look?"

"Don't be silly. I would have caught you. I'm quite strong, you know. I pump iron. Right now, I'm working on my biceps." She crooked her arm and clenched her fist. "Lars, my trainer, says my muscle definition is outstanding." She poked at her upper arm with her index finger and smiled. "Besides," she added distractedly, "it wouldn't do to have Jordan's intended breaking any bones a month before the wedding. Now tell me, how are your wedding plans coming?"

Elise stared at her openmouthed, then brought her elbows to her knees and buried her face in her hands, moaning softly. She felt as if she had just stepped into the Twilight Zone. Why was this crazy woman always appearing at the worst of times with her disturbing insights? And why was she so determined to encourage a marriage between Elise and Jordan?

"Plans for Mr. Prentiss's wedding are nearly complete," Elise mumbled through her fingers. "But I have no intention of walking down the aisle with the man."

The woman grabbed Elise's hands and gave them an affectionate squeeze. "Of course you'll marry Jordan."

"Don't say that! It's not true. It won't happen."

"You love him and he loves you."

"I do not—" Elise looked into her sparkling eyes. "He doesn't—" Tears threatened and she bit her lip, tipping her chin up in defiance.

"He does," the woman answered softly, patting her on the shoulder. "He doesn't know it yet, but Jordan is a clever boy. A bit thick at times, but one can't blame him for the traits he inherited from his grandfather, Jonathan. Lord, that man could be stubborn. That silly stock option plan is a perfect example. If he hadn't—" She stopped and smiled apologetically. "I do go on, don't I. Now, what were we talking about? Oh, yes, Jordan. He'll realize he loves you soon enough."

Elise gave her a morose look. "How can you be so sure?"

"Do you think I would waste all my efforts on a lost cause? You and Jordan belong together. It was meant to be. And on April 18, I plan to be there to watch you walk down the aisle to marry him. It's all very simple, Elise. Trust me."

"Trust you? How can I trust you? I don't even know your name. Who are you?"

"Why, my name is Esme. I thought I told you."

Elise swallowed, then stared at her. "No! I mean who *are* you?"

"I told you, dear. You must learn to listen more carefully. If not to me, then to your heart." Esme stood up and brushed off the seat of her sweatpants. "I really have to be going. I have a lot of work to do before your wedding."

"Work?"

She nodded. "If I expect to fit into my pink chiffon, I need to lose at least five pounds. Lars and I are going to work on my hips this week." She laughed. "Sounds deliciously sinful, doesn't it?"

"Wait a second. I have to ask you—"

Esme jogged up to the landing, then gave her a jaunty wave. "Can't stop for too long," she said. "Have to keep the heart rate up. Ta, ta."

"No, wait," Elise called. She slowly pulled herself to her feet, rubbing her sore backside again, then followed the woman. When she reached the next landing, the door to the hallway was just closing. Elise pushed it open and stepped into the hall, expecting to catch sight of Esme's pink jogging suit.

But the hall was eerily empty. She moved to the elevators and watched the lights beside the doors move from floor to floor. None of them was close to the twenty-second floor.

"Esme?" she called. The name echoed back at her from the glass-and-marble hallway. "Esme?"

Elise stood in the middle of the hallway, a frown of consternation on her brow. "Oh, Esme. What am I supposed to do? Can I really believe you?" She closed her eyes and tipped her head back, releasing a tightly held breath. "If only I could be as sure as you that Jordan would come to love me. What do you know that I don't? Tell me, Esme. Please tell me. What should I do?"

"Push the button," a voice replied.

"Push the button?" she whispered back. "I don't understand. What button?"

"The button by the door," the voice said.

Elise opened her eyes with a start. An elderly man in a business suit stood in front of her.

"If you want to go up, you push the button with the

arrow going up," he explained. "To go down, push the other button."

Elise felt her face color as she gave the man a quick smile. "Th-thank you. I'll remember that," she murmured. "But I'm in a hurry. I think I'll take the stairs." She reached the stairwell door just as a bell signalled the elevator doors were opening. For a moment, she hesitated, her gaze darting between the man and the elevator doors. But in the end she turned and took the stairs down one floor, too embarrassed to spend the trip down with the curious man.

As she waited for the elevator one floor below, her thoughts drifted back to Esme's declaration.

"You love him and he loves you."

Esme was right on one count. Elise did love Jordan. She had loved him from the moment she'd met him. But could she trust Esme's instincts about Jordan loving her? Could she trust the word of a stranger to make the most important decision in her life?

THE LIGHT from the television screen cast a blue glow across Jordan's darkened living room. He lay sprawled across the leather couch, his suit jacket crumpled on the floor beside him, his tie unknotted. A crystal tumbler of scotch and melted ice rested on his chest. With an impatient curse, he held out the remote control and fast-forwarded through the old black-and-white movie he was watching.

Elise had given him a list of Cary Grant movies to watch after their second romance consultation, claiming that the actor was the epitome of a romantic man. He had sent Stockton out to rent the videos. Along with the Cary Grant movies, Pete had returned with his own recommendations, advising Jordan that in his book, Cary Grant was a wimp.

Jordan had enjoyed the action movies on Pete's list. The men were tough and resourceful, rarely wore a shirt and carried rather large firearms. They avoided numerous explosions with amazing aplomb and managed to beat almost every bad guy to a pitiful pulp. And they had women falling at their feet like trees at a lumber camp.

Jordan had studied the movies, trying to ascertain how these action heroes had attracted such beautiful, willing women. There were no pretty gifts, no romantic dinners, no words of affection and not a single "I love you." Somehow these guys managed to avoid romance at every turn, yet still got the girl.

Too bad life didn't imitate art. Why couldn't Elise be more like the women he'd seen in these movies? Why was she so intent on a profession of undying love? Maybe Cary Grant had the answer, he had thought.

But after patiently sitting through four Cary Grant movies, Jordan was no closer to an answer. Pete had been right. Cary Grant was a wimp, always giving in to the woman, admitting his eternal devotion.

Jordan picked up the last movie on Elise's list and studied the cover. *Indiscreet.* An appropriate title, he thought to himself. Maybe that's just how she thought of their relationship. A foolish encounter. A momentary lapse in propriety.

And maybe that's how he should begin to think of it. At this moment, he didn't hold out much hope for resolving their differences. Elise was stubbornly clinging to her ideals and would settle for nothing less that a total surrender on his part. And he had no intention of hoisting the white flag and giving in to emotion.

I love you. Three simple syllables. Three simple words packed with unfathomable meaning. Why couldn't he say them? Why couldn't he *feel* them? All he felt right now was utter emptiness and anger. And longing—incredible, aching desire for her. It wasn't love; it was lust, pure and simple. When he was with her, he felt complete somehow, as if she filled him with warmth and surrounded him with satisfaction and contentment. And when they were apart, he felt cold and alone and numb to any emotion.

I love you.

"I—I love you." He frowned. He couldn't remember ever saying that exact combination of words before. Somehow he had thought they would be difficult to say. "I love you," he repeated. The words came without hesitation. But they were only words, without meaning and detached from any recognizable emotion he felt.

Jordan tried to remember if he'd ever heard the words before. His parents had never said them to each other in his presence. And he was sure his father had never uttered the endearment to him. But somewhere, in the back of his mind, he could hear his mother's voice. She had loved him, once, a long time ago. But then she had left and never come back.

How easily love could be tossed aside to make room for something, or someone, else. And how easily the words came out. He wondered why Elise set such store by them when they seemed to mean so little.

Jordan shook his head, then gulped down the rest of the watered-down scotch. Who was he to philosophize about love? He had never truly been loved, nor had he ever loved another. He wasn't sure he'd recognize the venerable emotion if it fell out of the sky and dropped at his feet.

What difference did love really make anyway? He had all he wanted in life, he had BabyLove...at least for another month. And then what? What if he lost the company? Jordan waited for the familiar rush of desperation and fear to twist in his chest and shatter his composure. He waited, and it came, but not with as much vengeance as it had in the weeks past.

He could live through losing BabyLove. He'd do what his grandfather had done years ago. He would start another company. Jordan closed his eyes and shook his head. Why waste time pondering what would never happen? He wasn't about to let his company go.

He stared at the video cover. He may not recognize love, but he'd be damned if he couldn't figure out something as simple as romance. If Elise thought Cary Grant was romantic, then Jordan would find out why. Even if he had to watch every one of his ridiculous movies all over again.

TEARS COURSED down Elise's cheeks, their warm saltiness mixing with the taste of green jelly beans. Elise grabbed a tissue from the box beside her on the bed and wiped at her watery eyes, before putting another handful of candy in her mouth. *Indiscreet* played quietly on the VCR and she watched the final scenes of the romantic comedy, reduced to mush by the perfectly romantic storybook ending.

Why couldn't life be like the movies? With a frustrated moan, she tugged at her twisted bathrobe, trying to cover her bare chest and thighs. Sexy lingerie was certainly not constructed for warmth, she thought to herself. But, then again, there was usually a source of warmth close by when dressed in a black Merry Widow, bikini panties and silk stockings with a seam running up the backs.

Just yesterday, Jordan's gifts were in the garbage. She wanted no reminder of him and their ill-fated relationship. But Elise's romantic nature had gotten the better of her, and she'd retrieved the gifts and hid them in her closet. Curiosity and a good dose of melancholy got the better of her and the empty boxes were now scattered across her bedroom floor.

She picked up the perfume and pulled out the stopper, then inhaled the exotic Oriental scent. A hint of jasmine drifted through the room as she dabbed a bit more of the scent on her throat and at her pulse points. The cat pin was fastened to her chenille bathrobe and the half-empty bag of jelly beans sat on her bedside table along with the filigree key in the rosewood box.

She reached over and picked up the key. Jordan had said it was the key to his heart. She smiled ruefully. If only it were that simple. Just turn a key, flip a switch, open a door, and Jordan would love her as much as she loved him.

Elise sniffled then pressed the remote to rewind through the final scene of the movie. The sophisticated story of two lovers torn apart by misunderstandings had always been a favorite of hers. Her affair with Jordan was much like that of the characters portrayed by Cary Grant and Ingrid Bergman, she mused. A creative, loving woman falls in love with a playboy businessman. The hero admits he's married to another...Elise shoved another handful of jelly beans into her mouth and continued to stare at the screen. Well, Jordan wasn't really married to another—yet. But he had told her he was engaged when he really wasn't.

And even though Ingrid knows he's married, she agrees to a discreet affair with Cary. Elise frowned. All right. So their stories weren't exactly alike, but they were pretty darn close. When Ingrid finds out that Cary really isn't married, that he's lied to protect his comfortable bachelor status, she plots her revenge. And when Cary shows up at her apartment...Elise sighed. And when Cary shows up at her apartment, Ingrid's plans for revenge fly out the window and she falls into his arms. And of course, Cary professes his undying love for her.

Elise smoothed the bedspread across her legs and leaned back against the pillows propped against the headboard. So much for the fortitude of the 1950's movie heroine. Luckily, the nineties woman was much more determined. But even though Ingrid gave in to the passion, love did triumph in the end. Love always triumphs at the ends of movies, she countered silently. Too bad real life didn't live up to the fantasies created in Hollywood.

She had left Jordan at his office earlier that day, and already it seemed as if they had been apart for weeks. Elise had looked forward to each and every meeting they'd had, even though she'd had to pretend differently. Elise felt a brief surge of guilt. She had even made some incredibly tasteless decisions for the wedding just so he would disagree and ask for more choices.

The thought of not seeing him again until his wedding day was almost enough to start the tears rolling. And the thought of him waiting at the front of the church for another woman nearly caused another fit of weeping.

Elise blew her nose. Maybe there was still hope. He hadn't chosen a bride yet, though by the files he had thrown at her, he had plenty of choices. So why hadn't he made a decision? Could Esme be right about his feelings? Could he be in love without knowing it?

With a groan, she burrowed beneath the covers. How did things get so incredibly confusing? She felt as if she were being pulled in a million different directions. One part of her was madly in love with Jordan Prentiss. Another part was rational enough to realize that he was the exact opposite of what she had dreamed of for a husband. Her practical side argued that at least he was being honest with her and honesty was one aspect of a relationship that she held in almost as much esteem as love. Then there was her optimistic nature. She, imagined it might be possible that, given time, Jordan could fall as deeply in love with her as she had with him. He did have his good points—he was dependable, handsome, smart, loyal. And she had to admit that her romance lessons did have an effect on him. She could do much worse.

What guarantees were there, anyway? Could she be certain that she would find someone better, someone she loved as much as she loved Jordan? Even if she fell in love with someone else and he loved her, who could say what the future would hold? At least with Jordan, what she saw was what she got. She knew exactly where she stood.

Yes, Jordan, I will marry you. The words were almost too unthinkable to say.

Her lips parted, the words forming of their own accord. "Yes, Jordan..." She cleared her throat. "I will marry you." She tried the sentence again. "Yes, Jordan...my darling, Jordan. I will marry you."

Elise threw the covers off and sat up in bed, her eyes wide with wonder. Suddenly the words had become easier to say. "Yes, yes, yes. Of course I'll marry you." A smile touched her lips. "I would love to marry you, Jordan Prentiss. I would love to be your bride."

Elise closed her eyes. Could she do it? Could she trust her instincts and Esme's assurances? The prospect of a future without Jordan was inconceivable. She loved him like no other and she could never forget him, no matter how hard she tried.

Yes! She would do it! She would marry Jordan Prentiss, and come hell or high water, they would live happily ever after.

Elise opened her eyes and grabbed the bedside phone. Now she just had to get him to propose once more. She giggled at the thought of his reaction when she finally said yes. Pausing to savor the image, she let her thoughts drift back over the past two months. The wedding plans were all made, each detail carefully considered with her own tastes in mind, right down to the wedding dress. It was as if fate had ordained that she would be his bride all along.

Maybe there was magic at work here, she said to herself.

She quickly dialed Jordan's home phone number as she concocted an excuse for them to meet just once more. The phone rang only once before she hung up, doubt slicing through her.

You're being rash and reckless.

Calming her nerves, she dialed his number again. This time she let the phone ring twice before she hung up. What if she was making a mistake?

Take a chance, Elise. You love him.

She dialed once again. The phone rang four times before she heard a click on the other end of the line. Her heart jumped into her throat. Jordan's voice sounded a stilted greeting and her heart fell back into place with a disappointed *plop* when she realized she had reached his answering machine. As the tone sounded, she opened her mouth, ready to leave a message. But the words refused to leave her lips, and in the end, she hung up.

With a moan of frustration, she got up from the bed and walked to the window, then pushed aside the lace curtains and gazed down at the street. Lazy snowflakes drifted on the midnight air, falling softly to the street below, dusting the gray concrete in glittering white. Snowfalls used to bring out the romantic in her, making her feel all cozy and safe. But now a smothering sense of loneliness swept over her and she shivered and wrapped her robe more tightly around her for protection against the draft of cold air at the window. She bent over the radiator and placed her palm on the barely warm cast iron.

No wonder she was cold. A nice cup of hot tea would set things straight. So would a good night's sleep. Maybe fate had stepped in again. Maybe she wasn't meant to talk to Jordan tonight.

Elise made her way to the dimly lit kitchen and set

the tea kettle on the stove to boil water. She slid onto one of the kitchen stools. Minutes later, the heat from a cup of chamomile warmed her face and hands and soothed her warring emotions.

Her mind roamed back to the final scene from the movie and she let her imagination spin a wonderfully romantic scene between Jordan and her. He would appear at her door. She would be stunned at first, then without a word, he would sweep her into his arms, kissing her deeply, enfolding her in his strong embrace. She would be spellbound, unable to speak. Then he would—

Her moony daydreaming was interrupted by the sound of the doorbell. Her heart stopped. Only one person would appear at her door after midnight. Elise walked slowly to the foyer. With a tremor of indecision, She reached for the doorknob, then pulled her hand away. Her fingers shook as she tugged the lacy curtain away from the window beside the door and peeked into the darkness. Her heart hammered in her chest.

A shadowy form stood on her stoop beneath the soft glow of the porch light, sparkling snowflakes falling against a familiar navy cashmere topcoat and dark hair. Slowly she unlocked the dead bolt, released the chain and turned the doorknob. A sweep of snow blew into the foyer as she opened the door.

An uncontrollable shiver ran through her, but it was caused by fear more than the cold, for Elise's future stood waiting on her front steps.

8

ELISE WASN'T SURE how she ended up in his arms or whether Jordan said anything to her before he covered her mouth with his. All thoughts of Ingrid Bergman and righteous indignation fled her mind the instant their eyes met. One moment, they stood on opposite sides of the threshold and the next, she was caught up in his embrace and swept away by his kiss.

Things she knew she should say dissolved in her throat and she realized that the time for talking was past. Talking had only brought them to an impasse, their words like bricks, building a wall between them. Now the wall lay demolished at her feet, breached by his touch and his taste, by the indescribably heady scent of him. It was a dream, a hazy cloud of romance, a fantasy come true.

The kiss went on and on, until the dream was gradually replaced by a very real passion that rose within her. Suddenly, she didn't want the fantasy, the perfect man; that wasn't enough. She wanted a real man, flesh and blood, driven by pure lust and desire. Hard muscle and smooth skin, warm breath and firm touch. She wanted Jordan.

With his mouth still melded to hers, Elise fumbled with Jordan's coat and scarf, until he impatiently yanked them off and threw them down on the foyer floor. He kicked the door shut with his heel and pulled

Elise back against his unyielding body, taking her breath away as he strained to eliminate all space between them. Parting the front of her robe with one quick, hungry movement, he skimmed his palms over her body. His fingers stilled when they came in contact with the lacy Merry Widow and he stepped back to look at her. A seductive smile curved his lips and he quirked his brow in appreciation, before he pulled her to him again with renewed urgency.

Elise sighed in pleasure, following his lead, running her hands beneath his suit jacket, over his ribs and torso, feeling his heat radiating through the crisp, starched fabric of his shirt. How many times had she imagined touching him with such delicious abandon, then chastised herself for such fantasies? But now it seemed so natural, so right.

Hesitantly she moved her fingers to the front of his shirt and pushed aside his tie. Slowly she worked at the row of buttons, her mouth still locked with his. Dragging herself from his kiss, she let her lips follow the trail of her fingers. With her forehead against his muscled chest, she inhaled the clean scent of his skin.

When her hands reached his belt, she stopped, then looked up into his eyes. For a brief moment, she was surprised at the undisguised vulnerability she saw there. It was as if she were looking at a different man, stripped of his icy armor to reveal the human beneath, a man she had only seen in fleeting moments when his guard was down. This was the man she wanted. This was the man she would spend her life with.

Her lips were numb from his kisses, and at first her mouth refused to work properly, but she felt compelled to speak, to set everything right between them.

What would happen this night would have meaning. This was the beginning of their life together. "Jordan, I—I have something I need to—to tell you."

He placed a finger firmly over her lips. "So help me, Elise, if you're going to grade me on my kissing, you'd better run for cover right now."

She looked at him, wide-eyed, then quickly shook her head.

"Good. Whatever you have to say can wait. Now, close that sweet mouth of yours and kiss me."

Her next words escaped from behind his finger. "Bub iz impordant."

"Elise." His voice held an unmistakable warning and he replaced his finger with his mouth, effectively stopping all further conversation. Without another thought, Elise wrapped her arms around his neck and threw herself into the kiss, reveling in the taste of him. She would tell him later.

He pushed her robe off her shoulders and it slid to the floor about her feet. His hands explored her body, her skin tingling beneath the lace, the garment transmitting the heat from his questing fingers yet barring his touch. As he drew her silk-clad leg up along his, she shivered at the delicious feel of his hard thigh against hers. For the first time in her life, she understood the appeal of lace and silk and sexy lingerie. The fabrics seemed to intensify every touch.

She tugged at his clothes, refusing to interrupt their kiss, until his jacket, tie and shirt lay in a heap on top of his coat. His skin was warm and smooth, his chest finely muscled. Then she moved to unbuckle his belt, hearing his sharp intake of breath as her fingers worked against the taut ridges of his abdomen. The belt slithered out of the loops and she dropped it on the floor.

Their kiss was suddenly broken when he scooped her up into his arms. With a tiny cry of surprise, she clasped her arms around his neck, afraid that he might drop her. But his hold tightened beneath her, strong and sure, and she nuzzled her face against his neck, enthralled by the pure romance of being swept off her feet. After all they had been through, she was amazed at how safe she felt in his arms, how right this all seemed. She belonged with him, now and forever.

He turned his head to the touch of her lips on his jawline. "Where's your bedroom?" he murmured as he moved down the long hallway to the back of the house and the kitchen.

Through the sleepy haze of her passion, Elise lifted her head and looked around. "No. It's upstairs."

He walked back to the stairway and stood at the bottom, turning his wary gaze to her. "Second floor?"

"Third," she said with a smile. "Maybe I should walk."

"Maybe you should go back to what you were doing."

With a low laugh, Elise playfully bit him on the earlobe, then traced the contours of his ear with her tongue. She heard his breath quicken and a moan rumbled in his chest as he reached the first landing. He wanted her as much as she wanted him. The bedroom seemed miles away.

"Are you sure you don't want me to walk?" she whispered into his wet ear. "You sound like you're tiring."

"Sweetheart, I'm anything but tired. Besides, I don't plan to let you out of my arms anytime soon."

Jordan started up the second flight of stairs as Elise continued her tender assault on his neck. When they reached the second-floor landing, he lowered her to the floor. Her heartbeat fluttered with nervous anticipation. "Why are we stopping?" she whispered.

"I need a break."

"Would you like me to carry you the rest of the way?"

He growled and settled Elise on the step above him, then moved between her thighs and pushed her back against the stairs, his arms braced on either side of her head. His voice was deep and husky. "I'm not tired. I'm just not sure I can go on in this condition." He pressed his hips between her legs and she could feel the solid ridge of his arousal as it made contact with her most intimate spot, separated only by the clothing they still wore. She somehow knew they would be doing a lot more than resting if he had his way.

He bent over her, outlining the shape of her mouth with his tongue, biting at her lower lip until she responded in kind, running her tongue along the smooth ridge of his teeth, sampling the flavor of his mouth. When she released him, he drifted down the length of her body and came to rest below her on the stairs.

With nimble fingers, he flipped each garter open, then slowly ran his palms along her legs, gathering the silk stockings in his fists until they bunched at her ankles. Then he drew them off her feet, one by one, and tossed them over his shoulder. A delicious shiver skittered up along her spine as his hands slid from her ankles to the soft skin of her inner thighs, gently kneading. Then his fingers grazed her satin panties and probed against the damp fabric until he found the hidden nub of her passion. Elise swallowed convulsively.

She had imagined this moment with Jordan so many times and each time the fantasy was bathed in a misty, magical haze. But that haze was gone. Instead her senses were sharpened until every touch, every sound shot pure sensation to her core.

"You're so soft, so warm," he murmured, his mouth against her knee, his breath soft against her bare leg. He tugged the black lace panties off.

With his gaze locked on her face, he began a gentle assault, his fingers dipping into and dancing over her pulsing center. His eyes smoldered with tightly leashed desire and she watched her every reaction reflected in his intense expression. She grasped his shoulders as the tension began to build, then pulled him more closely, desperate for more. She felt herself sliding down into a whirlpool of mindless sensation as her hips arched to his touch.

Jordan guided her legs around his shoulders and quickened his movements. When his touch was replaced by his tongue, she cried out his name once, low and urgent, before spasms of pleasure overtook her. Wave after wave of drenching sensation washed through her as she shuddered in release.

For a long time, she remained perfectly still, her eyes closed. Drawing deep gulps of air, she tried to steady her pulse. When she opened her eyes, he was beside her, watching her. He raised his hand to smooth a damp tendril from her temple, brushing his lips over her forehead and pausing a moment to taste the sheen of perspiration that dotted her brow.

When he drew back, she looked into his pale gaze. His eyes were dusky with desire and he smiled crookedly when she reached out to caress his cheek with her fingertips. A sudden, aching need twisted inside her and she caught herself stopping the words that she longed to say. She wanted to tell him how much she loved him, but she knew that her words would bring no response. He couldn't say what she needed to hear. And she would not ask him to lie.

She put her arms around his neck and he picked her up again, completing their trip to her bedroom. He set her down before him, then tugged the Merry Widow down over her hips until it rested on the floor at her ankles. She stepped out of it and heard his slow release of breath as he gazed up at her naked body. A sudden rush of modesty coursed through her.

"You're beautiful," he said as he stood, his voice filled with awe.

His words brought back the memory of the same declaration he'd made when he'd first seen her in the wedding dress. Then she had thrilled at the compliment as a naive girl might. But standing before him, flushed with passion, she felt a woman's pride in his appreciation of her body. He reached out to cup her breasts in his hands, languorously teasing at the nipples with his thumbs.

She ran her fingertips down his chest, feeling the light dusting of dark hair, soft and springy under her fingers, following the trail as it narrowed and disappeared beneath his waistband. How long would it take before she knew every inch of his body? She longed to take her time with him, to explore his skin and the muscles beneath, but the desire that had been so quickly sated was now building in her again.

With a flick of her fingers and a wicked smile, she unhooked his trousers and unzipped them with tantalizing leisure, casually brushing against the hard length hidden behind the fine fabric. She felt his hand clamp around her wrist and pull her away.

His movements were unhurried as he removed the rest of his clothes and she stared at him openly. Lord, he was beautiful. Wide shoulders tapered to a flat abdomen and narrow hips. Her eyes came to rest on the evidence of his arousal, smooth and hard, a shaft of silky steel.

His fingers gripped her shoulders and he pushed her back onto the bed. The heavy weight of his body sank down on top of her. Pulling her legs around his waist, he settled himself between her thighs and plundered her mouth with another exhausting kiss.

"I want you, Elise," he murmured against her swollen lips. "Here, now, so much I can't stand it."

She wriggled her hand between their bodies and wrapped her fingers around his throbbing erection, gently guiding it to her moist entrance.

"We need protection," he whispered.

"No, it's all right," Elise replied in a husky voice. They would be married in less than a month. And Jordan had wanted children. "You've been...careful in the past, haven't you?"

"Yes," he breathed. "Always. You're sure it's all right?"

"I've never been more sure of anything in my life." Her words were true on not just a physical level, but on an emotional plane, too. She was sure that she wanted

him, his body, his soul, his mind, his children. All that
the future held for them. Whether he chose to admit it
or not, she knew there were feelings between them,
deep and abiding. Maybe it would take a month or
maybe even a year, but he would say the words and he
would mean them. And there would be no lies between them, only the precious truth of his long-
awaited realization.

In an act of slow, carnal torture, he slipped inside of
her, expelling a tightly held sigh. As he began to move,
Elise felt her grip on reality loosen and once again she
was transported into a potent world of pure sensation.
She moved with him, absorbing his every thrust, feeling her world spiral upward until at last his body
tensed above hers. He froze, his muscles taut, his eyes
squeezed tightly shut.

With a soft plea of need, she urged him on until his
control shattered, carrying her higher until they both
found their release in a rare and precious moment of
exquisite intimacy.

JORDAN OPENED his eyes to the soft light that filtered
through the bedroom window, then closed them with a
contented sigh. A weight moved across his chest above
the blanket and he reached out to pull Elise's arm back
beneath the covers. Instead his hand came to rest on a
soft mass of fur. He opened his eyes again to find a
huge gray cat sitting on his chest, staring at him with
curious amber eyes. The cat began to purr and a soft
rumble vibrated against his ribs, mixing with the quiet
breathing of the woman tucked in the crook of his arm.
The other cat paced back and forth across the end of
the bed and pounced whenever he moved his toes.

"'Morning," he muttered, watching the cat guardedly and trying to remember the animal's name.

It stood up, walked the length of his chest and came nose to nose with him. Elise moaned softly in her sleep and the feline glanced her way before training her gaze back on Jordan. With an audible sniff of disdain, the cat flicked her fluffy tail and launched herself off his chest to land with a soft thud on the floor. Seconds later, the other cat followed suit, leaping from the bed and disappearing from the room.

He sank back against the pillows, closed his eyes and pulled Elise's pliant body closer to his, enjoying the petal-soft feel of her bare skin against the length of his body. They had made love through most of the night, tumbling from the bed to the floor and back to the bed again, until they were both exhausted.

He had lost himself in the warm depths of her body, drinking in her sweetness as would a man dying from thirst. It had never been like this with a woman before, so pure and intense, an unquenchable need that burned from deep within him. Their bodies had come together in one incredible passion after another. Yet it wasn't just his body that felt fully sated. His heart was content along with his soul. For the first time in a very long time, he felt happy.

A nagging thought crossed his mind and Jordan paused to consider a startling realization. Pushing himself up to a sitting position, he shook the sleep from his fuzzy mind. Though he tried to ignore it, the concept refused to leave his waking brain: he still wanted Elise more than anything in the entire world.

Good God. He was in love her. That was the only explanation for these feelings of raging desire and utter contentment. He found it almost impossible to fathom, but now, given the choice, he realized he would choose to stay in this bed forever. He would forgo his business, his former life. As far as he was concerned, Elise was all he needed to live, save food and water. Elise *was* his life.

Jordan rubbed his eyes and shook his head again. But there it was. He loved her. Could it be that simple? He grinned. If he hadn't been so damn determined to entice her into marrying him without a pronouncement of love, maybe he would have seen it sooner.

Jordan turned to Elise and shook her gently. She mumbled and turned away from him, snuggling her backside against his hip.

He poked at her shoulder. "Elise, wake up. Elise!"

"Umm," she moaned, burying her face in her pillow.

"Elise, we have to talk."

"Talk later," she murmured.

"Elise, I love you."

"I love you, too," she replied in a sleepy voice.

He raised his voice to a shout. "Elise, wake up!"

Elise jumped as if startled from a deep dream, then turned over, pushing herself up and staring at him through her tangled hair.

"I love you," he repeated.

She regarded him cautiously, as if she hadn't quite heard him, or had heard his words but didn't believe them. "What did you say?"

Jordan jumped out of bed, grabbed his trousers and yanked them on, then turned to her. A rush of self-doubt coursed through him at her wide-eyed stare and he raked his fingers through his hair excitedly. "It's all so simple. Don't you see? I don't know why I didn't say it before."

"Say what? Jordan, what are you talking about?" All traces of sleep had left her voice. She was alert and watchful.

Hesitation constricted his throat, but he ignored it and plunged ahead. "Elise...I—I love you...I think. No, I'm sure. I love you."

Hurt shot through her expression at his words and she backed away from him, pulling the sheet up around her naked body. "Don't say that, Jordan. You don't mean it."

Jordan looked at her, stunned by the cold tone of her voice. "Yes, I do."

"No, you don't. You're lying."

"I'm not lying."

"You're so desperate you'd say anything to get me to agree to your proposal. You don't love me."

"Dammit," Jordan shouted. "I'm sick and tired of other people telling me what to do and how to feel. For the first time in my life, I know exactly what I want. Elise, I want you to be my wife. If I say I love you, then I love you."

"You do not!" she shouted, scrambling out of bed and dragging the sheet with her. "How can you lie to me? You told me once that we would always be honest with each other. I thought I could trust you," she continued, her voice cracking with emotion. A tear sprang from the corner of her eye and she brushed it away with the back of her hand. "If there was one thing I could always depend on from you, it was the truth."

She wrapped the sheet around chest and tucked the edge in. The tears flowed freely now, yet she ignored them and laughed, a bitter contrast to her weeping. "To think I was going to accept your proposal. I figured if we didn't have love between us, at least we had honesty. But I guess I was wrong. We don't even have that."

"You were going to accept my proposal?" he asked increduously.

She nodded sullenly.

"And now you won't because you don't believe what I just said?"

She nodded defiantly.

Jordan could barely comprehend what she was telling him. She had steadfastly maintained that she wouldn't marry without love. Now, he was admitting his love for her and she didn't believe a word he said.

"Let me get this straight. I tell you I don't love you, yet I want to marry you, and you say you can only marry for love. Then I tell you I do love you and I still want to marry you. And you turn me down?" Jordan rubbed his eyes and looked at her in confusion.

"You don't mean it. You're just saying the words to get me to agree to marry you."

"What about last night? We made love. It was the most incredible night of my life. Doesn't that mean anything to you?"

"It certainly doesn't mean you love me. I'm sure your former girlfriends will attest to that, or did you flatter them with the same heart-felt declarations the morning after."

"Geez, I can't win, can I? I'm damned if I do love you and I'm damned if I don't. There's nothing I can do to get you to say yes, is there?"

He saw the uncompromising set of her jaw and he

knew what was coming next. She walked over to the dresser and picked up a silver-backed hairbrush. Nervously, she twisted it around in her hands, her back to him. Her voice was soft and unsure. "You could postpone the wedding and give us a chance to find out how we really feel, without this deadline looming over our heads."

Jordan paused before he answered. It wasn't as if the idea was completely new to him. The thought of giving up control of BabyLove had crossed his mind more than once over the past several weeks. But each time he had written the notion off as irresponsible and overly emotional. Still, the prospect of a future without Elise seemed much more dismal than the prospect of a future without BabyLove. Jordan felt his resolve waver for a moment, then steeled himself to reply. "No," he said flatly. "You know what this wedding means. I can't risk losing BabyLove."

She spun around and met his stubborn expression with one of her own. "So, admit you were lying," she challenged. "Then maybe I'll reconsider." She paused, then hiccuped once and wiped her nose with a corner of the sheet.

Jordan shot her an incredulous look then threw up his hands in disgust. "The hell if I'm going to play your games anymore like some loveblind knight jumping to your every wish." He strode over to her side of the bed and grabbed her by the elbow, pulling her against his body. "I love you. I know how I feel. You're the one who doesn't seem to have a handle on your feelings. Here it is, Elise, your last chance. Will you marry me?"

"If you think you can bully me into saying yes, think again."

Jordan released her arm and she stumbled back. "I give up. Go ahead and wait for your Prince Charming. Wait forever for your perfect man who says the perfect words at the perfect time."

He walked across the room and grabbed his shoes and socks from the floor, then paused at the doorway for a long moment, his back to her, his white-knuckled hand clutching the edge of the door, his pride at war with his heart.

"You don't want a man," he said, his voice choked with anger. "You want a myth."

With that, he walked out of the room, out of Elise Sinclair's house, and out of her life. For good.

ELISE CLUTCHED the note scrawled on BabyLove letterhead. The tersely worded missive had arrived by messenger an hour ago. She read the words again, trying hard to accept their meaning:

Dear Ms. Sinclair,
You will be happy to learn that I have chosen a bride and she has graciously accepted my proposal of marriage. I have passed along all the pertinent details of your wedding plans and she prefers to complete the rest of the wedding responsibilities on her own, including addressing and mailing the invitations. Consequently, she will have no need of your services.

Though my bride is quite confident that she can handle all the plans on her own, I would prefer that you confirm all arrangements and be present on the day of the wedding to ensure that all runs smoothly.

Enclosed is a check to cover your services, including the bonus I promised.

I wish you continued business success in the future.

Sincerely yours, Jordan B. Prentiss

P.S. I hope you find your prince.

Elise crumpled the letter in her fist and hurled it across the parlor. She watched as Thisbe pounced on it and batted it across the floor until she lost it beneath the sofa.

Well, he certainly worked fast. Just two days before, Jordan Prentiss had professed his devotion for her and made incredibly sweet, passionate love to her. Now he was marrying someone else.

Just what had their night together meant? Was it simply a manipulation on his part, another scheme to secure a bride? She had spent the past forty-eight sleepless, tear-filled hours doubting his actions and words, right along with her own, wondering if he had told the truth, wondering if she should have believed him. Now it was painfully obvious that Jordan hadn't lost any sleep over the entire incident. He hadn't meant a single word.

How could she have been such a fool? She had actually maintained hope that he would come to his senses and postpone the wedding for her. How many times had she picked up the phone to call him? How long had she stood by the window and watched for his car? She had even taken a taxi to his office building and sat in the lobby, hoping to run into him, before her pride got the best of her and she rushed home.

You don't want a man, you want a myth.

His parting words echoed through her mind. What was so wrong with wanting it all? Love, devotion, fidelity, commitment. Didn't every woman deserve that much? A man she could count on through thick and thin. A man who would put his wife before everything else in his life, including his business.

Elise brushed a tear from her cheek. Were her expectations that unrealistic? She knew, deep in her heart, how much BabyLove meant to Jordan. He had invested his life in the company and she was forcing him to chose. If he truly wanted her, he would have to choose; she couldn't give in.

But would it be so bad? Having Jordan on his terms would be better than not having him at all. At least she loved him. She might spend the rest of her life searching for a man that made her feel like Jordan did and never find another. Elise clenched her fists. No! It wouldn't work. She didn't want to spend her days playing devoted wife to a demanding mistress named BabyLove.

She felt a surge of tears clot in her throat, then swallowed them back, placing her hand on her chest. Why did it hurt so much? Her heart felt as if it had been torn in two, a sharp, ever-present ache stealing her breath and leaving her emotionally drained.

She hadn't eaten more than a bite here and there since the jelly beans she'd wolfed down before Jordan had arrived that night. Eating was the last thing on her mind, especially in the morning, when any thought of food seemed to induce nausea.

Would every day without Jordan be greeted with the same empty, sick feeling? It was nearly impossible to pull herself out of bed in the morning and face the day. Morning sickness. The naively humorous phrase for her tired and hungry state shot through her mind before she brushed it aside. Then a startling realization hit her like a sharp slap in the face. She and Jordan hadn't bothered to use birth control that night. She had been so certain they would be married and so sure he wanted children. Her common sense had been blurred by the overwhelming desire to feel him inside her, without barriers, to give him what he truly wanted, a wife and a family. Now that heedless decision had turned into a horrible mistake.

Elise frantically ran to retrieve the calendar from the kitchen, trying to remember dates that had meant nothing to her until now. She couldn't be. Morning sickness didn't start until much later in the pregnancy, did it? It was just nerves.

I won't worry about it until I find out for sure, she told herself as she fished Jordan's letter out from beneath the sofa. Thisbe sat beside her, waiting to reclaim her newest toy. Elise looked at the cat's expectant expression, then placed the wad of paper at Thisbe's feet. Slowly she reached out and gave the feline a gentle pat on the head. As she pulled her hand away, Thisbe rubbed against her palm and licked her index finger affectionately.

Elise sat on the floor, astonished by the truce that had been called. The cats had never approached her before; in fact, they had always maintained a wide berth. But now, this simple act of affection from Thisbe eased the aching hollowness in her empty heart.

She would survive. The hurt would gradually fade and the pain would dull over time. She would throw herself into her work, making a greater effort to find new clients. With Jordan's generous compensation, she wouldn't have to worry about paying her bills for a long time. Maybe she would take a vacation, get away from the cold, bleak Chicago winter. She could visit her father and Dorthi in Florida. She would try to build a relationship with her stepmother. The prospect of lying in the sun and taking long, solitary walks on the beach brought the first glimmer of hope into her desolate outlook.

She would plan to leave the day after Jordan's wedding. By that time she would be sure she wasn't pregnant. All her worries would be put to rest and she could go on with her life as it had been before.

9

ELISE STOOD in the center of the long aisle of Fourth
Presbyterian Church. Huge in scope and English
Gothic in design, the church was an oasis of tranquil-
lity, nestled among the skyscrapers and stores that
lined the Magnificent Mile. She had never attended a
wedding at Fourth Presbyterian but had wandered
through the church many times to admire the massive
pillars and soaring arches, the dark wood and lime-
stone walls. Elise wondered how many brides had
walked up the aisle and how many grooms had waited
at the altar since the church had been built decades before.

She glanced down at her watch. In about an hour,
the guests would all be seated, their presence filling the
church to barely a quarter of its capacity. To compen-
sate for the extra space, Elise had filled the nave with
flowers and greenery. The fresh fragrance pervaded
the still air.

The quiet was broken by the sound of the organ and
Elise looked up to the huge choir loft. The organist,
outlined against the glorious stained-glass window
that spanned the rear of the church, gave her a brief
wave before he began rehearsing some of the music
she had chosen for the service. She felt a stab of pain in
her heart as she recognized the majestic strains of Pur-

cell's "Trumpet Tune," the music she had selected for the processional.

How would she ever make it through this day? Given the choice, she would have stayed home in bed, eating a quart of ice cream for breakfast and trying madly to forget the significance of April 18. But—as she told herself again and again—she was a professional and it was her duty to make sure the Prentiss wedding came off without a hitch. She could fall apart on her own time. Besides, her masochistic curiosity had gotten the better of her and she wanted to see for herself whom Jordan had finally chosen as a bride.

"What a perfect day for a wedding," a familiar voice cried.

Elise lowered her gaze from the choir loft to see Dona walking slowly up the aisle, taking in the magnificent architecture and Elise's choice of floral decorations. "A sunny spring day with no chance of rain," Dona continued. "Elise, the church looks simply spectacular."

She smiled and nodded to her best friend. "It does, doesn't it? This has got to be the most wonderful wedding I've ever planned."

Dona laughed. "You say that about every wedding you plan."

"This time I'm sure," Elise replied in a soft, wavering voice. This would always remain the most wonderful in her memory, eclipsing those from the past and those yet to come. How could it be anything but perfect—this was supposed to have been her wedding.

"Hey, are you all right?" Dona rushed up to her, grabbing her hand and giving it a squeeze.

Elise brushed a tear from her cheek and forced a smile. Dona knew nothing about her relationship with Jordan, except that Elise had once had a passing infatuation with her wealthy and handsome client. His proposal and her refusal, the night they'd spent together and his declaration of love—all these Elise had kept locked deep inside her. "Of course I'm all right," Elise assured her. "You know I always get emotional at weddings."

"Usually you wait until the service starts before you open the floodgates, though."

"I'm just a little overwhelmed by the church and the flowers and everything."

"So, what do you need me to do?" Dona had assisted her on nearly all her weddings, helping Elise cope with the last-minute details and the minor crises that seemed to appear out of nowhere. Today her help would be the only thing that would keep Elise from losing her composure entirely. Dona would deal with the bride and groom and Elise would keep to the shadows, overseeing the other facets of the wedding.

"I need you to go over the usher's duties with them when they arrive. Then I need you to review the order of the service with the minister. Then, when the bride and groom arrive, brief them. They insisted on no rehearsal, but the service is very straightforward and the minister will guide them through it."

"Got it," Dona replied. "Anything else?"

"Yes. I'll need you to coordinate the processional."

"But you always do that."

"Well, I can't today. I have to...work with the photographer. It won't be hard—there's only one attendant. Just be sure the groom is in place with his best man at the front of the church, then run up and give the organist the go-ahead. Come back down and send them down the aisle. And don't forget the flowers."

"Elise, I really think—"

"You can do it, Dona. Now I have to go find a phone and clear up some final details for the reception. Why don't you find the minister?"

Elise rushed down the aisle, not waiting for Dona's reply, then took a left, heading toward the wing of chapels and meeting rooms that adjoined the church. Her hasty escape was thwarted by both the photographer and the florist as she stopped to answer their questions and make recommendations. When she could finally pull herself away, she ducked into the first open door she came to, closing it behind her with a sigh of relief.

As she turned slowly around, her eyes widened at the sight before her. Hanging from a portable coat rack in the middle of the room was the wedding dress, *her* wedding dress. Its wide skirt billowed beneath clear plastic, the tiny pearls and beads reflecting the light. The bridesmaid's dress she had chosen hung next to it, a pale sea-foam green gown with a tightly fitted bodice and gigot sleeves that mirrored the bride's dress.

As if in a trance, she walked across the room to gaze at the gown. It was more beautiful than she remembered. Her fingers gently traced the pattern of seed pearls that decorated the Alençon lace overlay. Taking hold of the wide skirt, she spread it out before her, unconsciously smoothing a tiny wrinkle from the folds of crisp, rustling shantung. With a shudder of emotion, she turned away, trying desperately to keep her tears in check.

She was drawn to two boxes perched on a small table. Opening the first, she found the beaded slippers she had worn that night at the bridal salon. To her surprise, the second box held the exact same veil she had tried on with the dress. A small velvet box revealed a hauntingly familiar string of pearls. Elise slapped the lids back on the boxes, then sat down on a folding chair beside the table.

A sense of unease came over her. What was going on? Hadn't his bride chosen her own accessories? Or had Jordan wanted his bride dressed exactly as Elise had for some perverse sense of revenge? For a long time, she stared at the dress, her mind and body numb. Then, at the sound of a door slamming in the hallway, she glanced at her watch.

Startled by the time that had passed, she stood up and brushed away the effects of her despondent mood. The guests would begin arriving any minute. And the bride, considering she would be dressing here, was woefully behind schedule. Elise decided to make a hasty exit, hoping she would be lucky enough to avoid meeting the woman. Just as she reached the door, it opened and her heart sank to her shoes.

But the figure who slipped into the room was not that of a strange woman, but that of an achingly familiar man. Jordan turned from the door, his face registering surprise at her presence. For a long moment, they did not speak, just looked at each other, gazes locked, expressions blank.

Jordan broke the silence. "You're here."

Elise opened her mouth to reply, but her voice had been taken away along with her breath. Her eyes scanned his body, marveling at the dashing sight he made in his charcoal-gray morning coat and pin-striped trousers. A white wing-collared shirt was a startling contrast to his smooth complexion and dark hair. And the pearl-gray waistcoat outlined the hard muscle of his torso. Her gaze came to rest on a dia-mond stickpin, twinkling from the center of his paisley ascot.

"Elise?"

She pulled her attention from the hypnotic gleam of the stickpin and back to his handsome face.

"Yes?"

"I didn't expect you to come."

"It's my job," she answered, her voice somehow de-taching itself from her body. She felt as if she were watching the scene from a distance, emotionless and remote. She realized this would be the only way she could cope with the feelings that threatened to break free from inside her.

"Elise, we have to talk."

She ignored his words, focusing her gaze over his left shoulder. "Your bride should be here by now. Maybe I should go look for her." Elise started for the door, but the touch of hard fingers grasping her wrist stopped her.

"Please, Jordan," she said in a choked voice. "Don't do this. You're getting married in less than thirty minutes. We have nothing more to say to each other."

"There won't be a wedding. There is no bride."

She snapped her head up and stared at him. "What?"

He reached out for her face and rubbed his knuckles across her cheek, as if he felt an urgent need to touch her. "No bride."

"Why?"

"I think you know why," he murmured. "There's only one woman for me."

She felt a sliver of relief shoot through her at his words, followed by a rush of anger. "But the church, the guests. Why didn't you call this off earlier?"

He shrugged and smiled crookedly. "I took a risk. I thought it best to play the hand out. And I hoped that you would change your mind."

"And the letter. Was that part of the game?"

"At the time it was a calculated bluff."

She was speechless, unable to decide whether to be angry or ecstatic, hurt or touched. Had he really been waiting for her to come back to him, to change her mind and agree to marry him?

"Elise, I need to ask you a favor."

His eyes were soft and pleading and she longed to reach out and brush away the lines of tension that creased his handsome features. She waited for the words, certain that he would say them just once more. *Marry me.* She could feel her answer forming on her lips.

"I want you to tell me the proper etiquette for calling off this wedding."

Her heart lurched in her chest and she tried to keep the disappointment from showing in her face.

Jordan grabbed her hands, pressing them between

his palms as he looked into her eyes. "I want to start all over. I want to make things work between us and I'm willing to wait as long I have to for you. These last few weeks without you have been hell. I sat in my office trying to work, but all could think about was you. BabyLove doesn't mean anything to me without you. You're my future, you're my life, not some corporation. I love you, Elise. I think I've loved you from the very moment I met you."

Elise felt her heart constrict in her chest. Oh, how she wanted to believe his words. "You'd give up BabyLove? For me? Jordan, I can't ask you to do that."

"I have a chance at something special with you, something real. When I think about losing BabyLove, I feel angry. But when I think about losing you, I feel paralyzed, like I can't go on. I can start another company, Elise, but I can never find another you. You're the only thing that matters to me now."

"Oh, Jordan." Tears ran down her cheeks unchecked. She wiped them away and took a ragged breath.

"Come on." He pulled her toward the door. "Let's put an end to this farce."

Elise shook her head, backing away from him, her pulse thrumming in her head. "No. I need some time. I have to think."

Jordan frowned, then nodded his agreement. "All right, but make it a good excuse. I would prefer to salvage at least a little bit of my pride. Of course, we'll let everyone enjoy themselves at the reception. That should help soften the blow. And we can return the wedding gifts."

By now, Elise's heart was pounding so loudly she barely heard his words. Steadying her hands, she tugged him by the arm, dragging him to the door. "Go," she urged in a shaky voice. "Wait for me upstairs. I'll be up in a minute." She pushed him through the doorway, then poked her head out. "Jordan. My assistant Dona is in the vestibule. Would you send her down here? I'd like to consult with her about the best way to do this."

She watched as he strode down the hall, his gait smooth and athletic. Then she softly closed the door and leaned back against it, taking a deep, cleansing breath.

Could she do it? A smile curved the corners of her mouth. Yes! She could and she would.

Elise hurried across the room and pulled the wedding dress from the hanger. Tearing off her clothes, she threw them on the floor until she stood in her underwear. Gingerly, she stepped into the heavy gown and pulled the rich fabric over her hips, then slipped her arms into the sleeves. A timid knock sounded at the door and she heard Dona's voice on the other side.

"Come in," Elise called, her back to the door. She reached back to attempt the tiny row of buttons.

The door opened and she waited for Dona to step in and help her.

"I'm sorry," her friend said. "I was looking for Elise Sinclair."

Elise slowly turned and watched an expression of alarm register on Dona's face.

"Elise," she gasped. "What are you doing? Are you crazy? What if the bride walks in here and sees you in her dress? She'll boot us both out of here." Dona crossed the room and grabbed a cuff. Tugging at it, she attempted to remove the dress from Elise.

But Elise pulled her arm away and smiled. "*I* am the bride."

Dona's voice was nearly a shout. "*What?* Elise, you have gone off the deep end. I knew you had a little crush on this guy, but you've gone way too far. Come on, get out of that dress and I'll take you home. We'll call my mother's psychiatrist, and he'll help you deal with this...this obsession."

"No, it's true. I'm going to marry Jordan Prentiss."

"Elise..."

"Dona," she shot back in the same patronizing voice. "Have I ever, ever lied to you?"

A confused scowl appeared on her friend's face. "No, I don't think so. But if you're really going to marry this guy, how come I haven't heard anything about it? What about that, huh?"

"That wasn't a lie. I just neglected to tell you the truth. Jordan asked me to marry him and I turned him down. Then we made love and he told me he loved me and I told him to get out."

"And the guy still wants to marry you?"

"He'd better." Elise turned her back to Dona. "Here, button me up. Then I want you to put on that bridesmaid's dress. I think it should fit, though it may be a little big. You're going to be my maid of honor."

"I don't know about this. If you want to make a fool of yourself in front of four hundred people, feel free. But I'm not about to get involved in one of your romantic fantasies gone berserk."

"It's not a fantasy, Dona. I love Jordan Prentiss, and he loves me." As soon as the dress was buttoned she spun around and kissed her best friend on both cheeks. Then she opened the the largest box, pulled the veil from its tissue paper nest and draped it over her arm. She grabbed the shoes and the string of pearls and rushed to the door. "I'll meet you upstairs. Now, hurry."

Elise carefully made her way down the hall to the vestibule, then stood behind a side door and tried to catch Jordan's attention. He stood in profile, his head bent to a young man also dressed in a morning coat and striped trousers. She waited until the ushers had cleared the vestibule of guests, then softly called Jordan's name. He turned to look at her. An expression of relief suffused his face as he walked toward her. "Elise, come on. Everyone's inside. We'd better tell them and get it over with."

She drew a deep breath, then stepped out from behind the door, pulling the long train out behind her. Her fingers tightened on the shoes she held in one hand as she watched for Jordan's reaction.

His initial look of astonishment slowly dissolved, giving way to an irresistible grin.

"Ask me again, Jordan."

He shook his head in disbelief and ran his fingers through his hair. "How do I know you won't turn me down again, Elise?"

"Just ask."

"Elise, will you marry me?"

She straightened to her full height in stocking feet

and smiled back at him. "Yes, Jordan, I will marry you."

With a shout of triumph, he pulled her into his arms and swung her around and around, his lips descending on hers.

He hugged her long and hard. She watched over Jordan's shoulder as the same expression of incredulity she had seen on Dona's face crossed the best man's face. Seconds later, her friend appeared in the doorway, dressed in the bridesmaid's gown, and tentatively walked toward them.

Elise breathlessly made the introductions. Dona relaxed visibly when she realized that Elise wasn't crazy and that Jordan actually did plan to marry her. Jordan's executive assistant, Pete Stockton, was introduced as his best man and he gallantly offered Dona his arm, pulling her away from Elise and Jordan and giving them a moment alone.

Elise fastened the veil to her hair, then placed her palm on Jordan's shoulder and handed him the beaded slippers. "Can you help me put these on?"

Jordan bent down on one knee and lifted her skirt, cupping her heel in one hand and sliding the left slipper on. "I seem to remember doing this once before. Only that time, you ran out on me." He looked up at her. "You aren't going to run away again, are you?"

"Not a chance."

"You understand that this wedding isn't legal, there's no marriage license. We'll have to do it all over again in a civil ceremony. You won't change your mind, will you?" She could feel his hand tightening on her ankle as he awaited her response.

Elise reached down and placed her palm on his face, caressing his cheek with her fingertips. The worried look on his face evaporated. "No, Jordan, I won't back out on you."

"We don't have to get married today. We can wait if you want."

"But you could lose your company."

"I could still lose my company. But better to risk losing my company than risk losing you."

Elise looked down at him in amazement. "You'd really give it all up for me?"

"For you and only for you."

"You're not going to lose me, Jordan. I'll be with you always, for better or for worse. Even if you do find yourself out of a job, we'll find some way to work it all out."

He slid the other slipper on her right foot, then stood up.

"I guess I'm ready," she murmured, smiling up at him. She threw herself into his arms and kissed him.

"Ahem. Mr. Prentiss, I presume."

Jordan pulled his mouth from Elise's and turned around, keeping his arm possessively wrapped around her waist. A dapper-looking man in a pin-striped suit and red bow tie stood before them.

"Yes, I'm Jordan Prentiss."

"Mr. Prentiss, my name is Lewis T. Stone of the law firm Schumacher and Stone. We handled your grandfather's personal and business affairs along with his estate."

"I'm aware of that, Mr. Stone."

"I have been entrusted to deliver this to you on your

wedding day." The man held out a thin envelope. "It is a wedding present from your late grandfather."

Jordan frowned, then took the envelope from the man's hand and placed it in his breast pocket. "Thank you, Mr. Stone. My bride and I will open it with the rest of the gifts."

"You may want to open it now, Mr. Prentiss."

Jordan looked at the lawyer warily, then pulled the envelope back out of his pocket. He handed it to Elise, keeping his gaze fixed on the lawyer. She tore the flap and unfolded an official-looking letter.

"What is it?" Jordan asked.

She glanced down at the signature. "It's a letter from your grandfather."

"Go ahead. Read it."

Elise held up the letter and began to read aloud:

Dear Jordan,

I suppose you're surprised to hear from me, seeing as how I'm dead, but an occasion as auspicious as your marriage cannot go by unnoticed. I have no way of knowing how long I've been dead, but suffice it to say, considering your aversion to marital commitment, it's probably been a long time.

BabyLove has always been run by a Prentiss and I intend to see that it remains so. As a wedding present, I wish to present to you a stock option that will allow you to purchase 150,000 shares of the company at $3.00 per share upon the first business day after your wedding.

Elise looked up in bewilderment, her eyes fixed on Jordan. "Did you know about this all along?"

"I'm afraid not, miss," the lawyer answered for him. "Apart from the executor of the estate, Jordan's great-aunt, I was the only person who knew of this."

Elise turned back to Jordan. "What does this mean?"

A smile replaced the look of surprise on Jordan's face as he glanced at Pete Stockton, standing just behind the lawyer. "It means that as soon as we are legally married, we will purchase $450,000 worth of stock in BabyLove."

Elise's mouth dropped open. "That's a lot of money Jordan. Do you think you should spend that much when you might lose your job?"

"We'll borrow the money from the bank."

She drew a sharp breath, grasping the sleeves of his coat with tense fists. "You want to borrow $450,000 from a bank! Good Lord, Jordan. I was worried about telling you about the $2,000 balance on my Marshall Field's charge card. And now you want to borrow nearly a half-million dollars?"

He and Pete were smiling as if they were sharing some private joke. A joke she had no way of understanding. "Don't worry. We'll pay it back the same day—right after we sell the stock. Of course, the stock won't be worth $3.00 a share."

Elise brought her fingers to her temples, trying to massage away a knot of tension that twisted there. "Oh, Jordan. This is not the kind of thing to be telling me on our wedding day."

"Elise, BabyLove stock is worth around $56.00 per share. I'll buy it at $3.00 and sell it at $56.00."

Elise's mind whirled in confusion. He was going to buy stock at $3.00 and sell it at $56.00. That meant he would make a profit. She mentally did the calculations. "That's $840,000!"

He laughed, then kissed her cheek affectionately. "No, Elise, that's $8.4 million. The company can't afford to repurchase the stock at market value, so the board will be forced to back down. And if they vote me out later, we won't have to worry. With that kind of money, I can start another company."

"Ahem." Lewis T. Stone requested their attention again. "I believe you'll want to hear the rest of the letter, Mr. Prentiss."

Elise looked down and continued to read:

"'Upon the birth of my first great-grandchild, you will receive a similar option to buy 150,000 shares. As I'm sure you have already deduced, this will give you controlling interest in BabyLove.

Jordan, you've always been a clever and resourceful young man. Now use some of that cleverness of yours and get me a great-grandchild!
Your grandfather,
Jonathan Bradford Prentiss'"

"So, it will be all yours," Elise murmured.

"**That** depends upon you," Jordan replied. He turned to the lawyer. "There's no time limit on this option?"

"The option will be available immediately upon your marriage, whether it takes place today or ten years from now."

"Don't you see, Elise? Now that we have the stock option, we don't have to get married today. We can take our time—we can plan the wedding you've always wanted, with your family and your friends. We will wait if you want to. I want you to be absolutely sure about this."

"Do you love me, Jordan?"

"Yes, Elise, I love you." His answer was as firm and certain as her question.

"That's all I need to hear. I want to marry you here, today. We can invite my father and stepmother to the civil ceremony." Besides, from the very start, this _was_ meant to be _her_ wedding.

"Ladies and gentlemen."

Elise turned to see the organist standing at the base of the stairs to the choir loft.

"The guests are getting restless. Let's get started."

Elise walked with Jordan to the far door, where he would take the side aisle to the front of the church. A sudden thought occurred to her and she felt a brief flash of panic. "Wait. There's just one little thing I have to tell you."

The sound of the first strains of the processional echoed through the church and Jordan grabbed her hand, giving it a squeeze. "It can wait, sweetheart. We've got a whole lifetime together." He stepped to the door leading to the sanctuary.

"No, it can't." Elise tried to calm her frantic feelings, pulling him back beside her. This could change everything. "It has to do with the letter."

"Elise, nothing you have to say is going to keep me from marrying you." He gave her a quick kiss on her forehead. "Nothing. Now, I'll meet you at the altar. Don't be late."

Elise watched Jordan pass through the door, with Pete right behind him. She turned to Dona. "I'm getting married," she said.

"Yes, you are," Dona replied. They rushed into each other's arms, hugging until Elise giggled and pulled away. Reaching up, she brushed the tears off her best friend's cheeks. "Why are you crying? I'm the one who always cries at weddings."

"Oh, I don't know," Dona said. "It's all so romantic. You always believed in happily ever after and now all your dreams are coming true."

"It is like a dream come true, isn't it?"

Dona nodded as she toyed with Elise's veil. Then she carefully fastened the string of pearls around Elise's neck and pulled the blusher veil over Elise's face. With a quivering smile, Elise watched her best friend move to open the wide central doors to the sanctuary. She followed her to the doorway, her heart hammering in her chest as her maid of honor began the long march up the aisle. Her gaze raced along the length of the church, beyond Dona, to the man who waited for her at the steps to the altar. Then she put one foot in front of the other and began to walk toward her future.

From that moment on, the wedding passed in a blur. There was a brief moment of confusion as the minister paused to get their names before beginning the service, but from then on, everything rushed by in a jumble of words and music and excitement.

Then the minister pronounced them husband and wife and she watched from behind her veil as Jordan turned to her. Gently he lifted the netting and pushed it over her head. Taking her face in his hands, he kissed her, softly and sweetly. As he pulled away, he murmured against her lips. "Now and forever, Elise."

She smiled up at him, tears spilling from the corners of her eyes. "Now and forever, Jordan."

Then they both turned and walked to the head of the aisle as husband and wife. They proceeded slowly, smiling and nodding at their guests as they walked.

Elise's gaze was drawn sharply to a pink-clad woman in the first row of pews. She clutched Jordan's sleeve. "Jordan, she's here! The lady in pink. That's her, in the wide-brimmed hat."

Jordan looked down at Elise, then followed the direction of her gaze. "Who, Esme?"

Yes. Who is she?"

"That's my great-aunt Esme. She's a major stockholder at BabyLove and is a member of the board of directors. She's also the Prentiss family matchmaker. She's been trying to marry me off for years. She'll stop at nothing for the chance to dance at a wedding."

Elise stopped and turned to Jordan. "She's your great-aunt? The same great-aunt that served as executor to your grandfather's estate?"

Jordan nodded.

"The same great-aunt that knew about the stock options?"

Jordan nodded again. "Yes, she knew about the—" A sudden realization dawned on his face.

They both turned to Esme. The older woman gave them a jaunty wave, then blew Jordan a kiss and winked at Elise. In that moment, Elise knew exactly

GET 2

HOW TO GET YOUR
2 FREE BOOKS AND FREE GIFT!

1. Peel off the MIRA sticker on the front cover. Place it in the space provided at right. This automatically entitles you to receive two free books and an exciting mystery gift.

2. Send back this card and you'll get 2 "The Best of the Best™" novels. These books have a combined cover price of $11.00 or more in the U.S. and $13.00 or more in Canada, but they are yours to keep absolutely FREE!

3. There's no catch. You're under no obligation to buy anything. We charge nothing — ZERO — for your first shipment. And you don't have to make any minimum number of purchases — not even one!

4. We call this line "The Best of the Best" because each month you'll receive the best books by some of today's hottest authors. These authors show up time and time again on all the major bestseller lists and their books sell out as soon as they hit the stores. You'll like the convenience of getting them delivered to your home at our special discount prices . . . and you'll love your *Heart to Heart* subscriber newsletter featuring author news, horoscopes, recipes, book reviews and much more!

5. We hope that after receiving your free books you'll want to remain a subscriber. But the choice is yours — to continue or cancel, anytime at all! So why not take us up on our invitation, with no risk of any kind. You'll be glad you did!

6. And remember...we'll send you a mystery gift ABSOLUTELY FREE just for giving "The Best of the Best" a try.

SPECIAL FREE GIFT!

We'll send you a fabulous surprise gift, absolutely FREE, simply for accepting our no-risk offer!

Visit us online at
www.mirabooks.com

BOOKS FREE!

Hurry!

Return this card promptly to GET 2 FREE BOOKS & A FREE GIFT!

The Best of the Best ™

Affix
peel-off
MIRA
sticker here

YES! Please send me the 2 FREE "The Best of the Best" novels and FREE gift for which I qualify. I understand that I am under no obligation to purchase anything further, as explained on the opposite page.

385 MDL C6PQ

(P-BB3-01)
185 MDL C6PP

NAME   (PLEASE PRINT CLEARLY)

ADDRESS

APT.#   CITY

STATE/PROV.   ZIP/POSTAL CODE

Offer limited to one per household and not valid to current subscribers of "The Best of the Best." All orders subject to approval. Books received may vary.
©1995 MIRA BOOKS

The Best of the Best™ — Here's How it Works:

what it was that had teased at her memory every time Esme was near. It was in her eyes. Those twinkling pale blue eyes. Eyes the exact color of Jordan's. Why hadn't she made the connection before?

"You don't think she orchestrated the whole—"

Jordan shook his head. "No...Well, maybe. She could have initiated the flap about my image. She could have talked Edward into the takeover attempt. And Esme knows me well enough to know I'd do whatever was necessary to maintain control of Baby-Love, including getting married. But how could she have known I'd fall in love with you? And that you'd fall in love with me?"

They turned to each other, then back to Esme. Jordan's great-aunt gave them a sheepish shrug.

"She knew," Elise answered with a laugh. "Believe me, she knew."

They continued down the aisle, through the vestibule and out the front doors into the sunshine of a perfect spring day. Pausing on the steps, Elise wondered whether this was the right time and place. It was the perfect place, she decided, and plunged ahead. "Jordan, there is one other thing we need to discuss. I tried to tell you before the ceremony, but you told me to wait."

"All right, Elise. You have my undivided attention for the next seventy years or so. Now what is bothering you?"

Elise took a deep breath. "I have a wedding present for you."

"That's very nice," he replied, kissing her softly on

the forehead. "What did you buy us? A toaster? A blender?"

"It's not exactly a traditional wedding present. And I can't give it to you right now, because I don't have it yet." She smiled. "At least, not in the literal sense of the word. You're going to have to wait another nine months or so before I can actually give it to you."

He frowned, a look of confusion etched on his brow.

Elise smiled at him and crinkled her nose. "You're going to get control of BabyLove back a little sooner than you thought. We'll have a vested interest in strained carrots by December."

He stared at her, dumbfounded. "Are—are you sure?"

"The doctor hasn't confirmed it yet, but by my calendar, our timing couldn't have been better. Or worse, depending upon how you feel about this."

"How I feel?" In one quick motion, Jordan scooped her up in his arms and walked down the steps to the street.

"We're going to have a baby," he shouted to any passerby who would listen. Pedestrians stopped and gawked as Jordan spun Elise around. Cabdrivers parked in front of the church honked their horns. A small crowd gathered to watch the groom and bride share a passionate kiss as the guests from the church began to fill the steps behind them. A smattering of applause broke out from several of the bystanders, and soon the crowd that surrounded them began to clap enthusiastically.

Rice rained down on them as they ran to the curb where a horse-drawn carriage waited. Jordan helped

Elise inside, then swung in beside her. The carriage pulled into the traffic of Michigan Avenue, amid the squealing tires of cabs and the roar of the city buses. But inside, Jordan and Elise were lost in their own private world.

A world where love *did* conquer all.

MARRIAGE IN JEOPARDY

Miranda Lee

CHAPTER ONE

THE first inkling Juliana had that something was wrong came with Stewart's telephone call to her office. Not that this was unusual. Blake's secretary often called her to relay messages from her husband. It was Stewart's tone of voice that disturbed her. He sounded almost…rattled.

'Mrs Preston, have you by any chance heard from Mr Preston today?' he asked after announcing himself.

'No, Stewart, I haven't. Why? Is there some problem?'

His hesitation to answer sent Juliana snapping forward on her chair. 'What is it?' she said sharply. 'What's happened?'

Her anxious quizzing seemed to shock Stewart back into his more characteristic role as Blake's unflappable right-hand man. 'No need to be alarmed, Mrs Preston,' he replied in that maddeningly phlegmatic voice he usually used. It's just that when I rang the Sydney office a minute ago they hadn't seen hide nor hair of Mr Preston all day. The manager sounded most relieved, I might add.'

'The *Sydney* office? Why would Blake be in the Sydney office? Wasn't he flying straight home from Manila today?'

'You mean Mr Preston didn't tell you of his change of plan?'

Juliana bit her bottom lip in a vain attempt to stop dismay from swamping her. This was one aspect of her marriage that had been bothering her more and more of late. Blake's obsession with personal space. He hated answering to anyone, especially his wife. Juliana knew *why* this was so, but knowing why did not make it any easier to bear.

'No, Stewart,' she admitted. 'He didn't.'

'I see.' The secretary was unable to hide the sardonic edge in his voice.

What do you see? Juliana agonised with a rush of fierce emotion. A marriage without love? A woman prepared to accept any kind of treatment in exchange for money and position?

Her heart ached with the desire to explain that her relationship with Blake was not really like that. OK, so maybe their marriage *had* been entered into with their heads, rather than their hearts. But that didn't mean they didn't care for each other, that they hadn't become the most important people in each other's lives.

If she came across as a cool, reserved spouse then that was because Blake liked her that way. Surely Stewart could appreciate that. He himself had been hired as Blake's secretary and assistant because he possessed the very qualities Blake demanded in all those close to him. He was self-sufficient, self-reliant, self-contained. Like herself.

Only she didn't feel self-contained at that moment.

She felt extremely vulnerable. And worried.

'Please, Stewart,' she went on, her voice unsteady. 'Don't leave me in the dark. Tell me what's going on.'

Once again, the man hesitated. Clearly, he'd been well trained by Blake over what the boss's wife should and shouldn't know.

Juliana felt the beginnings of panic. '*Please,*' she pleaded. Oh, God, if something had happened to Blake she didn't know what she would do.

'Mr Preston will be very cross with me,' the man muttered, 'but I suppose you have a right to know since my call has obviously upset you. Your husband sent me a fax yesterday to say he'd finished in Manila a day early and had decided to drop off at our Sydney branch for a totally unannounced visit on the way home, but that he would still be arriving in Melbourne by five-thirty.'

'But you said he *hasn't* dropped in at the Sydney office!'

'Which is no reason to panic, Mrs Preston. As you well know, it's not unlike your husband not to let even me know of last-minute changes of plans. Maybe he's stayed on in Manila. Or maybe he's gone to the Brisbane office instead. He's sure to turn up at Tullamarine airport as per schedule. The boss is very reliable like that. I'll just mosey on out to the airport to meet him and you pop on home and dress for dinner. I've booked a table for you and Mr Preston at Don Giovanni's for eight-thirty.'

'But what if his plane doesn't arrive?' Juliana cried,

unable to think of something as ridiculous as dressing for dinner when for all she knew her Blake might be in mortal danger.

'It will, Mrs Preston. Be assured of that. Now do stop worrying, and please…let this incident be our little secret. Your husband would be far from pleased if he knew I'd bothered you with this minor misunderstanding. Do I have your reassurance that you won't mention it to him?'

Juliana sighed. 'I suppose so, but please call me at home as soon as Blake's plane touches down, otherwise I'll worry myself to death.'

'I'll certainly do that, Mrs Preston,' he finished with far more warmth than usual.

Juliana hung up, aware that nothing would make her feel better till Blake was home again, safe and sound. Three weeks he'd been away. Three long, lonely weeks. She'd been so looking forward to tonight, to dinner, then afterwards. Now…

Her heart squeezed tight. What if something awful had happened? What if she never saw Blake again?

I'm being maudlin, she told herself abruptly. Maudlin and melodramatic and ridiculous. Just because I've been having some small doubts about my marriage lately. Stewart's right, Blake does this sort of thing all the time. He'll show up as he always does, smoothly elegant and totally unruffled. There's absolutely no reason to worry, let alone panic.

Still, Juliana could not settle to any more work that afternoon and was glad to leave the office at four-thirty, anxious to be home for Stewart's call. The Preston mansion was only a few miles from the city, overlooking the Eastern side of Port Phillip Bay, but Juliana caught the Friday afternoon rush, and the drive home took over an hour.

The telephone was ringing as she let herself into the house via the garages shortly after five-thirty. Since it was Mrs Dawson's night off, there was no one to answer it, and Juliana hoped it would keep ringing till she could reach the closest extension. Hurrying through the laundry and into the kitchen, she dropped her coat and handbag on the breakfast counter and snatched the receiver down from the wall. 'Yes?'

'Mrs Preston?'

'Stewart! Oh, thank God you didn't hang up. I was just letting myself in and I ran. But everything's all right now,' she sighed happily. 'Blake's jet landed on time, I gather?'

'Well—er—'

Juliana froze.

'Mr Preston's plane *hasn't* arrived as yet, I'm sorry to say, and I've been having some trouble locating him. I've been in contact with Manila, and it seems Mr Preston left on time yesterday, with Sydney as his intended destination, but the airports there are insistent he did not land anywhere in Sydney at all either yesterday or today.'

All the blood began draining from Juliana's face. 'Dear heaven…' She dragged over a kitchen stool and slumped down on it before she fell down. 'Have… have you contacted the various authorities?'

'I certainly have. They're making enquiries.'

'Making enquiries,' she repeated limply.

'Please try not to worry, Mrs Preston. I'm sure everything will be all right.'

'Do…do you think I should come out to the airport myself?'

'I don't think that would be wise,' came the firm advice. 'Especially if Mr Preston arrives shortly, as I'm sure he will. You know how he hates being fussed over. He'd much prefer you to wait for him at home, as you always do.'

Juliana flinched at what sounded like a reproof. The only reason she didn't meet or see her husband off at airports was because he always insisted she didn't, not because she didn't want to. This was another aspect of her marriage that was beginning to trouble her: other people's perceptions of it. Still, this was hardly the time to be worrying about appearances.

'You promise to ring me,' she said shakily, 'as soon as you know anything? Anything at all.'

'I promise, Mrs Preston. Must go. Bye.'

Juliana finally hung up the receiver. Oh, God… Blake…

For a moment she buried her face in her hands, terrified by the images that kept bombarding her mind. Blake…lying dead in a twisted mangle of metal on some mountainside. Blake…sinking to the bottom of the ocean in a cold coffin of steel. Or worst of all…his beautiful body charred beyond all recognition. Planes often burst into flames when they crashed.

Her loud cry of utter desolation shocked even herself.

Juliana's lovely hazel eyes opened wide. She sat

up straight in the stool. Dear heaven, she thought with a wild churning of her stomach. Dear heaven...

Juliana sat in the dark in her living-room, all alone. She was grateful that it was Mrs Dawson's night off, grateful that she didn't have to put up with the woman's scepticism over her distress. Blake's house-keeper had made it perfectly plain without being overtly rude that she didn't approve of her employer's wife, always calling Juliana 'Mrs Preston' in a stiffly formal manner.

Two hours had passed since Stewart's call. It felt like two years.

The sudden sound of the phone ringing sent Juliana leaping to her feet. Heart pounding madly, she raced across the room, hesitating fearfully before snatching the dreaded instrument up to her ear. 'Yes?'

'Stewart Margin here again, Mrs Preston. No need to worry any longer. Mr Preston is perfectly all right.'

Juliana swayed, gripping the edge of the telephone table as a steadier. 'Oh, thank the lord,' she whispered huskily. 'Thank the lord...'

She closed her eyes for a second to say another private prayer of thanks. Blake hadn't been killed in a plane crash after all! Soon he would breeze in through their front door, splendid as always in one of his immaculate business suits. He would toss aside his crocodile-skin briefcase before reefing his tie off then heading straight for the drinks cabinet where he would pour himself a hefty Scotch and call out to her. 'Come and join me, Juliana, and tell me about your day. Mine's been hell!'

Oh, Blake… What would I have done if something had happened to you? How would I have survived?

She paled as the realisation that had come to her earlier on struck again with sickening force, a realisation which could threaten her future happiness almost as much as Blake's dying. A small sob escaped her throat, her knuckles whitening as her nails dug into the wood.

'Mrs Preston? Are you all right?'

No, she cried in silent anguish. I'm not all right. I'm never going to be all right again. Don't you see? Somewhere along the line I've fallen in love with my husband! Why, if he walked in right now I would throw myself into his arms, weeping and making a complete fool of myself.

And what would Blake do? He would stare down at me in appalled horror, coldly withdrawing from such a display of emotional possessiveness. Oh, how he hated women who clung, who needed, who *loved* like that.

God! Whatever am I going to do?

Ask about your husband, you little idiot, the voice of common sense suggested. But ask *calmly*.

She gulped and set about gathering her wits. For if she didn't she might as well ask Blake for a divorce this very night.

'I am now,' she assured Blake's secretary. 'Has my husband's plane actually arrived?'

'No. He's coming in on a commercial flight that lands in…let's see now…in about ten minutes' time.'

'A *commercial* flight? What happened to his Learjet? Did it break down somewhere?'

'In a way. It appears that some time after take-off from Manila yesterday Mr Preston's plane went through a cloud of volcanic dust that clogged up the engines—and the on-board electronics—so badly that the pilot had to make an emergency landing.'

'An emergency landing? But *where*? Why weren't we *told*?'

'Fortunately the pilot knew of an American airforce strip on a nearby island, but unfortunately it was abandoned. It took some time for them to be able to contact authorities and get a helicopter to take them back to Manila. Blake had a message sent through to Tullamarine airport but it was misplaced temporarily during a change-over of staff. It's always rather hectic here during Friday evening peak hour. Not that that's any excuse really. Still, all's well that ends well, Mrs Preston. The boss is safe and sound.'

For the second time that day Juliana heard traces of emotion in Stewart Margin's voice. So he too had been worried. And he too was relieved.

A softly ironic smile passed over her lips. And why wouldn't he be? Without Blake as company director, Preston's Toys and Games would probably quickly revert to the almost bankrupt business it had been when he'd taken over a few years before. Without Blake, Stewart Margin might be swiftly without a job.

Without Blake...

Juliana shivered. If only her own relief weren't tinged with this awful apprehension.

If only this incident hadn't happened at all! she agonised. Then she might never have realised the depth of her feelings. She would have been able to go on in blissful ignorance, happily being the sort of wife Blake wanted without worrying that any moment she might betray herself and, in doing so, lose him.

But have you been happy being that sort of wife? came a dark voice from deep inside. *Really* happy? What about all those niggling little doubts of late?

'Mrs Preston? Are you sure you're all right?'

Juliana scooped in a steadying breath. 'I *am* still a little shaken,' she admitted. 'I'll be fine by the time Blake arrives home. But, as you mentioned earlier, my husband does hate any fuss, so best he doesn't know the extent of my concern over this matter.'

'Of course, Mrs Preston. I wouldn't *dream* of telling him.'

'Good. Let me know if there are any more delays, will you?'

'Certainly.'

When Juliana hung up the phone she didn't know whether to laugh or cry. She felt both elated and devastated. In the space of a couple of hours she had been through an emotional mill. She was *still* going through it.

She turned to walk somewhat dazedly out into the deserted kitchen, switching on the electric kettle for a cup of coffee. Would Blake still want to go out for dinner when he got home? she wondered distractedly.

She doubted it. He was sure to have been fed on the plane.

There was one thing, however, that he might want tonight after being away for so long.

Juliana shuddered. An odd reaction, she realised,

for a woman who had found nothing but pleasure in her husband's arms.

But with her newly discovered love burning in her heart Juliana could see that the intimate side of their marriage left a lot to be desired. Blake conducted their sex-life in a coolly clinical fashion, without any spontaneity or real passion. They had separate bedrooms, their sexual encounters always pre-arranged. He even marked the calendar in his study with the dates on which she would be…indisposed. Being on the Pill, Juliana could provide this information in advance.

She wished now that this were one of those days. But it wasn't.

Of course she could *understand* Blake's aversion to sharing a room with her. It was his way of keeping her at a safe distance, making sure she didn't start demanding any more than he was prepared to give.

But *understanding* did not make the situation sit better around her heart.

She cringed now to think of the way Blake would give her the nod before retiring whenever he wished to sleep with her; the way he didn't come into her room till she was showered and already in bed; the way he never stayed the whole night with her, going back to his own room once he was finished.

Juliana shook her head in distress. God, it was little better than legal prostitution.

No, no, she denied quickly. That was being unfair to Blake and their marriage. Their sex-life was only one aspect of their relationship. They were partners in more ways than just in bed. They went everywhere together. They were good friends. They always had been.

Was she going to ruin what they had simply because she'd been silly enough to fall in love? She would be crazy to. Her marriage was stronger than most. They were going to try for a baby next year. Madness to throw that all away by wanting the one thing she couldn't have.

So Blake didn't love her. He *did* care for her in his own peculiar way. So he wasn't swept away by passion for her at odd times during the day. He *did* make love to her quite beautifully when he came to her bed. And that was often enough.

For pity's sake, what did she want out of life? She had it good, had what she'd always wanted. Financial security; a solid marriage; a good job. All she had to do was keep her love under control and simply go on as before.

Which included not making any objections to the way Blake conducted their sex-life.

But, dear heaven, she hoped he would be too tired to come to her bed tonight. She didn't think she could bear to have him touch her just now. She was sure to do something silly, sure to give herself away.

There again, she did so long to hold him. Just hold him.

But Blake didn't know how to just be held. He never, ever touched Juliana at all except when he climbed into her bed. Not for him the simple holding of hands or the putting of an affectionate arm around her shoulder or waist. He was not, and never would be, a toucher.

And Juliana knew why.

Bitterness rose in her chest. His mother had a lot to answer for.

The telephone ringing again cut through the silence of the house.

Juliana stiffened.

It was Blake. She just *knew* it was Blake, ringing before he left the airport.

Though never liking her to call him at all, he often phoned her. It was another of his quirks about wives which Juliana fully understood. His mother had driven his father crazy with constant telephone calls, especially when he was away on business. They had not been chatty, affectionate calls, but jealously possessive calls, always wanting to know where he was, what he was doing, where he was going, when he would be home.

Then, once he *was* home, she never let him out of her sight, always touching him, kissing him, pawing at him. Noreen Preston had been a neurotically insecure women who'd loved her handsome husband to her—and everyone else's—distraction.

Juliana knew all this, not because Blake had told her. Her mother had told her. Her mother, who had been the live-in cook here in the Preston household for almost twenty years, her long employ coming to an abrupt halt a year ago when she was accidentally killed by a hit-and-run driver.

Juliana closed her eyes against the rush of tears.

Poor Mum…

Yet she knew her mother would not have wanted her pity. Or her grief. Lily Mason had been an open-hearted, kind-natured woman who'd embraced life with a naïve optimism that left little room for regrets and remorse. Unfortunately, however, this same naïve optimism made her vulnerable to certain types of men, ones whom Lily always thought loved and needed her.

All they had loved and needed, Juliana thought bitterly, was her mother's quite beautiful body in bed. Not one of them had ever offered to support her, or marry her, not even Juliana's father, who had apparently disappeared into the wide blue yonder as soon as he'd found out his teenage girlfriend was pregnant.

At least Lily hadn't made the mistake of letting any of these men live with herself and her daughter. Juliana was spared that. But even as a young child tucked up in bed she'd heard her mother sneaking men into her room late at night.

This had stopped for a while when Lily and her daughter had moved into the flat above the Prestons' garage. But not for long. Lily merely moved her assignation time to during the day, Juliana often smelling male aftershave and cigar smoke when she came home from school.

The insistent ring of the telephone brought Juliana back to reality. What on earth was she doing, mentally rumaging over all this dirty linen? The past might hold explanations for why people did what they did—herself and Blake included—but it didn't give her any weapons with which to handle the present and the future.

All she could do was gather herself and answer the

telephone, and, if it was Blake, show him that nothing had changed between them. Nothing at all.

She reached up and lifted the receiver down to her ear, telling herself to act as if she were taking a business call at work. As public relations officer for a large international cosmetic company Juliana had had plenty of practice at appearing cool under stress.

'Juliana Preston,' she said with superb calm.

'Blake here, Juliana.'

'Blake!' she exclaimed with a forced lilt in her voice. 'You bad man, you had me so worried.' Her tone betrayed not the slightest hint of any real worry.

He laughed his attractively lazy laugh, reinforcing her belief that this was the way to play the situation.

'And there I'd been,' she went on lightly, 'thinking you'd made me into a premature widow.'

'Thinking, or hoping?' he drawled. 'And don't you mean a *merry* widow? I'm worth a bundle. Even more after the deals I've just made.'

Juliana's skin crawled at the mention of money. It was bad enough having people like Stewart and Mrs Dawson believing she'd married Blake for his money, worse to have her husband voicing the same opinion.

Maybe it had been partly true. Once. But not now. Not any more...

How ironic that Blake would hate to think that was so. He *liked* the arrangement they had come to, the sort of marriage he'd insisted upon and which Juliana had thought she'd wanted too, at the time. God! If only she were able to take him into her confidence, to tell him of her newly discovered love.

But that was impossible. He didn't want her to love

him. In fact, he would hate the idea. The truth was, if she wished to continue being Mrs Blake Preston she would have to hide her love behind the sort of wife she'd successfully been up till now, but which she suspected would prove hard to be in the future.

'Everything went well, then?' she asked, keeping her voice amazingly cool.

'Fantastic!' he returned. 'I love doing business with the Asians—they're a real challenge.'

She forced a laugh. 'And how you do like a challenge!'

'Do I?'

'You know you do. That's the only reason you came back into the fold of the family business. Because it was on the skids. You liked to think you could resurrect it from the ashes like the phoenix.'

He chuckled. 'You could be right. But aren't you going to ask me what happened to my plane?'

'Stewart gave me the general idea. You can tell me more later.'

'Such restraint. Sometimes, Juliana,' he said with a dry laugh, 'I almost think you don't love me.'

Her heart squeezed tight. 'Whatever would give you that idea?' she tossed off.

He laughed again. 'Can I hope you'll be a bit more enthusiastic about my return later tonight?'

All her insides tightened. 'I would have thought you'd be too tired for that after your little adventure.'

'I slept on the plane.'

The implication behind his words was clear. He wasn't too tired. He would definitely be coming to her bed tonight.

Oddly enough, this thought didn't produce the reaction in Juliana that she might have expected, given her earlier apprehension. It actually sent a hot wave of desire racing through her body, bringing a flushed heat to her face.

She was shocked. She wasn't the easiest woman to arouse, Blake always having to take his time before she was ready for him. She suspected that her mother's promiscuous behaviour had instilled in her an instinctive fear of appearing sexually easy—hence the difficulty she had always found in surrendering her body to a man. Even with Blake, who seemed to know exactly what to do to relax, then excite her, she was still somewhat inhibited. There were several sexual activities and positions she not only would not permit, but which had previously repelled her.

Now, Juliana could hardly believe the images that kept flashing into her mind, or the way her heart was racing.

Had falling in love within the security of marriage finally released in her the sort of sensuality Lily's daughter should always have possessed? Had she subconsciously locked a highly sexed nature away within a tightly controlled shell, for fear of turning out like her mother?

Perhaps. Only time would tell, she realised shakily. Time. And tonight...

'Maybe I'll have a headache,' she said, seeking to defuse her tension with humour.

'I'll bring some aspirin home with me,' Blake countered drily.

'What if I just said no?'

'You never have before.'

'Maybe I've found somebody else to keep me happy while you're away.'

Blake laughed. 'Is that so? Well, you'll just have to tell him your hubby's home and he isn't needed any more. Now I suggest you have a nice relaxing bath and I'll be with you as soon as I can.'

After his abrupt hanging-up, Juliana stared down into the dead receiver, not sure how to take Blake's amused indifference to her taunt about another man. It crossed her mind that he might react the same way even if she hadn't been joking.

Wouldn't he *care* if she had an affair? she worried with a sudden and quite dampening dismay. Was he himself doing the same with other women during his business trips away?

She had never thought to question his faithfulness before, had never been ripped to pieces inside by the shards of jealousy that were even now slicing deeply into her heart. The thought of him touching another woman as he touched her...

A violent shudder ran through her before she was able to pull herself together with some solid reasonings.

Blake had *never* given her a reason to be jealous on his business trips. It wasn't as though he ever took a female secretary or assistant with him. He didn't have one. His faithful Girl Friday was a man—Stewart.

OK, so he didn't ring her every single day as some husbands would. And he never brought her a gift home, to show that he had been thinking of her while he was away.

But she fully understood why he didn't do either of those things.

Once he arrived home he always showed her in bed how much he had missed her, never missing a night for at least a week. Would he be like that if he was having other women on the side? No, of course not, Juliana reasoned. His offhand response was just his being as flippant with her as she had been with him. She was imagining things.

But her imaginings demonstrated perhaps what was to be feared in falling in love. She could almost understand Blake's deep aversion to it. Love made you irrational, panicky, insecure. Especially when that love was not returned.

The automatic kettle made a click as it switched itself off. Juliana stared at it. She didn't feel like coffee any more. A swift glance at the wall-clock showed it was ten to nine. Blake could be here in a little over an hour.

She shivered again. What to do?

Perhaps she should have that bath he'd told her to have. It might relax her, calm her nerves.

Juliana moved slowly from the living-room out into the large foyer from which the semi-circular staircase rose in all its magnificent glory. Hesitating for a moment on the first step, her hand curled over the knob at the end of the elegantly carved balustrade, Juliana's mind slipped back nineteen years to the first time she actually saw this house, and this imposing staircase.

Who would have dreamt that the little girl who had

stared with open-mouthed awe at the riches contained within the hallowed walls of the Preston mansion would one day be mistress of that same house? And who would have believed that she would ever find herself in the same situation as the tragic Noreen Preston, in love with a husband who didn't love her back?

For a moment, Juliana's stomach churned. But then she straightened her spine and continued up the stairs.

There was one major difference between herself and Noreen Preston. *She* was from tougher stock. Far tougher. No way would she ever commit suicide because she found out her husband was having an affair with another woman. She would fight for what she wanted, fight to the death.

And, as of now, she wanted Blake. More than she could ever have envisaged.

CHAPTER TWO

HALF an hour later, Juliana was lying in her bath, remembering that there had once been a time when she and Blake had been so close, she could have told him anything. But of course that had been years ago, and so much had changed since then...

The first time Juliana saw Blake he'd frightened the life out of her. She'd only been nine at the time. It was on her mother's second day as cook in the Preston household. Mr and Mrs Preston had kindly given Juliana permission to use their swimming-pool and, since it was an awfully hot day, smack-dab in the middle of the summer holidays, she had been only too happy to accept their generous offer.

So, garbed in her cheap multi-coloured costume, Juliana made her way out on to the vast back patio and pool complex. And it was while she was gaping at the Olympic-size pool, complete with extravagant surroundings, that the accident happened.

Blake, then fifteen, was making his first attempt at a backward somersault from the diving-board. Apparently, he didn't jump far enough away from the end of the board, for he banged the back of his head during the turn, splashing into the water then sinking like a stone to the bottom.

'Blake!' screamed a girl who was lying sunbathing on a deckchair. Juliana was to find out later that she was Blake's eleven-year-old sister, Barbara. But for now Juliana's attention was all on the unconscious shape at the bottom of the pool.

She didn't stop to think. She simply dived in, dog-paddled down to him and dragged him up to the surface. 'H...help me!' she spluttered out to Barbara, who was standing open-mouthed by the side of the pool.

Somehow, with her inept help, Juliana managed to pull Blake out.

'He's dead!' his sister cried. 'Oh, my God, he's dead.'

'No, he's not,' Juliana refuted, though frightened that he might be. 'Go and tell my mum to ring an ambulance!' she ordered. 'The *cook*!' she screamed when Barbara looked blankly at her. 'My mum's the new cook!'

Barbara ran while Juliana set about doing what she'd seen on television a few times but which she had no real experience with: mouth-to-mouth resuscitation. But she must have done something right, for by the time her mother ran out to tell her the ambulance was on its way Blake started coughing back to consciousness. By the time the paramedics arrived he only needed a little oxygen to be on the way to full recovery.

'I reckon you saved his life, little lady,' one of the paramedics praised.

'Really?' she grinned, widely pleased with herself.

'Yes, really,' the man said. 'Your mum should be very proud of you.'

Behind the ambulance officer's back Barbara

pulled a face at Juliana, which set the tone of their relationship from that day forward. Barbara never let an opportunity go by to express her disgust and disapproval that the cook's child was allowed the run of the house, let alone *her* pool. Blake, however, immediately became Juliana's firm ally, defending her against Barbara's bitchy snobbery and generally being very nice to her.

Oddly enough, despite the six-year age-difference, he really seemed to find Juliana's company enjoyable. Maybe because she was a bit of a tomboy, and would join in with his lcisure activities. They swam together, dived together, played board games together. Juliana also believed he found her a pleasant change from all Barbara's girlfriends who went ga-ga over him all the time. He clearly found their drippy drooling both embarrassing and repugnant.

Still, Juliana wasn't blind. She could see that at fifteen Blake was a well-grown and very handsome young man. His blue-eyed blond looks and well-shaped bronzed body drew the girls in droves. Barbara's classmates found any excuse to visit the Preston household. Not that he ever took any notice of them. They were too young for him, for a start. Generally speaking, he didn't seem to like girls at all. If he *did* have any girlfriends during his high-school years, he kept them a secret.

Juliana was the only female given the privilege of Blake's company and conversation, much to Barbara's friends' pique. They repaid her in a myriad spiteful little ways, from openly insulting her background to pretending to be friendly before cutting her dead. Once they even gave her an invitation to a non-existent birthday party.

Juliana could still remember her humiliation when she turned up at the address, only to be bluntly told there was no party there that day. Not wanting to upset her mother—who'd been so pleased by the invitation—she spent all afternoon in the park before returning home and pretending the party had been fantastic.

It was only when she told Blake later about the incident and he gave her a look of such pained apology that she finally burst into tears. He hugged her, something he *never* did, and told her not to worry, that people like that would eventually get their come-uppance.

But Juliana privately believed the privileged rich rarely got their come-uppance. It was the working-class poor who always suffered, who were put upon and discriminated against. The rich never lived in back rooms or wore hand-me-down clothes. They certainly didn't know what it was like not to be able to go on school excursions because they didn't have the money.

By the time Juliana turned twelve she'd decided that one day she was going to be rich too.

'When I grow up,' she told Blake shortly after her twelfth birthday, 'I'm going to marry a millionaire.'

Blake glanced up from his desk with a surprised look on his face. 'I don't believe you said that. I thought you despised the wealthy.'

Juliana was lying face-down on his bed, her face propped up in her hands. 'I'm going to start a different brand of wealthy. I'll give a lot of my money to charity and be kind to my servants.'

'What do you mean, be kind to your servants?' he said sharply. 'Mum and Dad are kind to your mother. Besides, you always said people shouldn't *have* servants at all.'

'Employees, then,' she argued stubbornly. 'I'll have to employ someone to clean and cook for me. I'm going to have a career.'

'Why have a career,' he scoffed, 'if you're going to marry for money? Rich men's wives don't work. They have lunches and their hair done.'

'I'm going to be different.'

'Are you, by gum?' He laughed at last.

'Yes, I am!'

'And what if you can't find a rich man to marry you?' he mocked. 'The rich marry the rich, or didn't you know that?'

Juliana frowned. She hadn't thought of that. But she wasn't about to have her dream shattered by cold, hard reality. Sitting up abruptly, she tossed her long straight brown hair back over her skinny shoulders, her pointy chin lifting defiantly. 'I'm going to be so beautiful when I grow up that millionaires will be hammering at my door!'

'*You! Beautiful*?'

His laughter cut to the quick. For Juliana knew she was a bit of a scarecrow, with her long, bony body and equally long, bony face. Only her eyes carried any promise of future beauty, being slanty and exotic-looking, their colour a chameleon hazel which changed colour with whatever she was wearing.

'You wait and see,' she pouted. 'My mother says I'm going to grow up quite lovely. She says I could be a model with my height and bone-structure.'

'Your mother has rose-coloured glasses,' Blake muttered. 'About everyone and everything.'

'You leave my mother alone. She's a fantastic person. You're just jealous because your mother hasn't time for anyone except your father!'

'I don't give a damn about my mother,' he scowled. 'Now get lost, rake-bones. I've got to get on with this study.'

'You're always studying these days,' she complained.

'Yeah, well, I want to grow up smart, not beautiful. My HSC is in a couple of months and I have to get well over four hundred to get into my course at uni next year. So for pity's sake get out of here, Juliana, and let me get some work done.'

She flounced out, thinking grouchily to herself that he didn't have to grow up beautiful because he already was, the lucky devil!

Juliana's dream of even becoming passably attractive came to an abrupt halt the following year. Puberty came in a rush and, horror of horrors, she broke out in a bad case of acne. All of a sudden she felt so ugly and awful that during her spare time she remained hidden in her bedroom. To make matters worse, that same year her mother sent her to the same toffee-nosed private school Barbara went to, the result of having saved like a lunatic during her four years' employ at the Prestons'.

Little did Lily know that the sacrifices she had

made for her much loved child's future were not bringing Juliana much present happiness. She was going through hell during her first year of high school among the daughters of millionaires. Never before had the difference between her world and the world of wealth and privilege been so painful. The children of the rich did not tolerate outsiders kindly.

The acne was the last straw for Juliana. Oh, how she would cry when she looked at herself in the mirror every morning. She was absolutely hideous!

Her only reprieve was that Blake was away on campus at university, doing his first year of an economics and law degree. She was afraid he might tease her about her skin. It was bad enough having Barbara calling her names like 'pizza-face' on the way to and from school every day.

But Blake was to be home soon on his mid-term break, and Juliana was simply dreading the day he would come over and call up to her to come swimming with him.

The day dawned, however, and when she refused to come down from the flat above the garages Blake thumped up the stairs, banged on the door and demanded to know what was the damn matter with her.

'I'm not leaving, Juliana,' he pronounced forcefully. 'So you might as well come out here and tell me what's what. And don't give me any garbage about your not liking the water any more because I won't believe you.'

Wretched with embarrassment and misery, she finally opened the door.

'Well?' he said, looking her in the face with only puzzlement on his.

'Can't you *see*?' she wailed.

'See what?'

'My skin,' she groaned.

The light dawned in his eyes. 'Oh, you mean the acne.'

She looked down at the floor in an agony of wretchedness and frustration. 'Of course I mean the acne,' she grumbled.

He put out a hand and tipped up her chin, scanning her face. 'They're not that bad, sweetie,' he said so tenderly that she promptly burst into tears.

'They are too!' she sobbed, and struck away his hand. 'What would you know? You've never had a pimple in your life! They're ugly. I'm ugly.'

Blake sighed. 'You're not ugly, Juliana. Fact is, I suspect you're going to become the beauty you always wanted to be. Why, you've grown so tall and graceful this past year. And you're not nearly as skinny as you used to be,' he added, flicking a rueful glance at her sprouting breasts. 'But if you're so unhappy with your skin, why don't you do something about it?'

'Like what? Mum says there's not much I can do except keep it clean. She said I'll grow out of it in God's own good time.'

'God helps those who help themselves,' he said sharply. 'Come on. I'm taking you to the doctor. I know there are things they can do for acne these days.'

'Do you really think so?' Juliana said hopefully.

'I know so!'

An hour later she came home armed with an antibiotic lotion for her skin which the doctor said had proved very successful with other patients, particularly girls. Juliana set about using it morning and night, and it wasn't long before she saw a quite dramatic improvement.

'It's a miracle!' she exclaimed to Blake in the pool a week later.

'I don't believe in miracles,' he returned with such a dark scowl that Juliana was taken aback. She frowned at him. He'd changed since going to university, she realised with a pang of true regret. Why did people have to change? First herself, and now Blake.

Her eyes followed him as he swam over to the edge of the pool and levered himself out of the water, the action showing a muscle structure in his back and arms she'd never noticed before.

'Have you been doing weights?' she asked.

He shrugged. 'A little. They have a good gym at the uni. It keeps me out of trouble.'

'What kind of trouble?'

His blue eyes flashed with exasperation, but he said nothing.

Juliana swam over and scrambled out to sit next to Blake, blushing when she noticed that one of her nipples had popped out of the tiny bra-top. She stuffed it back in, relieved that Blake wasn't looking at her.

There was no doubt about it, though. She would have to ask her mother for a new costume before the swimming carnival at school next week. This one was getting too small for her rapidly growing body.

'Can I feel your muscles?' she asked Blake, dripping water all over his thighs as she bent over to curve her hands around his biceps. 'Gosh, they're really something. Your back looks fantastic too.'

When she ran a quite innocent hand across his shoulder-blades, Blake stiffened. 'Cut it out,' he snapped, then abruptly dived into the pool.

Juliana stared after him, hurt and confused. What had she done?

But then she sighed her understanding. She'd touched him. Blake hated girls touching him.

Still, she would have thought he didn't think of her as a girl, just as she never thought of him as a boy. They were simply good friends.

It wasn't long, however, before Blake put aside his aversion to girls touching him. A never-ending stream of nubile young women began accompanying him whenever he came home from university.

Blondes, brunettes, redheads—Blake didn't seem to have any preference. The only thing the girls had in common was that none of them lasted very long. A few weeks at most.

At first Juliana had felt a sharp jealousy, for Blake never seemed to have time for her any more. But gradually her feelings changed to bitter resignation. Her close relationship with the son and heir to the Preston fortune had drawn to a close. She was once again nothing more than the cook's daughter, whose presence was tolerated though no longer sought out.

Only once during her school years did she cross

Blake's path in anything other than a 'hi, there, how's things, see you later' fashion. It was to prove a very memorable experience.

She was sixteen at the time. It was the night of her graduation ball to which she had worn Barbara's gown of two years before, given to her mother by an uncharacteristically sweet-tongued Barbara.

'Mummy paid a fortune for this, Lily,' she said as she handed over the exquisite ivory satin gown. 'It seems a shame that it's only been worn once. I'm sure Juliana would look divine in it. Much better than I did. She's so tall and slender.'

Naturally, her kind-hearted and still amazingly naïve mother had not seen the malice behind the offer. All she could see was a dress that she would never be able to afford for her own daughter, a dress fit for a princess.

'Just think, Juliana,' she had said excitedly. 'You'll be able to use the money I was going to spend on your dress to have your hair done and to buy a really good pair of shoes. Maybe an evening bag as well. Oh, you're going to look so beautiful!'

Lily would never have understood the fact that, at the fancy school she took such pride sending her daughter to, no girl would be seen *dead* in a dress another graduate had worn before, no matter how beautiful it was. Though not of this snobbish ilk, Juliana nevertheless shrank from the thought of turning up in Barbara's dress, for Barbara would make sure every girl in her class, as well as their partners, knew whose dress it really was. Blake's sister had already gone to great pains to make sure Juliana was treated like a leper by most of the other girls at school.

But Juliana wouldn't have hurt her mother for the world. So she staunchly wore the dress, ignored the other girls' snide remarks, holding her head high and looking as though she didn't give a damn what anyone said about her. Her cool, even haughty demeanour gave the impression that their snide remarks and sniggering whispers rolled off her like water off a duck's back.

Behind the cool façade, however, lay a deep well of hurt and anger. What right did they have to treat her like this, just because she hadn't been born into money? It wasn't fair! One day, she vowed, she would spit in their eyes, *all* of them—especially Barbara!

She left the ball as early as she could, but she couldn't go home. Her mother would be waiting up for her, anxious to hear the details of the night. So Juliana slipped quietly round the back of the main house instead of going straight up to bed, intent on filling in an hour or two just licking her wounds in private. Barbara and Mrs Preston were away for the night at relatives'. Mr Preston would be ensconced in his study at the front of the house. The pool area would be deserted.

So she was startled to find Blake sprawled in one of the deckchairs, for he wasn't expected home for the summer holidays till the following day.

Juliana quickly noted the whisky glass in his hand and the half-empty bottle of Jack Daniels on the cement beside the chair. This was another of his new habits. Drinking. Though it was usually only beer.

'Well, well, well,' he drawled, his eyes raking over her. 'Is this Cinderella home from the ball? And what a lovely Cinderella she is,' he went on in his now habitually droll fashion. University—or maybe life— had turned Blake into something of a cynic.

For once, Juliana found a retort just as cynical. 'I have no doubt the role of Cinderella fits me very well. But I can't see your sister as my Fairy Godmother, can you?'

Blake's eyebrows shot up in surprise at her acid tone. 'Meaning?'

'Barbara kindly presented my mother with her old graduation dress for me to wear tonight.'

'Aah... I see...'

'Do you, Blake? Have you any idea what it's like being treated like a charity case? No, of course not! You were born with a silver spoon in your mouth.'

'Sometimes one can choke on a silver spoon,' he said darkly, and quaffed back a huge mouthful of drink.

'I haven't noticed *you* choking. Not unless it's on grog,' she added, sweeping over to stand at the foot of the deckchair with her hands on her hips. 'What on earth are you doing, swallowing that whisky like water? Haven't you any respect for your kidneys and liver?'

He swung his legs over the side of the chair and stood up, tall and macho in tight, stone-washed jeans and a chest-hugging blue T-shirt. 'I'm not large on respect tonight,' he muttered.

'And what is *that* supposed to mean?'

'Nothing I can tell you, gorgeous.'

She drew in a sharp breath as his blue eyes moved hotly down her body to where the deep sweetheart neckline of the dress showed an expanse of creamy cleavage. Not a busty girl, Juliana's breasts were nevertheless high-set and nicely shaped. Blake's gaze was certainly admiring them at that moment. His narrowed gaze eventually moved on, travelling down to where the ivory silk ballgown hugged her tiny waist before flaring out into a romantically full, ankle-length skirt.

'That dress looks a damn sight better on you than Barbara,' he said thickly.

His gaze lifted to her face, shocking her with the stark desire she saw in their depths. No boy—or man—had ever looked at her like that before. Blake certainly hadn't.

'Juliana,' he said hoarsely, before doing something that both shocked and fascinated her. Dipping his finger into the glass he was still holding, he reached out to trace a wet trail around the neckline of her dress. This alone made her stand stock-still with eyes wide and heart suddenly pounding. But when he bent his head to start licking the liquid from her by now shivering flesh, a dizzying sensation made her sway backwards. He caught her to him, releasing the glass for it to smash into smithereens on to the concrete around their feet.

His head bent to kiss her with such deceptive gentleness that Juliana was momentarily disarmed. He sipped at her lips, over and over, his hands lifting to slide up into her hair, to lift its heaviness from her skull, his fingertips massaging her head with an almost hypnotically erotic action.

'Juliana,' he whispered against the melting softness of her lips.

'Yes?' came her dazed query.

'Yes,' he repeated huskily. 'That's all you need to say. Yes. I think you could be very good at yes...'

His mouth turned hungry, his lips prising hers apart. But when his tongue slid inside, the strong taste of whisky blasted her back to reality.

She wrenched her mouth away and glared up at Blake, furious with both herself and him.

His eyes were glazed as they opened to look down at her. 'What is it, honey? What's wrong?'

'You're drunk, Blake Preston! That's what's wrong.'

His eyes cleared to an expression of dry amusement. 'So if I weren't drunk, it would be all right? You'd let me kiss you?'

'Yes...no... Oh, don't be silly, Blake. You know we can never be anything but friends. Rich men don't become involved with the daughter of their cook! At least, not seriously!'

A black cloud darkened his face. He looked angry about something for a moment, then wearily resigned. 'I guess you're right.' A sardonic smile pulled at his mouth. 'So what's happened to your plan to marry a millionaire?'

'I know now that the only way I'll ever be rich is to earn it myself.'

'Oh? And how, pray tell? Your school marks have hardly been encouraging.'

'I'm going to study like a lunatic from now on. I can do it. I know I can!'

He cocked his head slightly on one side, staring at her for a few moments before giving a wry nod. 'Yes. I do believe you can. Come on, I'll walk you home...'

Juliana lay awake for ages that night, no longer thinking about the terrible time she'd had at the ball, or the white lies she'd told her mother when Blake delivered her to the door. Her mind was filled with memories of Blake's mouth moving over her cleavage, his strong arms pulling her hard against him, his tongue plunging between her lips.

Had it been the realisation of his drunkness that had made her stop him, or panic at the bewildering responses his actions had evoked in her body? She'd never felt anything like it before. There had been a rush of heat and excitement, combined with a momentary compulsive urge to let go every vestige of thought, to just let Blake do as he willed with her.

What bothered her most was that she seemed to have been responding to *Blake's* need, not her own. Why, she'd never looked upon him as anything more than a good friend before. She'd certainly never had any sexual fantasies over him as she had had over a few television and pop stars she liked. Yet all he'd had to do was look at her with desire in his eyes and she'd instinctively responded to that desire.

Juliana was stricken by the thought that maybe she was beginning to turn out like her mother, whose sexual vulnerability to men who *needed* her was quite pathetic in Juliana's opinion. She didn't want to be like that. She wanted always to be in control of her own actions, her own life. When and if she made love, she wanted it to be because *she* wanted and needed it, not the other way around. Anything else went against the grain!

By the time Juliana felt sleep snatching at her mind, she'd vowed to be on her guard against any repeats of tonight's incident. She would make sure she was never alone with Blake. She would keep other boys at arm's length as well, till she was older, and more in control of her silly self! She also vowed to do what she had boasted to Blake she would do—get a good pass in the Higher School Certificate, go to university and become a success, all by her own efforts!

Over the next two years she astounded both her mother and her teachers with her application. The boys did start hanging around, and even though she did find several of them quite attractive Juliana spurned their attentions, devoting all her time to study, and a smattering of modelling. Though she had not grown up into a classical beauty, her long, silky brown hair, tall, elegant body and exotically sculptured face gave her admission into a good modelling agency who found occasional work for her on the catwalk and behind the fashion photographer's lens.

After an excellent pass in her Higher School Certificate, Juliana began a marketing course at university, while still earning money from modelling on the side. Though not enough to live away from home. Blake, however, was doing well enough as a foreign exchange dealer to move out into a luxurious bayside unit. From gossip she had gleaned he'd quickly become quite the young man-about-town, working hard and playing hard.

It was while Juliana was doing her last year at university that tragedy struck the Preston household. Noreen Preston committed suicide with an overdose of sleeping tablets. Shortly afterwards, her husband Matthew succumbed to a heart attack, leaving behind a plethora of debts and a badly managed, almost bankrupt business.

Suddenly Blake and Barbara were parentless, and without any sizeable inheritance. Even the house carried a second mortgage. Barbara responded by marrying a middle-aged but very wealthy widower. Blake shocked everyone by chucking in his job, selling his flat and returning home to take up the flagging reins of the family company. With new ideas and a lot of hard work he eventually turned Preston's Games and Toys from an old-fashioned, non-profitable organisation into a modern, go-ahead concern whose stock was to become highly sought-after by investors and brokers all over the world.

By the age of thirty Blake Preston had become the toast of Melbourne's business and social worlds. Two years in a row he was voted Victoria's most eligible bachelor by a high-profile women's magazine.

He seemed to crown his worldly successes when he became engaged to Miss Virginia Blakenthorp, one of the débutante darlings of Melbourne's old-money families. It was around this time that Juliana herself—now gainfully employed in the marketing division of a chain of retail stores and living in a small but neat flat near the city—became engaged. To the younger son of the owner of the stores.

His name was Owen Hawthorne. He was twenty-eight and everything any woman could possibly want. Handsome. Polished. Rich.

It would have seemed that both Blake's and Juliana's futures were assured.

Yet one fateful night, the day before Juliana's twenty-sixth birthday and only a few weeks after her mother died, two engagements were broken and a third one entered into. Blake and Juliana were married a month later.

CHAPTER THREE

JULIANA was lying back in the bath, thinking about that strange night, when she heard Blake call out.

'Juliana! Where are you?'

She sat bolt upright, the abrupt action sending bubbles and water spilling over the edge on to the floor.

'I...I'm in here,' came her shaky reply. 'In the bathroom.'

Good God! she thought. Stewart must have driven like a lunatic to have dropped Blake off this early. Or had she been mulling over the past for longer than she realised? Since her wristwatch was out in the bedroom she had no idea of the exact time.

Juliana had just stood up to climb out of the bath when Blake opened the door and walked in.

'Julianna, I wish you'd...' His voice died when she swung round, giving him a full-frontal view of her nude body.

Wide-open hazel eyes found his startled blue ones. Juliana had never ever appeared naked like this before him. Not standing up. And certainly not with bubbles dripping from suddenly hard nipples. A fierce blush zoomed into her cheeks, her embarrassment finding voice in sharp words.

'For goodness' sake, Blake, haven't you ever heard of knocking?' In her haste to get out of the bath to wrap a towel around herself Juliana forgot about the water on the floor. As she hurriedly put one foot down on to the slippery tiles, it shot out from under her.

'Watch it!' Blake cried, racing forward to grab her. When she felt his hands close around her soap-slicked flesh she panicked, and tried to ward him off.

'Don't! I'm all right!'

But he already had a firm hold around her waist, lifting her right out of the water and setting her safely down on the mat in front of the vanity unit.

Did Blake deliberately slide his hands down over her bare buttocks before letting her go?

Juliana knew he probably didn't. Even so, her immediate sexual awareness produced further panic and every muscle in her body snapped tight as a drum.

'A towel,' she choked out. 'Get me a towel.'

Practically snatching the thing from his outstretched hand, she wrapped it quickly around herself sarong-style. Only then did she appreciate that Blake was staring at her in puzzlement.

Juliana knew she was acting exactly the opposite of how she'd vowed to act.

Her covering smile was not as sweetly soothing as she would have liked. 'Thank you. I—er—hope I haven't ruined your lovely suit. It's all damp down the front.'

Blake glanced down at the pale grey three-piecer which he wore most often when travelling, brushing at the waistcoat lightly. 'It'd take more than a few drops of water to ruin this little number.'

Which was true. Worth a small fortune, the mohair-and silk-blend suit fitted his broad-shouldered, slim-hipped body like a glove and never creased, even after the longest flight. Matched as it was at the moment with a crisp white shirt and a darker grey tie, in it Blake looked both coolly suave and utterly in command of himself.

Not so Juliana. She felt a mess, both inside and out. All she could hope for was that Blake would get out of here shortly and give her some breathing space. Meanwhile...

'You must have had a good run from the airport,' she said brightly, 'to get here so quickly.'

'We did. Caught every green light.'

'I thought for a moment I might have lost track of the time.'

When Blake made no attempt to leave the room, simply moving over to lean casually against the white-tiled wall, Juliana turned to face the vanity unit, though still made uncomfortably aware of his presence by his reflection in the mirror. Since they didn't share a bathroom, each having their own, Juliana was not used to being watched going about her everyday ablutions. To have Blake do so at this particular moment in time was unnerving in the extreme.

'Wouldn't you like to go and have a drink while I clean my teeth and stuff?' she asked with another pained smile.

'No. I'd rather stay here and talk to you.'

'Oh...oh, all right.' She shrugged nonchalantly, fully aware that this was to be her first real test. What would the Juliana of a few hours ago have done in the circumstances?

She had no idea. This particular circumstance had not even been in *that* Juliana's repertoire.

So what would a woman desperate to hide her love for her husband do?

Pretend he's not in the room at all, she told herself. Pretend you're quite alone. Pretend you're talking to him on an intercom.

Taking another of the fluffy cream towels from the nearby railing, she proceeded to dry her arms, then turned to lift one foot up on to the side of the bath. 'So tell me all about your little adventure,' she invited casually while she towelled down first one long, shapely leg then the other.

'Nothing much to tell, really. It—cr— Where on earth did you get those bruises?' he interrupted, straightening to frown down at three black and blue smudges on her thigh.

Juliana stared down at them as well, not having noticed them herself till now. 'I have no idea,' she said truthfully. 'Probably knocked into the side of a desk at work. You know how easily I bruise.'

'No,' he returned slowly. 'I don't, actually.'

Juliana was taken aback by the dark suspicion in his voice. Her surprise expressed itself in an edgy laugh. 'What on earth are you implying?'

She stared up at him, seeing a Blake she had never seen before. His face had an awful stillness about it, his normally lazy blue eyes narrowed and darkened till they were slits of cold steel.

Just as suddenly, however, his distrustful expression cleared, a sardonic smile dispelling the tightness around his mouth. He was his old self once more: coolly relaxed and casually indifferent.

'For a moment there I had a picture of you having

a rather different encounter with a desk,' he drawled. 'I should have known better. You're not into that type of sex, are you?'

Juliana's face flamed.

Blake's pat on her cheek was both indulgent and quite patronising. 'My sweet, innocent Juliana. Who would ever have believed it? But I rather like you as you are. It's most…reassuring. Still…'

For a long moment, he just stared into her startled eyes, his hand lingering on her jawline. Juliana could have sworn that he was going to kiss her, the prospect filling her with both dread and the most appalling excitement.

Yes, kiss me, her pounding heart urged him. Kiss me, touch me, take me…

Suddenly, his hand dropped away, his shoulders squaring. 'I think I *will* go down for a drink after all,' he said curtly. 'Join me when you're ready, if you like. If not…I'll join you later.' And, turning abruptly, he strode from the room, leaving Juliana to lean weakly against the vanity unit. When she glanced up into the mirror it was to see wide, glittering eyes, and lips already apart.

She groaned, leaning forward on to curled fists, shutting her eyes against the evidence of her own arousal. God! Whatever was she going to do?

Fifteen minutes later, she was going downstairs, dressed in her favourite dressing-gown, a rather ancient dusky pink velour robe that crossed over the bodice and sashed around the waist. It had deep pockets that one could slide one's hands into and feel very cosy.

Juliana's hands were indeed slid into the pockets as she moved across the entrance hall and towards the main living-room, but she felt far from cosy. Petrified would be closer to the mark. Still, she *looked* relaxed. And that was the primary requisite at the moment.

When she moved through the archway and on to the plush grey carpet that covered the expansive living-room floor, Blake glanced up from where he was stretched out on one of the chesterfields, giving her a small smile of approval.

'It always amazes me how good you look without having to try. There you are, with your face scrubbed clean and your hair pinned haphazardly on top of your head, garbed in a robe that's seen better days, and you still look fantastic. Of course you do move very well,' he remarked, watching her walk into the room.

'And you do flatter very well,' was her cool rejoinder.

'I have no reason to flatter you, Juliana. You're my wife.'

'Oh, charming.'

His chuckle was as droll as her tone. 'So!' Placing his own generous drink on the glass coffee-table in front of him, Blake stood up. 'What will you have to drink?'

'Something strong,' she answered, not without a touch of self-mockery.

'That's not like you.'

A nonchalant shrug disguised her inner tension. 'It's been one hell of a day.'

Blake laughed. 'That's usually *my* line.'

Moving over to the antique rosewood sideboard

they used as a drinks cabinet, he picked up the decanter of whisky and filled a clean crystal tumbler to halfway. Then came several ice-cubes from the silver bucket, cracking as Blake plopped them into the drink.

'This should soothe any frayed nerves you have.' He walked over to where Juliana was standing with her back to the empty fireplace. 'Here…'

She had to take both of her hands out of the shelter of the robe's pockets to accept the glass safely, cupping it firmly so that the drink wouldn't rattle. 'Thank you.'

'That's OK. Come and sit down.'

'I'd rather stand.'

Again, he darted her a sharp look. 'You *are* feeling out of sorts, aren't you? Anything I can help you with?' he asked as he retrieved his drink and joined her by the fireplace.

'Not really. Things didn't go as smoothly as I would have liked with a new product launch this week, that's all,' she exaggerated.

'What went wrong?'

'Oh, nothing major,' she hedged. 'Certainly nothing as dramatic as what happened to you yesterday. Want to fill me in on the details? You weren't in any real danger, were you?'

His lop-sided smile was rueful. 'Let's just say there were a few moments when I thought I might have to change my underwear.'

Juliana's stomach contracted. For Blake to admit as much meant he'd been very close to death and disaster. Very close, indeed.

'I…I'm glad you're home safe and sound.'

Blake's shoulders lifted and fell in a dismissive gesture.

'You *believe* me, don't you?' she urged with a weird flash of fear.

He surveyed her anxious face with a measure of surprise. 'Don't sound so serious, Juliana. Of course I believe you. Is there any reason I shouldn't?'

'Well, I…well, you…I mean…I wouldn't like you to think I would ever want you dead.'

'Of course I don't think that!' He chuckled, though a little darkly. 'You could get everything you want by simply divorcing me.'

She stared as he lifted his glass and quaffed a huge swallow. If she'd wanted evidence of Blake's current attitude to their marriage, she'd just got it. Nothing had changed since the night he'd proposed. Not a thing!

Her sigh was heavy as she lifted her own glass to her lips and drank.

'Tired?' he asked.

'A little.'

'Not *too* tired, I hope.'

'No…' There was a decided lack of conviction in that word.

A sudden strained silence pervaded the room, the only noise the clink of Blake's ice as he drained his glass.

'I think I'll go upstairs and have a shower, then,' he announced, depositing his empty glass on the mantelpiece behind them and striding from the room.

Several seconds later Juliana realised she was holding her breath. She also realised that, no matter how iron-clad her resolve to carry on as though nothing had changed in their relationship, there was one aspect where that was not possible. When Blake came to her bed tonight, it wasn't going to be the same. Not at all.

Would it be agony or ecstasy?

Either outcome worried the life out of her. For while Blake's lovemaking had always pleasured her, she'd never wanted it with this intensity before; had never been *afraid* of what her responses might be. She'd always been content to let Blake make the running, to just be swept along on *his* tide, never her own. Now, she'd discovered that love had its own tide.

Already, waves of desire were racing through her veins, their current strong and relentless. Never again would Juliana want to lie submissive beneath Blake, waiting resignedly for him to rouse her senses to an almost reluctant passion. She suspected that in future she would have to struggle to control a wildly escalating need for all sorts of intimacies, to hold herself in check lest she actually devour the man.

Common sense told her this was the last thing she should do.

Expelling the air from her lungs in a ragged rush, Juliana looked for fortification—and intoxication—in the glass her quivering hands were holding. A few swift swallows and it was empty, save some small bits of unmelted ice.

Whisky had always hit her system hard and fast,

making her mellow. And yes…sometimes quite sleepy. Juliana hoped tonight would be no exception.

No such luck. The whisky, if anything, seemed to spark a recklessness in her.

Why shouldn't I devour Blake if I want to? came the rebellious thought as she swept up the stairs. He's my husband, after all. Why should I hold back, pretend, fake being *less* passionate than I feel like being? It's crazy! Blake would probably be thrilled if I became more adventurous and aggressive in bed. A man of his experience and sophistication couldn't possibly be totally satisfied with our rather bland sex-life.

But no sooner had she decided this than another more sensible and quite insistent voice whispered to Juliana that Blake *was* satisfied; that he would look upon any change in her sexual behaviour with definite disapproval.

Juliana hesitated at her open bedroom door, her gaze ignoring the rest of the exquisitely furnished room to focus on the brass bed that sat proudly against the far wall. Queen-sized and fit for a queen, with its superb antique cream lace bedspread and hand-painted ceramic postknobs, Juliana's bed had once been Noreen Preston's bed.

Thank the lord she hadn't died in it, came the unexpected thought. Noreen's body had been found in a seedy motel on the other side of Melbourne. Still, Juliana suspected that a lot of wretchedness had been fostered between those sheets. If she closed her eyes she could almost hear the poor woman crying; *see* her clinging.

Odd. Juliana had never felt any real sympathy for

Noreen Preston before, the woman having always come across as a neurotic wife and simply dreadful mother. But one never knew the hidden secrets in a marriage, the whys and wherefores behind people's behaviour.

Had the handsome and selfish Matthew Preston enjoyed putting his wife through mental hell? Had he taken advantage of her obsessive love for him by greedily accepting all her attentions while callously dallying behind her back? Had he laughed at her insecurities, telling outrageous lies? Or had he thrown his infidelities in her face, till she couldn't bear any more?

'Juliana…'

She swung round at Blake's voice behind her, a nervous hand fluttering up to her throat. 'You startled me.'

'I didn't mean to.'

Her eyes flicked down over him, trying not to stare.

Some men might have looked funny in the fluffy white towelling robe Blake always wore after showering. He didn't, however. He looked gorgeous, the white colour emphasising the warm golden tan of his satin-smooth skin. If he'd been dark and hairy, the knee-length, open-necked style might not have been quite so flattering. But the adult Blake was no more dark and hairy than the adolescent Blake had been. He still looked like a young golden god, Juliana thought wryly. Her own private Adonis.

'What's the matter, Juliana?'

Blake's unexpected question snapped her eyes up

to his. Had she been staring too much? Frowning, perhaps? Grimacing, even?

Juliana recognised that her heart was pounding madly in her chest. There was no doubt about it. She *would* devour him. The realisation forced her to a decision.

'Actually, Blake, I'm not feeling the best. I really *do* have a headache.'

His steady gaze was disturbingly unreadable.

'It's been getting worse all day,' she went on in quiet desperation. 'First with the problems at work, and then after Stewart called I...I...' She swallowed. 'I was very worried about you, Blake. For a while there I was beginning to think the worst.'

'Is that so? As you can see, though...' he spread his arms wide for a second '...I'm fine.'

'And I'm very happy and relieved you are, but the after-effect of worry is often a headache. Look, you did ask me what was wrong, and I'm telling you.'

'So you are,' he said in a curiously flat voice. 'I'll see you in the morning, then.'

'*Morning*?' she repeated, eyes blinking wide. Blake had never come to her bed in the morning.

His smile was dry. 'For breakfast, Juliana. We usually breakfast together on a Saturday morning, remember?'

Her face flushed with an embarrassed heat. 'Yes, of course. I...I forgot. Tomorrow's Saturday...'

'Don't forget to take some pain-killers before you go to bed,' he advised curtly.

'I won't.' His message was quite clear. Don't have a headache tomorrow night...

Taking her by the shoulders, he planted a cold kiss on her forehead. 'Goodnight, Juliana. Sleep well.'

Again she heard the hidden message. You sleep well, wife, because I certainly won't. I wanted some sex tonight and you turned me away.

Juliana felt rotten. Yet she hadn't really lied. She did have the beginnings of a headache. Probably from drinking that whisky so quickly. She also realised that by tomorrow night her tension would be beyond a joke after spending all day in Blake's company. He would expect her to have breakfast with him, swim with him, go to the races with him, possibly go out to dinner afterwards with friends, then come home and sleep with him. Better she get over the sex hurdle tonight or it might grow too daunting for her to handle.

'Blake…'

'Yes?'

'Just because I have a headache it doesn't mean you can't—um—I wouldn't mind. Really I wouldn't.'

The curl of his top lip showed distaste at her offer. 'Well, *I* would. I'm not so desperate as to force myself on my wife when she's unwell.'

'You wouldn't be forcing yourself on me, Blake,' she said huskily.

'Wouldn't I?' His eyes narrowed as they scanned her strained face.

She couldn't help it. She looked away, for fear of all he might see.

'For pity's sake, let's not make a song and dance about a bit of sex,' he said with offhand brusqueness.

'Tomorrow night will serve just as well. I'm probably more tired than I thought tonight, anyway.'

Whirling away, he was in the process of stalking off down the hallway towards his own room when he stopped abruptly and turned to face a still frozen Juliana.

'One thing before I forget,' he said sharply. 'The door leading in from the garages was unlocked when I got home. That's being a little careless, considering the level of break-ins in this neighbourhood.'

His accusatory tone flustered her. 'I don't usually forget,' she defended, 'but the telephone was ringing as I was letting myself in and it distracted me.'

'I see. Well, try to remember in future. A woman alone is very vulnerable. I would hate to see anything happen to you, Juliana. You're very important to me, you know. Well, goodnight again.'

Juliana stared after his departing figure.

No, I *don't* know! she thought with sudden venom.

I must have been mad to go into a marriage like this, she agonised. Simply mad! Whatever possessed me to accept Blake's cold-blooded proposal that night?

It couldn't have really been his money. Money would never have induced me to put my self-respect on the line like this. It must have been love. I must have been in love with Blake all along!

CHAPTER FOUR

JULIANA blinked amazement at this new line of thought. Shaking her head, she moved slowly into the bedroom, shutting the door behind her. How could she have loved Blake all along without knowing it? It seemed impossible.

Sighing her frustration, she moved over to the brass bed, tossed off her dressing-gown and climbed in between the cool crisp sheets. The pillows welcomed her by now woolly head. Maybe if she could just sleep, things would be clearer in the morning.

Sleep, however, eluded her. It was as though, once this idea had implanted itself in her mind, it refused to let go. She found herself reliving key events in her relationship with Blake, trying to see them through more mature and less emotion-charged eyes.

Finally, Juliana had to accept that a romantic love, as opposed to a platonic love, *might* have lain dormant within her without her knowing it. Blake had come along in her life when she'd been only a little girl, a very lonely little girl. In the beginning, he'd been the father she'd never known; the big brother she'd never had; the close friend she'd always craved.

These roles had clouded the main role a handsome young man might have eventually played for a young girl once she reached puberty: that of boyfriend and lover. But by then the difference in their backgrounds had erected other barriers that made such a relationship undesirable and unwise.

Appreciating these barriers far better than her younger self, Blake kept his distance once Juliana started to grow up, thereby stunting the growth of any unconscious hopes and dreams she had probably been harbouring about him. After all, if she hadn't been secretly attracted to Blake, why had she been so fiercely jealous of his many girlfriends?

Juliana only had to look at the incident after her graduation ball to realise something could easily have flared between them that night if she'd allowed it to. *She* had called a halt to Blake's attempted seduction, put off by the fact that his interest in her was only alcohol-inspired lust. Which it undoubtedly was.

Her own sexual responses that night could not be so easily explained away.

Looking back, Juliana suspected that if she'd given in to those responses back then her love for Blake might have exploded from its platonic-coated shell. But where would that have got her at sixteen? Blake certainly wouldn't have felt impelled to marry her. He simply would have toyed with her, as he'd toyed with all his other girlfriends. She would have been dropped eventually. No doubt about it.

Other questions popped into her mind as she mused about her past behaviour. Why had she guarded her virginity so maniacally all those years, only to throw it away with a kind of despairing indifference the night she heard Blake had become engaged to another woman? And why choose that particular night finally to say yes to Owen's repeated proposals of marriage, if not because she subconsciously accepted that Blake was no longer a possible husband?

Blake…

Her secret hero. Her dream man. Her Prince Charming.

Yet he was hardly a Prince Charming.

Oh, maybe he had been once, before life tainted and warped his judgement of people and relationships. There'd been a kindness, an open-hearted generosity in the adolescent Blake that had drawn Juliana to him. The adult Blake, however, was ruled by a world-weary cynicism, not to mention a wariness of love, that made him capable of all sorts of things.

Juliana could still recall her shock when he'd proposed to her that night. There again, it had been a night of many shocks…

Owen had been the instigator of the first. They'd been about to go out on a dinner-date on the eve of her twenty-sixth birthday. She'd been running late because she'd been kept back at work to finish some problem or other. She remembered she had been putting the last touches to her appearance when Owen had come into her bedroom, watching her in silence while she applied some burgundy lip-gloss that exactly matched her burgundy crêpe dress.

She'd smiled at him over her shoulder as she put in her long dangling gold earrings. It was then that he'd come out with it.

'You do realise you won't be working after we're married, Juliana.'

Her hand froze on the last earring. She hoped she'd heard wrong. Frowning, she forced the last earring in then turned slowly to face her fiancé. 'I do realise I can't stay on at Hawthorne Bros once I'm your wife, Owen,' she agreed. 'That's company policy. But I intend finding another job.'

'No.'

'What do you mean, no?'

'I mean no, you won't be getting another job.'

She could not believe her ears. Owen, playing the controlling husband? If he knew her at all, he would know that was anathema to her.

His handsome face carried an appeasing smile as he came forward to take her in his arms. 'I want you free to travel with me, Juliana,' he said silkily. 'How can we just pack up and go off at will if you're tied down to a job?'

Juliana immediately felt a sense of panic take hold deep within her. She struggled against the awful suspicion that her engagement to this man was one big mistake. 'I have no objection to an extended honeymoon,' she compromised, 'but I can't envisage my life without my own job and my own money.'

'But you'll have all the money you want,' he argued softly. 'I'll open a special bank account for you to cover all your needs. You won't find me lacking in generosity, Juliana. You'll be kept in the manner to which I'm sure you'll quickly become accustomed.'

Juliana only heard one word. *Kept.*

She drew back to stare up at the man she'd thought she loved, thought she wanted to marry.

'I doubt I'd ever get accustomed to being *kept*,' she said shakily.

His laughter was dry. 'Come now, Juliana. You can't tell me you want to go on working in a dreary office when you can live the high life. Just think! You won't have to get up till lunchtime if you don't want to.'

'But I *hate* sleeping in!' she protested, further warning bells going off in her brain.

'That's because you're not used to it. Poor darling, you've had to work so hard just to make ends meet. It will be my pleasure to spoil you. All you have to do in return is be my loving wife. Now that won't be so hard, will it?'

He kissed her full on the mouth, his wet tongue demanding entry. Normally, Juliana didn't mind Owen's kisses. She usually found his ardour comforting, the body contact soothing the deep loneliness within her. Suddenly she found him cloying in the extreme.

Suppressing a shudder, she allowed him a few brief moments before pulling her mouth away, horrified at the growing repulsion within her heart and body. With an apologetic grimace, she eased herself out of his hold. 'Please, Owen, I can't think when you're doing that, and I need to talk to you.'

'I can't think when I'm doing that either,' came his desire-thickened reply. 'I'm mad about you, Juliana. You must know that.'

She stared at him. Yes, she did. But was madness love? And what of her own feelings? It was hard to keep telling herself she was in love with the man when his kiss just now had repelled her so. Just think-

ing about going to bed with him again made her feel
sick to the stomach.

There was no doubt about it. She could not go
through with this marriage.

'I won't ever give up working,' she said firmly.
'It's who I am.'

Owen's face showed exasperation. 'Who you are?
What kind of crap is that? You're Juliana, my fiancée,
soon to be my wife!'

'I don't think so…' Looking down, she began removing the diamond engagement-ring from her finger. 'I…I'm sorry, Owen,' she said as she held it out
to him.

He stared down at her outstretched hand. 'You
must be joking.'

'Unfortunately, no. But surely you can see that
marriage between us wouldn't work. We just don't
want the same things in life. It's best we found that
out now, before it was too late. Please, Owen…take
the ring.'

He backhanded her fingers with a vicious slap,
sending the ring flying across the room. 'Keep the
bloody thing!' he snarled. 'You might need it to pawn
when you're starving. And you will be, honey, if you
stay in this town. Come Monday you won't have a
job, a reference, or a reputation. You'll find life can
be pretty tough on the bastard daughter of a crummy
cook who hasn't the brains to know what side her
bread's buttered on. You stupid bitch! You could
have had it all! But what can you expect from the
gutter class? I should have listened to my friends.'

He stormed out of the flat, leaving Juliana to stare,

pale-faced and wide-eyed, after him. Shock was her first reaction, for she had never seen that side of Owen before, never dreamt he could be so violent and vengeful.

But shock was soon replaced by a crippling anxiety. Owen had the wealth and power to do what he threatened. She was a woman alone in the world with no one to turn to, no one to help her. No one except…

'Blake,' she whispered aloud.

She didn't stop to think if he would be home. She simply called a taxi and went over to the Preston house and rang the front doorbell. Blake's new cook-housekeeper answered, a dour widow named Mrs Dawson.

'Yes?' the woman asked suspiciously before recognising Juliana. 'Oh, it's you, Miss Mason.' Juliana had met Mrs Dawson when she'd come over to remove her mother's effects a few weeks before. Not that there had been a lot. Some clothes and jewellery. A few ornaments and photographs. Not much to represent a whole life. When Juliana had expressed as much to Blake that weekend, he'd said that *she* was her mother's legacy to the world.

'Lily was very proud of you, Juliana,' were his parting words that day.

Juliana closed her eyes for a second. Oh, Mum, I wish you were still alive. I need you, need your love and support. I'm frightened.

'Is there something I can do for you, Miss Mason?' the housekeeper asked.

'I have to speak to Blake. Is he home?'

'I'm afraid not. Would you like to leave a message?'

What possible message could she leave? Blake, I've jilted Owen and he's going to take revenge by blackening my name and making sure I can't get a decent job in Melbourne?

You didn't put such a message in the hands of a stranger.

'I need to see him personally. Can I wait, do you think? Will he be coming home tonight?'

Mrs Dawson looked dubious. 'He might be very late…'

'I don't mind. I really need to see him. It's a matter of life and death.'

Mrs Dawson sniffed down her not inconsiderable nose. 'Well, I suppose you can wait, if you must.'

'I must.'

'Come into the family-room then. There's a television there. I was about to watch the Friday night movie.'

Mrs Dawson retired at ten-thirty after the movie finished, an incomprehensible thriller that had about as much suspense as a parliamentary sitting. Not that Juliana was in a fit state to view television. Still, she had to do something while she awaited Blake's return. She was sitting there blankly watching the screen around eleven-thirty when she heard a car rumble into the garages.

Blake was home.

Jumping to her feet, she raced into the kitchen, where she practically collided with him on his way through.

'Juliana!' He smiled for second when he first realised whom he'd run into. But then a frown claimed his smile. 'What on earth are you doing here at this hour?'

'Waiting for you.'

'But why?'

'I...I need help.'

'What kind of help?'

'It's hard to explain. Do you think I could make us both a cup of coffee while I tell you? This could take some time...'

'To hell with coffee. Let's have a real drink. I'm in dire need. Follow me.'

'What's wrong with *you*?' she asked as she hurried after him into what had once been his father's study. It was not a room she'd been in often, certainly not since it had been redecorated. Gone was the old-world stuffy look, replaced by sleek modern lines to match its new occupant. The colours were predominantly grey and black, the curtains a dark red. Blake's black trousers and grey silk shirt blended perfectly.

He shot her a rueful glance from behind the built-in corner bar. 'I doubt you'd be interested. You'd only say it serves me right, that rich bastards like myself deserve all we get. Or has your attitude to rich bastards changed since you got engaged to the honourable Owen Hawthorne?'

Sighing, Juliana lowered herself into a squishy black leather armchair. 'Not exactly.' Her voice reeked with an acid bitterness. 'If anything, it's got worse.'

Blake's eyebrows shot up. 'I take it all is not well in lovers' land?'

'I'm going to flush his engagement-ring down the toilet when I get home! After I've found it, that is.'

Blake laughed. 'I take it you've had a little spat?'

'Hardly little. And it's not a laughing matter, Blake. The man's threatening to strip me of my job and my reputation. He says I won't ever get a decent position in Melbourne again.'

'Good God, Juliana, whatever did you do? Have you been playing around behind his back or something?'

Juliana shot Blake a savage look. 'Is that what you think of me? That I'm no better than a two-timing tramp?'

His shrug was irritatingly nonchalant. 'I think you're a very beautiful, ambitious young woman who always said she'd marry a millionaire. Can I be blamed for thinking that love might not have come into the arrangement, and that you might have become a fraction bored with Owen's performance in bed? I've heard rumours that he wouldn't get into the *Guinness Book of Records* as the world's greatest lover.'

Juliana wished she could have stopped the fierce blush coming to her cheeks. She'd often thought that Owen wasn't the most skilful of lovers. He was much too fast. But, considering her own tendency to be less than passionate in bed, she had brushed aside any concern over the matter. She'd already come to the conclusion that sex was overrated, anyway.

Still, Blake's assumption that a man's ineptness in

bed excused faithlessness annoyed her. As did his assumption that she was little more than a cold-blooded gold-digger.

'I'll have you know that I am not into the casual bed-hopping your lot seem to indulge in,' she countered sharply. 'I also would not dream of being unfaithful to the man I was engaged to. To me, an engagement is as serious a commitment as marriage. When I marry, it will be for life! That's why I broke my engagement. *I*, not Owen. I knew it wouldn't work out.'

'Why wouldn't it work out?' Blake came forward with a couple of glasses filled with whisky and ice. He pressed one into her hands and sat in a chair adjacent to her, watching her face as she struggled to find the right words.

'I...I...'

'Didn't you love him?' came the probing query.

Juliana sighed. 'I *thought* I did...'

'But you realised you didn't.'

'Yes.'

'When?'

'When he demanded I give up work after we were married.'

Blake laughed. 'Stupid man. That would have been the kiss of death with you. Clearly he doesn't know you very well.'

Juliana couldn't help it. She laughed too. But then she sobered. 'Whatever am I going to do, Blake?'

'It's quite simple, really, if you're prepared to put aside the romantic notion of marrying for love.'

She stared over at him. 'I'm not sure what you're

getting at. I'm not going to change my mind and marry Owen. Even if I loved him, I wouldn't marry a man who demanded I give up everything for him. I don't believe in that type of love.'

'Believe me, neither do I,' Blake returned drily. 'But I'm not suggesting you still marry Hawthorne. I'm suggesting you marry me.'

Juliana was lost for words. For a second, a strange elation swept through her. Till she remembered one crucial factor. 'But you're already engaged!' she burst out.

'Actually, no…I'm not. I broke it off tonight. That's why I was home early.'

'But…but *why*?'

His expression was deadpan. 'Would you believe I found out tonight that Virginia was planning to do what Owen wanted you to do?'

'What? Give up her job after the wedding?'

His smile held no humour as he nodded. 'Perverse, isn't it?'

She could think of nothing to say. Knowing Blake as she did, she knew that he would shrink from having a wife staying home and devoting herself entirely to him.

'Did…did you love her?' she asked at last, the question sticking in her throat for some reason.

He shrugged. 'What's love? I enjoyed making love to her. I also thought she would make a good mother. I want children, Juliana.'

'And Virginia didn't?'

'Not for donkey's ages. That was the straw that broke this camel's back.'

'I...I see.'

'I thought you would. You know me as well as I know you. So what do you say? If you marry me, Juliana, you won't have to worry about Owen Hawthorne's threats. I'll make sure they come to nothing. I'll also make sure you get a really good job, something even more satisfying than you have at the moment.'

Juliana could only shake her head. 'Blake, this is crazy!' Yet, crazy as it was, she could not deny she felt quite excited by the idea.

'Why is it crazy? You're everything I could possibly want in a wife—beautiful, intelligent, independent. And you'd make a good mother too. You *want* children, don't you?'

'Yes, of course.'

'I thought so. You had a good example of maternal love.'

'Aren't you worried that if I said yes I might be marrying you for your money?'

He smiled. 'Not at all. In fact, it would please me if that were the case.'

'Blake!'

'You don't honestly think I want you madly in love with me, do you?' he retorted curtly. 'I need that kind of marriage like I need a hole in the head. It will be quite enough if you like and respect me as much as I've always liked and respected you.'

She flushed with pleasure at his words. But the pleasure was tinged with worry. 'But...but what about sex?'

'What about it?'

'I...I don't think I'm very good at it.'

His eyebrows shot up. 'I find that hard to believe.'

She sighed. 'Well, believe me, it's true.'

'The girl I kissed on her graduation night was not even remotely frigid. You let me worry about the sex, Juliana. So what do you say? Will you marry me?'

Her lips remained pressed tightly together, even though the temptation to just say yes was quite strong.

'Think of the alternative,' he argued softly. 'No job; no reputation; no future. As my wife, you'll hold a position of power and privilege in this town. No one will turn their nose up at you, believe me. They'll kowtow and grovel. And no daughter of ours will ever have to wear a second-hand gown to her graduation...'

Was it this last incisively timed remark that made up her mind for her?

Juliana had thought so at the time; had thought her decision to marry Blake had been one of bitter practicality.

Now she knew different.

She'd wanted to marry Blake all along, loved him all along. But she would never have what she really wanted: his love in return.

'Oh, Blake...Blake,' she cried, and turned to bury her face into the pillow.

CHAPTER FIVE

'MORNING.' Blake breezed into the kitchen dressed far too sexily in a pair of tight stone-washed jeans and a blue windcheater the exact colour of his eyes. His thick tawny hair, Juliana noted, was still darkly damp from the shower, and trying to curl. It always did that when it was going to rain.

'Morning,' she returned crisply, and lowered her eyes again to the frying-pan, a silent groan echoing a painful acceptance that her sexual awareness of Blake had only increased overnight, as she'd feared it would. As though in readiness for this frustrating event, she herself was wearing a loosely fitting tracksuit in a very nondescript grey flannel.

Blake perched up on one of the kitchen stools. 'How are you feeling this morning?' he asked. 'Better?'

'Much better, thank you.'

Normally, Juliana liked Saturday breakfast, liked the relaxed informality of Blake chatting away to her while she performed her one cooking chore of the week. Today, she was far from relaxed.

'You don't look all that great,' he remarked.

Juliana gave him a dry look. 'I'm fine. Stop fussing. If I did that to you, you'd give me short shrift.'

He laughed. 'So I would. But maybe you should have a nap this afternoon. You've got dark rings under your eyes.'

'Aren't we supposed to be going to go to the races this afternoon?'

'Nope. Rain's forecast. I can't bear the races in the rain. Besides, I thought two trips to Flemington in one week might be too much for you. I know you're not *that* keen. Or have you forgotten what next week is?'

Juliana groaned out loud as she remembered it was the first week in November, Melbourne Cup week. Usually she avoided the famous spring racing carnival, because the crowds were horrendous, but the company she worked for, Femme Fatale Cosmetics, had booked one of the promotional marquees for Oaks Day on the Thursday—Ladies' Day. In her position as public relations officer, she would be obliged to go.

'Damn,' she muttered. 'I'll have to buy a new outfit, hat and all. Are you coming with me on the Thursday? You weren't sure when I told you about it before.'

'Sorry. Can't. From what Stewart told me last night, the Sydney branch could do with a good shake-up. I'm going to fly up there on Monday and stay the week.'

The news that Blake was going away so soon after his return did not depress Juliana as much as it would have done a day ago. She almost felt relieved. She certainly looked up at her husband with a brightening smile on her face. 'That's all right. I'll find someone else to go with me.'

She was startled by Blake's answering scowl. 'Well, you don't have to sound so happy about it. I thought you liked my company.'

'I *do*!'

'Do you? I'm beginning to wonder after last night.'

Juliana was taken aback—and somewhat annoyed—by his nasty tone. It was so unjustified. 'Blake, I had a headache. And, if you remember correctly, I didn't refuse to sleep with you. You *chose* not to.'

'Out of consideration for you,' he pointed out testily.

'Out of deference to your male ego, more likely!' she shot back. 'You don't consider *me*, Blake. You only ever consider *yourself*!'

For a long moment, they stared at each other, both angry, yet shocked as well. Blake especially. Juliana had never spoken to him like this before, had never accused him of callous selfishness.

His expression was unlike any Juliana had ever seen on Blake. He was pale. Shaken. Yet simmering with a barely held fury. 'My dear Juliana,' he said, his low monotone evidence of the difficulty he was having in containing his temper. 'You knew full well the sort of man I was when you married me. I *am* selfish, I admit it. But not in a sexual sense. If I were a selfish lover, I would have spent the night with you anyway, and to hell with your feelings!'

'You *never* spend the night with me,' she flung back resentfully. 'And it's *often* to hell with my feelings!'

He glared at her, his blue eyes getting colder by the second. The smell of burning bacon was filling the kitchen but both of them ignored it, each equally intent on venting their own anger.

'If by that remark you're saying I *don't* always satisfy you in a sexual sense, then you're the best darned faker in the business! Even on our wedding night, when you were as nervous as a kitten, I managed to do the right thing by you. If that wasn't my considering your feelings then I don't know what it was!'

Juliana flushed guiltily as she recalled her wedding night. Blake was right. That could have been a disaster, she'd been so nervous and uptight.

They hadn't gone away for a honeymoon after their simple register office ceremony; Blake had not wanted a big white wedding or any fuss. She had agreed at the time, since she had still been somewhat embarrassed over the speed of their marriage, a mere month after Blake had proposed.

Yet during that month not once had Blake touched her in an intimate or sexual manner, except for a couple of quick goodnight kisses. Juliana found herself on her wedding-day wishing that he had, so that the night ahead didn't loom as such unknown territory. Questions kept flashing through her mind all day. Would she be as hopeless as she had been with Owen in bed? Would she find herself tensing up as she always did once her clothes were removed? Would she always be left feeling inadequate and guilty?

She was an intelligent woman and knew that all the blame could not be put on Owen for her failure to find fulfilment on the occasions when she'd had sex with him. When she'd told Blake she wasn't any good at sex, she had meant it.

So when the time had come to undress, that first night, she'd been almost in a state of frozen panic. Blake had recognised that she was a cot-case, and in deference to her nerves—or so she had thought at the time—had told her to shower and pop into her own bed and turn out the light.

She had done what he suggested, but had still been literally shaking when he'd finally come into the room and slipped between the sheets.

'You're naked!' she gasped.

'And you're not,' was his dry reply.

'Yes, well, I...I...'

'Hush,' he said, and gathered her close. 'We'll just talk till you stop shaking.'

'T-talk?'

'Yes, talk. You were always pretty good at talking. Maybe if we start with something you *are* good at we'll get your confidence up and things can progress from there.'

'I wouldn't b-bet on it if I w-were you,' she returned, her teeth chattering.

'We'll see, honey, we'll see. So tell me about your new job. Do you like working in public relations rather than marketing?'

And that was how he went on, asking her question after question till her mind was totally distracted from the sex that was to come. It was only later that she realised that somewhere along the line he had subtly started touching her, stroking her, kissing her. First on her shoulder, then her neck, her ear, her cheek, her forehead, her nose, and finally...her mouth.

It was at that point that the question-and-answer technique had given way to a more direct line of action. Not that Blake had turned animal or anything. He'd remained patient and gentle, skilfully removing her nightwear without frightening her, after which he'd showed her that passion did not necessarily have to be either savage or wild. It could be slow-building and sweet. Blake whispered soft, tender endearments to her while he caressed her breasts and kissed her mouth, telling her she had a beautiful body and that he wanted to lose himself in it.

Which he eventually did. But not roughly, and certainly not quickly. She remembered how surprised she'd felt at first when it had looked as if he would never stop. Not that it wasn't pleasant. It was. No...*more* than pleasant. It was quite exciting, causing her heart to race and an alien heat to invade every corner of her body.

She'd felt vaguely embarrassed by her responses, the way her lips fell apart to let escape her rapid panting, the way her body started arching up to meet Blake's powerfully deep surges. And then... Oh, God, then she'd felt as if everything was squeezing so tightly inside her. She'd cried out in a type of startled shock, but soon her cry had turned to a sensuous gasp followed by an even, shaming moan, then finally to a long, contented, shuddering sigh.

Juliana flushed again at the memory of that

night, and all the nights since when she'd moaned beneath Blake's skilful hands.

But moans could mean many different things. Physical satisfaction perhaps, but also pain, as well as emotional torment. Would she moan a different type of moan tonight?

'You can't deny that I satisfy you in bed, Juliana,' Blake reiterated with some asperity.

'There are many types of satisfaction,' she muttered, truthfully but perhaps unwisely.

His glare was harsh. 'Meaning?'

Juliana finally realised that she had crossed over into very dangerous territory with this argument.

She shook her head and turned her attention to the already charred bacon. 'I'll have to cook some more. This is ruined.'

'Don't brush me off, damn you!'

Juliana stared up at Blake's now standing figure. The muscles in his face were taut, his jaw squared angrily, his fists clenched on the counter-top. God, he looked as if he wanted to hit her.

She scooped in a deep, steadying breath, letting it out slowly. 'I'm not brushing you off. You're right and I'm wrong. You're a wonderful lover and you always satisfy me, OK?'

'No, it's not OK. You're obviously disgruntled about something but won't come out with it!'

'It's nothing, Blake.'

'So you won't tell me.'

'There's nothing to tell!' she insisted.

'You're lying, Juliana. Something's troubling you and you don't have enough confidence—or *guts*—to tell me.'

She sighed. 'Don't make a mountain out of a molehill, Blake. It's nothing. Honestly. I've just been out of sorts lately, that's all. Please sit back down and I'll cook us some more breakfast.'

For a few startling moments she thought he was going to stalk out of the room. It would have been a most uncharacteristic gesture on Blake's part. He was not given to violent moods, or fits of temper. A dry sarcasm was the furthest he went in expressing disapproval or anger.

Juliana watched with a measure of astonishment as he battled with his emotions. Briefly it looked as if he *was* going to act like a typically infuriated spouse.

But then the old Blake resurfaced and he shrugged offhandedly, the tense lines in his face melting away. 'I guess I'm not used to your being temperamental,' he said with wry relief in his voice.

Juliana's fingers tightened around the plastic scoop she was holding, lest she lash out at him with it. If only he would show her for once that he really cared about her. If only he *would* storm out of the room, or just lose his temper. Anything would be better than this detached persona he hid behind all the time.

But she said nothing, did nothing, merely went on with cooking some more breakfast, letting Blake move the conversation round to less threatening topics. Yet all the while, underneath, she remained troubled. Where would all this end? How soon before she blew up again over some inconsequential matter, simply because she wanted more than Blake could give?

The problem seemed insurmountable. As much as she'd thought last night that she would do anything to save her marriage, Juliana now wasn't so sure. Maybe trying to save this marriage would prove too costly...

The telephone ringing towards the end of breakfast startled Juliana, making her jump up from her stool. Her nerves were obviously still on edge. Blake darted her an odd glance before reaching up to lift the receiver down from the wall. 'Yes?' he answered nondescriptly.

Nothing could be gleaned from Blake's end of the conversation, either who was calling or what it was all about.

'Hi, there... Really? That's thoughtful of you... Yes, we would... Send them over in a taxi... I'll pay for it... Thanks again... Yes, we will... Bye.'

'What was that all about?' she asked as he hung up.

'Jack Marsden had tickets for himself and Gloria to see *Phantom of the Opera* tonight but they can't go. Gloria's mother's ill and they have to visit her this weekend. He knows how much you like the show so he immediately thought we might like to go. He's sending the tickets over in a taxi.'

'Oh, how marvellous!' Juliana exclaimed, instantly excited despite the events of the morning. She'd seen the show for the first time earlier that year and had been dying to go again, but all the good seats were booked out months in advance.

'But how did he know I liked the show?' she asked, and started to clear up.

'I guess I must have mentioned it to him after we went last time, and, being the canny business-man that he is, he remembered. Jack wants me to invest some money in his construction firm. He'd go and buy tickets on the black market if he thought it would get him in my good books.'

Juliana could not help a sad little sigh. 'Why do you have to be such a cynic?'

'A realist, Juliana, not a cynic.'

'I can't see the difference.'

A dark cloud marred his beautiful blue eyes as he looked at her. 'You know, Juliana, I always thought you liked me.'

'Don't be silly, Blake, I *do* like you.'

'But not my so-called cynicism.'

'That's right.'

There was a short, sharp silence. Juliana bent to the task of clearing up.

'It will be our first anniversary in two months,' he resumed abruptly.

She looked up, forcing a smile to her lips. 'Yes, it will be. Why do you mention it?'

'I thought I might remind you of the agreement we made before we were married that if after the first year we thought our marriage wasn't working out, or if either of us did something foolish like fall in love with someone else, then we would call it quits.'

Juliana swallowed. She hoped she didn't look as sick as she felt. 'What…what are you trying to say? *Have* you fallen in love with someone else?'

His expression was startled. 'Don't be ridiculous. Love and I had a parting of the ways years ago. Good God, what a ghastly idea!'

'Then what *are* you trying to say?'

'I'm not exactly sure. I did think you were happy. But last night, and this morning...' He shrugged, clearly confused by the situation.

Yet his confusion touched Juliana. She wanted to stop what she was doing, take him in her arms, hug him, tell him she would never leave him.

Of course she couldn't do that. All she could do was try to verbally reassure him that she *was* happy, that she would *never* leave him. But before she could say a single word, he swept on, mocking in his self-reproach.

'Hell, what am I doing, asking you for reassurance like an insecure child, just because you're in a bit of a mood? I'm quite sure that if you wanted out of this marriage you'd tell me. You've always been as straight as a die.' His wry grin dismissed any lingering irritation. 'So! What are we going to do for the rest of the day?'

Juliana felt quite annoyed with him. There he'd been, about to lock horns with real emotions, real feelings, however confusing they might be. And what had he done? Once again darted behind that impenetrable shield, the one that closed tight around his heart, the one that shut out anything that could make him seem vulnerable in any way.

'I don't know about you,' she returned sharply, 'but I have to go shopping for clothes. Then I have to get my hair trimmed, after which I've been ordered to take a nap, since I have horrible dark rings under my eyes. But, since *you* have nothing to do, you can start by putting these dishes in the dishwasher!'

And with that she dropped everything, spun round and stalked from the kitchen, uncaring that Blake was gaping after her with his mouth open and blue eyes blinking wide.

CHAPTER SIX

JULIANA returned to the house from her shopping and hairdressing expedition as late as she possibly could, informing Mrs Dawson on the way through that she would have a small tray of toasted sandwiches in her room rather than a sit-down meal that night.

'What about Mr Preston?' the housekeeper asked. 'What will he be having?'

Juliana stopped and frowned. 'Hasn't he said anything to you about our going out to see *The Phantom of the Opera* tonight?'

'Not a word,' the woman sniffed. 'He left shortly after I arrived back this morning. I think he went out to play golf, since he took his golf-clubs with him.'

'Golf? In the rain?'

'Rain doesn't bother a man if he wants to play golf,' Mrs Dawson humphed. 'My Fred used to play all weekend, come rain, hail or shine. Can't see the attraction myself. A lot of walking and very little playing.'

'I couldn't agree more,' Juliana said with a small smile. She imagined poor Fred was only too glad to be out of the house and away from his bossy wife.

Suddenly, and quite unexpectedly, the other woman smiled too, showing good teeth behind her thin lips and quite attractive dimples in her cheeks. For once Mrs Dawson looked the fifty-five she was rather than a sour sixty-five. Then she did something else that astounded Juliana. She gave her a compliment. 'Your hair looks good that length, Mrs Preston.'

'Oh, do you think so?'

Juliana hadn't been too pleased with the hairdresser when she'd cut off much more than her usual one-inch trim, leaving it swinging just on her shoulders rather than resting down on her shoulder-blades. It wouldn't have happened if she hadn't been so distracted over Blake, and while all the girls in the salon had said it suited her she hadn't been too sure. Yet here was Mrs Dawson actually smiling at her and agreeing with them. In that case, it had to be true.

'It's still long enough to put up if you want to,' the housekeeper advised her with her usual practicality.

'Yes, I suppose so. I hope Blake likes it.'

'I doubt Mr Preston will even notice. Men don't notice such things about their wives. They only notice on *other* ladies.'

Juliana was inclined to agree with her. Still, the caustic comment underlined the fact that maybe dear old Fred had been doing a little more than playing golf during his lifetime. 'He certainly won't notice tonight, since I'm going to put it up.'

'When would you like me to bring up your tray, Mrs Preston?' the housekeeper asked with yet another astonishing smile.

Juliana found it hard to get used to the house-keeper's unexpected warmth, but she was not about to lose the opportunity to become friendly. The woman's stiff attitude towards her had been hard to live with. 'Not till six,' Juliana said. 'Oh, and Mrs Dawson...'

'Yes?'

'Please call me Juliana.'

The housekeeper was taken aback, yet clearly pleased. Perhaps she never disliked me at all, Juliana decided. Maybe Blake insisted when he employed her that she keep her distance. That would be just like him.

This last idea was almost confirmed by the woman's saying warily, 'But...but what about Mr Preston?'

'You can call *him* anything you darned well like,' Juliana said firmly. 'But in future *I* will only answer to Juliana.'

'In that case, you'd better call me Susanne.'

'Susanne. What a lovely name!' Juliana beamed. 'But enough of this girl-talk; I'd better get a move on if I'm to be ready on time.'

'Anything I can do to help? Any ironing?' Susanne Dawson nodded towards the parcels Juliana was carrying.

'No, these aren't for tonight. They're for Ladies' Day at the races next Thursday. I'm going to wear my green velvet tonight.'

'Ah, that's a lovely dress. But you're right, it would look better with your hair up. Then everyone can see the pretty sweetheart neckline. Better shake a leg then, Mrs—' She broke off with a wry chuckle. 'Better hurry, Juliana. I'll be up on the dot of six with a tray.'

Juliana laughed as she raced up the stairs. But, as

she swept into her bedroom and looked at that bed again, any feelings of buoyancy faded. Not even the prospect of seeing her favourite musical in a couple of hours could revive her spirits. All she could think about was afterwards…

'You're looking lovely tonight, Juliana,' Blake said blandly on the way to the theatre in a taxi.

She slanted a long, thoughtful look his way. He was sitting there, staring away from her through the passenger window to his right, casually resplendent in pale cream trousers and a shirt, a blue-grey blazer lending the outfit a slightly nautical look.

'Thank you,' she returned just as non-committally, thinking to herself how like Blake it was to come home shortly after she had that afternoon and not say a word about the morning's altercation; how like him not to question her arrangements about that night's meal; how *very* like him to compliment her appearance without really looking at her.

'Susanne thinks this colour looks well on me,' she added with a perversely mischievous smile. For she knew her remark would draw a reaction.

His head turned, his fair hair glinting as they passed under a bright street-light. 'Susanne? Who's Susanne?'

'Our housekeeper.'

He lifted a single eyebrow. 'Since when have you two been on first-name basis?'

'Since today.'

'And what brought that on? You know I like to keep my employees at arm's length.'

'Yes. But I don't.'

He stared at her for a few seconds. 'What in God's name is bugging you, Juliana? This can hardly be some sort of women's liberation kick, since you'd have to be the most liberated woman I know. I don't make you answer to me for anything.'

'Good,' she snapped. 'Then I don't have to explain why I've chosen to call Mrs Dawson by her first name, do I?'

She saw the anger well up in his eyes and revelled in it. Go on, she urged in silent desperation. Lose your temper with me, right here in this taxi, in front of a stranger. *Do it*!

He sucked in a ragged breath. His blue eyes glittered dangerously. His fists were clenched tightly by his side.

But, in the end, he didn't lose his temper. Taking a few moments to control himself, he eventually presented to her a totally composed face. Or was it a façade? Juliana had to admit that a muscle still twitched in his cheek. Was that evidence of the intensity of the struggle that was going on inside him? Or simply a sign of male anger that she should have put him in such an invidious position? Juliana knew Blake would be hating this.

'No,' he said in a low, deadly voice. 'You don't. Now if you don't mind I would like to terminate this conversation. *Right now*,' he bit out under his breath. 'I can't abide couples who make scenes in public.'

Juliana knew when she had pushed an issue as far as she could. Besides, what had she hoped to achieve? Was this how her love for Blake was going to take voice from now on, by her trying to goad him into an emotional response, no matter what it was?

She sighed her depression at living life on such a tightrope.

'They're still working on the road outside the theatre,' the taxi driver said just then over his shoulder. 'But I'll get you as close as I can.'

There was an atmosphere of excitement before each performance of *Phantom of the Opera*, the musical that had already become legendary, and in a way the traffic bedlam outside the old Princess Theatre only added to that air of excitement. Juliana found herself caught up in it the moment she climbed out of the taxi. People were pouring out of tour buses; others were being dropped off by car and taxi; still more simply walked up from where they'd either parked or alighted from trams.

'Do you want to fight your way through for a drink at the bar,' Blake asked as they made their way slowly towards the crowded entrance, 'or shall we go straight to our seats?'

'I suppose we might as well head for our seats,' she said with a frowning glance at the even more crowded bar on the left. Really, both the foyer and the bar were far too small, but it was the only theatre in Melbourne—in Australia for that matter—that had the kind of stage that could accommodate such a show as *Phantom*. It also brought an enormous amount of tourist trade to Melbourne, so Juliana supposed the locals couldn't complain. Still, she would have liked a drink, a fact which Blake must have noted.

'I'll get you a glass of champagne at half-time,' he promised.

The show was as marvellous as it had been the first time Juliana had seen it, even though there had been some changes of cast since then. When the lights came on for the interval she gave a huge sigh of ragged pleasure.

'Isn't it a wonderful show?' she said. 'Spectacular and stirring and oh, so emotional. You can't help feeling sorry for the Phantom; he does love Christine so…'

Blake turned to her with a sardonic smile on his face. 'I didn't realise you were such a romantic, Juliana. The man's a maniac and a murderer. My sympathies go to Raoul, not to mention the theatre owners.'

'Yours would,' she muttered.

His chuckle was dark. 'Because I'm an unfeeling bastard, or a businessman?'

'Aren't they one and the same?'

Juliana saw his eyes narrow with a flash of anger, but then he stood up to glance around the rapidly emptying seats. 'If I don't head for the bar post-haste I won't be back before the curtain goes up for the second half. Do you want to go to the Ladies'?'

'No. I'll just sit here.'

'OK.'

Juliana sighed as she watched him slip lithely through the groups of departing people. No doubt he would still get served fairly quickly. Blake had that effect on waiters and barmen.

She was sitting there, feeling unhappy with herself

for the way she kept making inflammatory remarks to Blake, when the sounds of merriment behind her drew her attention. Looking back over her shoulder, she saw that a group of young people several rows back were laughing and joking in that rather loud manner young gentlemen and ladies often engaged in when they got together. Not that they were being loud enough to be offensive. The theatre was practically empty, anyway.

Juliana was simply amazed, however, to see that one of the young men was none other than Stewart Margin. She stared as Blake's normally prim and proper secretary began acting the goat with his friends, pulling faces and puffing out a non-existent bosom, clearly taking off the role of Carlotta in the show. When he suddenly noticed her staring back up at him, a dark flush of embarrassment stained his cheeks.

For a moment he didn't seem to know what to do. She too felt embarrassed for him, so she swung round and stared blankly ahead, doing her best to hide her slowly spreading smile. Who would have believed it? Stewart Margin was human after all! In a way it reminded Juliana of what happened that afternoon with Mrs Dawson. You could have knocked her over with a feather when Blake's housekeeper had smiled at her.

An unexpected tap on her shoulder had her spinning round in the narrow seat. Stewart was sitting in one of the empty seats behind her, looking worried but not altogether remorseful.

'Good evening, Mrs Preston,' he said somewhat

stiffly, and somewhat in contrast to his performance of a few moments ago.

'Stewart…' Juliana could feel her lips twitching. Dear heaven, she was going to burst out laughing. She could feel it. In an effort to stop such a catastrophe, she bit her bottom lip.

'Is—um—Mr Preston with you?'

She nodded. It seemed the safest course.

'You—er—I mean…I'm sorry if we were annoying you just then, Mrs Preston. I know we were a touch loud but we were only having a little bit of fun. I mean…you won't tell Mr Preston, will you? He thinks that I'm—er—' He sighed his frustration. 'The fact is, one must act in a certain manner in front of Mr Preston, or one doesn't get along with him, if you know what I mean…'

Suddenly, any wish Juliana had to laugh dissolved into a longing to cry instead. She knew very well what Stewart meant. Very well indeed.

A sad little smile touched her lips as she reached out and patted the young man's hand. 'It's all right, Stewart. I fully understand. You weren't annoying me just now and I have no intention of telling Mr Preston. I suppose I was merely taken aback to see you—er—enjoying yourself so much.'

Now Stewart smiled. Grinned, actually. Juliana was surprised to see how attractive he was with his usually bland grey eyes twinkling. It came to her then that Blake's secretary would not be unpopular with women. 'You thought I was a stuffed shirt, I suppose,' he chuckled.

'You certainly give a good impression of one.'

His eyes flicked over her with such direct male appreciation that she was startled for a moment. 'And you, Mrs Preston, give a very good impression of a society wife. But I found out differently yesterday. You've got a heart, lady. Mr Preston is one lucky guy.'

Juliana flushed under the compliment. But along with the warm rush of pleasure came that longing to cry again. If only Blake *wanted* her heart...

'I'd better get back to my seat,' Stewart said when people started filing back into the row he was occupying. 'Thanks again, Mrs Preston. Look after yourself.'

She watched him make his way slowly along the row, wondering exactly how old he was. Twenty-six or -seven, perhaps? Younger than she'd always imagined. Before seeing him here tonight, she would have said thirty at least.

'Was that Stewart you were just talking to?'

Juliana swung back round to find Blake standing next to her, a tall glass of champagne in his hand.

'Er—um—yes—yes it was actually.' Dear lord, why did she have to sound so darned guilty?

As Blake handed the glass over to her she was stung by the coldness in his eyes. 'You two seemed to be having a very confidential little tête-à-tête. I had no idea you were so chummy.' He sat down, at last giving her some peace from the chill of his gaze. 'I also had no idea he would be here tonight. He certainly never mentioned it to me.'

'Well, why would he?' she defended. 'If you keep your employees at arm's length, they're not going to tell you about their private life, are they?'

'I suppose he tells *you* all about his private life, though,' he said silkily. 'Does he call you Juliana as well?'

'Don't be so ridiculous, Blake. You know he wouldn't dare.'

'Not in front of me, he wouldn't. But I've no idea what he might dare when I'm halfway across the world.'

Juliana's mouth dropped open as she turned to stare across at her stony-faced husband. 'My God, you're jealous!'

His top lip curled in open contempt of this suggestion, 'Now *you're* being ridiculous! I am not, however, a fool. And a fool I would be if I ever took a beautiful woman like you for granted. Now close your mouth and drink your champagne, Juliana. The curtain's about to go back up.'

It was to the credit of the show that within minutes Juliana forgot her emotional turmoil and became involved in the world of magical fantasy being played out on the stage. Though she would have been blind not to have seen the faint echo of her own situation in the storyline. The Phantom loved Christine to distraction, but it was to remain an unrequited love. Christine's heart belonged to another.

Blake's heart did not belong to another, Juliana conceded. It was simply incapable of loving her the way she wanted to be loved. Still…she shouldn't complain. He *did* care for her, in his own peculiar way. It would have to be enough.

They didn't spot Stewart in the crush of people after the show. Which was just as well, Juliana thought. Blake had been peeved by her chatting to his secretary. She didn't seriously believe he envisaged an affair between her and his secretary, but *nothing* was supposed to undermine the distance he liked to keep from those who worked for him. No doubt she'd already irritated the life out of him tonight by calling Mrs Dawson Susanne. Juliana was by nature a reserved person, but even she could see that Blake carried this obsession for insulation too far. Maybe it was time to quietly challenge it, to try to break it down somewhat. It wasn't a healthy attitude, she was sure of that.

Not tonight, however, she decided as they travelled home in a taxi in dead silence. She had done quite enough challenging for one night. Besides, she had other things on her mind.

'I think I'll go straight up to bed,' she said immediately they were inside the house.

'I'm having a nightcap first,' Blake returned. 'I'll join you shortly.'

Juliana did her best to keep her mind totally blank as she went through her night-time routine. She took off and hung up her clothes in the large Italian-designed walnut wardrobe; showered in her white-tiled gold-tapped bathroom; dried and powdered her body with a fragrant talc; cleaned her teeth; rubbed a light moisturiser into her face; took down and brushed out her hair.

This she stared at for a moment, thinking of Susanne's earlier comment about men not noticing changes their wives made to their appearance. It would be interesting, in a way, to see if Blake did notice. Hard not to. Several inches had been chopped off, leaving it to swing round her shoulders in a thick glossy curtain, the straight fringe lending mystery to her already exotic eyes.

Juliana never wore a nightie these days if she knew Blake was going to join her. It seemed coy to do so. Coyness was something she didn't like in women. If a wife was going to let her husband make love to her then why put clothes in the way? Maybe if he made love to her elsewhere in the house then it might be interesting to start with clothes on. But Blake had never done that.

What would she do if he ever did? How would she react?

Juliana's fingers tightened around her hairbrush as the most amazing fantasy started drifting into her mind. Agitated by it, she started vigorously brushing her hair, but soon her hand slowed to a stop and, while her eyes were wide open, it was not her reflection in the mirror that Juliana kept seeing, but another, heart-stopping vision…

Blake coming up behind her in the kitchen when she was cooking breakfast on a Saturday morning, wrapping his arms around her, pressing close so that she could feel his arousal through his bathrobe. She was also wearing a bathrobe under which she was similarly naked. He undid the sash, parting her robe to start playing with her breasts. Her breathing became very rapid, but she kept pretending to cook even though she was becoming uncontrollably excited inside. Only when his hands slid down between her thighs did she stop what she was doing. Whirling, she pulled his mouth down to hers in a savage kiss. Soon they sank down on to the kitchen floor, oblivious of the cold tiles, oblivious of everything but their passion for each other...

Suddenly, Juliana snapped back to reality, but the fantasy had left her with her heart pounding and her skin burning. She shook her head violently, trying to dispel more erotic thoughts from flooding her mind. Agitated by the effect they were having on her, she fled back into the bedroom, where she dived quickly in between the cool sheets.

Her mind, however, was relentless.

There followed the pool scenario...the dining-room...the sofa...

She squeezed her eyes tightly shut and huddled down under the quilt, but there was to be no peace in that either.

The shower...the stairs...

'Not asleep, are you?'

Her eyes flew open to encounter Blake closing the door, unsashing his robe as he walked towards the bed.

'No,' she gulped.

He smiled. God, but he was heart-stoppingly handsome when he smiled.

'And no headache?'

She shook her head.

He stared down at her. 'You've had your hair cut.'

Any satisfaction that he had noticed was overshadowed by the tumultuous feelings racing through her at that moment. Half of her wanted him to part that robe, to let her see him in all his glorious nakedness. The other half was petrified at what she might do if this madness inside her got out of control.

'It suits you,' he said.

Her smile was jittery.

He stared down at her some more, his eyes travelling down her face and over her bare shoulders. The quilt was pulled up tightly over her breasts, which was just as well for Juliana knew full well that they were swollen, the nipples hard peaks of arousal.

'You looked lovely in your green velvet tonight, Juliana,' he said thickly, 'but you look even lovelier without anything on. I didn't realise till I saw you getting out of your bath last night what a truly perfect body you had. Don't hide it away from me, honey. Let me see you…'

Juliana panicked when he tried to extract the blanket from her suddenly clenched hands, her eyes widening into large frightened pools as she gazed up at him in panic-stricken alarm.

'I…I don't want you to.'

He stopped, a dark frown instantly marring his handsome features. 'Don't want me to do what? *Look* at you, or make love to you?'

'L-look at me.'

His sigh was definitely disgruntled. 'Why are you so damned shy?' he said, shrugging out of his robe and climbing in beside her. 'I'd understand if you were ugly perhaps, but by God, Juliana, you're gorgeous!'

Juliana said nothing, her heart pounding wildly as she felt his arousal brushing against her. Dear God, if he only knew! Her fantasies had just shown her her secret longings. She was simply dying to touch him, to show him the extent of her passion.

Shy? She could see now that her so-called shyness had been nothing but a blind, hiding her true self. Now, she wanted to snap that blind up, throw open the windows, let the light shine in. She wanted Blake to see her for the sensual woman she really was, to take that sensuality and explore it to the fullest.

But wanting and doing were two entirely different things. She had no real experience to fall back on. Besides, how could she suddenly start acting differently? Blake would think it strange. Still, he *had* just given her the opportunity to be a little bolder...

'I'm not *that* shy,' she said huskily, and trickled a tentative hand down his bare chest and over his stomach.

His muscles flinched beneath her fingers, his stomach tightening as he sucked in a startled breath.

'Don't...don't you want me to touch you?' she whispered shakily. Oh, how quickly could one's confidence be shattered! Juliana suddenly felt stupid and clumsy and totally inadequate.

Steely fingers tightened around hers. 'God, yes,' he groaned, and carried her hand to his eager flesh, showing her what he liked. 'Yes,' he urged. 'Just like that.'

When he left her to it, Juliana continued for several minutes, fascinated by the thrill of power she felt every time she made him groan or shudder. She was beginning to contemplate a more intimate foreplay when he suddenly loomed up to throw her back against the pillows, kissing her with such savagery that she thought she might suffocate. But it would have been a glorious suffocation!

'You don't know what you've started,' he growled at last, capturing her wrists and holding them wide on the bed. 'By God, woman, you should have let the devils lie. Now I won't be content with less than everything. Do you understand me?'

She merely stared up at him, eyes wide, heart thudding.

'*Do you understand me?*' he repeated, and shook her.

'Yes,' she rasped.

'Don't stop me this time,' he ground out, and, discarding her wrists, he threw back the blanket and began sliding down her exposed body, his mouth hot and merciless on her shivering, quivering flesh.

There was no question of stopping him. He was unstoppable anyway. But it soon became obvious to Juliana that there was so much she didn't know about sex, and so much that Blake did.

He sent her over the edge within seconds of reaching his goal. But instead of it being the end, it was only the beginning. Sometimes she felt like a rag-doll, pushed this way and that, a mindless receptacle for his almost insatiable passion. He wanted her every way he'd never had her before.

Even after he'd seemingly spilled every drop of seed into her, and they were collapsed together on the bed, Blake did not leave her alone, trailing his nails lightly over her swollen nipples, making sure he never let her come down from that plateau of sexual sensitivity and abandonment he seemed to have taken her to. Soon the desire to touch him back took possession of her. But her hands were not enough for him. He wanted her mouth as well. He *insisted*.

Dazedly, she complied, finding it a surprisingly arousing experience. And this was the way she achieved the unachievable, stirring him again till he could stand it no longer. It was then that he lifted her on to him, kneading her breasts quite roughly while he urged her to ride them both to another exhausting climax.

Hours passed. Dawn came. And they finally slept.

Yet when Juliana awoke, Blake was not in bed with her. She lay alone and naked on top of the sheets, a picture of decadent disarray. Her hair was tangled, her lips puffy, her thighs and breasts faintly bruised.

'Will an apology do? Or do you want a divorce?'

Juliana's legs shot up under her as she scrambled into a semi-sitting position, swivelling round on the bed in the direction of Blake's voice.

He was in the window-seat, his back against the frame, his knees up, still as stark naked as she was.

Juliana swallowed, reaching for a pillow to hug against herself. 'Why…why would I want either?'

His head turned slowly till their eyes met. Juliana was truly shocked. He looked almost haunted as though he'd just committed the most dreadful crime, when all he'd done was make love to his wife as he perhaps should have all along. OK, so he'd managed to put ten months' worth into one night. And he had been a touch brutal at times. But she'd never been in any real pain. At least, not any that she hadn't enjoyed.

There was a fine line, Juliana had discovered the previous night, between pleasure and pain. She licked dry lips at the thought of some of those razor-edged moments.

Blake was staring at her.

'Are you saying that you didn't mind the things I made you do last night?'

Juliana flushed fiercely, for she could not deny that daylight had a tendency to make some of their love-making seem incredibly uninhibited. But she wasn't ashamed of it. She loved Blake. She was his wife. Nothing they did together was wrong. If he was a little forceful then maybe she had needed him to be. She certainly hadn't wanted to go on enduring the sort of antiseptic, clinical sex they'd been having. Her love demanded more than that now. At least she might find some peace in carnal passion, if that was all Blake was capable of.

'No,' she said simply. 'I didn't mind. We're married, aren't we?'

'Might I remind you that married men have been charged with rape before today?' he returned drily.

'But you didn't rape me last night!'

'It felt as if I did.'

'Did it?' She was totally astounded at his un-doubted sincerity. 'But why?'

He glared at her. 'You ask me that? You, who shook with fear on our wedding night, who shuddered whenever I tried to go past the most basic foreplay and intercourse, who even last night didn't want me to *look* at her. For God's sake, Juliana! What do you expect to think—that you suddenly went from prudish innocent to wanton whore in one night? Of course I forced you! If I didn't then…then—' He broke off and looked at her as though he were seeing a ghost.

Oh, my God, she panicked. He's realised I've fallen in love with him.

Apparently not, however. For suddenly he swung his feet down from the window-seat and stood up, hands clenched by his side, uncaring if she saw that in his anger he had become sexually aroused. He glared at her across the room, and if looks could kill she would have shrivelled up on that bed right then and there.

Juliana cringed when he strode menacingly across the room, but he did not touch her, merely swept up his bathrobe from the floor and pulled it on, sashing it round his waist with angry movements. By the time he looked at her again, however, his face was a stony mask, all emotions carefully hidden away.

'If I thought for one moment,' he said in a tightly controlled voice, 'that it was my loyal assistant who'd corrupted you over this last three weeks then I would tear him limb from limb. Only my knowledge of Stewart Margin's ambition puts my mind at rest on that regard. He might fancy you—after all, what man wouldn't? But he would not dare put any secret desires of his into action. He knows what the penalty would be. The same goes for my business friends and acquaintances. That only leaves someone you work with. Your resignation goes in first thing Monday morning, Juliana. If not, I'll start divorce proceedings immediately.'

CHAPTER SEVEN

JULIANA gaped up at him while the import of his words sank in.

'I take it by your silence that you will do as I say,' he drawled. 'After all, I'm sure you want to continue as Mrs Blake Preston, don't you, Juliana?'

Did she?

'In that case we won't mention the matter of your little indiscretion again,' he finished coldly, and, turning, strode from the room, leaving the door open behind him.

Juliana stared at the empty doorway for a few seconds before throwing the pillow away and dashing after Blake.

His bedroom was empty. Where had he gone? The sound of the shower running sent her hurtling into his bathroom, uncaring of his privacy, uncaring of her own nudity, uncaring of anything but the need to give voice to the fury welling up within her. She banged back the sliding glass door to reveal a naked Blake standing there under a steaming jet of hot water, his face upturned, his eyes shut. He didn't flinch an inch, or open his eyes, or turn her way.

'How dare you?' she spat. 'How *dare* you? I have not even *looked* at another man during our marriage, let alone slept with one. For you to imply...no, not imply, *accuse* me of being unfaithful while you were away, of doing with some other man the sort of things we did last night, why I...I...words fail me!'

She scooped in some much needed air. Her whole body was shaking uncontrollably. But even in her rage some inner instinct warned her to be careful with what she said, what she admitted. 'Has it ever occurred to you I might have become a little bored with our sex-life?' she ranted on. 'For it had become boring, Blake. Even you must recognise that. Boring and predictable. And maybe I've become dissatisfied with the way you never touch me unless it's in bed. A wife likes her husband to show outward signs of affection occasionally.'

Now Blake opened his eyes to look at her. They were hard and disbelieving. Juliana put her hands on her hips in a gesture of defiance and outrage. 'I have *not* taken a lover, either at work or any other place. And I will *not* resign on Monday! If that means you are going to divorce me, then so be it! Nothing, not being your wife or all the money in the world, is worth having to give up my independence and self-respect! To tell the truth, I can't imagine why I agreed to marry you in the first place, Blake Preston. You'd have to be the most selfish, cold-blooded, monstrous man in the entire world!'

The hands that shot out to grab her came so fast that she'd been yanked into the shower before she could say Jack Robinson. Blake slammed her hard against the wet tiles, holding her hands captive on either side of her, jamming one solid thigh between hers.

'Is that so?' he ground out, his sneering mouth only

inches from hers. 'Well, in that case you won't be surprised to hear I don't believe a word you've just said. But you've got guts, Juliana, I'll give you that. *And* imagination. Bored, were you? Dissatisfied, were you? Then why didn't you say something? You're an intelligent woman. You must have known any man would have wanted more than what you were giving me.'

His water-slicked knee lifted to start rubbing between her legs, making her breath catch and her stomach tighten. She knew she shouldn't respond beneath such an outrageous caress, but she did. Dear God, she did! His mouth curved into a cynical smile.

'You've suddenly discovered sex, Juliana,' he mocked. 'And you didn't discover it with me. That's the truth of it, my treacherous little wife. But I've always been a man to try to turn disadvantage to advantage. If it's imaginative sex you want, then I'm sure I can keep this new appetite of yours well satisfied.'

She gasped as he moved his other leg between hers, holding her there against the wall while he manoeuvred his impassioned flesh into her shockingly ready body. She turned her face away in appalled horror at the pleasure she felt, the mad excitement that took possession of her as he set up a relentlessly erotic rhythm. The water cascaded down over his head, splashing into her parted lips, trickling down over her distended nipples.

'Is this what you want?' he said, his voice slurred.

She wanted to scream her denial but no words came from her panting mouth. And then she was shuddering against the wall, her knees going from under her. He lifted her then, carrying her limp, wet body back into his bedroom, spreading her out across his bed where he continued quite mercilessly till he too spasmed with a violent release.

Almost immediately, he levered himself up from her shattered body, staring down into her utterly drained face with eyes like hell.

'Keep your job,' he grated. 'But God help you if I ever catch you with another man again.'

He turned and went back into the still running shower, this time locking the door behind him.

If she'd been in her own room, Juliana would have curled up where she was and cried her eyes out. But the possibility that Mrs Dawson might come upstairs at any moment to do the bedrooms sent her stumbling back to her own room and her own bathroom. She too locked the door, leaning against it and letting the tears run unashamedly down her face.

She spent ages in the bathroom, bathing at length. And thinking long and hard.

The marriage was doomed, she finally decided. Doomed...

Yet to simply throw in the towel when she loved the man so much seemed a cowardly thing to do. More than cowardly—extremely difficult, considering the changed nature of their sexual relationship.

Who would have believed she could be so easily and devastatingly satisfied as Blake had satisfied her in that shower? How did you turn your back on such pleasure?

But she had to if she was going to live with herself.

Life was more than the physical. And so was a marriage.

When she finally came out of the bathroom, the bed had been made with fresh sheets, the room tidied and dusted. Juliana blushed to think of what Susanne might have thought about the state of the bed. She pulled on jeans and a top, and was standing there, trying to decide what to do next, when there was a knock on the door.

'Juliana... It's Blake...'

'C-come in,' she stammered, instantly nervous. Now was the moment to tell him she could not go on if he really believed she was an unfaithful wife; if he was going to continue to treat her with contempt.

Surprised to find him dressed as though for work in a business suit, Juliana was at a loss for words for a moment. Blake, however, was not similarly indisposed.

'I've decided to fly to Sydney this afternoon,' he began straight away, standing with his hand still on the doorknob. 'I'll be back on Wednesday evening in time to take you to the races on Thursday. Before you say anything, I want to apologise, not for my behaviour—since you undoubtedly enjoyed what I did,' he inserted drily, 'but for my accusations of adultery, and my rather lack-lustre performance during this marriage so far. I mistakenly thought the type of sex-life we had was all you could handle. Obviously I didn't see the signs of change. Maybe I've also left you alone too much, a factor which will be remedied.'

He sighed then. It was a weary, troubled sigh. 'I don't want to lose you, Juliana. I value our marriage and I want it to last. Maybe it's time we started trying for a child.'

A *child*? A child would bind her to him forever. There would be no escape. Juliana needed that escape for a while. Much as Blake's words just now had soothed most of her doubts and fears, she still wasn't entirely convinced their marriage would last.

'I…I think we should wait a while for that, Blake,' she returned hesitantly. 'At least till the New Year, the way we planned.'

His gaze locked on to hers, his eyes intent. What was he trying to see?

'Very well, Juliana,' he conceded matter-of-factly. 'Goodbye. I'll see you on Wednesday. You can tell Mrs Dawson I should be home for dinner.'

And then he was gone.

Juliana sighed. What had changed? No goodbye kiss. No asking her to accompany him to the airport. No doubt she would not hear from him during the days he was gone, since three days would hardly warrant a phone call in Blake's opinion.

Juliana was wrong about that. He did call. Every night. At first, she was thrilled, but then not. The calls were brief and rather brusque. Clearly he was checking up her, seeing if she came home every evening. When he called her again at work on Wednesday morning she was quite sharp with him, even though he was only telling her that he would be taking her out for dinner that night and that she was to inform Mrs Dawson not to cook for them. After she'd hung up, she regretted her sharpness, but she couldn't help suspecting that Blake had been trying to catch her out at something at work.

As luck would have it, she was kept late at work that day. Blake was already home when she turned into the driveway for there was a light on in his bedroom. As Juliana used the remote control to open the garage doors, a nervous agitation churned her stomach.

She knew why.

Not a night had gone by since Blake left that she hadn't wanted him. Quite fiercely. Yet, with the passing of the days, that mad night she'd spent with him, plus the incident in the shower, had taken on an unreal feeling. It was as though it hadn't happened to her and Blake, but to two other people. Strangers. Juliana worried that Blake would never be like that again, that *she* would never feel like that again.

The kitchen was deserted as Juliana walked through from the garage. She had given Susanne the night off in view of her not having to cook for them, and the housekeeper was happy enough to visit her sister who lived in the Dandenong Hills. She wouldn't be back till the next day.

There was only herself and Blake in the huge house. The thought excited Juliana. She hoped it would excite him.

He didn't look at all excited, standing at his dressing-table, putting his gold cuff-links into the sleeves of an ivory silk shirt. The front buttons were undone and the shirt hung open, showing an expanse of smooth golden flesh down to where his charcoal-grey trousers stopped the unconsciously sensual display.

He glanced up once he became aware of her standing in the doorway, watching him. It was a very fleeting glance.

'Ah, there you are, Juliana.' Not a word of enquiry or reproach about her being late. 'I've booked a table for seven-thirty. You've only got thirty minutes. Look, why don't you leave your hair up, have a quick shower and put on that green velvet dress you had on the other night? I really liked that on you and it won't need ironing.''

He finished with his cuff-links and started buttoning up his shirt. When she continued to stand there, staring at him, he lifted an eyebrow at her. 'Is there something I can do for you?' he drawled.

She tried not to flush at the image in her mind.

'No. I was going to ask how things went in Sydney but it can wait, I suppose.' And, whirling away, she fled to her room, closing her eyes in pained humiliation as she shut the door behind her.

Twenty-five minutes later she was struggling to pull up the back zip of the emerald-green velvet when Blake materialised behind her. 'Let me…'

Her eyes flew to his in the dressing-table mirror, but he merely smiled that enigmatic smile he sometimes produced and zipped her up. Yet his hands lingered on her shoulders, his gaze admiring as it travelled slowly over the reflected dress in the mirror. Juliana found herself looking at the dress as well, trying to control the wild fluttering of her heart.

It was a simple style, cut to hug the line of a woman's body, the skirt pencil-slim and just above the knee. The sleeves were three-quarter-length and tight, emphasising the slenderness of her arms. But it was the neckline that drew the eyes, the wide sweetheart shape showing a good deal of creamy flesh and just a hint of cleavage.

Juliana had first discovered the style suited her figure when she'd worn Barbara's graduation gown, and since then she had often bought dresses with that neckline. The only drawback was that bra straps often showed, so the right underwear was required.

Juliana always wore a strapless corselette of stretch black lace with this particular dress, since such a garment also enhanced the hour-glass shape that best displayed the tightly fitted style. Her years of modelling had taught her how to show her figure off to best advantage. Such underwear pulled in her waist, giving her slender hips a fuller look, and pushing up her limited bust.

Thinking about her underwear, however, especially with Blake standing so close behind her, was making Juliana hotly aware of her body.

'I have a little present for you,' he astonished her by saying.

She went to turn around but he held her there with an iron grip. 'No, stay right where you are...''

Drawing a long green velvet case from his suit jacket pocket, he unclipped it and placed it on the dressing-table in front of her. In it was the most beautiful emerald and gold necklace Juliana had ever seen.

'Oh, Blake! It's magnificent!' she exclaimed, reaching out to run her fingers over it. Clearly, he had had the green dress in mind when he'd bought it. 'But...but what's it for?' She glanced up at his face

in the mirror. 'It's not my birthday for another
month.'

His smile was odd as he lifted the necklace from
its velvet bed and secured it around her neck. There
was no doubt that it looked spectacular against her
pale flesh but Juliana had the strangest feeling that
with this gift Blake had just paid for services rendered. Or was it for services still to *be* rendered?

'Does it have to be for anything?' he said suavely.
'Can't I give my beautiful wife a gift?'

'Yes, but…'

She froze when he bent to kiss her neck. 'Do shut
up, Juliana, and just let me do things to please you.
Isn't that what you said you wanted? Outward dis-
plays of affection? From now on I will give you whatever takes my fancy. And *do* whatever takes my
fancy…'

His mouth trailed lightly back up to her right ear,
where he blew softly into the shell-like cavern.
Juliana shivered.

'Perhaps we'd better be going,' he said softly.

Dinner at the restaurant was agony.

First, Blake had booked one of those ghastly places
where people went not so much to eat, but to be seen.
Celebrities and millionaires abounded. Most of the
men had little dolly-birds on their arms: not wives—
mistresses and girlfriends. And they all dripped with
expensive jewellery.

Juliana's new emerald necklace felt as if it was lit
in neon around her neck, especially after one abom-
inable woman made caustic mention of it. *Kept*

woman, Juliana felt it was screaming out to everyone. Which was crazy really. Blake was her husband. How could that make her *kept* in any way?

Yet by the time they left the restaurant Juliana was very much on edge.

'I didn't like that place, Blake,' she said with a little shudder. 'I don't want to go there ever again.'

'Oh? What was wrong with it?'

'The food stinks and so does the clientele.'

He laughed. 'You don't like the rich and famous any more?'

'I never did like them, as you very well know. I merely envied the power they had.'

'So if you couldn't beat them, you joined them, is that it? After all, might I remind you that your husband is a very rich man?'

'No, you don't have to remind me...' Her hand lifted to finger the necklace.

He slanted her a dark look but said nothing. Silence was maintained till they were climbing out of the car inside the garages.

'The night's still young,' Blake said. 'Care for a swim?'

'I...I don't think so.' The pool had become the focus of Juliana's most persistent fantasy lately.

'What, then? You tell me what you want to do.'

His eyes clashed with hers over the roof of the car. Why did she get the feeling he was taunting her, trying to make her say that she wanted him to make love to her? Was this to be her punishment for changing the status quo in their relationship? Constant humiliation?

Juliana fiercely resented being put in such a position. No way was she going to beg, or grovel, or even hint.

'I don't know about you,' she said casually, 'but I have a good book to read.'

'Oh? Anything I've read?'

To be caught out in a lie made Juliana's teeth clamp down hard in her jaw. 'I doubt it,' she bit out, vowing to snatch up anything from the family room on the way through. Susanne was always reading.

'You don't want a nightcap?'

'Well…maybe a port before I go up.' To race away would seem as if she was frightened to be alone with him.

'You didn't ask me what happened in Sydney,' he remarked while he poured them both a port.

Juliana was settled in one of the three gold brocade armchairs that matched the sofa. The sofa, like the pool, had been put on her list of no-nos for a while. She took the glass with a stiff smile on her lips. 'Sorry, but I'm sure you handled things with your usual panache.'

'*Panache*? What kind of business term is that? Panache, I ask you!' He dropped down in one of the other armchairs, stretching his legs out in front of him and loosening his tie. 'I gave those lazy, inefficient idiots up there a blast that could have been heard all the way to Melbourne. I doubt they'd be telling their wives tonight that their boss has *panache*.'

'Sounds as if you were in a bad mood,' she pointed out.

'Maybe.' He shot her a knowing look. 'Maybe I had good cause…'

'Meaning?'

'Meaning I would have much rather been here, making mad, passionate love to my wife.'

Juliana's hand shook as she lifted the port to her suddenly dry lips. She sipped the drink, her gaze finding Blake's over the rim. There was self-mockery in those glittering blue eyes, but real desire as well. Her stomach lurched.

'Take off your clothes,' he said abruptly.

Some of the port spilt into her lap. 'Oh, my God, my beautiful dress!' She shot Blake a savage glance. 'You made me do that,' she accused. 'You, with your pathetic suggestions.'

He laughed and stood up. 'It's you who's pathetic, Juliana.' He came over and dabbed at the spilt port with the scarlet hankie he had in his pocket. Leaning over, he kissed her full on the mouth then fixed ruthless eyes upon her. 'You've been on fire for sex all night and what have you done? Complained. Quibbled. *Lied*. Why not come right out and say you want me to ravage you? Why not stand up and take that damned dress right off? It's what you want to do, isn't it? Or would you really prefer to go to bed with a good book?'

He lanced her stunned face with a furious glare before straightening to stride back over to the bar. 'To hell with this port. I need a real drink!'

He rattled the whisky decanter, even spilling some as he filled a fresh and very tall glass. 'Here's to a return to prudery!' he announced, and lifted the glass in a mocking toast. But when he turned around to further deride the woman who had ignited such an uncharacteristic display of temper and emotion, Blake froze.

She stood before him, the dress on the floor, her body the epitome of erotica in the black lace corselette, her long slender legs encased in sheer black stockings that ran all the way down to her black high heels. The emerald necklace around her neck looked exotic and somewhat depraved. Her breathing, he noted, was rapid, and there was a wild light blazing in her eyes. She had never looked more dangerously seductive or more breathtaking beautiful.

'You bitch,' he rasped, and, putting the glass down, moved slowly towards her, a smile on his lips.

CHAPTER EIGHT

JULIANA'S chin lifted. 'If I'm a bitch, then what are you?' she countered, well aware that she was being deliberately provocative. But, having taken up Blake's challenge, no way was she going to back down.

'Oh, I'm a bastard through and through,' her husband agreed, his smile turning rueful as he reached out to touch the emerald necklace around her throat. 'But a very rich bastard, you must admit,' he added, and, curling his fingers around the necklace, he began pulling her towards him.

The taunt over his wealth added a fiery fury to Juliana's already heated bloodstream. When her head was yanked indignantly backwards, the clasp gave way and Blake was left holding the broken necklace in his hand.

'Don't you ever throw your money in my face again!' she hissed. 'And don't you ever parade me in front of other people like some cheap whore!' Snatching the necklace from his stunned fingers, she flung it across the room. 'That's what I think of your thinking you can buy me!'

Too late Juliana realised she had finally done what she'd always thought she wanted to do to her unruffable husband: make him really lose his temper. But the actuality was not quite as desirable as she had once imagined. Blake looked as if he wanted to kill her.

'I don't have to buy you,' he ground out savagely. 'You're my wife! I can damned well have you any time I want you.' And, with his face flushing an angry red, he scooped her up into his arms and dumped her on to the sofa, pinning her there with a knee across her stomach while he began reefing his clothes off: first his tie, then his jacket and shirt till he was naked to the waist.

Only then did he turn his attention to *her* attire, reefing open the hooks that ran down the front of the black lace corselette and wrenching both flaps aside, exposing her body to his glittering gaze. Holding her shoulders down, he sat on the edge of the sofa, effectively stopping her from escaping. When his mouth started to descend towards one of her hard-tipped breasts Juliana lashed out with closed fists, striking the side of his head, his shoulders, his chest.

'No you can't damned well have me any time you want me!' she screamed at him. 'Not unless I agree.'

His smile was frightening as he gripped her flailing hands in an iron grasp. 'You'll agree all right, my sexy Juliana. You'll agree...' And, pinioning both her wrists within one large male hand, his free hand set out to make his prophecy come true, sliding down over her flat stomach and under the elastic of her tiny black lace bikini briefs.

'No,' she groaned once he found his target.

'Yes,' he bit out, and ruthlessly continued.

'You're a bastard.'

'We've already established that.'

'I...I won't give in,' she cried, but her voice was already unsteady, her heart hammering away like mad.

Gritting her teeth, she tried to ignore the sensations his knowing hand was evoking, tried not to let her thighs fall evocatively apart to give him easier access to her body. But she was fighting a losing battle. In the end, pride demanded she not let him win, even as she lost.

Catching his heavy-lidded gaze with a desire-charged look of her own, she smiled a smile as perversely wicked as his had been. His eyes widened, that tormenting hand stilling for a moment.

'Don't stop,' she husked, and arched her back in voluptuous surrender.

His hand withdrew as he stood up, his breathing as ragged as her own. 'No,' he said thickly. 'You won't get what you want that easily. You'll earn your pleasure, wife.'

'What makes you think I won't enjoy earning it?' she rasped, and levered herself up into a sitting position, her hands going to the belt on his trousers.

His fingers closed over hers, then tightened. Her eyes flew upwards, locking with his. The pain of the buckle digging into her palm was intense but she refused to make a sound. Finally, he laughed and drew her upwards till she was standing, trembling, before him. A few violent movements and he had stripped her totally naked, except for the long black stockings and her high heels.

For an interminable time he simply stared at her, his torrid gaze roving over her softly parted lips, her swollen breasts, the triangle of damp curls that so ineffectually guarded her desire. When he reached out to touch her there, she sucked in a shuddering breath.

'Juliana,' he said, and with a groan of raw need moved to crush her against him, grabbing the back of her head and covering her mouth with his till she was weak and pliant in his arms.

'And now, my incredibly beautiful wife,' he muttered at last against her panting mouth, 'let's see just how far you'll let your bastard of a husband go…'

'Wake up, sleepyhead.'

Juliana yawned and stretched, then buried her face back in the pillow. 'Can't,' she mumbled. 'Too tired.'

'I don't doubt it,' Blake muttered drily. 'But we have to get going. If we're not at Flemington by eleven we won't get a parking spot, even in the members' area. It's nine already.'

'Nine!' Juliana shot upright, pushing her hair out of her face. 'My God!' she exclaimed, looking around her. 'I'm in *your* room. When did we…?' Her frown was puzzled, for the last thing she recalled was falling asleep in Blake's arms on the sofa.

'I carried you up,' he told her on a sardonic note. 'And believe me, I won't do it again in a hurry. Either you weigh a ton or I was a little—er—done in at the time.'

Laughter bubbled from her lips. Some time during their crazed lovemaking session last night all the anger and frustration associated with their changing sexual relationship had been routed. They'd mocked each other, taunted each other, dared each other. They'd even hurt each other. Juliana could remember slapping Blake once, and he'd slapped her right back.

But the final outcome had been a purging that left them both exhausted, yet at peace with each other. Afterwards, Blake had cradled Juliana in his arms and told her that there would never be another woman for him. Never.

It might not have been an avowal of love, but it was as close as he would ever come to it. Juliana had drifted off into a deep sleep, happy and content.

She had woken just as happy. 'You should know better than to challenge your old diving mate, shouldn't you?' she teased.

Blake smiled from where he was lying next to her, his arms linked behind his head. 'They were great days, weren't they, Julianna?'

'Marvellous…'

'Too bad we had to grow up and become part of the world at large. It's not a very nice place.'

Juliana's heart turned over at Blake's sudden bleakness of spirit. She much preferred the man he'd been last night, the lover who'd cuddled her close and said the sweetest of things.

'No, it's not,' she agreed, 'but we can make our own little corner a nice place, can't we?'

His head turned towards her, and a small smile tugged the grimness from his mouth. 'My darling Juliana…the eternal optimist.'

'I'll settle for being just your darling Juliana,' she whispered, and kissed him on the cheek. 'I do so love being your wife, Blake. I love everything about it. Now more than ever.'

She saw his hesitation to accept her love, despite her having skirted around saying straight out that she loved him. In the end, he couldn't help withdrawing from any open acceptance, defusing a situation he obviously found awkward with a flash of dry humour.

'I know exactly what *you* love, Mrs Preston, and I'm not going to be conned into any more. As it is, I'm going to have to take a bottle of vitamin E tablets with breakfast, plus a swag of oysters for lunch. Speaking of lunch, up you get, lazy-bones. The gee-gees await!'

He himself bounced out of bed and headed straight for the shower without looking back. Juliana noted that he carefully locked the door behind him.

She shrugged away any upsurge of dismay. Blake was not about to change in a hurry. But he *was* changing. After all, he hadn't put her in her own bed when he'd carried her up, had he? He'd put her in *his*.

'This place is madness today!' Juliana exclaimed, looking at the cars pouring into Flemington. And it was only ten-forty!

Blake had managed to squeeze his turquoise Mercedes sports car into a smallish spot near a fence, not far from the members' entrance into the track. As was the tradition during the Melbourne Cup carnival, people had set up picnics behind and between their cars, with caviare and chicken and champagne on the menu, but still more people were surging towards the gates of the course proper, anxious to soak up the atmosphere inside the grounds.

'It was worse on Tuesday, I heard,' Blake said,

coming round to join her at the back of the car. 'Something like a hundred buses parked down along the Maribyrnong River, and countless limousines dropping off Arab sheikhs and their entourages all morning.'

'How would you know?' she frowned. 'You were in Sydney.'

He grinned. 'Stayed in the motel and watched it on telly. Can't miss the Melbourne Cup, you know. I'm a Melbournian!'

'I suppose you even backed the winner.'

'Of course. I had half the field.'

'Blake! You can't win punting like that.'

'Juliana, my sweet...'

She caught her breath when he put a protective arm around her to steer her safely through the milling crowd.

'...one doesn't try to win on the Melbourne Cup. One tries to end up with a ticket on the winner. That's totally different. After the race, one surreptitiously slips all the dead tickets into nearby waste-paper baskets then produces the winning one. Everyone thinks you're a genius!'

Juliana laughed and shook her head. 'I won't from now on. I'll know the truth.'

'Ah, yes, but...' he gave her an affectionate squeeze—in public! '...I don't mind *you* knowing the truth. There shouldn't be any secrets between a husband and wife, should there?'

Juliana's heart turned over. Tears hovered, but she quickly blinked them back and lifted a dazzling smile to his handsome face. 'No, Blake. No secrets. None at all.'

He stared down at her for a second, and she could have sworn a dark cloud flitted momentarily across his eyes. It worried her. Did he still think she might have had an affair? Oh, surely not.

'Blake…'

'Mmm?'

'I…' She glanced around her. People were pressing close. The words died in her throat. Which was just as well, perhaps. The more she protested her innocence, the more guilty she might sound. Best say nothing.

'Oh, nothing,' she went on with an offhand wave of her hand. 'It's going to be warm, isn't it? I'm glad I wore something reasonably cool.'

The pink linen suit she had on was very simple, with short sleeves, a straight skirt and big black buttons down the front of the jacket. Teamed with a saucy black hat that dipped over one side of her face, and other black patent accessories, Juliana thought she looked chic and cool.

'It'll probably storm later,' Blake remarked, glancing up at the sky. 'I hope that hat doesn't ruin.'

'The lady in the hat shop warned me it would go like a limp rag if I ever got it wet. Do you honestly think it will rain?'

'Sure to by the end of the day.'

'We can stay under cover, sipping champagne.'

'I came here to have a bet, Juliana, not sip champagne.'

'I thought you came here today to be with me!

Truly, Blake, everyone from work is dying to meet you. Now you tell me you're going to be slipping away to spend all afternoon fighting your way through to the bookmakers or standing in long totalisator queues. You do realise the promotional marquees are in the middle of the course proper, don't you?'

'Good God, why didn't they get one of the decent ones down the end of the straight?'

'Don't be such a snob. There's nothing wrong with our being in the centre. Firstly, you'll get a much better view of the races. Special tiered seats are being set up near the finishing-post. You couldn't be in a better spot. And the company has hired a couple of hostesses whose job it is to go round putting everyone's bets on for them. What more could you ask for?'

'You…and me…naked…on a desert island?'

Heat zoomed into her cheeks. 'Don't say such things out loud,' she hissed, aware of the people all around her.

Blake's chuckle was cynical as he leant close. 'You can't fool me any more with that prim and proper act. I know the real you, Juliana. I only hope none of the other gentlemen here today knows the real you as well…'

Her eyes jerked up to his. 'You…you still don't trust me, do you?'

'I put trust in the same category as love, my sweet. It's very nice in theory but awfully suspect in practice.'

Any further chit-chat was terminated by their arrival at the toll gates. Blake withdrew his wallet and paid the entrance fees, after which he took her elbow and urged her inside.

'Don't get your knickers in a knot, Juliana,' he pronounced brusquely on seeing her distress. 'I don't believe in worrying about things one can't change, which includes the past. We've started our marriage anew this past week with a clean slate and a damned sight more interesting sex-life. Let's leave it at that, shall we?

'Of course,' he added darkly as they walked together past the beds of roses and down towards where they could cross into the centre of the track, 'I would cast a dim view if any man here today showed any more than a work-like interest in you. A very dim view indeed...'

No man dared.

Blake, in full millionaire mode, was a formidable husband and companion. It would have taken a brave male to try to muscle in on the woman on *his* arm, especially when that woman was his wife! Juliana still gained the impression that Blake sized up every one of her colleagues, from the nineteen-year-old mailboy to the thirty-three-year-old field sales manager to the national sales manager, who was pushing fifty and very happily married.

Juliana had to work hard to hide her frustration with Blake. What did she have to do to persuade him that she hadn't been playing around while he was away?

Nothing, she finally realised. He would believe what he wanted to believe. To change her behaviour for fear of feeding his ill-founded suspicions was not only non-productive but extremely stressful. She felt tense enough as it was, having Blake give everyone the once-over with that penetrating gaze of his.

The women, she noticed, stared at him openly and swooned behind his back. And why not? He was like a young Robert Redford with his classically featured face, blond hair and blue eyes, not to mention his tall, athletic body, encased very attractively that day in an elegantly casual tan suit and open-necked blue shirt. All this, plus the fact that he was as wealthy as any Onassis, made her handsome husband pack a pretty powerful punch.

'I think it's the wrong spouse doing the worrying,' she muttered under her breath on one occasion.

Blake shot her a dry look over his shoulder then returned to give his bet to the simpering hostess.

They all traipsed out to see the race in question— the third of the day. Juliana's choice stumbled out of the barrier and was never sighted. Blake's was beaten by a short half-head.

'If I'd been putting on my own bets,' he grumbled, 'I'd have had the winner.'

'Sure,' she said ruefully. 'You'd also have had every other horse in the race, even the donkey I bet on.'

'True,' he grinned.

They were still sitting on the seats near the winning-post, everyone else having gone back inside their respective marquees.

Juliana glanced up at the sky. Black clouds were sweeping in from the west, a sure sign of the storm Blake had predicted earlier.

She sighed. 'I suppose we'd better get back under cover. It's looking mighty ominous overhead. Good grief!' she suddenly exclaimed. 'Do you see who I see over there?'

She nodded over to where Owen Hawthorne was standing near the rails on the other side of the track, arm in arm with none other than Virginia Blakenthorp. It was the first time Juliana had seen either of them since her marriage, which was not surprising, she supposed, since Blake didn't socialise with his old crowd any more.

'If you mean our respective exes,' he said in a bored tone, 'then yes…I see them.'

'Do you think they might be going out with each other now?'

'I certainly should hope so. They're engaged.'

Juliana sucked in a startled breath. 'Owen's *engaged* to Virginia?'

Blake settled narrowed eyes upon her. 'Yes. Why? Does that bother you?'

'Well, I…I…no, not really. I'm sure they're admirably suited. But if you knew that, why didn't you tell me?'

He shrugged. 'I didn't think you'd be interested.'

'I'm not *interested*. I'm just…just…'

'Jealous?' Blake suggested blandly.

Juliana glared her exasperation. 'It's not a matter of jealousy, but of guilt.'

'*Guilt?*'

'Yes, guilt. I felt guilty getting married so quickly after I broke my engagement to Owen. He loved me, you know, despite his shortcomings. I wasn't totally

insensitive to his feelings. Virginia I wasn't so concerned with. Girls like her rarely stir me to sympathy.
But I didn't like either of them to think I only married
you for your money.'

'But you *did* marry me for my money, darling. I
knew that from the start. It was my ace card in se-
curing your services as a wife. Of course, it has taken
some time for my investment to bear fruit...'

He leant over and kissed her with almost insulting
tenderness. Juliana gasped when his lips finally lifted
from hers, her eyes pained as she looked up at him.
But her pain soon changed to a justifiable anger.

'There are many wealthy men in this world,' she
snapped, 'whom I wouldn't touch with a barge-pole,
let alone marry. If it were just your money I wanted,
Blake, then why do I still work, why do I always
insist on buying my own clothes and paying my
way?'

His shrug was indifferent. 'Very well, so I used the
wrong word. You married me for my position and
power. Why deny it? I've never minded, Juliana. You
know that. I've always admired your honest ambition.
I especially admired your refusal to pretend love,
quite unlike that lying bitch over there.'

The venom in Blake's voice gave rise to the unnerving suspicion that he might really have been in
love with Virginia. Maybe he still was. His assertion
that night that he'd broken his engagement because
Virginia wanted to become a lady of leisure after their
marriage suddenly didn't ring true.

'What really happened with Virginia, Blake? Did
you find out she had another lover?'

'No,' he returned coldly. 'I found out her family was stony-broke, yet the day before she'd been telling me what a killing her daddy had made on the Stock Exchange that year. I suddenly realised she wouldn't look at me twice without my money. Hell, during those months of near-bankruptcy most of my so-called friends deserted me in droves. I thought Virginia was different from the usual society girl because she worked. But she was only working because she *needed* to work, not because she wanted to. I was nothing to her but a meal-ticket, a means for her to embrace the type of empty, lunch-flitting, charity-committee existence females of her ilk thrive on!'

He lanced Juliana with a savage scowl. 'Now, if you're finished with the third degree about *my* life, why don't I hear some truths about yours? Have you been seeing Owen Hawthorne while I've been away?'

'No!'

'Who, then?'

'No one!'

'Don't lie to me, Juliana.'

'I am *not* lying to you.'

'You'd better not be. I thought I could let bygones be bygones but I've suddenly realised I'm not that noble. There are some things in life that a man just cannot tolerate being deceived about, and his wife's extra-curricular activities is one of them. If I ever find out you *have* lied to me in this, Juliana, you might discover a Blake you've never seen before.'

He stood up abruptly. 'Come on, let's go back inside before this storm breaks right over our heads.'

Stunned by Blake's clearly jealous warning, Juliana

said very little for the rest of the afternoon. Was his jealousy inspired by male ego and possessiveness? she kept wondering. Or something far deeper and more vulnerable?

She dared not hope Blake was falling in love with her, but somehow she couldn't help hoping. It was what she wanted more than anything else in the world. Why, if Blake loved her, she could endure anything. Anything at all!

Not, however, his sister Barbara, who was waiting for them when they arrived home that afternoon.

CHAPTER NINE

THERE was no warning of Barbara's presence inside as Blake parked his car and cut the engine. No strange car taking up one of the two empty spaces in the four car garage, or parked in the street outside. The first they knew of their unexpected visitor was when they came into the kitchen.

'There's someone to see you, Mr Preston,' Susanne announced in her starchy Mrs Dawson voice. 'Your sister. She's in the study.'

Juliana grimaced, turning away to place her hat and bag on the breakfast bar. Susanne saw the reaction and almost smiled, but managed to hold herself together. Clearly, she didn't like Barbara any more than Juliana did.

'She seemed upset,' the housekeeper added.

Blake frowned. 'I see... Maybe I'll go in and talk to her alone, Juliana,' he said, glancing at her over his shoulder.

'Be my guest,' she returned drily.

He shot her an exasperated look. 'Women!' he grumped. And marched off.

'What's up, do you know?' Juliana asked as soon as Blake was out of earshot.

Susanne shrugged. 'Mr Preston's sister wouldn't confide in me. Maybe she's left her husband. Or maybe he's thrown her out.' She turned away and continued her preparations for the evening meal. 'I presume I should cook enough for one more for to-night's dinner?'

Juliana groaned silently. Having Barbara over for the odd meal was bad enough. But to have her stay didn't bear thinking about.

'I suppose so,' she sighed. 'I sure hope that's all you'll have to do for her.'

The housekeeper's eyes jerked up. 'I hope so too! If there's one woman I can't stand it's...' Suddenly she bit her bottom lip and busied herself back on the vegetables. 'Sorry, Juliana. I shouldn't have said that. It's none of my business. Mr Preston can have here whomever he likes. My job is just to do the house-work, not voice opinions.'

Juliana patted the other woman on the shoulder. 'It's all right, Susanne, I understand your feelings en-tirely. The woman's a right pain in the butt. But, as you say, she is Blake's sister and we must make her as welcome as we can. Of course, if you decide to short-sheet the bed and add the odd funnelweb spider to her night-time glass of water then I'll turn a blind eye.'

Both women burst into laughter, and were still gig-gling when Blake strode back into the room, looking like thunder.

'Might I request a pot of black coffee?' he said sharply. 'That crazy female in there has been downing my Johnny Walker like water, along with some damned tranquilliser or something. I can't get any sense out of her. Bring the coffee in when it's ready, would you, Juliana? Maybe you, being a woman, might be able to get to the bottom of the problem. All Barbara's done since I walked in is cry! And before you tell me you and she don't get along—as if I didn't know that already—then just do it for me, OK?'

'Of course, Blake,' Juliana agreed. 'I'll do what I can.'

'Thank you.' And, whirling, he was gone as abruptly as he'd come.

Susanne shook her head then started making the coffee. 'Men aren't too good at just listening, are they?'

Juliana frowned. 'Blake used to be when he was younger…'

'Was he? Oh, well, I didn't know him them.'

'He was very nice. Very kind and considerate.'

'*Was* he?' There was no doubting the surprise in the housekeeper's voice.

Juliana's smile was rather sad. 'He's still like that underneath,' she said. 'It's just that life's been hard on him, what with his mother's suicide, his father's premature death and then his having to work so hard to save the family company from bankruptcy. He had to become tough to survive, I guess. When men have to be like that at work all day, they don't always know how to switch off when they come home.'

'You're probably right. My Fred was a bus driver. He used to tell me that by the time he came home after driving in the traffic all day his nerves were shot to pieces.'

'That's probably why he played golf,' Juliana suggested. 'It's supposed to be a very relaxing game.

Your husband would have especially appreciated all that walking in wide open spaces.'

'Yes…' Susanne seemed thoughtful while she put the finishing touches on the coffee-tray. 'Yes, I suppose that could have been so.' She brightened as she handed Juliana the tray. 'I always thought he just wanted to get away from me. But I can see now that he might have *needed* that relaxation. As it was, he still had a heart attack before he should have…'

Now her face started to fall, tears pricking at her eyes. Juliana was happy to leave her to her memories, hopeful that she might have given the poor woman a different slant on what had clearly been an unhappy marriage. Maybe that was why Susanne had never had children. Or maybe the not having children had created the unhappy marriage. Who knew which came first, the chicken or the egg?

Juliana hesitated at the study door, taking a deep breath to prepare her for the fray. With both hands full, she had to kick the door instead of knocking on it. Blake swept it open, smiling in rueful relief at her.

'Thank the lord,' he whispered.

Juliana peered over his shoulder to where Barbara was slumped in one of the deep armchairs, her face buried in her hands. By the shaking of her body she was still weeping, though quietly. Despite her strong dislike for Blake's sister, Juliana was moved to some sympathy. Not much. But some.

'Why don't you make yourself scarce?' she suggested to her husband. 'I'll call out if I need you.'

'You have no idea how grateful I am that you're doing this. You're a grand girl.'

'Don't thank me till later. I might just murder Barbara if she turns on me the way she used to.'

'I think you've finally turned the tables on *her*, Juliana.'

'We'll see, Blake. We'll see...'

Juliana allowed her husband to escape while she moved into the room with as much enthusiasm as a man going to the gallows. Barbara, she knew from experience, was not given to accepting gestures of kindness with a good grace. Blake's sister saw kindness as weakness. Juliana scooped in a breath and braced herself.

'Some coffee, Barbara?' she offered as she put the tray down on the sleekly lined grey desk.

Barbara muttered something unintelligible.

Juliana poured the coffee anyway, dropped in two cubes of sugar, stirred it thoroughly then presented it under Barbara's nose as a *fait accompli*. She waved it away with dismissive impatience.

'Blake said you were to have coffee, Barbara. So damned well take this and drink it!'

And so much for my sympathy, Juliana berated herself.

Barbara grudgingly mopped up her tears with what looked like a man's handkerchief, took the cup and saucer and started to drink, hiccuping after every mouthful.

Despite the ravages of the tears she was looking pretty good, her diet-slim body encased in a black silk dress that must have cost a king's ransom, especially with the matching coat that was draped over the back of the chair. Her hair, Juliana noted, was a more flattering shade of blonde than the last time she'd seen her, and her skin was clearly the skin of a woman who'd always had the best of facials. Barbara, at twenty-eight, was no raving beauty. But she was a classy-looking woman. No doubt about that.

'Feel like telling me what's wrong?' Juliana suggested once Blake's sister had finished the first cup and had started on the second.

'No,' Barbara pouted.

It was reminiscent of many pouts Juliana had been on the receiving-end of before. A bitter resentment welled up inside her. What in God's name was she doing, taking pity on this woman, trying to help her?

'Fair enough,' she said brusquely, standing up from where she'd been balancing on the arm-rest of a nearby chair and heading for the door. No way was she going to beg or cajole Blake's spoilt brat of a sister into womanly confidences. No way was she even going to stay around and watch her sulking.

'Where…where are you going?' Barbara wailed.

Juliana stopped, gritted her teeth, then turned slowly around. 'Upstairs to my room. It's been a long day and I'd like to change.'

'But Blake said…I know he asked you to…to…'

'To what? Listen to your problems? Give you advice? Let's be honest, Barbara—you don't want my advice. You can't stand me any more than I can stand you. This was a hopeless idea of Blake's from the start. Tell *him* your problems. I can't deal with them, or you.'

'Please don't go,' she cried out with such desperation that Juliana hesitated. 'Blake won't understand

and I...I don't know what to do. Henry's cut off all my credit cards. He...he says he doesn't care where I go or what I do as long as he doesn't have to pay for it.'

'And why is he acting like this? Don't go telling me he doesn't love you, Barbara. The man loves you to distraction.'

'Because he's a jealous old fool!' Barbara burst out. 'He thinks I'm having affairs behind his back.'

'And are you?'

Barbara looked uncomfortable for once in her life. 'Not really affairs...'

'But there have been other men.'

'Well, of course there've been other men! Do you honestly think I could go my whole life only sleeping with that old coot?'

Juliana sighed. 'So you *did* only marry Henry for his money.'

'Don't you come the high horse with me, Juliana. You're not so lily-white yourself. If ever there was a girl who's always had her eye on the main chance then it's you!' She wiped her nose again and gave Juliana one of those supercilious, scoffing looks she specialised in. 'You weren't exactly in love with Blake when you married him, were you? Good God, you were engaged to another man a couple of weeks beforehand! So don't you start looking down your nose at my marriage, madam. You married my brother for his money and don't think everyone doesn't know it!'

Juliana sucked in a hurt breath for a second till she decided not to let this woman do what she had always done: make her feel rotten. *She* knew she hadn't married Blake for his money, and that was all that mattered. Having re-gathered her composure, she eyed Blake's sister with a mixture of contempt and pity. The woman really was a pathetic creature.

'Don't presume to judge my marriage, Barbara,' she said with as much forbearance as she could muster. 'Or the reasons behind it. Blake and I are a very special case.'

'Oh, I don't doubt that! You and he were always as thick as thieves, even when you were kids. And so secretive! All those afternoons you used to spend in his room,' she sneered. 'I mean, girls like you start young, don't they?'

Now Juliana had heard enough. There was a limit to everything. 'Get out,' she said quite calmly.

'W-what?'

'You heard me. Get out. Right now.' Striding over, she swept the coat up from the back of the chair and threw it at the open-mouthed woman.

Barbara got unsteadily to her feet. 'You have no r-right to do this. Blake...Blake said I could stay till I s-sorted myself out.'

'He will retract that once I've told him what you just said. Now *move*!'

'I will not!' she resisted stubbornly. 'I have a right to stay here if I want to. This is my *home*.'

'You left this home when you married,' Juliana pointed out icily. '*I* am mistress of this house now.'

Barbara's upper lip curled in open contempt. 'Too true, you little slut. That's all you are. All you'll ever be to my brother. His mistress! Oh, you might have a marriage certificate, but he never wanted you as his wife! All you are is a legitimised whore! Blake will never want any woman other than sexually. Darling Mummy screwed him up good and proper. And what she didn't screw up, darling Daddy did!'

Her laughter was quite lewd. 'Speaking of screwing, I'll bet you never guessed who was one of the many *ladies* Daddy was having on the side, did you? Oh, I see it's dawning on you. Yes, your own darling mother. Our own sweetly caring cook, Lily! Don't look so shocked, Juliana, dear. You couldn't have been ignorant of your mother's appetite for sex. Like mother, like daughter, eh, what? *You* certainly must be good at it for Blake to marry you. He always told me he'd only ever marry for money. That's why he dumped poor old Virginia as soon as he found out she was flat chat. Yet he married you!'

She smiled an ugly smile as she slipped into her coat. 'I guess some habits die hard. Maybe he decided to install a nice regular bedmate for him to have between trips overseas. Yes, that must be it. He has his little black book full of international good-time girls to cater for him while he's away and good old reliable Juliana to fix him up at home, the way she always did.'

Juliana grimaced as she gulped down the rising nausea in her throat. Her head began to whirl.

It wasn't true. Mum couldn't have been sleeping with Matthew Preston. She would have known it if she were!

But, even as she denied it to herself, Juliana remembered the cigar smoke she used to smell when she came home from school. Matthew Preston had smoked cigars.

As for Barbara's accusation about Blake and other women overseas…

Juliana swallowed again, then lifted her chin proudly. 'I don't believe a word you've just said, Barbara. You're a jealous, vindictive bitch. You've always been a jealous, vindictive bitch. In your hate for me you don't even care if you ruin your own brother's happiness. For we *are* happy. I know that won't go down too well with you, since you've made such a mess of your own life. Not that I give a damn about that! Blake always told me people got their come-uppance. I didn't believe him before. Now I do. You've made your bed, Barbara. Go home and lie in it. Meanwhile, I'm quite happy to lie in mine, with Blake by my side. He cares about me. Whether you believe that or not is immaterial. *I* do. And he does not sleep around!'

Barbara laughed. 'Really! Well, why don't you check out the top drawer on the left-hand bedside chest in his room? That's where he keeps his little black book. You'll find all the women in it plus their phone numbers. I dare you to have a look tonight before you curl up in your cosy little bed. Maybe you won't be so smug then. Maybe you'll realise exactly what you are to Blake. Why, you're no more to him than your mother was to my f—'

Juliana slapped Barbara's face so hard that the sound reverberated in the room. Or was that Barbara's scream?

She would have slapped her again if Blake hadn't raced into the room.

'What in God's name is going on in here?' he demanded to know.

'Barbara is just leaving,' Juliana said with stunning outward calm. 'Aren't you?'

Barbara was staring at her, frightened perhaps by the look in her sister-in-law's eyes.

'And she won't be coming back,' Juliana finished.

Blake looked first at his pale-faced wife, then at his defiant sister. For a long moment the air tingled with electric tension. Which way would his loyalty go?

Finally, he turned to Barbara with a hardening expression. 'I don't know what you've just said to Juliana, but if it's what I think it is I'm going to strangle you with my bare hands.'

For the first time, Barbara looked worried, then she became aggressively defensive. 'What *I* said to *her*? You should have heard what *she* said to *me*! Called me a bitch, told me I had made my bed and now I had to lie in it. She's cruel and horrible, Blake. I don't know why you married her. You didn't *have* to marry her to get what you wanted, you know. She would have been as easy as her...'

She gasped as she realised she'd really put her foot in her mouth.

'You have five seconds to get out of here,' Blake said in a low, steady voice that was infinitely terrifying. 'Out! Don't walk. Run! As fast as you can or I won't be responsible for what happens to you.'

Panic-stricken now, Barbara glanced from one to the other, then, with a sob, ran from the room. They heard her high heels clack hurriedly across the marble foyer, heard the front door bang.

'Juliana,' Blake said thickly, and gathered her into his arms.

She went, collapsing, unable to think of anything but what he'd just confirmed with his action. Her mother *had* been his father's lover, had perhaps contributed to his mother's suicide. It was all so appalling, so...shattering.

'I...I never knew,' she sobbed. 'I never knew...'

'Hush, my darling. Hush. It's all in the past and quite inconsequential now. There's nothing to feel too terrible about.'

Juliana struggled out of his arms, tears streaming down her face. 'Nothing too terrible? Good God, how can you say that? My own mother was responsible for your mother's death!'

'No...' Blake shook his head. 'She never knew about Father and Lily. I swear to you. They hid it very well. I only found out quite by accident when I came home unexpectedly from university one night and saw Dad slipping down the back stairs from your flat. He only had trousers on. It didn't take much to put two and two together. I knew Dad had been having affairs for years.'

Juliana stared at him. 'You're talking about the night of my graduation, aren't you?'

Blake sighed. 'Yes.'

'Oh, God...' She pressed her fingers against her throbbing temples. 'How you must have despised him. And my mother!'

'I never despised Lily, Juliana. She was the nicest

woman I ever knew, but she was also lonely and vulnerable. My father was a handsome, charming, sophisticated man. She didn't stand a chance against him. As for my father…I didn't despise him either. I knew what he was, knew he had this weakness for warm, beautiful, giving women like your mother. Sure, I was disillusioned for a while. What son doesn't want his father to be a paragon of perfection? And the young do judge harshly. But eventually I understood why he craved escape from my mother's relentless jealousy and possessiveness. Women like that make men want to run, and run and run. They kill all that's good in a relationship. They make loving anyone a living hell!'

'Which is why you've never loved anyone,' Juliana said, and looked away. 'Nor wanted them to love you.'

'I certainly don't want that kind of love. But I do want *you*, Juliana. I have ever since you were thirteen.'

Her eyes snapped back, rounding with shock.

His own expression was self-mocking. 'Remember that day by the pool when you felt my muscles?'

She nodded, her mouth dry.

'I wanted to grab you then, kiss you, force you. I was a virgin myself, would you believe it, but it was your virginity on the line that day, Juliana. It took every ounce of my control to dive into that pool and swim away from you.'

'I…I had no idea…'

'Do you think I didn't realise that? You were still a child, despite your rapidly growing body. But I was nineteen, and a nineteen-year-old boy's desires are very strong. Still, I soon found a remedy,' he finished almost bitterly.

Juliana was silent for a few seconds.

'I...I was very jealous of all those girls,' she said softly.

Blake smiled. 'Were you? I'm glad.'

'Glad?'

'Glad that you suffered as much as I was suffering.'

'You weren't suffering, Blake Preston! You were having the time of your life!'

'Was I? Oh, Juliana, if only you knew...I used to watch and wait for you every time I came home from university just to catch a glimpse of you, to marvel at the way nature was turning you into such a beauty. I kept thinking to myself, Soon...soon she'll be sixteen, soon she'll be at the age of consent...'

Juliana was startled. 'You...you planned to seduce me when I turned sixteen?'

'Do you want me to deny it?'

'Well...no, I suppose not. Not if it's true.' Yet she did feel somewhat dismayed at the thought.

'Good lord, Juliana, I was a spoilt, sex-crazed rich kid who thought he could have any girl he wanted. Believe me when I say I had never been knocked back. Yet the only girl I really wanted was you, probably because you were forbidden; a challenge. Why do you think I came home early from university that night? I couldn't wait another day to see you. I had no idea that was the night of your graduation ball. I thought, it being a Wednesday, you'd be home. Then there was my father, coming down from a rendezvous with your mother.'

His laugh was derisive. 'Seeing him changed everything. Oh, I still wanted you. I might even have seduced you that night if you'd let me. But you didn't, Juliana. You told me off and made me see reality, which was that we could never be happy together while my father was having an affair with your mother. It was an impossible situation. As much as I tried telling myself that I could still have you if I wanted you, I couldn't bear to see the look in Lily's eyes when and if she found out both she and her daughter had been ill-used by Preston men. I also thought it was only a matter of time before *you* found out about them. But you never did.'

'No, I never did,' she murmured, still astounded by all that Blake had told her. She had no idea she'd been the object of such a long sexual obsession. He'd certainly hidden it very well. There again, she'd hidden her own love for just as long, even from herself.

'Barbara only knew because I told her one night in a drunken binge shortly after Dad's death.'

'I'm surprised she didn't tell me sooner,' Juliana said with a catch in her voice.

'I warned her not to.' Blake gathered her still shaken self back into his arms, laying her head on his shoulder. 'I never dreamt she would come out with it at this late stage. I'm sorry, Juliana. I won't let her hurt you again. I promise.'

'She's always hated me.'

'No, she's always *envied* you. Your beauty; your honesty; your love of life.'

'I don't love life very much tonight.'

'You will. I'm going to make you forget Barbara, and the past. I'm going to make you forget everything, Juliana, but here and now.' And, tipping up her chin, he kissed her with such passion that she was well on the way to forgetting before they left the room.

CHAPTER TEN

JULIANA woke the next morning, once again in Blake's bed. His side was empty, the bedside clock said seven-fifteen and his shower was running.

Friday, she thought. And groaned. Friday was not her favourite day at work. The sales teams came in for their weekly meeting and she never seemed to get anything done. To tell the truth, she didn't feel like going to work at all that day. She felt tired and troubled after the happenings of the night before.

Blake had not been able to dispel all her distress over what she'd found out about her mother and his father, no matter how hard he'd tried. In fact, the more passionate he became, the more perturbed she felt underneath, about a whole lot of things, the main one being what exactly did she mean to Blake? Was Barbara right? Was she no better than a legitimised mistress?

Juliana breathed in sharply. Oh, my God, the book... The little black book. That was one thing she *had* forgotten about.

She stared at the top left-hand-side drawer, then at the bathroom door. The shower was still running strongly. Dared she look?

And what if the book was there, with a whole lot of women's names and phone numbers in it? What would that prove? It did not mean Blake was still using either the book, or the women. He might simply not have thrown the rotten darned thing away after they were married.

Her stomach twisted. The urge to know if it was there, a reality, and not another one of Barbara's malicious inventions, was compelling.

I won't look inside, Juliana vowed. I just want to know if it exists.

Her hand trembled as it reached for the knob on the drawer, but there was no turning back now. The decision had been made.

She yanked it open.

Three neat piles of various coloured handkerchiefs greeted her, behind which lay a battered copy of *The Power of One*. Peeping out from under the novel was the corner of—not a little black book—but a little dark blue one.

Juliana frowned. Was this it?

There was only one way to find out.

Holding her breath, she eased the small leather-bound note book out from under its hiding spot. As she started to flick through it, her heart began to thud. Her fingers slowed. Her eyes widened.

Each successive page revealed a stunning array of women's names and numbers, listed under the city they lived in. Jennifer in London; Simone in Paris; Carla in Italy; Maria in Greece; Ellie in Bangkok; Jasmine in Hong Kong; Midori in Tokyo; Cindy in New York.

And that was only a sample.

The list was staggering. There were even some interstate numbers. Girls in Sydney and Brisbane and Canberra and Adelaide and Perth.

The sudden snapping off of the shower sent Juliana into a panic. Shoving the book back, she banged the drawer shut and dived back under the sheets. With some difficulty she resisted the silly urge to pretend she was still asleep when Blake came back into the room, a towel slung low around his hips.

'You still in bed?' He smiled wryly and walked across the room to fling open his wardrobe, well aware, Juliana thought despairingly, of how incredibly sexy he looked like that. His daily twenty laps in the pool, plus all his other sporting activities kept his broad-shouldered, slim-hipped frame in top condition. The skiing in winter, the tennis in summer, not to mention the odd hit of squash and the occasional game of golf, all kept the fat away and those gold-skinned muscles well-toned and rippling.

'You're going to be late for work if you don't get up,' he remarked as he dropped the towel and casually drew on brief black underpants.

'I...I think I'll take a sickie.'

This brought a sharp glance over his shoulder. 'That's not like you. Aren't you feeling well this morning? Your period's not due today, is it?'

'You know damned well it isn't,' she snapped before she could stop herself.

Blake frowned at her for a moment, then with a casual shrug turned back and kept on dressing.

Juliana watched him with a gradual sickening in her stomach. He was so beautiful, yet perhaps so frighteningly amoral. His dark suspicions over *her* having an affair probably reflected the fact that he was having them himself, right, left and centre. Men were renowned for their double set of standards where sex was concerned. And it wasn't as though Blake's father had set him a good example...

Juliana cringed inside again to think of what had been going on under her nose all those years. Not that she blamed her mother—Blake was right about that. A woman of her nature and susceptibility to men wouldn't have stood a chance against a man like Matthew Preston. Any woman would have found him hard to resist. Lily would have been putty in his hands.

Just as I am putty in Blake's hands, Juliana thought with a growing sense of despair. He hasn't fallen in love with me. He only *wants* me. I've been fooling myself where that's concerned. Oh, maybe he almost meant it when he said there would never be another woman for him. The women in those books probably weren't *women* to him. They were merely bodies. There were too many of them to be anything else.

Weren't?

Who said they were in the past tense? Juliana mocked herself. They could be well and truly present, *and* future.

Still, the lingering hope that Blake no longer used that little book and would not have any need to use it in future revived her naturally optimistic nature. She could cope with Blake's not loving her if he didn't cheat on her. And really, she had no evidence of any actual cheating. The book's existence proved nothing.

Barbara's knowledge of it actually proved that Blake had had that book for years!

'Do you want me to ring your office for you?' he offered as he tucked a white shirt into his pin-striped navy trousers.

Suddenly the prospect of moping around the house all day, worrying about everything, was too awful to contemplate. What could she achieve by it, except get herself into more of a mental and emotional muddle?

'No, thanks,' she told him. 'No need. I've decided to go in after all. I'll just have to be a little late.'

'I'll say. You usually take ages getting ready. Well, I'm off downstairs for breakfast. See you tonight.' He came over and pecked her on the forehead. 'Don't forget, we've got that dinner-party at Jack's tonight.'

Juliana pulled a face. 'I had forgotten. Oh, well... It won't be too bad, I suppose. Jack's good fun, and I do want to thank him personally for those tickets to *Phantom.*'

Blake patted her cheek. 'That's my girl.'

Juliana's heart sank as she watched her husband stride confidently from the room, putting on his suit jacket on the way. He was already in his business mode, his bed and its occupant quite forgotten.

There would be no inner turmoil while *he* sat at his desk that day, no more worries over his wife's loyalty. He had her now in the palm of his hand. And how he knew it! She would be ready and waiting for him when he came home tonight, both for the dinner-party and any other party he might want afterwards.

Juliana swallowed at this thought. Blake had certainly turned her heightened sexuality to his advantage. He seemed to be enjoying the power he now had over her in bed to have her do whatever he desired, to reduce her to a wildly willing partner who didn't know the words 'no' or 'stop' or 'don't'. Not that she could blame him, she supposed. What man didn't want a woman to be his sexual slave? And what woman didn't want her man to be as skilled and imaginative as Blake was? The situation was a double-edged sword all right.

With a sigh Juliana climbed from the bed, gathered her clothes up from where they were scattered over the floor and made her way slowly back to her room. She wished she could be really happy about the way things were going in her marriage; wished she could dismiss all thought of that infernal notebook. But she knew its existence would be a constant thorn in her side. She also knew that the next time Blake went away on business she would be sorely tempted to see if he had left it behind or taken it with him.

He left it behind, and she was ecstatic.

The occasion was the last week in November. And, while Blake was only away three short days in Hong Kong, the days leading up to his trip had been the wrong time of the month for Juliana, and she figured if Blake was ever going to be suspect it might be after he'd been deprived of sex for a while.

Juliana hadn't dragged up the courage to actually look in the drawer till the very evening Blake was due back. She felt so elated at finding that book still in its hidey-hole that she impulsively decided to go and meet him at the airport, despite there being barely enough time for her to make it by the time Blake's plane touched down shortly after nine o'clock.

Some impulses, she realised after she saw Stewart Margin's reaction to her last-minute appearance, were not such a good idea. Blake's secretary was sitting in the waiting lounge next to Gate Three, his nose buried in a newspaper, when she stepped from the moving walkway and hurried over.

'Hello, Stewart,' she said, quite happily at that stage.

His eyes snapped up, his face showing instant alarm. 'Mrs Preston!' He shut the newspaper noisily and scrambled to his feet. 'What...what are *you* doing here?'

'Just thought I'd come along and meet my husband.'

'Does—er—Mr Preston know you're meeting him?'

'No. Why? Is he late again?'

'No. His plane's already landed. It's just that... well—um—' He shrugged uncomfortably, looking as though he wished he were anywhere else but here.

Juliana started wishing the same. She shouldn't have come. It had been a stupid thing to do. Naïve and stupid.

Her earlier elation died. How could she have believed Blake would be pleased she was here, waiting for him like an adoring little wife? Their relationship might have changed, but not *that* much. Just because they now slept together in his bed every night, all night, it did not mean he would want her fawning all over him in public.

Stewart's muttering something under his breath added another dimension to Juliana's dismay. Dear heaven, surely Blake wouldn't start thinking things, because she was here with Stewart, would he?

Though not having openly continued with his crazy accusation about her having had an affair the last time he'd been away, Blake *had* become more possessive—even watchful—over her. When Jack had mildly flirted with her the night of his and Gloria's dinner-party, Blake had glared at his host with a withering coldness.

On one other occasion he'd questioned her rather sharply when she'd been very late home from work. Half-flattered, half-frustrated, Juliana had impatiently explained that she'd left the office on time, but had been caught in a traffic jam. Blake's considered and very chilly silence for several minutes afterwards had given her the disquieting feeling that he hadn't believed her.

A premonition of impending doom swept through her.

She might have turned and fled if passengers hadn't started filing from the flight tunnel into the lounge where she and Stewart were standing. Blake was the third person along, his blue eyes narrowing when he saw them both together.

Juliana gulped, plastered a bright smile on her face and determined not to let her inner disquiet show. After all, she *was* innocent.

'What are you doing here, Juliana?' were Blake's

first words. His tone was measured. Not exactly accusing, but definitely not happy.

'I couldn't wait to see you,' she said, truthfully enough. And, stepping forward, she held him by the shoulders while she kissed him on the cheek. His body felt stiff beneath her hands, his skin coldly unwelcome.

She drew back, her smile strained now.

'How nice,' was his flat reply. 'How did you get here? You always said you'd never drive at night in the city.'

'I caught a taxi.'

'You should have asked Stewart to drive you. After all, you did know he would be meeting me, didn't you?'

Juliana could feel her discomfort developing into a fully fledged fluster. 'Well, yes, I did, but I—er—it was a last-minute decision to come...'

'Oh?' His smile was blackly sardonic. 'Was it quicker to come here than go home?'

Stewart, Juliana knew, lived in the northern suburbs of Melbourne, a long way from their bayside home.

An angry exasperation cooled her embarrassing blush. She straightened her shoulders and gave Blake a reproachful look. 'No,' was all she said, determined not to be verbally bullied like this. Hopefully Blake's nasty innuendoes were going over poor Stewart's head, though from the look of the young man's obvious agitation she didn't think so.

Truly, Blake was being unforgivably horrible. Yet there she'd been, less than half an hour ago, dying for him to go home. Now she felt absolutely wretched.

Blake at last acknowledged his secretary's presence. 'Hello, Stewart. Everything all right here while I was away?'

'A few small problems, Mr Preston. Nothing I couldn't handle.'

'Where are we parked?'

'The usual spot.'

'Fine. Let's go, then. Sorry, Juliana, but Stewart and I will be talking shop during the drive home. I hope you don't mind sitting in the back on your own, but, let's face it, neither of us had any idea you'd be here, did we, Stewart?'

'We certainly didn't,' the secretary agreed quite forcefully.

'I don't mind,' she said, as civilly as her fury would allow. Never again, she vowed. Never again!

It began to drizzle on the way home, the temperature dropping as well. No one, other than Melbournians, would have dreamt summer was only two days away. Dressed only in lightweight forest-green casual trousers and a cream silk blouse, Juliana hugged herself in the back seat of the company Ford, wishing Stewart would turn on the heater. He didn't, and she stubbornly refused to ask.

She glared, first at the back of Blake's head, then out at the rain-spattered pavements, her nerves stretched to breaking-point by the time Stewart dropped them off at the house. She wasn't sure which of them was going to snap first, but it was obvious, by the tension between them as they went inside, that a fight was brewing.

In a way, Juliana would have appreciated the chance to clear the air, but Blake, it seemed, was content to let silence be his weapon. After delivering his luggage to Mrs Dawson for her to do his washing, he strode into the living-room to pour himself his usual nightcap. Juliana trailed after him, strung up and irritated. She wandered around the room while Blake downed a very stiff drink, then poured himself another. Not a word had passed between them. Suddenly, it was too much for her and she whirled on him.

'Don't you ever do that to me again!' she burst out.

'Do what?' he returned blandly.

'You know what, Blake. Don't play the innocent with me.'

His laughter was bitter. 'I thought that was my line.'

'See? You're doing it again. Making nasty innuendoes.'

'Is that what I'm doing?' He quaffed back half the second whisky then topped up the glass.

'You know that's what you're doing. And it's so unfair. I have never been unfaithful to you. Not the last time you were away, nor this time!'

'Is that so?'

'Yes, that's so!'

'In that case you won't mind coming upstairs with me now, will you?' He turned and stared at her over the rim of his glass while he drank. His gaze was hard and cold, yet appallingly sexual. Juliana felt her skin begin to crawl with a ghastly excitement. 'I feel like making love to my wife.'

He placed the empty glass on to the coffee-table with a clunk, then began to walk towards the door. Checking mid-stride halfway across the room, he turned to eye her still standing there. 'Aren't you coming, darling?' he asked in a softly mocking tone. 'A faithful wife who is so anxious for her husband to come home that she meets him breathlessly at the airport must surely be in need of a little loving.'

He held out his hand to her.

She stared at it for a long moment, then slowly lifted her eyes to his.

'Yes, Blake,' she said, her heart breaking. 'I am. But that's not what you're offering, is it? What *you're* offering I can get in *any* man's bedroom.'

She could see that she had stunned him with her counter-attack. Stunned and infuriated him.

'I don't doubt it. You've become quite the little sensualist lately, haven't you?'

'And that bothers you?'

For a second, his nostrils flared, his eyes glittering angrily. But he quickly gathered himself. 'Why should it? Do you think I was *happy* with our previous sex-life? Good God!'

Juliana looked away from his scathing contempt. '*I* was,' she said brokenly.

He scoffed his disbelief.

'At the time,' she added, her gaze returning to his.

'And what happened to change all that, if you don't mind my asking for the umpteenth time?'

She simply stared at him, unable to think of a reason other than the truth. And she couldn't tell him that.

He started walking slowly towards her. 'Cat got your tongue, Juliana? Shall I fill in the blanks for you?'

He stopped right in front of her, his face mocking. 'I know exactly what happened,' he said in a low, dark voice. 'You met some bastard, some wicked, clever bastard who took no notice of your ice-princess routine, who took no notice of your prudish little ways, who simply *took*!'

His hands were busy on her blouse as he spoke, unflicking the buttons, parting the material so that he could easily unsnap the front fastening of her bra. His eyes darkened as they swept over the rosy tips, already hard with arousal.

'You found out you liked it that way, didn't you? Nothing too gentle or sweet for this new Juliana...' And his hands started putting his words into actions.

She bit her bottom lip to stop any sound from escaping, her eyes pained when he bent to replace his hands with an even less gentle mouth. The appalling thought that Susanne could come into the room at any moment only seemed to add to her excitement. And her shame.

The shame finally escalated when his hands went to the waistband of her trousers.

'No...' she said shakily, and staggered backwards, fumbling as she did some of the buttons back up. 'No!' she cried. 'You're wrong. About me. About everything! It...it wasn't like that. I'm not like that. Oh, I can't stand this any more. I can't stand it, I tell you.

I have to get out of here, away from you. I...I have to...'

She left him, standing there with his jaw dropped open. She didn't stop to pick up her bag, just swept her car keys from where they hung on a peg on the kitchen wall and raced for the garage. Susanne, luckily, was nowhere in sight. No doubt she was busy washing in the laundry or watching television in the family room.

Pressing the remote-control panel that opened the garage door and the front gate, Juliana leapt into her car and fired the engine. Blake must have thought she'd run upstairs, for he hadn't followed her into the garage. It wasn't till she was roaring up the street that her rear-view mirror caught him racing out on to the wet pavement, waving his arms at her to stop.

But she did not stop, and after a couple of intersections she knew he wouldn't be able to find her. She swept the small sedan up several side-streets and screeched to a halt in a dark lane, only then realising she was shaking like a leaf.

Slumping across the steering-wheel, she started to cry. And once she started she could not stop.

Finally, she was all cried out, but the weeping, she found, had not solved anything. It simply left her drained of every ounce of strength, both physically and emotionally. There was no energy left, no fight, no will. She really could not go on. She also could not go home. Not yet. No...certainly not yet...

Like an automaton, she started up the car and drove slowly, aimlessly. Somehow she found herself going towards the city on the road she usually took to go to work, the water on her left, houses on her right. Swinging round a curve she spotted St Kilda pier in the distance stretching out into the grey waters of the bay.

Juliana remembered how, as a teenager, she'd often spent hours walking along that pier, idly watching the horizon or the student artists who used to sit there, painting the boats. It had been a type of refuge for her whenever she'd been troubled in some way. Usually, by the time she left the pier, things had seemed more in perspective. Less catastrophic. The water, it seemed, had had a soothing, calming effect.

Despite the late hour, she pulled over and parked in one of the parking bays across from the pier, making her way over via the arched walkway that spanned the busy road. Down the steps she went and along on to the pier proper.

Practically deserted, the place was, yet she didn't find it creepy. There was one man—a drunk by the look of him—leaning on one of the posts, and further along a lone fisherman was trying his luck. The rain had temporarily stopped and a faint moon was shining through the clouds. The water looked pretty black, but still peaceful.

Juliana walked over to a private spot and leant against the railing to peer blankly out to sea. The water lapped softly around the posts underneath her pier. Moored boats rocked gently in front of her. Gradually, a peace stole over her tormented soul. Yes, she'd been right to stop here.

She was standing there, reviving her spirits and the will to go on with her marriage, when something hit her on the back of the head.

CHAPTER ELEVEN

'SHE'S coming round...'

Juliana moaned again when some person—a doctor, presumably—pulled up successive eyelids and shone a bright light into each eye. She lifted an uncoordinated hand to push the pencil-thin torch away.

'Hi, there, Mrs Preston. I'm Dr Trumbole. How are you feeling?'

'My...my head aches,' she managed to get out, her voice sounding slurred.

'I'm sure it does. But don't worry. You've got a nasty bump on the back of your head and a mild concussion, but you'll live.' He smiled down at her. 'I'll get the nurse to give you something for the headache.'

'How long does my wife have to stay in hospital?' Blake asked from where he was standing at the foot of the bed, looking almost as bad as Juliana was feeling.

'We'll keep her in for another day, just as a precautionary measure.'

'So she might be able to go home tomorrow?'

'I don't see why not, provided she can go home to nothing but strict bed-rest for several days. No work of any kind. She shouldn't even walk around much. I trust that won't be a problem?'

'She won't lift a finger.'

'Good. I must go and start my rounds. The nurse will be back shortly with some tablets for you, Mrs Preston. Now don't worry if you feel sleepy soon after taking them. They'll contain a sedative as well. Goodbye, Mr Preston.'

'Goodbye, and…thank you, Doctor. You've been most kind.'

The doctor patted Blake's shoulder. 'Someone had to reassure you that your wife was not going to die.'

Once they were alone Blake came forward to sit on the side of the bed, picking up her hand between his. His sigh was weary. 'God, Juliana, don't ever do anything like that again. You had me so darned worried. When you didn't come home all night I rang the police. They told me you answered the description of an unconscious lady found on St Kilda pier. Apparently some old bum contacted them about you but he'd done a flit by the time they and the ambulance arrived. Since you had no ID on you, they had no idea who you were.'

As she stared at his grim expression, a horrible thought came to mind, making her stomach churn. 'Blake, I wasn't…I mean…whoever attacked me…he didn't…didn't…'

'No, no. He didn't touch you other than to hit you. From what the police have gathered he just took your keys and stole your car. Must have followed you from where you'd parked it. They've already located the car, stripped and burnt out in a park somewhere.'

Tears pricked at her eyes. 'My poor little car…'

'I'll buy you another car.'

A type of resentment welled up at his offer. Did he

think he could solve every problem that easily? Just whip out his chequebook? Well, it would take more than money to erase the memory of last night. Much more than money...

'No, Blake. I'll buy my own car.'

He dropped her hand and stood up, exasperation on his face. 'For pity's sake, Juliana, would it hurt you to let me buy you a damned car? There's a limit to independence, you know, especially for a man's wife!'

She just looked at him, not having the energy to argue. Eventually, he let out a disgruntled sigh and sat back down. But he didn't pick up her hand again.

'All right, all right, I'm being irrational,' he admitted. 'But I feel so rotten about last night. I acted like a pig out at the airport. Then, when we got home, I treated you abominably. There was no excuse for what I did. I hope you will accept my apology, Juliana. I assure you nothing like that will ever happen again.'

He'd barely finished his stiffly formal and not really appeasing words when the ward sister bustled in with a glass of water and two huge white capsules.

'Here we are, Mrs Preston. If these don't shift your headache, nothing can. Only problem is getting them down. Drink plenty of water with them. Here...let me help you sit up.'

Juliana gulped the bombs down, lying back afterwards with a ragged groan. Her head was killing her.

'Poor dear,' the sister soothed, and straightened the bedclothes. 'You'll feel better soon. Did the doctor tell you you'd probably drift off to sleep?'

She nodded.

'Nice nurse, that,' Blake remarked after she left.

'Mmm.'

'I'll go once you get sleepy.'

'All right.'

A heavy silence descended. Juliana was in too much pain to make idle chit-chat, let alone tackle the problems that still beset their personal relationship. Blake's apology did not alter the fact that, underneath, he believed she was an adulteress. Maybe he thought he would now magnanimously push this belief to the back of his mind, but Juliana knew it would lurk there, poisoning what could have been so good between them.

How could she happily go to his bed knowing he thought she'd done all those intimate things with some other man—or men? And what of Blake, being prepared to sleep with a wife he thought was a two-timing tramp? What did that make her, if not what Barbara had accused her of being? Blake's legal whore...

Juliana's heart sank to an all-time low. She might have wept if her aching eyes and whirling head hadn't started feeling so heavy. A yawn captured her mouth. She closed her eyes.

Though almost asleep, she flinched slightly when she felt Blake's lips on her forehead.

She thought she heard a sigh. Was it hers, or his? She didn't hear him leave the room at all. By then, the sedative had done its work.

Juliana did go home the next day, despite still feeling exhausted. Though maybe it was more an emotional exhaustion than a physical one. Depression had taken its hold and she could not seem to throw it off.

Susanne, perhaps sensing that all was not well with her, fussed like an old mother hen. Nothing was too much trouble. A television and video were set up in Juliana's bedroom. Piles of books were collected from the local library. Magazines appeared in droves, donated by Susanne's sister.

Juliana was only allowed out of bed to shower or to go to the bathroom. Her own local doctor visited daily to check on her progress. Vitamins were prescribed along with tablets that looked suspiciously like tranquillisers. Juliana flushed them down the toilet. Flowers arrived in abundance from people she worked with, with a couple of the girls dropping by regularly for visits after work, bringing good cheer, chocolates, fruit and more magazines.

But, despite everything, Juliana remained depressed.

Blake, of course, was the reason. Juliana would have liked to talk to him about their relationship. Really talked in a deep and meaningful way. But he was so unapproachable in his manner and attitude that it was impossible.

Though superficially kind and considerate, he began treating her more like a distant invalid relative than a wife. She felt he did what he did through duty, not true caring, their meetings awkward and strained.

He would stop by briefly in the morning for a few moments' stiff conversation before breakfast, telephone her once during the day with a couple of brisk questions about how she was feeling, then condescend to eat his meal with her in her room at night, though he silently watched the news on the television while they ate. He also suddenly seemed to have to retire to his study every evening after dinner to work or make phone calls. There was certainly no question of his ever coming into her bed at night, not even just to hold her or be with her.

Juliana began to fear that Blake was using the situation to regress to their earlier separate-bedrooms, separate-lives status. And, while she didn't want to be used like some whore, the intimacy of sex might have broken down the emotional barriers Blake seemed to be re-erecting. But making love never came up in their meagre conversations, though admittedly the doctor might have told Blake that was out for a while. She was lucky if she got a peck goodnight, let alone a hug or a proper kiss.

It depressed Juliana further to think that if Blake couldn't actually sleep with her he didn't want to touch her at all. Was that marriage?

Well, they had never had a real marriage, she decided unhappily, and it had taken this crisis to show up the weaknesses in their relationship. Yet she had once deluded herself into thinking that their marriage was strong. How crazy could one get?

But of course that had been before she'd realised she loved Blake, before she'd started wanting so much more than her husband had been prepared to give. Well, she *had* got more, in a physical sense, but Juliana was gradually coming to the conclusion that, even if they resumed their sex-life, their marriage was still doomed to failure. It was like a time-bomb ticking away, waiting to self-destruct. Her problem now was, did she want to wait for the time-bomb to explode, or take her future into her own hands and walk away with her self-respect and pride intact?

When Saturday came and Blake still went into the office, Juliana almost despaired.

'I can't take much more of this,' she muttered to herself, and, throwing hack the covers, she drew on her old pink dressing-gown and slowly made her way downstairs.

Susanne was busily polishing the foyer floor when she looked up and saw Juliana. 'You're not supposed to be coming down here,' she scolded. 'The doctor said maybe tomorrow you could sit by the pool in the sunshine. Tomorrow is not today. And you don't even have slippers on! Oh, truly, Juliana, do you want to catch your death of cold?'

'You sound just like my mother used to,' Juliana said, a lump forming in her throat. 'She...she was the cook here, did you know that?'

The housekeeper looked up at her with real surprise. 'No...no, I didn't know that.'

Juliana traced her hand over the elegantly carved knob at the end of the balustrade, a knot in her stomach. 'I'm not really cut out to be the lady of the house, I suppose. I should have known it wouldn't work...'

'Juliana, what are you talking about? You're one of the nicest ladies I've ever worked for. Why, you're a *real* lady, not like some of those stuck-up madams who think money has given them class. All I can say is, your mother must have been a real lady too, because you're a credit to her. Don't ever let me hear you putting yourself down again, do you hear me?'

Juliana blinked her shock at the other woman's giving her a right dressing-down. But maybe that was what she needed to jolt her out of this crippling depression.

'And another thing,' the housekeeper raved on, her face flushed with emotion. 'I think that after Christmas you and Mr Preston should plan a little holiday away together. If my Fred and I had spent more time alone together we would have been a lot happier. Your Mr Preston works too hard. And so do you. There comes a time, you know, when if a couple don't have a baby it gets too late. They drift apart and everything becomes just awful.'

She stepped forward and touched Juliana compassionately on the sleeve. 'Now I know how much you love that handsome husband of yours. My heart almost breaks with the way you look at him sometimes, but there's no use thinking *you* can change his cold little ways. Mr Preston is one of those men who doesn't want to appear weak in front of a woman. But put his own flesh and blood in his arms, and he'll melt to mush. I'll bet my lotto money on it!'

Juliana stared at the other woman.

A baby…Blake had asked her to have a baby. But she hadn't been prepared to take the risk.

But loving someone was always a risk, and she prided herself on not being a coward.

Tears of gratitude filled her eyes as she looked at this stern-faced but kindly woman whom, till recently, Juliana had held at arm's length. 'You could be right.

Yes, you could be right. I'll discuss a second honeymoon with Blake when he comes home. Thank you, Susanne. I feel much better now.'

But she didn't really get the chance to discuss a second honeymoon with Blake. He came into her bedroom late that afternoon with a big cardboard box in his arms, 'Hello, there,' he greeted. 'You're looking much better.'

She put her book down with a ready smile, remembering her new resolve not to give up on this marriage till she had fired every bullet she had. 'I went downstairs for a while. What have you got there?' she asked with real curiosity in her voice. Blake was the only person who hadn't brought presents to her sickbed, maybe because everyone else had inundated her with them. Of course, it was typical of Blake not to give presents.

'A little get-well gift,' he told her.

As he carried the box across the room, whimpering sounds emanated from the holes in the sides.

'Oh, Blake! It's a puppy, isn't it?' She clapped delightedly. 'Show me, show me!'

'Patience!' he commanded, and placed the box on the bedcovers next to her, opening the lid flaps to reveal the most adorable bundle of black canine fur she'd ever seen.

'Oh, Blake!' She swept the puppy up into her arms, whereupon it immediately started madly licking her face as if to show its gratitude at finally escaping that awful prison of darkness.

'What breed is it?' she asked.

'Labrador.'

'You're cute as a button, aren't you, darling? That's what I'm going to call him—Buttons.'

'I thought he might keep you company while I'm away.'

Juliana's eyes jerked up. Blake was looking down at the puppy with no readable expression on his face. He looked, as always, incredibly handsome in a dark grey business suit. But his handsomeness no longer mattered to Juliana. It was his heart she coveted.

'You're not going away again before Christmas, are you?' she asked with a catch in her voice.

'Have to, I'm afraid. There have been some problems with a shipment of video games. When the container ship arrived last week we only had half the stock. The best and quickest way I can sort this out is to go over there personally.'

'Over where?'

'Tokyo.'

'I…I see…'

'I don't want to go, Juliana. I have to.'

'Of course you do!' She forced a bright smile to her lips. 'And you're right, Buttons will keep me company, won't you, sweetheart?'

Buttons reacted enthusiastically to her attention with some more manic licking.

'When do you have to leave?' she asked, keeping her eyes down.

'Tonight.'

'*Tonight*!' she gasped, her eyes snapping up.

'Yes. My flight leaves in a little over an hour. If I go immediately, there's still a chance I can get the rest of the stock flown over and into the stores before Christmas.'

'Are…are you packed?'

'Yes. I called Mrs Dawson from the office this afternoon.'

'She didn't say anything.'

'I asked her not to.'

'And when will you be back?'

'No later than next Thursday.'

'That long…'

'I should be finished in Tokyo within a few days but I'm going to drop off at Hong Kong on the way back.'

Juliana's stomach tightened. What had been the woman's name in Hong Kong? Jasmine, wasn't it? Jasmine… God, but that was a depressingly sensual and feminine name. No doubt Jasmine had everything else to match as well.

'So, what's the attraction in Hong Kong?' she asked a touch sharply.

'I have some business to do there as well.' He bent down to kiss her lightly on the cheek. 'I'll be as quick as I can.'

Juliana bit her tongue to hold her silence. She had no evidence that Blake was dropping off in Hong Kong to see some woman. He hadn't taken the address book last time he went overseas. Why should he this time?

Because you haven't been living as husband and wife for quite some time, came a darkly cynical voice. Not since a week before the *last* time he went overseas. Maybe he *needs* to see this woman.

'Blake!'

He was striding from the room when his name burst from her lips. Checking, he turned to frown at her obviously emotional outburst. 'Yes?' he asked. Almost warily, she thought. Or was it wearily?

She had wanted to tell him how much she would miss him, but suddenly the words would not come. 'Th-thank you for the puppy.'

His smile was definitely wry. 'My pleasure. *Au revoir*. Look after yourself, and don't go walking along deserted piers in the middle of the night.'

Within moments of his leaving, the terrible temptation to race into his room and see if that little blue book was still there gripped her in its tenacious hold and refused to let go. Juliana didn't know which would be worse—not looking and so keeping her optimistic hopes alive, or risking seeing that empty spot in the drawer.

In the end she could not stand the not knowing.

Clutching the puppy in her arms, she made her way shakily into Blake's room and opened the drawer. All the breath rushed from her body. It was there! Dear heaven, it was there!

She sank down on to the bed and buried her face into the pup's furry side, her whole body trembling with emotion. But gradually the strange feeling that something wasn't quite right started wiping the relief from her heart, replacing it with an increasing unease. Lifting puzzled eyes, she stared once again into that drawer.

And then it struck her. The book wasn't where it had been before, peeping out from under the novel.

The novel was still there but the address book was sitting on top of it in full view. Someone had recently taken it out then put it back in a different spot.

Why?

There were a host of innocent explanations, but somehow Juliana wasn't comforted by any of them. Finally, she put the pup on the bed, picked the notebook up and started flicking through it again, not knowing what that would prove, but doing it anyway.

She saw the torn-out page straight away, and knew, before a closer inspection confirmed it, that it was the page which had included Jasmine from Hong Kong. Pale but oddly composed now that she knew the awful truth, she replaced the book, picked up Buttons and returned to her room.

She sat on her bed, staring dry-eyed into space.

Five days, she had to think about all this. Five days in which to make up her mind whether she could live with, and continue to love, a man who was unfaithful. Five days to find a way to survive this utter, utter hell.

CHAPTER TWELVE

JULIANA lay back on the deckchair by the pool, doing her best to keep calm. Blake would not be home for a few hours yet. If she started becoming agitated now, she would be a mess by the time he arrived.

But it was hard to stay calm on the day one was going to ask for a divorce.

She had decided not to tackle Blake about Jasmine, or any of the other women in that book. Really, they were only a symptom of the true disease that was destroying their marriage, which was that Blake no longer trusted or respected her. She could have coped without his love. She could not cope with his lack of respect.

Buttons' sudden barking had her twisting round to see what was upsetting the little devil. Already that week he had chewed up two shoes, one fluffy slipper, the leg of a chair and anything else anyone left lying around. Susanne had forbidden him to come inside till he'd learnt to behave himself.

Juliana squinted over to where the barking was coming from. But the sun shining in her eyes made it difficult for her to see into the shadows of the wide patio. She could just make out someone sliding the glass doors back and scooping up the frantic animal, someone tall and…

The light glinting on his blond hair as he broke out

of the shadow sent a panicky rush of air into Juliana's lungs.

'Blake!' She scrambled to her feet, hastily drawing a see-through floral wrap over her brief red bikini. 'What are you doing home this early?'

He came forward, idly stroking the puppy while he frowned at her fluster. 'I caught an earlier flight. Is there a problem with that? Are you going out?' His narrowed gaze flicked over her scantily clad form. 'You don't look as if you're going out.'

'No, I'm not going out, but I…I…' She was floundering, for how could she say that she wanted to be more formally dressed to face him with her news?

'You what, Juliana? Have I come home at an inopportune time? Is that it?'

His sarcasm was the last straw. Her eyes carried total exasperation as they raked over him. She shook her head in a type of weary frustration. 'Yes, Blake,' she agreed grimly. 'You came home at an inopportune time. I had a plan, you see, a timetable in my mind. I was going to be so calm and reasonable about everything. Mature and, yes…as kind as I could be. Because I thought the way you were was probably not your fault. But I can see now that I would have been wasting my time. So I'll just say it out straight. I want a divorce, Blake. I can't take it any more.'

He said nothing for several seconds, his face stiffly unreadable, his hand frozen mid-air above the dog's head. Finally, he lowered the pup gently on to the cement then straightened to glare at her. 'You can't take *what* any more?'

Juliana sighed. 'Not here, Blake. Not here…' And she turned to walk back towards the house.

His hand shot out to grab her arm, twisting her back to face him. 'Who is it?' he demanded to know. 'Tell me!'

She shook her head again in utter defeat. 'Please, Blake, I don't want a scene. I just want a divorce. You promised me we would call it quits after the first year if our marriage didn't work out. Well, the year's almost up and I'm not happy with you. That's the kindest way I can put it.'

His eyes widened with a look of dawning horror, his hand dropping from her arm. 'My God, you've fallen in love, haven't you?'

Her lips parted in surprise before she realised he meant fallen in love with someone else. But by the time she recovered her composure, the damage had been done. A guilty blush had already joined her goldfish gasp.

'It's not bloody Stewart, is it?' he ground out. 'Or Hawthorne again? For pity's sake, don't tell me it's Hawthorne!'

Juliana's eyes mirrored her deep sadness. 'It's no one, Blake. You've got it all wrong, as usual.'

'No, I haven't,' he pronounced with ironic insight. 'I've got it right, at last. You had an affair with someone while I was away those three weeks, and now you've fallen in love with him.'

Juliana stared up at him in total disbelief. 'Do you honestly think I would have been making love with you the way I have been if I was in love with someone else?'

'You *haven't* been making love to me lately! As for those other times…you wouldn't be the first woman to hide her guilt behind a burst of passionate lovemaking. You probably hadn't fallen in love with the bastard back then. It was probably only another grotty little affair. For God's sake, why don't you admit it? You've already asked me for the divorce. The least I deserve is the bloody truth!'

'All right, Blake. You want the truth? You can have it. Yes, I have fallen in love with someone. And yes, he is a bastard! You're so right about that. But you're wrong about the timing. I already knew before our sex-life improved that I loved him. There was no doubt in my mind at all. It was a certainty. And the reason it was a certainty was because my secret love was none other than my own husband. You, Blake! I'd fallen in love with *you*!'

All the blood had begun to drain from his face during her speech, only to have colour jerk back at the end.

'Me!' he exclaimed, clearly stunned.

'Yes, you.' Her laughter was only just this side of hysterical. 'Funny, isn't it? Most men would adore to have their wives love them as I realised I loved you, have *always* loved you.'

'You've…*always* loved me?' he rasped.

She shrugged with the sort of indifference despair brought. 'I didn't realise it till I thought you might have died in a plane crash. It's amazing how almost losing a person makes you aware of what their value is to you. I…I…' She swallowed and tried to gather what inner resources she had left, looking up at two very shocked blue eyes with a growing bitterness. 'Yes, Blake, I've always loved you. Maybe from the very first moment we met.' Now her laughter was mocking. 'Blake Preston...my hero...my prince. Only my prince doesn't *want* my love. He never has. Love and he parted company a long time ago.'

'Juliana...darling...'

'Oh, don't ''darling'' me, you unfeeling, unfaithful rat!' she exploded, anger a much safer emotion than maudlin sentiment.

'*Unfaithful!*'

If she'd thought he was startled before, he was totally flabbergasted now. 'Since when have I ever been unfaithful?' he demanded, black clouds quickly gathering behind those momentarily wide eyes.

'Since you went to see your precious Jasmine in Hong Kong for starters!' she countered, and knew immediately by his face that she had hit the mark.

'Did you think I didn't know about your book of names?' she scoffed. 'Well, I did! Barbara was only too happy to tell me about them. She even told me where to find them. And I looked! Oh, yes, I looked more than once. It's amazing what a woman in love will do when she's desperate. And you almost got away with it this last time. If I hadn't noticed the rotten thing had been moved, if I hadn't picked it up and saw the page missing, I wouldn't have...have...'

Her voice trailed away when she found herself staring down at a small velvet box resting in Blake's outstretched hand. He also had the most peculiar look on his face, as though he was trying not to cry.

'Jasmine and I were once lovers,' he said shakily.

'A million years ago. All those women were my lovers...a million years ago. That book hasn't left my drawer for so long that I'd almost forgotten it was there till I had cause to look up a number again, the number of a certain woman who is married now but who is also a top jeweller. I needed Jasmine's number, Juliana, because I wanted to buy you this.'

And he flicked open the box to reveal an incredibly delicate but beautiful diamond ring. 'I never bought you an engagement-ring the first time round. I was going to court you properly this time, *make* you fall in love with me, because...you see...I had discovered how much I loved *you* the night you ran away. When I saw you lying unconscious in that hospital bed I knew that if you died, if I ever lost you, I would simply stop wanting to live...'

He dragged in a deep breath, letting it out with a shudder. But then his mouth curved back into a wry smile. 'Of course I had trouble admitting any of these radical feelings. How could I possibly have done the one thing I'd vowed never to do? Especially with my beautifully cool, independently ambitious wife, who didn't love me back, and who I mistakenly thought was having an affair, or affairs! I fought my feelings all that next week but, once I accepted that they wouldn't go away, that they were *real*, I decided to do something about them. Since you were still with me, I rationalised that this other man—or men— meant nothing to you. It was only sex. Yet *our* sex was better than ever! So I decided then and there that I would make you fall in love with me if it was the last thing I did. And now…now you tell me you loved me all along!'

Tears flooded Juliana's eyes. 'Oh, Blake…is it true? You really love me?'

'Do I really love her…?' He shook his head and for a split-second she saw a flash of pain that told her he'd been through as much hell as she had. Which he must have, she conceded, thinking all that time that she was being unfaithful to him, grappling with his jealousy, but still deciding that if he could win her back he would try to forget her infidelities and go forward.

He took the ring from its bed, tossed the box away then picked up her left hand. Both their hands were trembling. He slipped the diamond on her ring finger till it rested against the plain gold band.

'With this ring,' he said, 'I thee wed. With my body, I thee worship…'

And, sweeping her hard against him, he kissed her as though he would never let her go.

And he never did.

In April 2002
Get ready for a wild ride from

Western ROGUES

They were knights in shining...Stetsons!

A mercenary, returning to his hometown,
finds the woman he never *could* forget,
in Annette Broadrick's
LEAN, MEAN & LONESOME.

An upstanding physician insists on a marriage
of convenience—or is it?—to save a woman's
reputation, in Cathy Gillen Thacker's
A SHOTGUN WEDDING.

*They may not have been conventional
cowboys, but they sure lived by
the code of the West....*

Available at your favorite retail outlet.

Silhouette®
Where love comes alive™

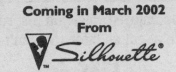

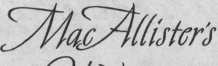

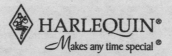

COOPER'S CORNER

In April 2002 you are invited to three wonderful weddings in a very special town...

A Wedding at Cooper's Corner

USA Today bestselling author
Kristine Rolofson
Muriel Jensen
Bobby Hutchinson

Ailing Warren Cooper has asked private investigator David Solomon to deliver three precious envelopes to each of his grandchildren. Inside each is something that will bring surprise, betrayal...and unexpected romance!

And look for the exciting launch of *Cooper's Corner*, a NEW 12-book continuity from Harlequin— launching in August 2002.

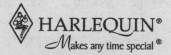

HARLEQUIN®
Makes any time special ®